Reminiscences
of an Accidental
Embezzler

Reminiscences of an Accidental Embezzler

Howard E. Hallengren

To order additional copies of this book, contact:
Xlibris
1-888-795-4274
www.Xlibris.com
Orders@Xlibris.com
749371

Footfalls echo in the memory
Down the passage which we did not take
—T. S. Eliot

CHAPTER I

New York—April 1990

Fingerprinting! I should have considered the possibility that I might have to be fingerprinted when I applied for this job. But there I was, waiting to be "processed," as they called it in the Human Resources Department. And fingerprinting was one of the main steps in the process. I had been fingerprinted once before back in 1977 and never thought that I would have to do it again.

I sat looking around the waiting room—the walls painted a washed-out cream color, a worn, bilious green carpet on the floor, and rather nondescript modern prints on the walls. Couldn't a supposedly major US bank do better than this in their Human Resources Department? And the name—Human Resources Department. I could only shake my head as I thought about the pomposity of naming what used to be called simply the Personnel Department the "Human Resources Department."

I wanted this job; I needed this job. But I felt that there was just no class, no style to the place. How could a bank with such a proud history as that of the Second National Bank of New York come to appear rather shabby and commonplace? I felt that it had to reflect on the present management. I was really upset as I sat in that depressing room; if only I could go back to Switzerland and work there again. Swiss banks had class; they had style—everything that this place seemed to lack. But I know all too well that I can't go back to Switzerland. I can sneak in for a visit now and then, but I can never work there again. So I'm stuck with New York and I'm stuck with this bank. I guess Thomas Wolfe was right: "you can't go home again."

And then the fingerprinting problem loomed up in my mind. The whole job interview process had gone remarkably well, and I know that I had really impressed everyone that I had talked to. It wasn't often that the management of Private Banking got to talk with someone who had the international background that I have. So I had been approved all the way along the line, and now all that was left was the processing: a drug test, being photographed, and being fingerprinted. There was nothing for me to do but to sit there, staring

1

down at the horrible green carpeting and wondering how long I would have to wait. It took close to fifteen minutes more before I heard my name.

"Mr. Wenner. Mr. Kurt Wenner."

"Yes."

"Would you come with me please?"

A very attractive young woman came out into the waiting area, and said, "Hi, Mr. Wenner. I'm Irmane Garcia. My office is just down the hall."

She was really quite attractive, and I was happy to follow her out of the waiting room and into what was apparently the main office area. We walked down a long aisle, past a sea of desks and I was really turned off by the look of the place. The decor was the same in this room as in the waiting room: the same drab walls, the same nauseous carpeting, and the same type of cheap-looking modern prints on the walls. Only here everything was cluttered and messy: boxes piled in the aisles and papers falling off desks. But I could not take my eyes off Irmane Garcia; this young Hispanic woman whom I was following had a tremendous figure and the movement of her hips was almost hypnotic as I followed her to her office. I smiled to myself as it occurred to me that maybe my luck was changing after all.

As she led the way, Irmane turned to look back at me and, as I quickly caught up with her, I took the opportunity to say, "You pronounced your name 'Ear-mon.' But how do you spell it?"

She smiled as she replied, "Well, it's spelled 'I-r-m-a-n-e' but just about everyone here in New York pronounces it 'Er-main.' However, I think I'm making progress since at least most of my friends get it right now."

"It's quite a nice name. Is it a family name?"

"Not really. I'm from Barbados, and it's not all that uncommon there. . . OK, here we are—where I work."

She led me into a large room, which originally must have been planned as a conference room. There were several large tables loaded with various brochures explaining the employee benefit plans of the Second National Bank, piles of papers, a camera on a tripod, and a smaller table with what appeared to me to be the fingerprinting materials. Irmane walked behind her desk that was in one corner of the room and said, "And you must be from overseas too, Mr. Wenner, since you seem to have a slight accent."

"Yes, of course. I'm originally from Switzerland—from Zürich to be precise. But since I've lived in California for the last ten years, perhaps I have somewhat of a Los Angeles accent."

She laughed and said, "I didn't know that there was such a thing as a Los Angeles accent, but I suppose there must be."

I felt that I had to be particularly nice to Irmane, at least until I could decide what to do about the fingerprinting. If my prints and my application were sent off to the FBI, I knew I'd be sunk. But at this point, I didn't know what else I could do. I couldn't refuse to have my fingerprints taken. I knew that I'd have to think of something, but, in the meantime, I had to concentrate on being nice to Irmane. Fortunately, I had had enough experience playing up to women of all ages that charming Irmane should not be a problem.

To show that I was being cooperative, I said, "Well, what's the first thing I have to do to be 'processed' as you personnel people put it?"

"Let's start with the fingerprinting, and then we can take the picture for your ID card. Would you come over here, Mr. Wenner."

Irmane stood by the small table and began getting some cards out of an envelope, and she also opened an inkpad. She motioned me to come over and stand next to her, and I could feel my heart pounding as I stood there. I really couldn't tell if I was afraid of the fingerprinting or excited by the young woman. The pursuit of young women such as Irmane always excited me, and whether that was it now or whether it was simply fear of the fingerprinting, I didn't really know. But I knew that I had to make every effort to control myself.

Irmane took my hand and I was impressed by how soft her hands were as she held mine. She immediately said, "Relax. I won't hurt you." She looked at me with a rather knowing smile as she said it. She then took one of my fingers at a time and began the slow process of putting each of my fingerprints on the cards, making duplicates of each print.

It was almost an erotic experience for me, at the age of fifty-eight, to be having a young woman manipulate my fingers like this, and I felt that I had to discipline myself to keep my mind on the immediate problem. But it was a hard thing to do. Irmane seemed to me to be about twenty-eight or thirty years old, maybe half my age, with jet-black hair and dancing brown eyes. To try to break the spell, I finally asked her, "What do you do with the prints after you've taken them?"

"Oh, I put together a package of eight or ten of them and send them off to the FBI. It depends on how many new employees we have in a given day. I only have a few appointments today, so I'll probably wait until sometime tomorrow before sending them over. And the second set—I keep that one for our files here at the bank." As she finished the job, she took the two sets of prints and put each set into a three-by-five envelope with my name on it.

As she did this, I asked, "When do you get the results back? I mean, I was wondering if I could start work right away, or if I had to wait for the results. We know how slow government bureaucrats can be."

Irmane smiled at me again. "No, they're really not. The FBI is actually pretty good. They get the results back to us in just a couple of days. You know that they don't really check the fingerprints though, at least not at first. It would be very difficult for them to do that. So what they do is check all the personal data we give them ——the name and all of that—and if they find a match there, then they check the fingerprints."

"Oh, I didn't know that. I just assumed that they had a way of comparing the prints."

"I understand that that's very hard. So they run the personal data through their computers, and then check the fingerprints later if the computers come up with something. But to get back to your question, you don't have to wait to start your job. We'll take your photo now and I'll give you your ID card, and if the head of your department agrees, you can start work tomorrow, or even this afternoon if you want. I assume you took the drug test in the Medical Department already."

I nodded in agreement. "Yes, I did. So I guess that if any of the tests come back negative, the bank will fire the employee right away. Do many people fail the tests?"

Irmane sat down at her desk and shook her head. "Well, as you can imagine, lots of the young kids that we're hiring for clerical jobs and the like, many of them fail the drug test. Pot smoking will show up in the urine even if a person hasn't smoked any for over a week. But I can't remember anyone ever being rejected because their fingerprints or personal data revealed some kind of criminal record. Anyone who's got a record is never going to apply for a job at a national bank. It would be stupid. . . It's pretty common knowledge that banks have everybody checked."

Irmane then handed me a small package with a wet paper towel inside, such as airlines sometimes give out, and, as I stood wiping the ink off my hands, Irmane leaned back in her chair and her eyes seemed to sparkle as she asked me, "You're not afraid of flunking one of the tests, are you?"

I quickly replied, "No, of course not." My rather abrupt reply seemed to surprise Irmane, and I immediately tried to soften it by adding, "I don't take drugs, you know, or smoke pot, or any of those things that all the young people seem to do. So there should be no problem." I waited for a few moments and, when she didn't say anything, I asked, "Well, what's next?"

She moved over to the camera, and she then asked me to pose for the picture for my identification card. She had a special machine that put the picture together with my typed name and social security number into a laminated ID card. After she took the picture, it was only a minute or two before the machine produced a card. As Irmane handed it to me, she said, "Now that wasn't so bad, was it?" I did not answer, but just stood looking down at my picture on the card. I was clearly disappointed at how the picture had turned out, I guess because it was hard to think of myself as being close to sixty years old. Some people might think that I looked fairly distinguished, or at least European, with gray hair, a strong chin, and only a slightly receding hairline. But I could only think of myself as I used to be thirty or more years ago—the epitome of a vigorous, young, blond German youth.

As I kept looking at the picture, Irmane went on, "Incidentally, I see that you'll be in Private Banking. What's your job going to be?"

"Oh, I'll be a portfolio manager in the investment area. It will be in International Private Banking so all of my customers will be from abroad. I think the fact that I speak four languages—French, German, and Italian, in addition to English—was one of the main reasons I was hired. And then I think they liked my Swiss background since I've spent my whole career giving investment advice in foreign exchange and in the global bond markets, which foreign investors really like. I don't think that the people here at the Second National Bank know very much about these things. Of course, I probably shouldn't say that because I don't know them very well yet, but that was my impression from the three or four people who interviewed me in Private Banking."

There was an awkward pause after I said this, while I stood staring at the woman, still admiring her quite extraordinary dark beauty and trying to figure out what else I might learn about the fingerprinting process. She looked up and met my eyes briefly before saying, "Well, that's it, Mr. Wenner. Good luck in your new job." We shook hands quickly, and I felt I had been dismissed. Under the circumstances, all I could do at that point was to thank her and to find my way out.

CHAPTER II

Once on the street, I really did not know what to do. It was only a little after eleven in the morning, and I felt that I could not go uptown to my new office and try to start work while the fingerprinting issue remained unresolved. So I began walking south on Broadway toward Battery Park. The Second National Bank's Human Resources Department was at 79 Broadway, within walking distance of the bank's Wall Street headquarters, and it was just a few blocks down to the park at the very southern tip of Manhattan.

As I crossed Battery Place to go into the park, I looked back at One Broadway, a building I had always admired when I lived in New York the first time. I knew it had been built just before the turn of the century and had been the headquarters of a major steamship company. The building was decorated with the colorful official crests of a number of the major seaports of the world: Venice, Genoa, Nice, Montevideo, Cape Town. And the building itself was a handsome limestone building in the classical "Belle Époque" style with a mansard roof. It almost looked out of place now, with all of the tall, glassy, modern buildings looming over it. This building always reminded me of Europe and particularly of Zürich, where I was brought up and where I had lived for so many years.

I walked down to the water's edge and looked out at the Statue of Liberty. It was a beautiful fall day, and there was a slight haze over the water. As I stood there, gazing out at the Statue, I thought how nice it was of the French to provide the United States with this much admired and much needed symbol. Unfortunately, as far as I was concerned, the Statue did not represent liberty, as it was intended to. For me, it represented my exile. I had come to the United States in 1963, not because I had wanted to, but because I had been forced to flee Switzerland. Some stupid mistake that I had made at that time had gotten me into trouble with the law, and I had to get out of Switzerland or else I would have had to spend time—and it was a ridiculously long period of time—in jail. There was no way that I was going to go to jail, so my only alternative was to get out of the country while I could. That had been almost twenty-five years ago, and even though I had been in the States ever since, it still bothered me that it was very difficult for me to even visit Switzerland.

Ironically, I had been born in the US since my parents were living in New York in 1932 at the time of my birth. But they had gone back to Zürich in 1934, and I had grown up there, had gone to the university at Berne, and had learned to be an avid Swiss patriot. And even after being forced to flee Switzerland, and spending all these years in the US, both in New York and California, I never really considered this country my home. I always felt that Europe was better, that Switzerland was better, and, above all, that Zürich and the Schweitzer Deutsch were the best. And I could never forget the fact that Ingrid is there. I have to laugh when I think that, after all these years, we never got a divorce. I guess I must have loved her once, and she was, after all, the mother of my daughter. And I really don't know why I keep thinking about her; maybe it's because we had a really good relationship at one time. But like so many of my relationships, it really did not last all that long.

However, I could not think about that now. I had to figure out what to do about those fingerprints. Back in 1977 I had been fingerprinted at the US Courthouse, which was just a few blocks away from where I now sat, and since it was Federal marshals taking my prints at that time, there was no point in trying to do anything about them. But now, Irmane said that she would not send them off to the FBI today, so there was still time for me to do something. I sat on a bench looking out at New York harbor for almost an hour trying to decide what to do, and then got up and walked along the promenade. A plan started to form in my mind and I decided to kill some time by taking the ferry to Staten Island and back. I walked over to the nearby terminal and went in and bought a ticket. There were not many people taking the ferry in the late morning, and the rather shabby terminal was not crowded. I only had to wait a few minutes before the next ferry began to load, and I walked through the boat and up to the front, where I could stand in the sun for the trip across the harbor.

It was a really good day, and the sun and the salt air seemed to revive my spirits. I started to see a way to handle the fingerprinting problem, as the ferry crossed the harbor and as I watched through the haze to see Ellis Island and the Statue of Liberty pass on the right. There were other ships in New York harbor that morning, and I wondered idly where the outbound ones were heading. When the ferry reached Staten Island, I simply stayed on board with some other people, who were probably tourists, and the boat soon began the trip back to Manhattan. On the way back, the plan became clear in my mind and I decided what I had to do. I obviously knew that my plan would be somewhat risky, but I also knew that I had no choice. I prided myself on that fact that I had never been afraid to take chances in the past, and I certainly could not afford to be afraid now.

When the ferry arrived at the Manhattan pier, I decided to try to find a place for lunch, so I walked back up along the promenade, and headed up West Street to Battery Park City. Whenever I was down in this part of Manhattan, it always amazed me to see what had been created here. Battery Park City was a whole new community, with hundreds of apartments and condominiums and, at the north end, the huge office towers of the World Financial Center. The promenade along the Hudson River had a great deal of charm, which the developers had obviously intended. But even though it seemed to me that it was somewhat contrived, I felt that it really worked, and I felt that it was surprisingly restful.

A great deal of construction was still going on, but I found an outdoor restaurant near the World Financial Center, and had a leisurely lunch with a half bottle of wine. I ordered a California Chardonnay, one that I had gotten to know when I lived in Los Angeles, and it was not at all bad—in fact, it was maybe even a little better than the Swiss Fondant that I usually had. However, I was not willing to give the Americans all the credit for the wine since the vines undoubtedly came from France in the first place.

The afternoon passed slowly, but it was finally five o'clock and I began walking over to Broadway, and then up the street until I was opposite #79. I waited across the street and watched all of the employees hurrying out. As opposed to Los Angeles, where people seemed to begin rushing home long before a hypothetical 5:00 p.m. quitting time, people in New York tended to work somewhat later. As I stood there, I was hoping to see Irmane leaving the building and at about 5:40 p.m., I did see her rush out and head up Broadway, probably to the Wall Street subway station. I continued to wait, since I wanted to give the office more time to clear out, but at exactly 5:50 p.m., I crossed the street and went in. I knew that this would be an ideal time, since the security guards at most buildings in New York did not require people to sign in until six o'clock. And it was still late enough so that the Second National's offices should be fairly empty.

I went up the elevator to the 17th floor, where the Human Resources Department was located, and got off into the glass-enclosed elevator lobby. The door to the waiting room was locked, and there was no one that I could see in that room. I waited a few minutes since I was fairly sure that someone would come out shortly, and it didn't take long before a young woman came rushing out, clearly in a big hurry. I could tell just from looking at her that she was one of these terribly self-important young women who probably had an MBA from one of the top American universities, was on an accelerated management training program, and was so self-important that she could not be bothered to even look at anyone else. I smiled at her in my most engaging way and said, "Pardon me, I wanted to see Irmane Garcia." I thought it might make an impression if I pronounced Irmane's name correctly as "Ear-mon."

"I left something in her office this morning."

She looked irritated to have to reply, "Sorry, I'm afraid she's already gone."

I said, "Well, let me show you my bank ID card. I'm with the bank, you know."

The woman was in too much of a hurry to argue with me, particularly since I was a distinguished-looking, gray-haired gentleman, and I had a very fashionable tan, having just come from California where I had lived for so many years. And I certainly appeared to be a prosperous bank officer in my expensive European-cut suit—a suit that I had bought on Rodeo Drive in Beverly Hills just a few months previously. And since I had a Second National ID, she could have no question about my being a fellow banker. She quickly used her access card to unlock the door and let me in, just as the down elevator came and she hurried into it and was gone.

I walked through the waiting room and back into the main office area, managing to act as if I owned the place. There were still several people at their desks, and those who did glance up paid no attention to someone who looked as if he could be one of the bank's many vice-presidents.

I held my breath as I got to Irmane's office, afraid that the door might be locked. But it opened when I turned the knob, and as I went into the office, closing the door behind me, I exhaled with a sense of relief, realizing that one of the major risks was behind me. I started looking through Irmane's desk for the envelopes with the fingerprint cards and the reports that were to go to the FBI. There was nothing in the desk, but I quickly found what I wanted in the first file cabinet that I tried. The two envelopes containing my information were in different files—one for the FBI and one for the bank, just as Irmane had said. I opened both envelopes and checked to make sure both sets of prints and both reports were in fact there, and then tried to decide what to do with them. The two envelopes were too large to put into my coat pocket, as I would have liked to do, but I finally saw some large bank envelopes on Irmane's desk, and I took one of those and put the reports containing my fingerprints and personal data into the envelope.

There was still one more thing to do. Irmane was a pretty sharp woman, and I was sure that she would have kept a record of the employees whose prints were being sent to the FBI, and that she would check that list to make sure that she got all of the reports back. I had not seen any report on her desk or in the files that I had checked up to that point, so I again began looking through the file cabinet. The files were not in very good order, but I could find nothing that referred to fingerprinting. I was really beginning to worry when I again went back to her desk, and was afraid that she had already sent a report off to some other department of the bank. However, I suddenly noticed the computer terminal on Irmane's desk and realized that she must keep her records in her PC. I should have thought of the computer right away, instead of spending all that time looking through the file drawers. I turned the computer on and scrolled through her files, quickly finding a reference to the FBI lists. As soon as I accessed that list, I found my own name, the date of my fingerprinting, and the number of the batch in which it would be included for shipment to the FBI. I immediately deleted my name from the list and then checked the PC's directory to see if there could be other places where my name might be included. Finding nothing, I turned the machine off, feeling that I had done just about everything I could to protect myself.

I had been in Irmane's office about forty-five minutes and it was now 6:40 p.m. I hoped the office would be empty when I walked out because the last thing I wanted now was for anyone to question me as I left. I picked up the envelope containing the reports, took a deep breath, opened the door, and stepped back into the main office area. I saw no one at any of the desks and walked toward the reception room. Just then two young men were coming in, and I instinctively straightened up before nodding at them and saying, "Good night." They mumbled something in reply, but I never stopped as I hurried back out through the glass doors and into the elevator lobby.

Once back on the street, I was really relieved and I thought to myself, "Well, I've done all I could. Let's just hope that Irmane does not remember that my name should have been on that list." She was undoubtedly a competent young woman, but I had to rely on the fact that she was fairly busy and probably would not examine her lists to see if the name of every new employee was there. I would start my new job the next day and would not know for two or three weeks whether or not the Human Resources Department had been able to find out anything about my past.

ZÜRICH: THE SWISS EXPERIENCE

CHAPTER III

Zürich—January 1965

I had been a really hectic morning—the phones never seemed to stop ringing. I sat at my desk trying to keep up with the rapidly changing situation in the foreign exchange markets. I was a trader in those markets and had shorted the US dollar. And I had taken a position that was a good deal larger than I was authorized to take for the bank's own account. I had been hoping that the Swiss Franc would rally this morning and bail me out, but it was pretty clear now that that was not about to happen. So I was intently phoning portfolio managers in the bank's Investment Management Division imploring them to find customer accounts into which I could lay off part of my losing short position.

I was merely following the practice among Swiss banks of managing customer monies without, what in the United States is called, the "Chinese Wall" that segregates customers' money from the banks' own money. What I was trying to do with my losing foreign currency position was similar to what the banks frequently did with bond underwritings, where the Swiss banks would earn an underwriting fee from the corporation selling the bonds, and then turn around and place the bonds in customers' discretionary accounts, whether it was a good deal or not. One of the main reasons for the tremendous profitability of Swiss banks was that they rarely incurred losses and usually made substantial profits on their bond underwriting and trading activities. They all had very large amounts of customer assets under management, and could use those assets to bail out their own positions. As foreign exchange trading became more important, the banks found that their customers' accounts could be used to bail out unfavorable F/X positions as well.

On the other hand, if the underwriting or trading position was profitable, the banks would keep most of the position for their own accounts. Practically all of the customers of the Swiss banks were from other countries and had accounts in Switzerland to take advantage of Swiss bank secrecy laws, and many of these clients had obtained their money in ways that did not bear close examination. Therefore, the customers were hardly in a position to complain about the performance of their accounts, and as long as that performance was at least half way decent and the customers were allowed to make a little money here and there, they were satisfied. And so what I was doing this morning was not particularly unusual.

The foreign exchange market, however, kept going against me and the phones were ringing nonstop. It was a particularly hectic morning, and the other traders at the trading desk were as busy as I was. However, since none of them had shorted the dollar, they were not particularly concerned by the dollar's continued strength. The phone at my desk, like all of the phones at the trading desk, had several incoming lines, one of which was a private line that only I could pick up. I was busy talking on the other lines, but I finally became aware that my private line was blinking, and I quickly punched that button and yelled into the phone, "Yes?"

"Mr. Wenner. This is Mrs. Jendricks, Dr. Hofbeck's secretary. I've been trying to reach you for at least ten minutes. Dr. Hofbeck is waiting to see you. Please come up to his office at once."

I did not get a chance to reply, since the line immediately went dead, and I sat there momentarily startled. What could Dr. Hofbeck want? He was the Managing Director of the Schleswigbank of Zürich, and a very austere and commanding figure. I think I had only been in his office twice in the five years that I had been with the bank, and both of those times it had been for meetings with clients, where I was present to assist one of the portfolio managers. I couldn't believe that Hofbeck could know about my losing F/X position already. And even if he does know, I already have most of it laid off in individual accounts. Why would he want to see me? I couldn't figure it out, but I began to hope that maybe I'm going to be promoted. That had to be it! They've finally recognized that I'm the best bond and F/X trader that they've got, and I'm to be promoted to an account management position.

I got up from my desk and put on my coat. One of the other traders at the desk yelled, "Hey, Kurt. Where the hell do you think you're going? The phones are crazy this morning!"

I paid no attention to him and just walked away, not bothering to reply, leaving the other traders shaking their heads. I went to the men's room, which was just on the other side of the elevator lobby, to comb my hair and to straighten my tie. I always had trouble with some hairs at the back of my head that kept standing up straight, and I plastered them with water to hold them down. I really wanted to look the part of a young Swiss banker when I went in to see Hofbeck. I stood for a minute considering myself in the mirror, and was pleased with what I saw: a good-looking thirty-three-year-old, with high cheekbones and a strong chin. I had been told for years that I was the epitome of the young, blond German archetype, and I knew that this was an advantage in dealing with senior management in a bank as German-oriented as Schleswigbank. I quickly decided that I looked all right, and I headed to the elevators for the ride up to the twelfth floor—the top floor of the Schleswigbank building.

Dr. Hofbeck's secretary grimaced in disapproval when I arrived. "I'll let Dr. Hofbeck know that you are here now."

Mrs. Jendricks had an office adjacent to Dr. Hofbeck's and I stood waiting in her office while she went into the Director's office to let him know that I was there. I was again struck by the size and furnishings of her office as I had been the first time I was there, actually wishing that I had one at least as impressive. A minute later she re-appeared and told me to go in. Like his secretary's office, Dr. Hofbeck's office was furnished in surprisingly good taste. It seemed both traditional and modern at the same time, since the Director, or his decorator, had combined several different styles of furniture. There were two very impressive carved wooden pieces as focal points: a massive desk in front of the windows and a large breakfront that dominated one wall. These were heavy, traditional pieces, and they had been combined with a large glass and chrome coffee table and a glass and chrome étagère that stood against another wall. In addition, the use of colors had been well considered, from the large leather desk chair, and the two guest chairs in front of the desk, all in a deep burgundy, to the obviously expensive multi-colored oriental rugs that lay atop the beige carpeting. This was not the traditional office for a banker in Zürich, and I was sure that it said something about Dr. Hofbeck that he had chosen this style of decoration.

Dr. Hofbeck was a tall man with sharp features, gray hair, a receding hairline and wearing steel-framed glasses. He was an imposing, even aristocratic-looking man, and I was more than a little nervous as I faced him now across the massive oak desk.

The Director told me to sit down—"Sit down, Wenner"—and then surprised me by saying, "You've heard about Mr. Poëhl?"

I did not know how to respond at first, so I shook my head, and finally said, "No, sir, I have not."

"Well, I'm afraid he had a rather serious operation yesterday—something to do with his pancreas, and not at all promising."

Gerhart Poëhl was one of the portfolio managers with whom I worked closely, and I had not been aware that he was even ill. All I could say was, "I'm sorry to hear that."

"Yes, well we're all most upset, and I've phoned his wife to let her know that we will help her in any way we can. But there seems to be little that we can do. However, that is not why I sent for you. You know that Poëhl was about to go on a trip to South America—Argentina, Bolivia, Paraguay—those places. Schleswigbank has quite a few customers in that part of the world, and they have not been called on for quite some time. And so I have asked Mr. Steiner to make the trip just as Poëhl had scheduled it. Steiner has, of course, agreed, and will be leaving on Saturday."

As I heard this news, I started to tense up, knowing immediately that this discussion was going to affect me personally. I started to say something, but it was clear that Dr. Hofbeck had not finished.

"Mr. Steiner is very good at dealing with customers—and particularly with our German customers—but he is not very current on the bond and foreign exchange markets, and these are the markets that our customers are most interested in. Steiner is a very good account administrator, but, as I'm sure you appreciate, he is not an investment specialist.

"And so I have suggested to him that he take you along to handle the technical investment questions. I believe that you know Mr. Poëhl's accounts, and I am sure that you can discuss the current situation in the markets. That is why I have decided to send you. I assume that you will be able to accompany Mr. Steiner." It was a statement, not a question.

This was really tremendous news for me, absolutely tremendous, and I could only respond, "Oh, yes, of course. I must tell my wife, but yes, there's no reason not to. I can certainly go."

"Good. Since you must leave at the end of the week, both of you will need to do a lot of work to get fully prepared, so there will be no need for you to stay at the trading desk—the other traders can handle things."

"Thank you, sir. I'll see Mr. Steiner, and make certain he has everything he needs. And I assume that I should talk with him about the travel arrangements."

"Yes, talk to Steiner. And if there is anything else that is needed, let my secretary know. This is an important trip and we want it to be a success."

Since he had clearly finished, I rose to leave, again saying "Thank you, sir," but as I got to the door, Dr. Hofbeck's voice hit me like a knife in the back: "And one more thing, Wenner. Be sure to close out that short dollar position by the end of the day." I mumbled something in reply, and went on out of his office.

This was such fantastic news that I had to think about what it all meant, and I could not do that back at the trading desk. I took the elevator down to the ground floor and walked out onto Bahnhofstraße. I headed down to the lake, passing the elegant stores and the sedate banks that lined the street. Schleswigbank was just two blocks north of the Paradeplatz, and I crossed the plaza and the baroque headquarters building of Credit Suisse, and continued down to the landing stages at the Zürichsee. I stood for a few minutes watching the swans and ducks that were swimming around in the lake and expecting to be fed. It was a cold, raw January day, however, and I realized that I had to keep walking to try to keep warm, so I began to pace back and forth along the shore. It was too late to do anything about it, but I realized that I should have taken a coat when I left the bank. Being sent to South America, however, was such a bombshell for me that I simply had to get away from everyone, if only for a few minutes.

South America! I had never been there, of course but, as Dr. Hofbeck said, Schleswigbank had quite a few customers there, many of whom were probably ex-Nazis who had fled there after World War II. Being asked to go there was clearly a feather in my cap. The bank not only recognized my abilities, they needed me. As I thought about it, I realized that they must be grooming me to take Poëhl's place, if Poëhl was as sick as Hofbeck implied.

From what my supervisor had told me at the time of my semi-annual review, Schleswigbank considered me to be a very good bond and F/X specialist, and, with my language capabilities, they undoubtedly felt that I would make an ideal account administrator. Fortunately, I can speak several languages—German, French, Italian, English—as most Swiss do. That must be it. This trip would be like a try-out—they would be giving me a chance to deal with customers, and if I did well, I would almost certainly take over for Poëhl.

But what about Steiner? Helmut Steiner was a cold fish. I really did not like the guy and was not anxious to spend a lot of time with him. However, it was clear that I would have to impress Steiner so that a favorable report would go back to Dr. Hofbeck. It occurred to me that I'd better go and see Steiner right away and find out what he needed. In my opinion, the man doesn't have a brain cell working, but I'll have to play up to him and try to make him look good on the trip so that at least he won't complain about me to Hofbeck. I hated the politics of the institution, but knew that I had to deal with that situation if I wanted to get ahead.

Ingrid should be happy about this. I don't think that I had ever been able to satisfy her with anything that I had done since the day we were married. But the trip to South America would provide a great conversation ploy for her when talking with other bank wives—"Oh yes, Kurt is traveling in South America. Dr. Hofbeck thinks so much of him, and when poor Mr. Poëhl became ill, why the very next morning, Kurt was asked to take his place on this trip." I could hear her bragging that way, but I knew that Ingrid would only be happy if the trip meant a new job, and the new job meant more money. She never had all the things she wanted, and she was always complaining to me that our apartment was too small and in the wrong part of town. Trying to impress her and to satisfy her had been the overriding goals of my life, and this trip might just possibly be a step toward meeting those goals—at least, that was my hope.

The next few days were hectic. Practically all of the work in preparation for the trip fell on me. I was really surprised that Poëhl had done so little, particularly since Poëhl was generally very conscientious. I got the impression that Poëhl had known that he would not be able to make the trip, and therefore had not really prepared for it. Whatever the reason, I had to make up investment reports for each of the customers that Steiner and I would be visiting. And I also had to put together some material on the bond, stock, and foreign exchange markets. I had to work every evening that week, and was really glad that Steiner left it all to me. There was no question that I knew the markets and the accounts far better than he did; it would only have irritated me if Steiner had tried to tell me what needed to be done.

Unfortunately, I had little time to spend with Ingrid. She had, of course, been delighted when she heard the news, but her next reaction had been just what I had predicted: "But Kurt, darling, this must mean a promotion. Doesn't it?" A promotion would mean more money, but she left that unsaid. In some ways she was more excited about the trip than I was. She wanted to know all about the preparations, particularly about what cities we were going to and what hotels we would be staying at. And she was dying to know how everyone else in the office reacted when they heard the news that I was going on the trip. She kept asking if Dr. Hofbeck had talked to me again, and she was quite upset that Steiner was doing so little to help get ready for the trip. "They don't really appreciate you, darling. You're smarter than anyone there and you do all the work, and people like Steiner and Poëhl get to be vice-presidents. It's really not fair." I hadn't seen Ingrid so excited since we were married, and I realized how disappointed she would be when I returned from the trip, even if I did end up with Poëhl's job. Recognition came very slowly at Schleswigbank, and financial rewards slower still.

While I got all of the material ready for the client meetings, Steiner spent most of his time talking with the bank's travel agent about the plane and hotel reservations. He wanted to be particularly sure that we had a suite in the best hotel in Buenos Aires. Schleswigbank's policy did not permit employees, even one of Steiner's rank, to stay in suites, but he insisted that it was necessary to do so since we would be meeting most of our clients at the hotel. In a country like Argentina with foreign exchange controls, those clients who did have accounts abroad did not want their Swiss bankers coming to their homes or offices. They would meet their banker at a hotel, usually in the banker's own room. It was somewhat inconvenient for the client, but it was the most discreet way to handle their, of necessity, very "private" banking. The matter was finally referred to Dr. Hofbeck, and he agreed that Steiner and I could take a suite in Buenos Aires, where we would be meeting most of our clients, but not in any of the other cities. And surprisingly, he also directed that we should fly first-class. He could not envision any Schleswigbank employee traveling on bank business, being seen in coach.

Chapter IV

Argentina, February 1965

As the McDonald Douglas DC-8 slowly descended over the Rio de la Plata on its approach to Buenos Aires, I sat in my seat next to the window and could not take my eyes away from the view below. It was evening as we were landing, and lights reflected on the water, creating a truly beautiful scene. It had been a good flight and an exhilarating experience for me, and the real excitement was yet to come. Steiner and I had flown from Zürich to Frankfurt, and boarded the Lufthansa flight there. The DC-8 was one of the first of a new series of jet engine planes that had just been put into service, and there was a real feeling of excitement as it roared down the runway. When I had walked to the plane and climbed the stairs into the first-class section, I had noticed that the four jet engines were made by Rolls Royce, and I could feel the power of those engines as the plane lifted almost effortlessly from the Frankfurt airport. Even Steiner seemed caught up by the excitement of the takeoff as the plane soared into the air.

It was a very long trip from Frankfurt to Buenos Aires, and the plane made only one stop, in Dakar, primarily for refueling. A few passengers from coach got off, but there was no change in the first-class cabin. After about an hour on the ground, the DC-8 took off again, and it seemed to me that the time passed very quickly from the time we took off from Frankfurt until we reached the coast of South America. First-class on Lufthansa was really great, and I certainly hoped that I would never have to fly in coach on a long flight like this one. I had ventured back into the coach section several times during the flight to try to get a little exercise, and I thought it was oppressively crowded and hot, and everyone looked extremely uncomfortable. It was a relief for me to return through the curtains dividing the two sections and once again be in the spaciousness and comfort of first class.

Everything on the flight—the food, the wine, the service—had been truly first-class, and if it was not with regret, it was at least with some apprehension that I watched as the plane descended to Buenos Aires. It was really impressive as the plane slowly landed at the Buenos Aires airport. I was convinced that this would be a trip that would stay in my memory forever.

Passport control was a mere formality. Both Steiner and I had obtained our visas in Zürich, although it had taken several phone calls from Dr. Hofbeck to the Argentine consulate to get them at the last minute. It occurred to me that I could have used my American passport, and I wondered if it would have been any quicker had I done so. Having been born in the United States, I was, of course, a US citizen, and my parents had gotten an American passport for me, which had always been kept current. But this was just a fleeting thought, and I knew it would not be very smart politically to let Schleswigbank know that I had two passports.

As Steiner and I rode into the city from the airport in our taxi, we maintained an almost total silence. Steiner had said very little on the plane, and I did not feel that I should take the initiative to start a conversation. Steiner might have preferred to come on the trip alone, and to that extent I was all too aware that Steiner might resent me. However, I knew that it probably bothered Steiner even more to realize that he needed me on this trip, and that his meetings with customers would be far more productive as long as I was there than if Steiner had come alone.

As the taxi came into the center of the city, I was really amazed at Buenos Aires. I don't know what I had expected, but I had not expected that the city would look like something straight out of middle Europe. The layout of the streets and boulevards, and the architecture of the buildings were completely European. And when we pulled up to our hotel, the Mirador, a late nineteenth century baroque building, even Steiner had to laugh and break the ice by saying, "We fly halfway around the world, and it looks like we're right back where we started in Zürich."

After checking in, we were ushered up to our suite, and I was relieved to see that it was a two-bedroom suite, since I would have hated to share a bedroom with Steiner. It was elaborately decorated, with very ornate furniture, and I could immediately understand that it would be a perfect spot to meet with our customers. Tonight, though, the only thing that I was interested in was getting to bed, and I'm sure that Steiner had the same idea. So, with a quick word about meeting for breakfast in the morning, we retired to our respective bedrooms, and I was relieved to be by myself again, at least for the night. As I lay in bed that night, I really had to smile before I went to sleep as I thought about what I was doing. Flying first-class from Frankfurt to Buenos Aires, and now staying in a suite at one of the best hotels in town, wasn't all bad. There certainly was some compensation to working for a Swiss private bank.

Both Steiner and I were up fairly early the next morning and had breakfast served in our suite. Steiner had made a number of appointments with clients before leaving Zürich, but he also spent much of the morning on the phone contacting others and arranging times to see them. While Steiner was doing this, I checked with Schleswigbank's correspondent in Buenos Aires, the Banco de la Plata, and got an update as to what was happening that Monday morning in the bond and foreign exchange markets. Finally, about 10:30 Steiner came to me and showed me our schedule for the balance of the week, and it was clear that we would have very little time for sightseeing. Schleswigbank did have a great many private banking customers in Argentina, and Steiner had filled almost every hour of our time in Buenos Aires with appointments.

We started seeing customers that day at lunch, and, as appointment followed appointment for the rest of the week, it seemed to me as if there was an unending parade of customers descending on us. The customers were virtually all German; they were all elderly, only a few being as young as their fifties; they had all gone into business since moving to Argentina, and most had become quite prosperous. All of the meetings were conducted in German, and the customers' interests focused primarily on the bond and foreign exchange markets—my particular areas of expertise.

The meetings themselves followed a pattern, with each customer being given a statement on his account, which was identified by a number. Those were the statements that I had prepared before we left Zürich. Many of the customers only received statements when they visited Switzerland or when a bank representative came to see them, since they did not trust the Argentine mails, even though Peron was no longer in power. Having assets outside of Argentina was not illegal, but the customers did not want the government to know about those assets, in order to protect them from any government attempt to tax or to otherwise confiscate them. The military junta that had succeeded Peron was a great stabilizing influence from the viewpoint of most wealthy people in the country, but inflation was rampant and one never knew whether or not the Peronistas might return to power. So investing money outside of Argentina was essential for the wealthy, just as it was essential to be absolutely discreet about such investments.

The discussions also followed a pattern as the customers asked questions about the investments in their accounts, what was going on in the markets, and what Schleswigbank planned to do during the next year to try to improve the performance of their account. As the week wore on, I soon realized that not a single customer ever expressed any satisfaction with the way in which his account had been invested or with the investment results. No matter how well the account might have done, the customer always felt that the bank should have done better. I heard myself repeating the same explanations over and over again, and having to listen to the same complaints endlessly repeated throughout the week. It did not take long before I began to wish that I was back on the trading desk in Zürich, and not here talking with these all-too-smug German expatriates.

One thing that did impress me, however, was Steiner's performance. The man was always charming to the customers, and he gave every appearance of really enjoying the meetings with them. I quickly saw how valuable to the bank this was, and I decided to make a similar effort to try to be just as upbeat as Steiner throughout the week. Another thing I noticed was that, after listening to me talk about the markets to a number of customers, Steiner soon picked up much of my current market analysis, and began to break into my explanations or even to answer investment questions on his own. This clearly annoyed me, and it was an effort not to let the customers see just how annoyed I was. And so for the last half of the week, Steiner and I were verbally fencing with each other in front of the customers.

Toward the end of the week, I finally realized Steiner's motive in rehearsing the answers to all the investment questions, when Steiner announced that he was going to go to Asunción, Paraguay, to see several important customers there. He also said that it would not be necessary for me to go with him. He rather patronizingly said, "I really think I've heard your spiel on the markets so often I could repeat it in my sleep."

Needless to say, I was more than a little upset that Steiner was going off without me to see these customers, at least one of whom I suspected had been a fairly important ex-Nazi official. I wondered why Steiner was so insistent on going to Paraguay alone, and it occurred to me that he might have a personal relationship of some kind with these clients. But there was nothing I could do about it, so my main concern was how I could kill time in Buenos Aires waiting for Steiner to return. We both had appointments the following week in Punta del Este, across the Rio de la Plata in Uruguay, where wealthy Argentineans vacationed, and I knew Steiner would not and could not cut me out of that trip. This was late January, the height of the South American summer, and Punta del Este would be jammed with vacationing Argentineans—all of whom would be actual or potential clients of the bank.

Steiner, however, suggested that I should spend the time that he was in Paraguay by going to a small town in northwestern Argentina, near San Miguel de Tucamán, to see a customer who was somewhat of a problem. This man, a Herr Gustav Reinsdorf, had a fairly small account with Schleswigbank of about 250,000 Swiss francs. Normally the bank would not have gone out of its way to call on him, but he had written several letters to Gerheart Poëhl about his account, indicating that he wanted to do something with it. Steiner couldn't be bothered to go there himself, but the bank was trying to close small accounts or get the customers to bring them up to the 500,000 SFr minimum, and Steiner said that I could carry this message as well as he could.

I had been irritated with Steiner all week as he horned in on the investment discussions with customers, but this suggestion really upset me since it appeared to be a deliberate slight on Steiner's part. Being sent off to a remote corner of the country to call on one of the bank's smallest customers really put me in a foul mood. It was becoming hard to remember how excited I had been less than a week before as Steiner and I had flown into Buenos Aires. But there was nothing I could do since I knew it would be a terrible mistake to argue with Steiner and give Steiner a reason to complain about me when we got back to Zürich. So I accepted the assignment as graciously as I could, and set about making the necessary arrangements for the trip.

Chapter V

Since I had been assigned the job to go and meet this person somewhere out in western Argentina, almost in the Andes, I had to find out where it was and how to get there. I had the client's phone number so I called and talked with his housekeeper, who gave me some basic directions as to where it was. But then I had to find a way to get there, since it was a small ranch, about 15 miles west of the town of Santa Maria, itself about 20 miles west of San Miguel de Tucamán. I had never heard of any of these places and had no idea where they were or where I had to go. However, I finally found out from the concierge at the hotel that the Argentine airline had a daily flight to Tucamán at eight in the morning. It arrived in Tucamán at eleven-thirty every day and returned to Buenos Aires that afternoon. This was a little awkward since this did not give me enough time to travel to Santa Maria and complete my business in time to get the return flight the same afternoon. Under the circumstances, it looked like I would have to stay overnight someplace, and I was not at all pleased by this. When I called the second time to say that I was coming, I talked with Herr Reinsdorf himself and he insisted that I stay at his home. He also told me that he would send his car to meet me at the Tucamán airport. At least the client seemed pleased that I was making the trip, even if I was not.

I have to confess that my humor did not improve when I got to the Buenos Aires airport early the next morning. I discovered that the Areoliñeas Argentinas plane that I was to take was an old DC-3. The plane was a rather sad sight as it sat outside the terminal with its tail on the ground, and with its two propeller engines leaking oil on to the tarmac. It provided a striking contrast to the sleek, new, jet-powered Lufthansa DC-8 on which Steiner and I had arrived just a few days earlier. However, since I could see no alternative, I resignedly boarded the plane and struggled up the steeply inclined aisle to my assigned seat. The DC-3 was designed with its tail close to the ground, so that the inside of the plane was at a fairly sharp upward angle. Fortunately, the plane was not very crowded, and I had two seats to myself. The stewardess on board seemed to do everything—directing the passengers to their seats, taking baggage on board to stow in a compartment behind the cockpit, and, after the plane was air-borne, serving dark, strong coffee to the passengers. She had gone up into the cockpit for takeoff, and I could only wonder if she was helping fly the plane too. Needless to say, I did not consider it to be a pleasant flight.

The plane landed in Córdoba as the first stop on the flight, and most of the passengers got off. Again, the stewardess was very busy, as she helped unload some of the luggage and then reload baggage going to Tucamán. As I watched her, I really became fascinated with her since it was rare that I had seen anyone work so hard, and I wanted to kick myself as I realized, now that the flight was almost half over, that she was quite attractive and that I had made no effort to get to know her. She was not a very big person, and yet she carried the bags and did all of her other jobs with seemingly little effort. After the plane left Córdoba, I found my spirits improving and I really could not understand why I had not paid more attention to her before. I then tried to strike up a conversation and, while she was pleasant, all I was able to find out was that she would be going back to BA with the plane that afternoon. I did discover, however, that she would be on the flight again the next day, and I decided to make a more concerted attempt to get to know her on the return trip.

As the plane neared San Miguel de Tucamán, I could see the Andes Mountains beginning to rise up in the distance. It was still morning and the sun was hitting the snow-capped peaks, providing me with a beautiful and dramatic picture. Although Tucamán itself was at a fairly high altitude itself, the mountains were all to the west, and I knew from having looked at a map that Herr Reinsdorf's ranch was still farther to the west and probably well into the foothills of the Andes. I was surprised as the plane descended to see how green and lush the area around Tucamán was. It was in stark contrast to the barren desert of so much of northwest Argentina.

The old reliable DC-3 bounced to a stop on the runway, and taxied up to the small terminal. I deplaned with the few passengers on board and told the stewardess that I would see her the next day. She merely smiled and said something in Spanish that I did not understand.

Inside the terminal, a young man came up to me and said, "Señor Wenner?'
"Yes."
"Good morning, I'm Toni. Herr Reinsdorf sent me to meet you."

The young man was probably in his early twenties, and with his dark coloring I decided that Toni must be either Italian or Spanish. Toni seemed friendly enough, but did not make much of an effort at conversation. He led me out to the car—an old Mercedes—and held the door for me as I got into the front passenger seat. Toni put my bag in the back seat, and got behind the wheel of the car and took off. And it seemed to me that we almost literally took off, since I can't remember ever being in a car with anyone who drove as fast as Toni did. We sped out of Tucamán heading toward Santa Maria on a good two-lane blacktop road all the way to Santa Maria. I could see the speedometer and Toni drove that stretch at well over 130 kilometers per hour. The young man seemed to revel in the speed, and took some fairly risky chances in passing slower farm vehicles on the road. All I could do was to hang on tight and hope that he knew what he was doing.

Santa Maria was a very small town; a sign as we entered said that there were just over 5,000 people. I was unable to get any impression of the place, however, since Toni barely slowed as we went through. Exiting Santa Maria to the west, I saw a road sign indicating that we were on the way to Antofagasta de la Sierra, and I could tell that the land was gradually rising toward the nearby mountains. There had been a great deal of farming near Tucamán, but here the land became much rockier and Toni told me that it was used mainly for grazing sheep. I tried to keep my eyes on the mountains, which were really impressive, but it was hard to do as our car careened along the road.

The road now became gravel, but this did not slow Toni down at all, and he maintained his almost breakneck speed. I had to hang on as tight as I could as the Mercedes sped over the increasingly rough surface. I was really getting scared, and finally decided that I had to say something.

"Is it really safe to go this fast on this kind of road?"

Toni flashed a big smile at me, and said, "Don't worry. I drive this road almost every day, and I know every bump in it. There are a few big ones up ahead here, but I'll take care of those."

A few minutes later, Toni suddenly veered off the road, down into a gully alongside the road, and then quickly back up onto the road again. I was really frightened now, but Toni kept on smiling and actually laughed as he said, "What did I tell you? If I hit one of those holes at this speed, the least I'd do is blow a couple of tires, or maybe worse. So I just go around them—it's quicker. There are only a couple more like that, but don't worry, like I said, I drive this road all the time, and I've never had an accident yet."

All I could do was to silently curse Steiner for sending me out to this God-forsaken corner of Argentina on what could only be a wild good chase. So I closed my eyes and prayed to whatever God it was that was supposed to be watching over us to see me through so that I could get back to my nice, quiet trading desk at Schleswigbank.

As promised, Toni veered off the road twice more to avoid deep holes or gullies in the road's surface, and he expertly brought the car back to the road each time. Finally, I was very relieved as Toni slowed appreciably and then turned off on the dirt road leading to Herr Reinsdorf's home. The road was immediately blocked by a wooden fence, and Toni brought the car to a stop, and I can't begin to say how utterly relieved I was when the car was finally completely stopped. Toni got out and opened the gate, and, after we passed through, he had to get out again to close it. However, it only took a minute before he was back in and we were moving into the ranch. Toni pointed out that the land on both sides of the trail belonged to Herr Reinsdorf and that he, Toni, was the one that did all the work on the ranch and took care of the sheep. There seemed to be quite a few sheep on both sides of the road, with some wandering across the road itself. I was very relieved that Toni drove very slowly now, since he clearly did not want to risk hitting any of the animals. I had the feeling that he was more concerned about the well-being of the sheep than he was about me.

We drove for about half a mile, and I could finally see a grove of trees ahead, with a rather imposing two-story stone house in the center. As we drove up to the house, I could see that the grounds were nicely landscaped, with some evergreen shrubs and several flowerbeds. Whoever had done the landscaping had left much of the rocky ground untouched, but the overall combination of bushes, flowers, and rocks was striking and partially offset the rather grim impression given by the house itself. Getting out of the car, I was surprised at how much cooler it was here than it had been in Tucamán.

I commented on the weather and Toni said, "Well, Tucamán is only about 7,000 feet high, but here we're at about 9,500 feet. And then because the humidity is so low, you'll find that it's much warmer in the sun than it is here in the shade."

Toni led me into the house, and I was immediately struck by the heavy, dark feeling of the interior. The front hall was paneled in dark wood, and there were several carved chests and benches in the same finish. There were a number of old, traditional oil paintings on the walls, and it seemed to me that they were scenes of Bavaria and the Black Forest. The pictures were not very well done, and they contributed to the somber atmosphere of the hall. Toni then led me into a room that seemed to be either a library or an office and that was furnished very similarly to the front hall. It was clear that Herr Reinsdorf had made a great effort to recreate an old German atmosphere here in northwest Argentina.

As we entered this room, I could see that Herr Reinsdorf was seated behind his desk, and I was almost shocked at how poorly the man looked. He seemed very frail, and sat slumped forward in his chair. I had seen in the bank's file that the man was in his mid-80s, but I had not expected that Herr Reinsdorf would look as bad as this. From what Steiner had told me, I had been afraid that this would be a difficult meeting, that dealing with Herr Reinsdorf might be awkward, and that he would have complaints against the bank or would make some unreasonable requests. But I immediately realized that this was a very different situation, and that I would have to be very careful how I dealt with this man who looked as if he did not have long to live.

Toni went up to the desk and said, "Sir, this is Mr. Wenner."

Herr Reinsdorf had watched us as we entered and said, "Oh, thank you, Toni, and Mr. Wenner, thank you so much for coming. Please sit down, but pardon me for not rising. At my age, my legs are not what they used to be."

I went up to him and we shook hands; at his suggestion, I then took the chair immediately in front of the desk.

"It is really very good of you to come all the way here to Santa Maria to see me. I cannot tell you how much I appreciate it."

"Not at all. It's been an interesting trip for me so far, particularly in getting to a part of Argentina that I had never seen before, and being so close to the Andes and getting such a wonderful view of them."

"Yes, the mountains are beautiful. I think the Andes are more dramatic than the Alps. It was one of the main reasons I chose to live here after the war—the mountains, the wonderful climate, and what I might call the remoteness."

It occurred to me that Herr Reinsdorf might look frail, but that his mind was certainly sharp.

Herr Reinsdorf than turned to Toni who was still standing near the door. "Toni, will you get a bottle of that wine we talked about. I'm sure Mr. Wenner would appreciate a little something to drink before lunch."

Toni nodded and quickly left the room, only to return a few minutes later with a wine cooler and several glasses. He proceeded to uncork the bottle, and let Herr Reinsdorf taste the wine before pouring a glass for me. I was just thinking that Toni was an accomplished servant, when I was surprised by Herr Reinsdorf suggesting to Toni that he have a glass of wine with us.

"Thanks, but I'd like to do a few things before lunch, so if you will excuse me, I'll see you at lunch."

The wine was an excellent Rhine wine that had been imported from Germany, and it had been chilled perfectly. Having a glass of wine was just what I needed after that rather wild drive from the airport, and I seemed to relax rather quickly. And I was surprised that I really enjoyed sitting in this room that looked as if it had been transported piece by piece from Bavaria, drinking a very good white wine, and engaging in small talk with this elderly gentleman. And it was just small talk before lunch. Herr Reinsdorf asked about Mr. Poëhl, and I merely told him that Mr. Poëhl had not been feeling too well, and that the bank had decided it would be better if he did not try to make the trip. Herr Reinsdorf expressed rather perfunctory regrets, but he seemed a good deal more interested in asking a great many questions about conditions in Europe. He was particularly interested in asking about the financial markets—stocks, bonds, and foreign exchange—and finally about the Cuban missile crisis that had occurred two years previously and had scared the whole world. I was impressed by how well informed he was, and asked how he kept up on everything.

Herr Reinsdorf said, "Well, I have *La Prensa*, of course, sent up from Buenos Aires, but I also have *Der Stern* sent over from Germany, and then I have the *Economist* sent from London. And I also have a short wave radio, and can pick up stations from all over. It has become a sort of hobby with me to try to stay on top of world events. I can't do too much around the ranch anymore—Toni really does everything now—so it keeps me occupied." We chatted for quite some time, and Herr Reinsdorf asked me if I would mind pouring some more wine. "The doctor in Tucamán tells me not to drink anything alcoholic, but I can't believe that a little wine will hurt. In fact, I try to tell him that I really think I feel better after a glass or two, but, of course, one can't tell doctors anything."

As we were talking, an elderly woman came to the door, and Herr Reinsdorf said, "Ah, Maria, I want you to meet Mr. Wenner, the young man from Switzerland that I told you about. Mr. Wenner, this is my housekeeper, Maria." Maria seemed to be a rather stolid figure, and, after a very brief greeting, she immediately announced that lunch was ready. I got up and stood for a second wondering if I should help Herr Reinsdorf, but Toni quickly came back into the room, and virtually lifted the old man out of his chair, supporting him as they walked into the dining room. Toni helped Herr Reinsdorf into the chair at the head of the table and suggested to me that I take the chair to his host's left. Toni sat to Herr Reinsdorf's right, and Maria then came in and began to serve what turned out to be a wonderful lunch. After serving the first course, a rich, homemade vegetable soup, she sat with us. The pattern was repeated with each course: Maria would serve, and then sit at the table and eat with us. The food was excellent; following the soup there was green salad, and then thick lamb stew that I have to say was just about as good as anything I could remember having. Toni served more of the Rhine wine with the soup and salad, but switched to a Chilean cabernet with the stew. I had never had a Chilean wine before; in fact, I really did not know much about wines, but I was very impressed with this wine's heavy, dark body.

It turned out to be not only an excellent lunch, but a rather pleasant one, since Toni seemed to be a very friendly and talkative young man, losing whatever inhibition that had kept him relatively quiet on the drive from the airport. As Herr Reinsdorf had done earlier, Toni seemed eager to ask me a great many questions about things going on around the world. And, I have to say, that I was truly impressed at the openness in the relationship between these three people since it seemed pretty apparent that they were very much like a family, one that seemed to get along with each other much better than most. Finally, Herr Reinsdorf suggested that he and I take coffee in the study, so that we could get down to the business that needed to be taken care of.

CHAPTER VI

After Toni had again settled Herr Reinsdorf in his chair in the study, he left and then Maria brought in coffee and some pastries. She served the coffee and quickly slipped out of the room, leaving the two of us to ourselves. Herr Reinsdorf started the conversation by observing, "You seem to be a rather young man, Mr. Wenner. Schleswigbank must have a great deal of confidence in you to send you on this trip and to have you deal with their customers."

"Well, as a matter of fact, this is my first trip abroad for the bank. I have been working with Mr. Poëhl on his accounts and, when he became ill, the bank asked me to go to Argentina along with one of Mr. Poëhl's colleagues, a Mr. Steiner. I think they felt that I had more experience in the bond markets and in foreign exchange than Mr. Steiner did."

"Do you mind my asking how old you are?"

"No, not at all. I was thirty-four last September. I was born in 1930."

"I'm sorry if I embarrassed you, but I thought you and Toni might be a little closer than that in age. He's twenty-six, but working out of doors all the time has probably made him look a little older. Then again, dark people like Toni perhaps look a little older than someone as fair as you are."

I did not feel that any response was necessary, and busied myself with my coffee.

Herr Reinsdorf also remained quiet for a few minutes, and then said, "I do envy both of you for your youth. It's not easy to be eighty-five, as I am, and to be in poor health. But one has to be philosophical. And while I don't mean to be morose, it is necessary to face the facts."

Again, there was a rather prolonged silence before Herr Reinsdorf went on. "As you have probably guessed, I came to Argentina after the war. And I came, not because I was a Nazi, which of course I was, but because I had no reason to stay in Germany. But perhaps I should explain, and I hope I won't bore you."

"No, please go on."

"I had been an administrator in occupied Norway through most of the war, and was able to make quite a bit of money. Permits were required for almost any type of business transaction, particularly imports and exports, and it was understood that the German administrative officers, particularly those who were members of the Nazi party, would be taking payments—bribes, if you will—to issue those permits. It was primarily the Swedish businessmen anxious to do business with Germany who were the ones seeking those permits. I always find the Swedes, with their professed neutrality and moral superiority, quite intolerable. They were just using their neutrality to make as much money as they could, and they traded with either side indiscriminately. But I was trying to make money too. So it was a wonderful situation. I established several bank accounts in Switzerland, and had the Swedish companies deposit my "commissions," as we called them, directly to my Swiss accounts. As you might guess, I built up quite a sizable fortune between 1941 and 1944. But it ended then as the war turned against Germany, and I was transferred to the Russian front. The next year was really horrible, and I was taken prisoner by the Russians as we retreated through Poland.

"But I survived, and was finally released in 1946. When I got back to our home in Augsburg, however, I found that my wife had been killed in an air raid in Munich early in 1945—she was working there at the time. And my son simply never returned from the war. To this day, we have never heard what happened; he was on the Russian front too, and all the Government has ever said is that he was presumed dead. So there was only my daughter. But she seemed to resent me as one of the Nazis who had brought all that ruin to the country, and who caused the death of her mother and brother. At least, that is my impression. She had married during the war, and her husband was able to get a visa for Nicaragua, and they went there in early 1947. So what was left? I decided to get out too, and got a visa for Chile. One had to pay for them, but I had all that money in Switzerland, so it was no problem.

"I spent a few months in Santiago, but could not find anything I wanted to do, so I came to Buenos Aires and settled there for a time. I have to confess, however, that I was never comfortable there. I worried about the Israeli agents who were looking for ex-Nazis, and although I personally had done nothing to the Jews, I decided to move out of the city. I looked all over Argentina and finally found the little town of Santa Maria, and was quite taken with it. Did you see it on your way here?"

"Not very well, I'm afraid. You know how Toni drives."

"Yes, of course. On your way back, insist that he slow down so that you can see it. It's really quite charming,—it has a wonderful little museum—and it's because of that town that I decided to come here—over fourteen years ago, in 1949."

"And Maria and Toni, you found them here or in Tucamán?"

"No . . . No, Maria worked for me in Buenos Aires—she cleaned my apartment, and things like that. She's Italian, of course, and had a young son. I'm sure you've guessed that Toni is her son. She was a widow, and when I told her I was moving here, she asked if they could come with me. It seemed such an easy solution for me that I agreed at once. It has been one of the best decisions of my life. We've become quite a little family, and I could never have gotten on all these years had I been alone. As I told you this morning, Toni does all the work around the ranch now, and I plan to leave it to him when I die."

There was another long pause, and I waited for the old man to resume.

"Please don't mention that to him. I haven't told him, but this place should be his, he has more than earned it and I must tell you that he has certainly helped to ease the pain of the loss of my Hans."

"Yes, I can see that he must be a great consolation to you—both Toni and his mother."

"It's very strange to think of Hans as I sit here talking to you. You really look a great deal like him. Like you, he was the model of a young, blond German youth—at least he was the last time I saw him. Toni is so different in some ways, but he has really become like a son to me. I think I've helped him, but he and Maria have certainly helped me. It's a good relationship since we have helped each other. . . And we like each other."

"So, Mr. Wenner, there you have my story. I guess my only regret is that I rarely hear from my daughter. She and her husband live in Mexico now, in Cuernavaca, and they seem to have become quite rich. There is nothing she could do with this place, so I would not think for one minute of leaving it to her. But I want her to have the money that is in my account at Schleswigbank. I believe there is a total of about 250,000 Swiss francs, isn't there?"

"Yes, there is."

"I want to transfer that money to her bank account at a small bank in Schaffhausen. Do you know the place?"

"Yes, it's near the German border, and not far from Zürich."

"Yes, it's right on the border, in fact. It's really quite a charming town, directly on the Rhine and there's a rather dramatic waterfall there—probably the most impressive one on the Rhine. I had heard about Schaffhausen long before the War because it was a place that Victor Hugo had loved, and when I was reading one of his books, I came across the passages he had written raving about its medieval character. And then during the War, it had a brief moment in the headlines when the Americans bombed it, mistakenly thinking that it was in Germany. President Roosevelt actually wrote a letter to the mayor of Schaffhausen apologizing for the bombing, and the Americans, as they usually do, paid all kinds of money to anyone who suffered any damage in the bombing.

"At any rate, aside from the town's history and charm, it was very convenient, being right on the German border, so I opened one of my Swiss bank accounts there during the war. When Elsa was married, I transferred that account to her, and I now want to close my account at your bank and move that money to Elsa's account at the Schaffhausen bank."

"Do you want to do this right away, Herr Reinsdorf?"

"Yes, in my condition, it is never too early to make these kinds of plans. I hope there won't be any difficulty in making such a transfer."

"Oh no, none at all. I have a form here that we can fill out right now, and I'll take care of the transfer as soon as I get back to Zürich. Now the only thing

I need is the exact name of the bank in Schaffhausen and your daughter's account number there."

"Yes, I expected you would. I've written down the name of the bank, and you can copy it from this paper, but I don't have her account number. I used to have it when it was my account, but the number was probably changed when I transferred the account to her. Can't I just give you my daughter's married name? It's Elsa Wilhelm—Mrs. Dieter Wilhelm."

"Well, I assume that this is a numbered account, so the name will not help in making the transfer. In fact, we should not even use the name of the account, just the number."

"Unfortunately, my daughter is traveling now. She's in New York, but I don't know where she's staying. I tried to phone her after you called to tell you were coming, but she had already left for the States. I really feel that it is so important that I do this now. Isn't there any way I can fill out the form and sign it, and send you the number later."

I thought for a while about what he was suggesting. I liked Herr Reinsdorf, and it was pretty easy to see that the old man was not well. Getting this transfer taken care of would be a great relief for him, but Schleswigbank required that forms such as this one not be accepted unless they contained all of the required information. Not having an account number on the transfer instructions would be the same as accepting a blank check. But I also knew how anxious the bank was to get rid of some of these smaller accounts, and I also knew that I would get some credit for getting it transferred. So I finally said, "When will your daughter be back in Cuernavaca?"

"I believe next week."

"I'm not supposed to do this, but we can fill out the entire form, except for the account number, and I'll have you sign it. Then next week after I return to BA from Punta del Este—I'm going to spend most of next week in Uruguay—so when I get back, I'll call you and you can give me the account number at that time. If you don't have it before I leave BA, I'm afraid I'll have to tear up the form, and we will then have to start all over when you do get the number."

"But this form will indicate that the money is to go to an account at the Schaffhausen bank?"

"Oh yes. It will specify the Schaffhausen bank, and will only lack your daughter's account number."

"Good. I will call her as soon as she gets back, and then we will talk before you leave Buenos Aires and you can fill in the right number."

It was a very simple form that took me only a few minutes to complete, after which Herr Reinsdorf immediately signed it and dated it. When the form was completed, Herr Reinsdorf said, "I think we should have a little brandy to celebrate. Please, would you get the brandy and glasses from the cabinet?"

I went over and found a bottle of brandy on the cabinet that must have been forty or fifty years old—the label was so old and faded that I could barely read it. I poured a small brandy for each of us, and we toasted each other before drinking. Herr Reinsdorf said, "I feel so much better to know that everything is taken care of now. I made a new will last month, and now this account will be transferred, so I really have no worries left."

I did have a few worries, however, since I knew that I was breaking a bank rule. But it seemed pretty clear that I would either get the proper account number before I left Argentina, or I would simply destroy the form. And with Steiner off in Paraguay, he would know nothing about this, so I felt that there was really no possibility that doing this for Herr Reinsdorf would become a problem.

CHAPTER VII

After the transfer instructions had been signed, we talked for a few minutes, but it was clear that Herr Reinsdorf had become quite tired. Therefore, I helped him up to his room as he said he would like to rest for a while. Since there was now nothing else to do, and it was a beautiful day outside, I decided to go out and explore the area around the house. I did not know where Toni was, so I just began walking up the steep hill behind the house. I soon discovered that I had to stop repeatedly to catch my breath, and I remembered that at this altitude the air was quite thin and that climbing was particularly hard. I kept going, however, stopping now and then to take a deep breath, and I finally sat on a rock at a point near the very top of the hill that gave me a great view of the whole ranch. It was late afternoon, and the sun had moved to the west behind the mountains so that the ranch was now in shadow.

It was really a very strange experience as I sat and absorbed the peace and serenity of the place. I could see the sheep down below, and I thought I could see Toni doing something near the barn, but the sheep and Toni and all living things seemed remote and almost unreal to me. I seemed to feel a quietness on that hill that was really unique—a stillness that I had never felt before in my life. As I thought of going back to Switzerland and returning to the pressures of the trading desk, I wondered if I would ever feel anything like this again. There was no wind, there were no birds, there seemed to be nothing but the harsh rocky land—and silence. It was truly unique since I had never before realized that silence could be palpable. All I could do was sit there and gaze out over the ranch to enjoy that silence for as long as possible.

Sitting there, my thoughts turned to Ingrid, and I realized that, much as I loved her, she could never appreciate this spot and this moment. I knew that I could not even tell her about it since she would not understand what I was talking about. It was certainly because of her, and because of her drive and her ambition, that I worked as hard as I did at the bank and that I strove to get ahead. I was obviously ambitious myself, but she always gave me an extra push. What if I went back to Zürich and suggested to her that we come back to some little ranch like this and raise sheep? What would her reaction be if I told her about the quietness, about the peace and solitude, and about the silence?

There was no question in my mind; I knew what the answer would be—she would just laugh. I knew I was being foolishly romantic, but for some reason some part of me seemed to respond to this remote spot, to its austere beauty and to its silence. I wondered if there was something in my life that was lacking, something I knew that I could not find back in the harsh reality of Zürich, Schleswigbank, and Ingrid. It was funny; I had not wanted to come here, and now I felt that I might be able to find something here that I could find nowhere else. It was such a far cry from the life I was leading in Zürich that, for a moment at least, I felt that I would have to find a way to come back.

I continued to sit there while the sun slowly sank behind the mountains to the west and while the early evening chill became more insistent. Finally, very reluctantly, I got up and began to work my way down that hill, finding the descent much easier than when I had walked up. It was almost dark when I got back to the house, and I found Toni in the dining room, getting ready to set the table.

Toni greeted me in his usual friendly way, "Oh, there you are, Mr. Wenner. I was beginning to wonder if you had wandered off and gotten lost."

"No, I had walked up the hill or, rather, struggled up the hill. I'm not used to the altitude, and it takes one's breath away. And please, I would much prefer if you called me Kurt."

"OK, if that's what you'd like. As to the altitude, when we first came from BA I had the same problem too. But after a time, I guess that your lungs adjust. I never notice the altitude anymore. What did you think of the view from up there?"

"It was tremendous." I paused for a minute, and then added, "But did you ever notice the total silence?"

Toni stopped gathering the plates and silverware, and looked at me for a minute. "Yes. It's why Elena and I go up there. She's my fiancée, and it's great when we can just sit there together. I don't think we ever feel closer than when we're up there."

Nothing was said for a couple of minutes as the two of us seemed lost in our own thoughts. It was broken as Toni began to set the table.

I asked him, "Are there just the two of us for dinner?"

"Yes. Gus usually doesn't come down for supper anymore, we have our big meal in the afternoon. And tonight my mother took her meal up to her room."

"It would be easier if we ate in the kitchen, wouldn't it?"

"You don't mind?"

"Of course not."

"Well, we're just having a light meal."

The kitchen was very comfortable, and as we sat talking over our cold chicken and beer, I became more and more impressed with Toni. This young man seemed to be so at peace with himself, so self-confident, so personally secure. He told me of his ambitions—of his wanting to make a better life for himself and his mother, of wanting to get married and raise a family, and of having the financial security to give his children all the things that he had lacked in his childhood. And he spoke of his tremendous indebtedness to Gus—Herr Reinsdorf.

"I'm uncomfortable calling him Gus in front of other people. But when we first came here thirteen years ago I was only thirteen, and he insisted that I not call him Herr Reinsdorf. So we finally hit on Gus. He's been the only father I've ever known, and I really worry when I see how his health has been declining."

"Well, I'd never seen him before, but I was surprised at how weak he seemed to be."

"It's gotten worse in the past few months. And I hate to think what will happen. Starting over someplace else will not be easy, although it won't be too bad for me, but it will be very hard on my mother."

I tried to reassure him by saying, "I don't think you have to worry about that, do you?"

"I really don't know. Even if he wanted to leave the place to me, and my mother thinks that he would do that, he has that daughter of his, and I don't know what she would do."

"Have you met the daughter?"

"God, have we met her! What's her name, Elsa something? She came here about four years ago, and she's nothing like her father. A real bitch. My mother heard her arguing with Gus when she first arrived because she refused to have us sit at the dining room table with her. When Gus was alone, my mother went in and suggested that he would probably want to talk with his daughter as much as possible while she was here, so my mother suggested that she and I would take our meals in the kitchen. Gus understood, but he thanked her, and that's the way it was. The daughter wanted to be waited on all the time, like she was a duchess or something. She's a cold, hard bitch. I just pray that I don't ever have to have a run-in with her. But we shouldn't even be talking this way. I'd hate to think of anything happening to Gus—I know I'd really miss him."

The two of us continued talking for a while, and I finally said, "Well, all I can say is that I'll probably have to have more to do with the daughter in the future than you will."

Toni looked at me and nodded slightly as he said, "I hope you're right."

The next morning I had breakfast with Herr Reinsdorf and Toni, and I was surprised at how relaxed everyone seemed to be. After being here for less than twenty-four hours, I felt as if I were a part of this family. I really regretted having to leave that morning, but I had to be at the airport in Tucamán by noon for the one o'clock departure of the flight back to Buenos Aires. As I was leaving, Herr Reinsdorf said, "Thank you again for coming. It's a great relief to know that everything is taken care of."

"I can't tell you how much I've enjoyed being here. You have a delightful spot, and I'm only sorry that you won't be a customer of Schleswigbank anymore. Now I won't have an excuse to come visit you again, but I will call you next week from Buenos Aires, as we agreed."

Toni drove a little more slowly on the return trip, and even pointed out the sights of Santa Maria as we passed through. When we got to the airport, Toni said, "I was surprised that you said to Gus that he wouldn't be a customer of yours anymore. I don't know what that's all about, but please come and visit us any time you're able to."

We shook hands and I turned and walked into the tiny airport building. The same old DC-3 was there on the tarmac, with the same crew and the same stewardess. I had planned to try to get a date with her on the way back to Buenos Aires, but I was now totally preoccupied with my thoughts of Herr Reinsdorf's ranch and the people I had met there, and I sat looking out the window for the whole return trip. It was only when we had landed in Buenos Aires and I was getting off the plane that I remembered my intention to get a date with the stewardess. But when I tried to strike up a conversation with her, she just smiled sweetly and turned to the next passenger who was deplaning.

CHAPTER VIII

Back at the hotel in Buenos Aires, I returned to the suite Steiner and I had been staying in, since I had not given it up when I went to see Herr Reinsdorf. I knew I would be back in just one day, and Steiner was expected to return a day or two later, and it was easier to leave the luggage in the suite. However, Steiner did not come back. Instead, he sent a telex from Ascunción indicating that he had to remain there longer than planned, and was then going to go on to La Paz. He told me that I should go to Punta del Este myself, and that he hoped that we could meet in Buenos Aires a week later for the return flight to Frankfurt.

I was actually relieved to learn that Steiner was not going to join me in Uruguay, and was pleased that I would be handling the calls there on my own. I wondered what Steiner was up to in Paraguay and Bolivia; it seemed to me that there must be something more than just meeting with clients. It was possible that even the bank was not aware of the real identity of the clients he was dealing with in those countries. Fortunately, all of the customer files for the meetings in Punta del Este had been left in Buenos Aires, so I began immediately to prepare for those meetings. This took quite a bit of time, and I was not able to do any sightseeing, as I had hoped to do.

Two days later, I flew across the Rio de la Plata to Montevideo, and hired a car to drive me to Punta del Este. Immediately upon my arrival, I plunged into another round of nonstop customer meetings. Maybe because Punta del Este was a vacation resort and all the customers were more relaxed there, or maybe they found it easier to deal with me because I was relatively young, and there was no one else from the bank there, but whatever the reason, the meetings went extraordinarily well. I was really elated that I had managed to get several customers to add substantial amounts to their accounts, and I also picked up two new accounts for the bank. I was sure that Dr. Hofbeck would be pleased with my accomplishments—and I had done this entirely on my own.

Since Punta del Este was a vacation spot, everyone spent the late mornings and the afternoons at the pool, on the beach, or on the tennis courts. As a result, I found that I could only have meetings with the clients in the early morning or late in the day. It was easy for me to decide to follow the same kind of schedule as the clients did, and as a result, the whole week in Punta del Este became very much like a vacation for me. In addition, I was invited to have cocktails and dinner with one of our customers every night that I was there, so relaxing by the pool in the afternoon was a great relief. I spent so much time at the beach that I had to worry about getting sunburned. I knew that when I got back to Zürich, everyone would notice my tan.

The week in Uruguay passed by all too fast, and I was soon on my way back to BA. As I sat on the plane returning to BA from Montevideo, I realized that the week in Punta del Este and the day that I had spent at Herr Reinsdorf's ranch had been the best part of the trip. I had originally been irritated when Steiner had decided to go off to Paraguay alone, but that had really given me the opportunity to make my own mark from a professional viewpoint, and it had also given me the most enjoyable part of the trip.

When I got back to the Mirador, I found another message waiting for me saying that Steiner would not be able to return to Buenos Aires in time for the return flight to Frankfurt. But he said that I should go on alone. I was not surprised to hear this, and only wondered how Steiner was going to explain things to Dr. Hofbeck when he got back to Zürich. Since I had given up our suite when I went to Punta del Este, I now decided that I would only need a single room for one night. I knew that the plane would be leaving early the next morning, and I wanted to get to bed early. It was just about 9:00 p.m. when I retired, but I suddenly remembered that I had to call Herr Reinsdorf to get the daughter's account number at the Schaffhausen bank. God, I thought, I hope the old man's not sleeping. I had to get that number, or we would have to start the process of closing that account all over again.

I placed the call with the operator and the call went through fairly quickly. Toni answered the phone and I said, "Toni, it's Kurt here. I hope it's not too late and that Herr Reinsdorf has not gone to bed. But I do need to speak with him."

Toni replied, "I'm afraid that it is too late, Kurt. Gus died two days ago."

While the news was not totally unexpected, I was still shocked. "He died? Toni, I'm so sorry. I don't know what to say. What happened?"

"We think he had a stroke a day or two after you left, and there was just nothing to be done. The doctor came from Tucamán, but we decided not to move him, and then the day before yesterday, he just died in his sleep."

I didn't know what to say since so many things were going through my mind. "I feel so helpless down here in Buenos Aires. Is there anything I can do?"

Toni hesitated a minute, but then said, "Well, we haven't been able to get in touch with his daughter. I've tried to call but her housekeeper says she's in New York. We'd like to go ahead with the funeral, although my mother feels we should wait until we've talked with the daughter."

I immediately said, "Go ahead with the funeral. It may be several weeks before she can get down to Argentina. You and your mother were more family to him than she was anyway."

"Yes, you're right about that—I think we will. She may give us hell later, but we've got to do something. Although she'll probably kick us out as soon as she gets down here."

I felt that I needed to reassure him, so I said, "Toni, I'm sure you don't have to worry about that. You must have driven Gus into Tucamán to see a lawyer in the last month or two, didn't you?"

"Yes, why?'

Since Herr Reinsdorf had died, I decided it would be all right for me to at least hint at what he had told me, so I said, "Gus told me he had made a new will. Toni, go and see the lawyer—I'm sure you'll find everything is all right."

He replied, "You must know something."

"Look, I promised Gus—here I am calling him Gus—that I wouldn't say anything. But he did look upon you as if you were his son, so go see the lawyer and don't worry about the daughter."

"Well, I'd been thinking that I had to do that anyway, and you're right—I'll do that the first thing tomorrow. Incidentally, was there some particular reason you called?"

I could not possibly tell him the reason for my call, so I answered: "No. . . No, nothing in particular. I'm leaving in the morning for Europe, and I just wanted to call to see how Herr Reinsdorf was, and to thank him again for his hospitality. But Toni, write to me sometime and let me know how everything turns out. I left my card on the desk in the study and it has my address on it."

"Thanks for calling, Kurt. It's been a big help, and I will write to you soon."

I was really saddened by the call, but I felt that what I had been able to tell Toni had probably provided some reassurance to him, at a time that he certainly needed someone his own age to talk with. I thought that it would be good idea if I called him after I get back to Zürich to see how things were going. It had been a long call, and as I got into bed, I remembered the account closing form that was the real reason for the phone call. I knew that I couldn't possibly find it now, and I simply thought that I would have to tear it up when I got back to Zürich.

CHAPTER IX

Zürich, February 1965

I had arrived back in Zürich on a Saturday morning, after a flight from Buenos Aires to Frankfurt the previous day, an overnight stay in Frankfurt and an early morning flight to Zürich. Coming out of the warm Argentine summer into the middle of a cold Swiss winter was something of a jolt, but I hurried home and spent the whole day in the apartment with Ingrid. I was really happy to be with her again after the first real separation of our marriage, and was eager to tell her all about the trip. Sitting close to her again, holding her in my arms, inhaling her scent,—this was a wonderful feeling, familiar, reassuring, and exciting, and one that I had sorely missed. She could be a chameleon at times, changing her personality and mood to reflect mine. And this particular morning, she struck the perfect note for my return, being about as sexy as I could ever remember her being.

We sat together in front of the small fireplace in our apartment, and for several hours I told her about the trip—about the customers in Buenos Aires, about Steiner taking off for Paraguay and Bolivia alone, about my trip to Punta del Este, and about my overnight trip to Herr Reinsdorf's ranch. However, I did not tell her about the thoughts that I had as I sat on that hill behind the ranch house of possibly wanting to live in a spot like that. I did not tell her since I knew that she would not understand, and I did not want to spoil the memory for myself. But I did tell her that Herr Reinsdorf had died a few days after I had been there and met with him.

We were having a glass of wine, and Ingrid lay with her head on my shoulder. So in this very relaxed situation, I said, "As a matter of fact, the old man signed transfer instructions to close his account with us and move 250,000 francs to his daughter's account at some bank in Schaffhausen. He didn't have her account number, but he signed the form in blank anyway—he was supposed to give me the number when I called him from Buenos Aires. So, darling, if you want 250,000 francs, go over to Schaffhausen and open an account, and I'll fill in that number on the form."

Ingrid laughed as she replied, "Oh, Kurt, it would really be easy, wouldn't it? Is that all you need, the number of an account? And with Swiss bank secrecy laws, no one could ever find out."

As I leaned down and kissed her again, I said, "That's right, no one could ever find out."

We made love that afternoon and, after the long separation, we were both really overjoyed at being together again. Afterward, we lay in bed for a long time, not talking, not even thinking, just glad to be together again. Later in the evening, Ingrid fixed a light supper that we ate in front of the fire. We talked some more about the trip, but I was totally exhausted, and we decided to go to bed early. I was feeling on top of the world after what I felt was a very successful trip and now being home again and lucky to have a wife as great as Ingrid.

In the morning, I was lying on my side, with my arm across Ingrid, holding her tightly to me. She was still sleeping and I really felt blessed holding her warm body against my own. *If there is a God, he has been good to me,* I thought. To have a woman like this next to me in bed, to have her as my very own, to have her as my wife—what more could I ask? We lay that way for a long time, and I tried to remain as still as possible to avoid waking her.

She did move finally, and she took hold of my arm and held it more tightly against her body. We did not talk for some time, until finally Ingrid said, "Kurt, you know we could do it, don't you?"

"Do what?"

"Take that 250,000 francs."

I was surprised at what she had said, and I replied, "You're not serious."

"Yes, I am. Think about it. You have the account closing form. It's been signed by Herr what's-his-name. I could go up to Schaffhausen and open an account and get a number, and all you have to do is put that number on the form. Then you just send the form off at Schleswigbank to be processed. Who could ever find out?"

"Ingrid, the man is dead."

"But they don't know that. And he was obviously alive when you saw him, and you don't have to let on that you found out that he was dead. There was no reason for you to phone again after you had been to that God-forsaken spot."

I did not like the way this conversation was going, and I said, "It was not God-forsaken. It was a beautiful place."

"All right, it was beautiful. But the man signed a form closing his account and instructing that the money be sent to an account in Schaffhausen. And you are simply carrying out his instructions. Who will ever know the difference?"

Instinctively, I felt that I had to argue with her, and said, "He has a daughter. That's who the money is supposed to go to."

"Does she know about the account at Schleswigbank?"

"I don't know. They weren't very close."

"How do you know that?"

"He told me. The daughter was bitter because of the war. Her father was a Nazi, and both her mother and brother were killed in the war. She seemed to hold it against her father. So he hardly ever saw her."

Ingrid was persistent, as she asked, "Where does she live?"

"In Mexico, actually in Cuernavaca. But she's in New York right now."

"You certainly found out a lot about her."

"Well, her father told me that the reason he couldn't get her account number was that she was traveling in the States. And then when I talked with Toni—the young man who runs the ranch—he told me that they had been trying to reach her about her father's funeral, but that she was still in New York."

"So her father may not have talked with her at all about transferring the money."

"He maybe didn't."

"Would she know that the account existed?"

"I don't know. She had only been to see him in Argentina once, and that was years ago. But there are the bank statements. I just brought him the statements covering the last two years. We never send them to him, of course, because of the mails, but there would be statements right up to the end of 1964 probably on top of his desk."

"And you think she would find them when she goes through all of his papers?"

"I don't know that either. She doesn't inherit the ranch—Toni does."

Ingrid sounded a little out of sorts, as she said, "I can't believe that you know everything about these people, and you were only there for about twenty-four hours."

I had to smile at her irritation, and said, "Well, they all seemed to like me. And neither the old man nor Toni ever really had much of a chance to talk with anyone about their personal affairs. So Gus—that's what Toni calls him—Gus told me that he was leaving the ranch to Toni, and that's why he wanted the account at Schleswigbank to go to Elsa."

"Elsa. That's the daughter's name? You know that too?"

"Yes, as a matter of fact. It's Elsa Wilhelm. Mrs. Dieter Wilhelm."

Ingrid seemed a little more irritated as she said, "I suppose you like her too."

"No. Toni said she was a real bitch. She wouldn't eat at the table with Toni and his mother, and she wanted to be waited on all the time."

"Toni's mother. Where does she come in?"

"She was Herr Reinsdorf's housekeeper when he lived in Buenos Aires. Then when he decided to move up to Santa Maria, she asked if she could come along and bring her son, who was only thirteen at the time."

"Well, it's just one big happy family. I'm surprised they didn't adopt you too."

I couldn't resist saying, "I asked, but they wouldn't have me."

Ingrid tried to hit me after I had said that, and we struggled playfully for a few minutes, before settling down again into a comfortable embrace.

"But Kurt, the daughter's in Mexico, she has not been close to her father, she's not inheriting the ranch, there is no reason for her to go to Argentina, and she may not even know about the Schleswigbank account. She would probably be surprised if the money ended up in her account in Schaffhausen. Isn't that right?"

"Yes, I guess so. And she doesn't really need it."

"She doesn't need the money? Who told you that?"

"Her father. He said that his daughter and her husband had become quite rich."

"All the more reason not to worry. She will hear that he's dead, and that he has left everything in Argentina to the young Italian—he is Italian, isn't he?"

"Yes."

"So why should she come to Argentina? Would the young man invite her there?"

"No. No, he wouldn't do that. He didn't like her."

"Think about it Kurt, it's the perfect situation. We've been handed the chance to take 250,000 francs, and no one will ever know."

We lay in bed together for a long time, neither talking, but both of us thinking about what had just been said about the money. I know that Ingrid started to fantasize about all the things she could buy with the money, but I had very mixed thoughts. On the one hand, I was thinking of finally being able to provide a lifestyle for Ingrid such as I had never been able to provide before, but, on the other hand, the fact that taking the money would be both legally and morally wrong was something I could not ignore.

We finally got out of bed, and later over coffee at the kitchen table, Ingrid said, "Kurt, you know all about Swiss banking laws. Let's say she did find out and she did complain. What would happen?"

"Well, we would probably tell her that we had valid transfer instructions signed by her father several days before his death, and that the account was closed. And she might have to have a lawyer to get even that much information."

"Would she be told that the money had gone to the Schaffhausen bank?"

"No. I'm sure that would violate Swiss bank secrecy laws. We'd never tell her that."

"So what could she do?"

"Probably nothing. She could go to the authorities, but if they inquired at Schleswigbank, we would have his signed instructions to show them. You're probably right, Ingrid. She either would never know about the account and about the transfer, or even if she did, she couldn't find out where the money went. And even if she found out that the money went to the Schaffhausen bank, they would never in a million years tell her whose account it went into. That would be a clear violation of the secrecy laws."

Ingrid was persistent, and went on, "Kurt, we would be fools if we passed up this chance. It's as if God or fate or someone wanted us to have this money. I'll go up to Schaffhausen in the morning and open an account, and on Tuesday you can fill in the number that I get and put the transfer through. Oh, and isn't it lucky that Steiner is still off in Bolivia or wherever he is. If he had been in Buenos Aires with you, you probably would have told him that the old man was dead, and we wouldn't be able to use the form. Everything has worked out perfectly."

I felt that I had to argue with her, and said, "It is wrong, though. Don't you think that it's at least morally wrong, Ingrid?"

"No, I don't. She's been a terrible daughter, and she doesn't deserve the money. So let's not start getting all moralistic or religious or something about this. We've got a great chance to change our lives—just think, Kurt, how it will change our lives—and there's absolutely no risk. You will do it, won't you?"

"I'll think about it, Ingrid. I want to be sure in my own mind that there really is no risk, and I want to think about every angle. I don't have to put in the transfer instructions on the first day I'm back at work, so let's take our time and be sure that this is something that is as riskless as you say it is. I'll think about it."

CHAPTER X

On Monday I returned to work, and immediately faced the problem of what desk I should sit at. I did not think that I should go back to the trading desk, and I thought that it would be presumptuous of me to move into Gerheart Poëhl's office. So I went back to the temporary desk I had used while preparing for the trip. I spent most of the morning writing call reports and doing other follow-up work from the trip, until late in the morning when I received a call from Dr. Hofbeck's secretary. I went up to the Managing Director's office with a good deal more confidence than when I had been summoned there just a few weeks before.

After some perfunctory inquiries about the trip, Dr. Hofbeck said, "I would like you to fill in for Mr. Poëhl, at least temporarily. His condition has worsened while you were away, and I must tell you that I doubt if he will be able to return. Of course, we cannot make any announcement about that for the present, so your assignment will be temporary for now.

"I might mention that I had a few telexes from Steiner, and he indicated that you were doing an excellent job in Argentina. He must have had great confidence in you to send you off to Uruguay on your own, while he went to Paraguay. Do you know why he did that?"

"No, I was somewhat surprised."

"I'm sure he had his reasons, but bank policy does require that there be two officers calling on customers when traveling abroad. I will have to talk with Steiner about this. At any rate, I hope things went well for you in Uruguay."

"As a matter of fact, I think that they did. I was able to obtain additional deposits to some of our accounts, and even got two new accounts."

"Oh really. Well, give me a complete report, and when Steiner returns I will want to meet with both of you again."

I left Hofbeck's office feeling truly elated. I was getting Poëhl's job, I was able to show concrete results from the work I had done in Uruguay, and Hofbeck was clearly irritated with Steiner. The rest of the day passed quickly as I moved into Poëhl's office, and continued to try to get caught up on everything after the trip. As I headed home that night, I realized that I had not had time to even think about the Reinsdorf money.

The next day, Tuesday, was very similar. Monday night Ingrid had pressed me for a decision, but when I got to the bank on Tuesday morning, I was swamped trying to get caught up on all of Poëhl's work, and, again, I put the money out of my mind. It even occurred to me that I was deliberately trying to keep myself busy so as not to think about the possible embezzlement. And as that thought came into my mind, I realized that what Ingrid and I had been talking about was, in fact, an embezzlement. There was no other way to describe it.

When I got home that night, Ingrid rather abruptly asked, "What did you do about the money? What have you decided?"

I did not like the pressure that that question entailed, so I said, "I just don't know. It's risky, you know that. And why should we take that risk when everything is going so well?"

I could not recall seeing Ingrid so adamant as she argued, "We've talked about the risk, and we know that there's virtually none. I don't see why you're dithering. If you wait much longer, the bank will find out that he's dead, and then we will have lost our chance. Kurt, of course, things are going well at the bank—they're finally beginning to appreciate you. But with 250,000 francs, think what we could do. We could move to a better apartment, I could dress better, and you could too. You know we'll have to go to a lot of dinners and things like that now, and I can't go in dowdy old clothes. I'll bet Steiner and Poëhl have entertained in their homes—we can't do that here. We need this money a great deal more now that you've been promoted than we did before. We're moving up into a different class, and we have to show that we fit in."

I hated to argue with Ingrid, so my answer was a form of concession: "I know that, but you were going to go to Schaffhausen and open an account, and you haven't done that. So don't blame me for not moving ahead. You're not doing anything either."

"Darling, let's not quarrel. If you really don't want to do this—if you don't want to take this money that has been virtually handed to us—well, then I'll have to accept that. But I don't want to quarrel with you. I love you too much for that. So we'll just have to forget it."

It seemed to me that some sincerity was lacking in both of our arguments, as I said, "Ingrid, I don't want to quarrel with you either. Maybe I'm afraid, I don't know. I want the money too, and I do realize what it can mean to us. But if we're caught, it's the end of everything for us. You do know that, don't you? It will really be the end of everything."

There was clearly a strain between us all evening, and while we each made an attempt at conversation, the attempts were forced and there was no spontaneity. We went to bed that night with neither of us having any idea as to what we were going to do about Herr Reinsdorf's money.

The strained silence carried over to the next morning, and as we sat having coffee in the kitchen, I could only think back to that time on that hill at the base of the Andes at Herr Reinsdorf's ranch and the serene silence that I found there, as opposed to this gray, angry silence here in my own apartment with my wife. I thought Ingrid might say something about the money when I left for work, but she said nothing and we merely exchanged the most perfunctory of kisses as I went out the door.

At the bank, I threw myself into work again, although I did look at Herr Reinsdorf's signed transfer instructions several times, hating the idea of making a decision about what to do with it. I kept the signed instructions in the bottom drawer of my desk, but I had taken them out and put them on top of my desk just before Steiner came into my office. I was surprised to see him.

He greeted me by saying, "Well, I see you've taken over here."

"So it seems. Dr. Hofbeck told me to fill in for Poëhl, at least temporarily."

"I'm sure you know that it won't be temporary. So congratulations."

I was not sure that they were the most sincere congratulations, but I said, "Thanks. When did you get back?"

"Yesterday morning, but I was too exhausted to come into the bank."

"Did things go well in Paraguay and Bolivia?"

"Very well, and I assume that everything was OK in Uruguay."

I realized as we talked that I was practically on an equal footing with him now, and replied, "Yes, business was good and it was almost like a vacation."

It sounded to me as if he was trying to needle me as he said, "I see you got quite a tan—you must have enjoyed the beach." When I didn't react, he added, "But I have to tell you that Dr. Hofbeck wants to see both of us this afternoon to get a complete report on the trip. Three o'clock in his office."

Steiner left and I looked again at Herr Reinsdorf's transfer instructions that were still lying on top of a pile of papers on my desk. I really did not know what I would have said if Steiner had asked about that document.

At three o'clock, Steiner and I were shown into Dr. Hofbeck's office and with very few preliminaries, the Managing Director asked about the trip. Steiner told about the meetings in Buenos Aires, giving Dr. Hofbeck a detailed list of the customers with whom we had met and the size of their accounts. Hofbeck asked a number of questions about different customers, addressing the questions both to Steiner and to me. Hofbeck then added, "I've talked with Mr. Steiner about going off to Asunción and La Paz alone, and he explained to me earlier today that several customers asked him to come, but demanded complete discretion. We have agreed, and Mr. Wenner, I want you to understand this as well, that if it is required to travel alone in this way in the future, you should get my approval first. Fortunately, Mr. Steiner has been able to bring back some rather valuable new business, and for this we can forgive him.

"Now, you told me, Mr. Wenner, that you had gone to Uruguay by yourself while Mr. Steiner was in Paraguay and Bolivia."

"Yes, and here's the report of my trip. As I told you, I did get some additions to several accounts, as noted on the report, and was able to obtain two new accounts."

"Well, it seems to have been a productive trip."

Steiner then ventured, "And Kurt also managed to get rid of one of our small accounts, didn't you Kurt?"

Dr. Hofbeck said, "And what was that?"

"Helmut—Mr. Steiner—suggested that I go to a little town up in northwest Argentina to see a Herr Gustav Reinsdorf."

"Reinsdorf? I may have known him. A German, probably a Nazi."

"Yes, he told me that he had been a member of the Nazi party. I stayed at his place for a day—it was rather remote and I had no alternative—and he agreed to transfer his account to a bank up in Schaffhausen."

"Schaffhausen?"

"He said that he had opened accounts there during the war since it was so near the German border."

"As many of his compatriots did. How much was it?"

"Just about 250,000 francs."

"Good. We have to keep pressing to get rid of those small accounts. Well, gentlemen, I think that all in all you had a good trip, and you should plan to go back about every six months, particularly if you're able to pick up new business. Thank you again. I think that that will be all for now."

When I got back to my office I felt remarkably calm. I knew that the die was now cast as to Herr Reinsdorf's money, but the nervousness I had experienced earlier in the day was gone. I felt as if the decision had been taken from me. I was certainly not going to admit at that meeting what had actually happened—not with Steiner present, and probably not even to Hofbeck. As an up-and-coming young officer of Schleswigbank I had to show that I was successful in all that I set about. I was not going to confess that I had permitted Herr Reinsdorf to sign an incomplete transfer form, a form that I still had, and I certainly saw no reason to tell them that Herr Reinsdorf was dead. I would now have to transfer the money to an account at the Schaffhausen bank, and either Ingrid or I were the only ones who could open that account. The die had been cast.

I arrived home that evening and was greeted by the same coldness as I had felt from Ingrid in the morning. I decided to say nothing at first, and I changed into more casual clothes and, without asking what she wanted, made drinks for both of us. I brought the drink to her in the living room and said, "It's done."

She looked up as I stood over her, her eyes widening, and she began to understand. "I told Hofbeck and Steiner that Herr Reinsdorf had closed his account."

"Kurt, you didn't."

"Hofbeck wanted to know about the trip and Steiner and I were in his office, and it just came out. I told him that I had gotten some new accounts in Uruguay, and incidentally, that I had convinced one customer to close a small account. Hofbeck was very pleased."

Ingrid jumped up to embrace me, and I yelled, "Watch the drinks."

"Darling, how marvelous, how wonderful, I can't believe it! Now there's no question—the money will be ours."

We hugged each other fervently, glad that our brief estrangement was over. I sat down on the sofa and Ingrid immediately sat on my lap. We toasted with the drinks that I had made, and continued to savor the moment, knowing, as we each did, that the money was as good as ours and that it would, in fact, change our lives.

After we had sat together for a while, I said to Ingrid, "So in the morning, you must rush to Schaffhausen and open an account at the bank, and then phone me with the number so I can complete the transfer form."

"Kurt, I know I said I would do that, but I would be so nervous. I could ruin everything if I said the wrong thing. I hate to back out on you now, but it will be much safer if you open the account. You know banking, and you would be sure to do everything right."

"Don't be silly. There's nothing to opening an account. I'll give you all the information you need. You don't have to be nervous."

But Ingrid was not to be persuaded, and it ended up that I had no choice. I had told Hofbeck and Steiner that I had obtained a transfer form on Reinsdorf's account, and I would have to produce a completed form in the next day or two, or risk having questions asked. So there was nothing else I could do. Since Ingrid did not want to go to the Schaffhausen bank, I would have to do it myself. The next morning I left home at about 8:00 a.m. for the drive to Schaffhausen, and Ingrid phoned Schleswigbank to tell them that I was not feeling well—she explained that it was probably exhaustion from the trip—and that I would not be at work that day.

Schaffhausen was only about fifty kilometers from Zürich, but the road went through a succession of small towns, and traffic was heavy in the morning, so the trip took over an hour, as I had planned. During the drive, I devised a story that I would tell the bank, and I decided that maybe it was better, after all, that I open the account, rather than Ingrid. I finally arrived in Schaffhausen, a town to which I had never been before, and as Herr Reinsdorf had said, it was as quaint and picturesque a medieval town as one could imagine. It looked so much like a picture postcard, that it was hard to believe that I had come here to finalize an embezzlement. I had some trouble finding the bank, at first mistaking the Kantonalbank for the Schaffhausen Bank. I kept driving around the old town center, and finally found the building that I was looking for on Grabenstraße. I drove several blocks down the road to park my car, not wanting to risk anyone seeing Swiss license plates on my car since I intended to tell them at the bank that I was from Germany. I then walked slowly back to the bank and went in, asking to see an officer about opening an account.

I was shown into a private room, in true Swiss banking custom, and waited for an officer to join me. The room was not opulent, as were the physical quarters of many of the big Swiss banks in Geneva and Zürich. In fact, the furnishings were rather sparse—just a plain, functional wooden table, and several leather-upholstered chairs. I didn't have to wait very long, and after a few minutes, one of the bank's officers came in and introduced himself.

"Good morning. My name is Hans Eberhard. I am an account officer here at the Schaffhausen Bank."

I responded, "Good morning. I am Johannes Reinsdorf, from Augsburg, in Germany, and I have come here at the suggestion of my uncle, Gustav Reinsdorf."

"Yes."

"My uncle lives in Argentina now, but he used to have accounts here at this bank, and he still may, for all I know. I do know, however, that my cousin, Elsa Wilhelm of Cuernavaca, Mexico, still has an account here."

"Well, as you know, we can't comment on that, but I can say that you seem to have some excellent references."

"Thank you. My uncle has written me to say that he would like to transfer some money to me—I'm not sure how much—and when I wrote to him that I really did not want the money to come into Germany, for tax reasons of course, he suggested that I open an account at this bank. He said that he had had a number of accounts here back in the 1940s. I've never been to Schaffhausen before, but from what I've seen, it is as charming as my uncle indicated."

"Thank you. As you can imagine, we now work very hard to retain the town's character."

"I understand that it was bombed by the Americans during the war, although when I came into town this morning, there did not appear to be any post-war buildings, at least in the town center."

"That's right. I was a boy during the war, and the Americans primarily bombed the IWC factory—the International Watch Company plant—probably thinking it was some German factory, although even there they caused very little damage. The odd thing is that IWC was founded by an American and everyone here in Schaffhausen always felt that that was one reason that President Roosevelt apologized and the Americans paid reparations so quickly."

"Well, I'll look forward to spending more time here on my next visit."

Mr. Eberhard said, "As to your account, we will, of course, be happy to open one for you, and I assume then that you will want to have a numbered account."

I concurred, saying, "Yes, very definitely, a numbered account."

"And you will not want statements sent to Augsburg."

"Oh no, no it will be much better for you to hold them here, and then I can pick them up whenever I travel to Switzerland."

"Or one of our officers could bring them to you in Germany."

This was not a difficult question, but I was glad that I was handling the matter rather than Ingrid. I quickly said, "No. I think not. I really do not want any records to be brought into Germany."

"As you wish. Now if you would just fill out this application, and if you could make a deposit to get the account opened, I will go and get the number for the account, and some temporary checks. And one other thing. Could you tell me the name of the bank from which the transfer is to come."

"Yes, my uncle said that it will be the Schleswigbank in Zürich. As a matter of fact, I have been rather remiss in getting the account opened so that the transfer could be made. He wants me to phone him with the number tonight, and he will then immediately instruct the bank in Zürich."

In less than thirty minutes, I was back on the street with a numbered account at the Schaffhausen bank. It was so simple; no identification was required, virtually no questions were asked. All I had had to do was to indicate that some money would be coming, and the bank was happy to open the account. There were very few places in the world with banking laws as easy, and as secretive, as those in Switzerland.

CHAPTER XI

Zürich, 1965

The money was transferred into the account I had opened at the Schaffhausen bank on February 25, 1965, and for the next six months Ingrid and I suddenly had everything that we had ever wanted. It was a tremendously heady experience for both of us. I decided that I wanted to get our new wealth out of the Schaffhausen bank as quickly, but as discreetly as possible, so I drove to Schaffhausen frequently over the next few weeks to withdraw large sums of cash. By the end of April, I had withdrawn everything and had closed the account. Most of the money went into a safe deposit box at a bank in Küsnacht, just south of Zürich on the east side of the Zürichsee. Even though I trusted Swiss bank secrecy laws, I felt that it was more prudent to put cash in a safe deposit box so that there would be no record of it at all.

I tried to impress upon Ingrid that we should not suddenly start spending a great deal of money since this would inevitably start speculation as to where the money came from. And I did prevail upon her to show quite a bit of restraint. However, we jointly decided to move into a new and larger apartment in a better part of town; we bought a new car; and both of us bought some new clothes. We spent a little over 25,000 francs on the furnishings for the apartment, the car, and the clothes, but this hardly made a dent in our new-found fortune.

Shortly after the money transfer, Poëhl died and I was formally confirmed as the new account administrator, and was also designated as an officer of the bank. At thirty-four, I was the youngest man ever to attain such a position at Schleswigbank, and I was very proud of that fact, as was Ingrid. I managed to hear some of the tidbits from the rumor mill at the bank, and it was clear that I was now generally considered to have tremendous potential for future promotions. My experience on the trading desk was unique as far as senior management of the bank was concerned, and it gave me an excellent understanding of the bond and currency markets, both of which were very important to the bank. This background, combined with the fact that I was almost certainly a good deal sharper than any of my professional colleagues, made me one of the best investment professionals in the department. I immediately became a member of the bank's investment committee, and I am pretty sure that everyone sensed from the moment that I became a member of that committee that I was one of its most important members.

The other members of the committee were older, stodgier, and more averse to risk than I was, and I was surprised to discover very quickly that they were hesitant to disagree with me. As a result, everyone seemed to wait until I expressed an opinion and it was then generally my opinion that carried the day. But no matter what I thought of the other members of the committee, my manner was always deferential to them and I believe that I handled myself in such a way that the only person who was irritated by my success was Steiner. Steiner recognized the formidable competition he now faced, but he could think of nothing to try to combat it.

In June, the Swiss Bankers Association held its annual meeting at the Dolder Grand Hotel in Zürich. In the past, Schleswigbank had been represented by Dr. Hofbeck and several other senior officers. This year, however, both Steiner and I were also invited, along with our wives, for the formal dinner that opened the conference. I told Ingrid that this would be a great opportunity for us to make a major impression not just on Dr. Hofbeck and other senior bank officers, but probably more importantly on their wives. There wasn't much I could do other than to wear a tuxedo as required, but I told Ingrid that she should find an elegant new dress for the occasion—with the emphasis on conservative elegance, since it was the older bank directors and their wives that we wanted to impress. Ingrid found a fairly simple black gown that seemed to me to show both sophistication and good taste. It was also tight-fitting enough so that it showed off her great figure. I don't think that there was any question that that night, Ingrid and I were far and away the handsomest couple in the grand ballroom. And we must have been the youngest, since I was only thirty-four and Ingrid was twenty-nine, so that we were twenty or thirty years younger than most of the stodgy bankers from around Switzerland.

I learned later from Mrs. Jendricks that Dr. Hofbeck and his wife were also impressed by Ingrid and me, particularly when several officers of other banks commented on the favorable impression that we had made. Mrs. Jendricks said that Dr. Hofbeck felt that Schleswigbank was finally getting some attention at one of these meetings, instead of having all of it hogged by Credit Suisse and Union Bank of Switzerland. He apparently felt that I could be valuable to the bank in the long run, and Mrs. Jendricks attitude toward me seemed to have improved quite a bit since our first meeting a few months earlier. I quickly realized that Mrs. Jendricks really liked to gossip, and I tried to be particularly nice to her so that I could learn as much as possible as to what Dr. Hofbeck was thinking.

Shortly after the Swiss Bankers Association meeting, we received an invitation from Mrs. Hofbeck to have dinner at their home. That dinner, which occurred in early August, really put an official seal of approval on Ingrid and me. It seemed pretty clear to me that, considering the various invitations and my promotions at the bank, that both Dr. Hofbeck and his wife were very interested in us, and I have to give Ingrid credit for doing everything she could to ingratiate herself with Mrs. Hofbeck. The Director's wife apparently led a rather dull or routine existence, and Ingrid started inviting her to various art exhibitions and to some of the museums in Zürich, and this level of attention clearly made a very favorable impression on her. From time to time, Dr. Hofbeck would mention to me how much his wife had enjoyed one of the outings that Ingrid had suggested.

Throughout the summer and fall, the Hofbecks saw to it that Ingrid and I were included in most of the important social events that took place in Zürich. The rumor mill within Schleswigbank was apparently operating at full speed, and it was reported back to me that I had been established as Dr. Hofbeck's protégé, and even as his heir apparent. When we were alone in our new apartment, Ingrid and I talked about how our status at the bank had changed in just a few short months. We both agreed that having the additional money had been a significant help since it enabled Ingrid to be dressed beautifully on every occasion. However, I attributed the major part of our success to my own abilities as a bank officer. Whatever the reason, there was no question that things were really developing very favorably for us.

During the last week in August, I had to take my semi-annual military leave of two weeks, which was required of all Swiss men. I was able to come home twice during the period to see Ingrid, but I did not go into the bank on either of those occasions. When I did return to the bank, on September 9, I found a mountain of mail that had accumulated during my absence. I did not have time to go through it during the first few days that I was back, however, because of the need to see Dr. Hofbeck on a number of urgent issues. I also had to attend meetings of the Investment Committee that had been postponed while I was away, and to see several customers who had delayed visiting the bank until I had returned.

Finally, late on Wednesday, my third day back, I finally worked my way down through the pile of mail to find a handwritten letter that had been sent to me from Cuernavaca, Mexico.

August 25, 1965

Dear Mr. Wenner:

I am the daughter of Gustav Reinsdorf, who lived near Santa Maria, Argentina. I am not sure whether or not you know that my father died in early February, but I understand that you had been to see him in late January, shortly before his death.

I visited his home after he died and discovered that he had left everything he owned in Argentina, including his ranch, to a young man who worked for him. I do not know what this person might have done to influence my father to leave him far more than the young man had any right to expect, but we all know that old people can be easily influenced in the last days of their lives by those who are anxious to profit from their death.

It is not because of this that I write you, however. On visiting the ranch, the only items I was able to obtain that had belonged to my father were some of his papers (the young man and his mother having appropriated everything else). In reviewing those papers, I found the statements covering his account at Schleswigbank, showing that the account had a balance of 250,000 Swiss francs as of December 31, 1964. Your card was included among the papers, and I was told that you had left it when you were there in January. I assume that his account was discussed during your visit.

My father's will indicated that he was leaving everything to this person in Argentina since he was making other provisions for me, outside of the will. To my knowledge, the only other asset that my father had was the account with your bank, and I have been waiting to hear from you as to its disposition. My fear, of course, is that the same young man who prevailed upon my father to leave him the Argentine assets may also have managed to obtain control of the funds that were held in your bank.

Accordingly, I would very much appreciate your letting me know exactly what disposition has been made of the funds that were held in this account. Should you need proof of the fact that I am my father's only descendent, I am sure that I can provide that. As I mentioned, I do have the statements on the account, and to verify that, I will mention that its number is 763-294-759-AG. Looking forward to hearing from you in the near future,

Elsa Wilhelm

I have to confess that I was a little upset upon reading this letter, even though it was not entirely unexpected. Ingrid and I had discussed the possibility of the daughter's inquiring about the money, and I was now in the fortunate position of being the bank officer who would respond to her. I knew that my reply was something that would require very careful consideration, but before I started to think about that, I saw another handwritten envelope in the pile of mail on my desk. This one was from Argentina, and I realized at once that it must be from Toni.

August 16, 1965

Dear Kurt:

I have wanted to write to you for some time, but have been very busy ever since Gus died. First, let me thank you for reassuring me as to the ranch. It was very upsetting to know that Gus did not have long to live, but the added worry of not knowing what would happen afterwards was starting to get to me. The conversations that we had really helped.

I have to tell you that his daughter, Elsa, did come down here. We had talked to her on the phone a few times, and she tried to give me a hard time about going ahead with the funeral. She just assumed, though, that this place would be hers, and I finally had to tell her that Gus had left it to me. She really carried on when she heard that, and made all kinds of crazy accusations about how I had tricked her father into doing that.

We did not hear from her for a while, but she finally called from Tucamán last week. She was staying at a hotel there (and it's not a very good hotel) and she had been to see Gus's lawyer. She said she wanted to come out to the farm in the next day or two to look over her father's personal things, and I told her to come ahead. Of course, she showed up the next afternoon when I was out working with the sheep. I'm afraid I made kind of a bad impression, since it was a hot day, and I only was wearing a pair of shorts and was pretty dirty and sweaty. My mother had put together a lot of Gus's personal things, like his watch and rings and some other things, but all that the daughter wanted to look at was his personal papers. I really hadn't touched his desk, and she went through it with a fine-toothed comb.

She took a number of papers that had to do with the account at your Bank, or so she said. She kept asking what had happened to the money in that account, and wouldn't believe that I didn't know anything about it. She said she was going to contact your Bank and find out if I had gotten the money, and that she would sue me if I had. It got so bad with her accusing me of being a thief, and things like that, that my mother finally came into the room and told her to get out. Fortunately, the taxi that brought her from Tucamán was waiting, and she went off in that.

I have to laugh when I think of it now, because there I was standing like some kind of savage, with virtually nothing on, while she was screaming about some money that ought to be hers. Well, I hope that that's the last I ever see or hear of her, but you may not be so lucky, since she said she was going to get in touch with you about the money.

On a happier note, Elena and I are going to be married in September. I'm not very religious myself, but my mother and Elena's parents all want a church wedding, so we decided to have it at the church in Santa Maria. Then everyone will come back here for a big dinner. Gus left me enough money along with the ranch so that we can go on a honeymoon, and we are going to go to Italy. I still have

grandparents in a little town in Umbria, and I think this is a great
chance to go and see them.
　　Well, that's about all for now. I hope everything is going well for
you, and that Elsa doesn't give you too much trouble.

Toni

　　I had to smile at how differently the two letters had described the same events. I had no doubt that Toni was telling the truth and that Elsa was bitter at having lost the Argentine inheritance. The fact that she thought that Toni might have gotten the money from Schleswigbank was not all bad from my viewpoint. As long as she had that obsession she would probably continue to bemoan Toni's influence over her father, and never suspect that there had been an embezzlement involved with the loss of the money. Instead of waiting, I decided to respond to her right away, and quickly drafted the letter that I had actually thought about on several different occasions since Ingrid and I decided to take Herr Reinsdorf's money.

September 12, 1965

Dear Mrs. Wilhelm:
　　I have just returned to the Bank after an absence of two weeks and found your letter of August 25 waiting for me. First of all, please accept my sincere sympathy on the death of your father. I had only met him on one occasion, when I visited him at his home in January, but he was a very gracious host during my visit and I had quickly come to have a very high regard for him. I need not tell you what a real loss you have suffered.
　　In normal circumstances, I would not be able to respond to your questions about accounts here at Schleswigbank. As you undoubtedly know, Swiss banking laws are very strict in prohibiting the release of any information as to accounts at Swiss banks, particularly as to so-called numbered accounts. In this case, however, you already have information about your father's former account with our Bank, and we understand that you are your father's sole living descendent. Therefore, our legal department feels that it is appropriate for me to answer your questions.
　　It is, of course, true that your father did have an account at this Bank, and I did visit your father in Argentina to discuss that account with him. At the time of my visit, your father gave us explicit instructions concerning the disposition of the account, and those instructions have been carried out. Under Swiss law, it would not be possible for me to divulge what those instructions were, but you may

rest assured that Schleswigbank has followed his instructions precisely as he directed.

I hope that this letter will assuage any uncertainty that you may have felt about this matter, but if you have further questions, please let me know.

Kurt A. Wenner

That night I told Ingrid about the letter, but neither of us was particularly concerned about it. Ingrid agreed that Elsa sounded frustrated at losing out on her father's inheritance, and she felt, as I did, that Elsa was directing her anger at Toni. We both hoped that we had heard the last of her.

Chapter XII

Several weeks passed without anything happening, until in early October I received another letter from Elsa.

September 28, 1965

Dear Mr. Wenner:

I received your letter of September 12 concerning my father's account at your Bank, and I must tell you that your response was totally unsatisfactory. I have no intention of being so easily brushed aside. My father indicated in a will made just about a month before he died that he was making provision for me with assets outside of Argentina, and I am convinced that he intended that I should have the money that was in the account at your Bank.

This is a matter of principle to me—it is not a matter of money. My husband is quite well off and 250,000 Swiss francs more or less will not change our style of living. But the money should have been mine, and I insist on knowing what happened to it. It is quite possible that the young man in Argentina, who managed to convince my father to will him his estate there, was able to get these funds also. If that is the case, I will take legal action against him in Argentina. It is also possible, however, that your Bank, knowing that my father had died, simply did what Swiss banks are famous for (or infamous for) and transferred the money to its own account. In either event, I need to know what happened to it.

If you continue to decline to answer my questions, I will have to retain a lawyer in Switzerland to represent me in taking whatever action is necessary to find out what disposition was made of my father's account.

Elsa Wilhelm

I realized that this letter was a good deal more serious, and I knew that another letter from me would have no effect on Mrs. Wilhelm. I also felt that for me to send another letter to her probably would not be wise from my own personal viewpoint. It would be much better to get the bank itself to begin to fight this battle for me. That night when I got home, I told Ingrid about the new letter, and she immediately became alarmed.

"This is becoming serious, isn't it Kurt?"

I tried to reassure her, although I was not 100 percent confident myself. I said to her, "No, I don't think so. We can still handle it. You know Friday night we're going to that dinner party at Jurgen Kohl's home. Dr. Hofbeck said it will be quite a bash—everyone will be there. I'm sure that Rudolph Schnabel and his wife are invited. You remember them, we met them a few weeks ago at the Hofbeck's. He's a director of Schleswigbank and the bank's outside counsel. The party will be a great time to talk to him and tell him about my little problem and ask his advice."

"Kurt, you don't want to bring in bank management, do you?"

"Why, of course. She's threatening legal action, and I'm just being the good, honest employee in bringing this to the attention of our general counsel."

The dinner on Friday night was being given by Jurgen Kohl, a director of Zürich Bank Corporation, to honor a visiting governor of the United States Federal Reserve Board. There were about forty people at the party, an elaborate cocktail party and buffet dinner, and, in my opinion, Ingrid and I were again the youngest and most glamorous couple at the party. The party was held at the Kohl's home, a great old estate on several acres of landscaped grounds along the Zürichsee about ten miles south of the city. An enormous buffet table had been set up in the dining room, and, after the cocktail hour, the guests were asked to begin serving themselves. Ten tables had been set up in the living room, the library, and a small sitting room; Ingrid and I sat with an American couple from the US embassy in Berne. The American was an economic attaché and he and I had a spirited discussion throughout dinner as to economic growth trends and the direction of the currency markets. When we finished eating, the American and I exchanged cards and agreed that we would have to get together again.

I was quite anxious to talk with Mr. Schnabel, but I wanted to talk with him when no one else was around. So I waited until after dinner, when brandy was being served and guests were moving around from room to room before I approached him.

I found Mr. Schnabel standing by himself off to the side of the living room, and I went up to him and started out by saying, "I'm sorry that I haven't had a chance to speak with you tonight, Dr. Schnabel."

He politely replied, "I'm sorry too. I enjoyed talking with you and your lovely wife when we were together at the Hofbeck's a few weeks ago. How is everything going at the bank these days?"

Since he asked about the bank, I decided to bring up the Elsa problem right away. "Well, I hadn't intended to bring it up tonight—I don't like mixing business and pleasure—but I do have a problem that I think I should discuss with you."

He frowned as he said, "Really. Nothing serious, I hope."

"I don't think so. We closed a small account a few months ago, acting on the customer's instructions to transfer it to another bank. It was one of those small accounts we were trying to get rid of. Unfortunately, the man died shortly after giving us the direction to close the account, and now his daughter is insisting on knowing what happened to the money."

He shook his head as he said, "That can't be very serious. Just tell her we aren't able to give out that kind of information."

"Well, I've already done that. But now she's threatening to get a lawyer to try to get the information. Under the circumstances, I thought I ought to come and talk to you about it."

"Yes, I see, she's threatening to make a fuss. Well, yes, you're right I should look into it. Call my secretary and make an appointment for next week—probably Tuesday—and bring along all of the papers and correspondence. I'm sure we can take care of her fairly easily."

I was very relieved by his response, and early on Monday morning I made the appointment as instructed. His secretary scheduled it for Tuesday afternoon, and so I had to wait for a day before getting to see him. But on Tuesday I went to his office, and I showed him the form signed by Herr Reinsdorf on January 26. The form, of course, included the transfer instructions that I had put on to the form after my return to Zürich. I also showed Dr. Schnabel the letters that I had exchanged with Elsa Wilhelm, and her last letter in which she indicated that she intended to retain a lawyer in Switzerland to pursue this matter.

I decided that I should set the record straight as to when I had learned that Herr Reinsdorf had died, and said, "There is one other thing that I have to confess. Herr Reinsdorf died on February 1, and I was informed of that before I left Argentina. I hope I did the right thing in putting through the transfer anyway. I really thought that we were obligated to carry out Reinsdorf's instructions, even though he had died."

Mr. Schnabel looked down and thought about what I had said for a minute, and then said to me, "Well, you probably should have referred the question to my office before you made that transfer, and we'll have to be more clear about this in the future in our instructions to the staff. But you're right. We had the man's instructions, and we would have been remiss if we had not carried them out, even though he had passed away in the meantime." Dr. Schnabel studied the papers for a few minutes, and then asked me, "Who do you think got the money?"

I was glad that he asked this question since it would enable me to make a few points that would support my position. I replied, "I don't really know, of course. In retrospect it's kind of funny because he wanted to give me the name to put on the form. Obviously, we did not want the name on the transfer form, and I was not all that curious. I know he did not want anything to go to his daughter—he told me that they had been estranged since the war and that he had only seen her once in the last fifteen years or so. He also told me that she and her husband were quite rich and really didn't need any more money. But he did mention a nephew, or a cousin's boy—some distant relative—whom he had not heard from in years. In fact, he didn't even know that the young man existed, but the man had sent Reinsdorf a picture and Reinsdorf was struck by the fact that the young man looked so much like his son, who had died in the war.

"It's my suspicion that he told this nephew, or relative or whatever he was, to open an account at the Schaffhausen bank because that bank was so convenient for someone living in Germany, and he decided to transfer this money to him. Reinsdorf was very sick and probably knew that he did not have long to live. He had just made a new will, and he told me how relieved he was to have this account taken care of as well."

Mr. Schnabel nodded and said, "I'm sure you're right, it sounds very logical. Now, how do we convince Mrs. Wilhelm of that?"

I felt my best course was to remain silent, and finally Dr. Schnabel pressed the intercom and asked his secretary to come in. "I'll dictate a letter while you're here and you can make sure that everything I say is correct."

October 12, 1965

Dear Mrs. Wilhelm:

Your letter of September 28th addressed to Mr. Kurt Wenner of Schleswigbank has been referred to me for reply. I am a director of the bank, and am its outside counsel.

I have carefully reviewed the instructions that were given to Mr. Wenner by your father when Mr. Wenner visited him in Argentina in January, and the subsequent actions of the Bank in carrying out those instructions. Let me assure you that my objective review of the Bank's internal documentation indicates beyond a shadow of doubt that your father's instructions were faithfully executed.

You indicated that you may wish to retain counsel in Zürich to pursue this matter further. That is, of course, your decision. I must tell you, however, that under Swiss law you cannot be given the information that you seek. All that your counsel will be able to do is to verify that we had appropriate instructions from your father, and that those instructions were carried out.

If you or your counsel have any other questions concerning this matter, please direct them to me.

Dr. Rudolph Schnabel

I left Dr. Schnabel's office feeling tremendously relieved. There was no reason for anyone at the bank to think that this was anything but a case of a disappointed daughter who did not get the inheritance she had expected. I went home that night and told Ingrid what had happened, and she came and sat with me on the sofa, both of us feeling tremendously relieved.

After a while Ingrid said, "You were right, Kurt. It's much better for the bank's counsel to tell her that everything was done properly than for you to be the only one arguing with her. And we were right too. The bank has no reason to suspect that anything is wrong, and Elsa has no way of finding out the truth."

I couldn't help saying, "But I'll bet we haven't heard the last of her."

"Why?"

"Because I think she will get a lawyer, and we'll have to deal with him before this is all over."

And my feeling was, of course, correct since it was only a few weeks later that I received a call from Mrs. Jendricks asking me to come up to Dr. Hofbeck's office again. When I got there, Dr. Hofbeck said, "That Wilhelm woman won't give up. She has hired a lawyer and they want to come in and see us."

I said, "I guess I expected her to do that."

"Rudolph sent her the last letter, didn't he?"

"Yes."

Dr. Hofbeck said, "Good, then I'll have him here too. He can deal with the lawyer."

I was curious about her lawyer, so I asked, "Who did she hire?"

"Someone who specializes in criminal law. His name is Hans Brandt."

"But don't you think that when Dr. Schnabel explains the situation to Mr. Brandt he will tell her that there's nothing she can do."

"Undoubtedly. It's a waste of money on her part, but she's apparently a very determined woman."

I had not realized until I was about to leave Dr. Hofbeck's office that the meeting with Elsa and her lawyer was to take place the very next day, and it took place in the conference room next to Dr. Hofbeck's office. Elsa arrived with her attorney precisely at 11:00 a.m. as scheduled, and I finally met this woman with whom my life had become so intertwined. The one word that came to my mind immediately upon meeting her was "formidable." She was a woman with a striking appearance: tall, somewhat thin but with a good figure, blonde hair pulled back tightly against her head and tied with a black ribbon in back, and a face that just missed being described as attractive. She managed to convey a stern, aloof, almost regal feeling as she entered the room. I assumed that she had to be around fifty since she must have been about thirty in 1945 when the war ended, and that was now twenty years ago. Age, however, was not what came to mind when one met Elsa—it seemed to me that her overall appearance, including her manner and her expensive clothes—these were the things that indicated to me that this was a very impressive woman.

She was introduced in turn to Dr. Hofbeck, Dr. Schnabel, and finally to me, and she acknowledged each introduction merely with a nod of her head, without saying a word. It occurred to me that for all her regal manner, she was probably trying to hide the fact that this confrontation made her nervous. I have to confess that I was nervous myself as I sat across the conference room table from her—a woman from whom, quite literally, I had recently stolen 250,000 francs. I knew that at this meeting she had to be convinced that Schleswigbank had acted properly, and that there was nothing else for her to do to find out what had happened to her father's account at the bank.

As the meeting began, Elsa turned to me first, and said in a very strong voice, speaking perfect German, "I've wanted to meet you, Mr. Wenner, ever since I found out that you had seen my father shortly before he died. I feel sure that you talked with him about the disposition of his account with your bank." As she talked to me, I felt as if she was appraising me and passing judgment upon me. The look that she focused on me was intense, as she then asked me, "What did he tell you about his intentions as to that account?"

I managed to appear perfectly calm as I answered her, since I knew that, as a Swiss banker, there was only one answer I could give, "I'm afraid, Mrs. Wilhelm, that my letters have told you all that I can as to what became of your father's account. We did discuss it, of course, but—and I hate to fall back on bank secrecy laws—but those laws do prevent me from saying anything more than that the bank carried out the instructions that we were given."

Still focusing on me, Elsa went on, "I don't know, Mr. Wenner, if you can appreciate what it's like to find that a parent has died, and then to find out that some farm worker and his mother have managed to get control of most of his property. And on top of that, you're unable to discover what happened to any other money that they didn't manage to take for themselves. You are a young man but I hope that when your parents die, you are not faced with this kind of a cruel situation."

I had to smile to myself at Elsa's rather transparent gambit to gain sympathy, and immediately deflected that by replying, "My parents died when I was very young, Mrs. Wilhelm, and I can certainly appreciate how upsetting this entire situation must be for you. As I told you in my letter, I had only met your father on that one occasion, and then only for one short day, but I did find him to be a charming and gracious man, and I am sure that all of these uncertainties make his death even more difficult for you."

Elsa now turned to Dr. Hofbeck, saying, "I hope you understand, and I mentioned this in one of my letters, that the amount of money involved here is not great, and I am not pursuing this matter because of the money. I really believe that the young man and his mother, who worked in Argentina for my father, took advantage of him in the final months of his illness. I am sure that they persuaded him to leave them everything he owned in Argentina. There were a great many things in my father's house that I wish I could have had: some of the furniture from our home in Augsburg, paintings that meant a great deal to me, some of my mother's jewelry—things like that. But the lawyer in Argentina tells me that his will is unassailable, and so my only avenue to try to right what I consider to be a terrible wrong, is to pursue the money he had here at Schleswigbank."

I was unable to repress a smile as Elsa talked about the furniture, paintings, and jewelry that she had been unable to get since I knew that Herr Reinsdorf had brought nothing with him from Germany—it would have been impossible as he went first to Santiago, then Buenos Aires, and finally to his ranch in Santa Maria. Again, Elsa was trying to gain the sympathy of her audience. She glanced at me as she finished this statement, daring me to contradict her.

Dr. Hofbeck then spoke up and said, "Mrs. Wilhelm, I must tell you that we do sympathize with you. This whole situation is undoubtedly extraordinarily difficult for you. If there were any way that Schleswigbank could resolve your doubts about your father's account, I can assure you we would do so. But, as Mr. Wenner has pointed out, Swiss banking law absolutely prohibits us from giving you the kind of information that you want. It simply cannot be done."

Mrs. Wilhelm retorted, "I merely want to know if that person in Argentina— Toni DiSantis—was the one that got the 250,000 francs from this account. You merely have to tell me yes or no."

Dr. Hofbeck answered, "And that is precisely what we cannot tell you because, in fact, we do not have the slightest idea who got your father's money. I don't think I'm breaking any law by telling you that your father only instructed us to transfer the money to an account at another bank. We have no idea to whom that account belonged."

There was a silence for a few minutes that was finally broken as Dr. Schnabel said to Mrs. Wilhelm's lawyer, "Mr. Brandt, as a lawyer in Switzerland you are bound by our bank secrecy laws. I'm sure you agree that if I were to show you the appropriate documents, you would not be able to reveal their contents to your client. Isn't that correct?"

"Yes, I would agree with that."

"But, after seeing them, you could assure her that we had her father's directions and that we had acted properly. If you agree, let me take you into one of our conference rooms and I will show you the form of direction that we have from Herr Reinsdorf, and the internal bank documentation that supports our contention that Schleswigbank acted exactly in accordance with those instructions."

Then turning to Mrs. Wilhelm, Dr. Schnabel said, "If your attorney and I do this, he could then assure you, Mrs. Wilhelm, that the bank has acted properly in this matter. Would that be acceptable to you?"

Elsa and her attorney spoke together for a minute, and he then said, "Yes, that will be acceptable to my client." Dr. Schnabel and Mr. Brandt left the conference room, and Elsa and Dr. Hofbeck and I were left to await their return. Dr. Hofbeck immediately excused himself and told me to let him know when the lawyers had returned. It was a rather awkward situation, but I tried to make conversation with Elsa, offering her coffee and trying to comment on the weather, but she clearly preferred to wait in silence. I quickly decided that there was nothing to be done, other than to sit quietly and wait for the lawyers to return.

As I sat there across from Elsa for about fifteen minutes, I wondered what she was thinking. Was she still focused on Toni as the culprit or did she suspect that Schleswigbank itself might somehow be at fault? I wondered if she realized that she was about to reach a final dead end in her quest to find the money. As far as I was concerned, I felt a rising elation. She had pursued this matter much further than I had expected, but my initial analysis of the whole situation had been correct, and Ingrid and I were safe. And as the knowledge that we were getting away with it—that we had successfully embezzled 250,000 Swiss francs—I realized that there was a certain thrill in this whole escapade—in getting away with something as audacious and as daring as this had been. It took a great deal of self-discipline to keep from showing the elation that I felt as Elsa and I awaited the lawyers' return.

The two lawyers finally came back and I went and told Dr. Hofbeck that they were ready. When we were all again seated at the conference table, Mr. Brandt said, "Mrs. Wilhelm, it appears to me that the internal documentation here at the bank is absolutely incontrovertible. The transfer instructions were certainly signed by your father. I am not a handwriting expert, but his signature was clearly similar to the signature on the account opening forms, as well as to some of the samples of his handwriting that you gave me. Also, I do not believe that there is any possibility that the transfer instructions had been tampered with in any way. There was no evidence of that at all. And finally, the bank had clearly transferred the money as he had instructed. Now that transfer did happen after he had died, but I agree with Dr. Schnabel that Schleswigbank had no alternative but to follow those instructions, even had they known that your father had passed away.

"Therefore, Mrs. Wilhelm, I really do not think that you can go any further with your inquiry. If you were to go to the banking authorities they would, I am sure, come to the same conclusion that I have. And Swiss law simply will not permit anyone to give you the information as to where the money was sent."

Elsa sat there for a long time, and finally said, "I will have to accept your advice, Mr. Brandt, but I must tell you I don't like it." And looking over the other three men, she added rather defiantly, and I felt rather impolitely, "One just can't trust these Swiss bankers." She then rose and shook hands with Dr. Hofbeck and Dr. Schnabel without saying anything more. As she shook hands with me, however, she looked directly into my eyes saying, "It is so frustrating for me to think that you know what became of the money, and I don't. If only I could convince you to tell me."

This comment was expressed so forcefully that I was thrown for a loss momentarily, but I quickly recovered to respond, "As Dr. Hofbeck told you, Mrs. Wenner, we do not know who got the money, so there really is no way that I can help you. I hope you believe me when I say that I am truly sorry." With that, Elsa turned and left the room, indicating that she would wait for her lawyer outside.

Mr. Brandt said, "I want to thank you very much Dr. Schnabel and Dr. Hofbeck for your help in reviewing this situation for my client. I do think that Mrs. Wilhelm will continue to wonder who actually got the money, but I hope that she will now realize that her father did not intend that she receive it."

Dr. Hofbeck said, "It is sometimes hard for a person to accept a situation like this, and I'm afraid Mrs. Wilhelm is a very strong-willed woman so that it is doubly hard for her."

"Well, again, thank you, and I would expect that this will be the end of the matter."

I was, of course, enormously relieved at the conclusion of the meeting and went back down to my office feeling a mixture of elation and exhaustion. I was unable to concentrate on work for the rest of the day, and I finally decided to leave the office early to head home. On the way, I bought a bottle of champagne, already chilled, and burst in on Ingrid. "It's over—we can celebrate." I grabbed her and held her tightly, repeating, "It's over. We're safe, she's finally gone." Ingrid, of course, wanted to know all the details of the meeting with Elsa, and I was only too happy to relive the whole experience.

For me the great joy was being free of the threat of being found out, and of ruining my career at the bank. The money had never been all that important to me; I had taken it for Ingrid. Now that the danger was past, I could celebrate what seemed to be my renewed freedom and again concentrate full time on getting ahead at Schleswigbank. The fact that we could go on enjoying the money was only an incidental matter for me. I know that for Ingrid the money was tremendously important, but I was primarily concerned with saving my career. In the back of my mind, however, I kept having the thought that the entire embezzlement had been a real experience and, while I would never do it again, I was glad that it had happened. There was a real thrill in doing something as daring and as illegal as what we had done, and there was an even greater thrill in getting away with it. Ingrid and I celebrated with the champagne that night and quickly adjourned to the bedroom, where we made love passionately before finally falling into an exhausted sleep.

Chapter XIII

Zürich – 1966

During the next few weeks life began to return to normal for me. The fear of being found out, which had hung over me for the preceding five months, had dissipated, and I could once again focus more clearly on my job and my career. As the year drew to a close, I suggested to Ingrid that we take a vacation and go away for the holidays. We thought about going someplace where we could lie on the beach in the sun, but decided instead to spend Christmas in Taormina in Sicily. We flew down to Palermo, which was on the other end of Sicily, and rented a car. This gave us the opportunity to drive very leisurely across the island, visiting all the amazing things to see there. It seems that every group had conquered Sicily at one time or another—the Greeks, the Romans, the Moors—and all have left behind remnants of their occupation. Taormina itself was a charming little town overlooking the Straits of Messina, with the volcano Etna looming in the background. And being there for the Christmas holidays was really great since bonfires were lit all around the town, many up in the hills overlooking the town, and people gathered at the fires to sing Christmas carols. The weather was very good, and it ended up being a really good vacation.

When I got back to my desk at Schleswigbank, I found that an enormous amount of work had accumulated and I had to work late several evenings to try to get caught up. There were constant meetings during the first week that I was back, and I had still not been able to clear up the backlog on my desk by Tuesday of the second week. That Tuesday afternoon, Mrs. Jendricks called and asked me to come up to Dr. Hofbeck's office. I had not seen Dr. Hofbeck since returning, and I assumed that he might want to know about my vacation. In fact, that was the Managing Director's first question, and he and I spent some time in discussing all of the many interesting things to see in Sicily.

I was quite relaxed, and totally unprepared for Dr. Hofbeck's next statement: "Mrs. Wilhelm is coming in this afternoon."

"Mrs. Wilhelm? I'm very surprised. I thought that we had seen the last of her."

69

"Yes, so did I. But she called Rudolph Schnabel and said that she had one more thing that she wanted to discuss with us, and she wanted all three of us to be together. So she will be here in about ten minutes, at three o'clock, and Rudolph should be here also."

"Did she say what she wanted? I don't believe that there is anything else we can tell her."

"No, and I really did not want to see her, but she can be quite insistent."

I immediately felt all the old tension come rushing back, all the tensions and worries that had evaporated over the past month. And I was irritated that Dr. Hofbeck had waited until just minutes before she was due to arrive before telling me that she was coming. I could not imagine what Elsa could want now, or why she would be coming back one more time. Her own lawyer had been convinced that there was nothing more she could learn, and it seemed inconceivable to me that she simply wanted to go over the same old ground one more time.

Dr. Hofbeck and I sat making small talk for the next few minutes until first Dr. Schnabel and then Mrs. Wilhelm arrived. As at the first meeting, Mrs. Wilhelm dominated the room when she walked in with that aura of calm superiority that she always seemed to have, but this time I thought that I sensed in her more excitement or nervousness than before.

After a few introductory preliminaries, Dr. Hofbeck said, "Now Mrs. Wilhelm, we thought this had all been settled. We really cannot continue going over this matter time and again."

She rather haughtily replied, "I appreciate that. When I left here a month ago I thought the matter had been settled too. I was not happy, but I felt that I had run into a brick wall and that I would not be able to get any further information. But something rather surprising happened. About a week after we last met, I went to Schaffhausen en route to visit some relatives in Germany. I have an account at the bank there." My heart started pounding when I heard her begin talking about Schaffhausen.

Elsa went on, "As I was concluding my business, my account officer mentioned that earlier last year a young man had opened an account at the bank, using my name as a reference. The young man said he was my cousin. At first I expressed surprise, and asked what his name was. My account officer, a Mr. Meier, said that he was unable to give me that information. So then I took a shot in the dark and described my so-called cousin: fairly young, about thirty, blond, rather good-looking, with strong features, and a cleft chin, and Mr. Meier agreed that the young man did indeed look like that."

I absolutely froze as Elsa came close to describing me. She went on, "Then I said to him, 'I had forgotten. My father intended to give some money to my cousin and had him open an account here so that funds could be transferred from Schleswigbank in Zürich.' And Mr. Meier said, 'Oh, I see you know about that.' I then tried to get Mr. Meier to give me the address the young man had given when he opened the account since I claimed to have lost track of my cousin, but, of course, he refused. And I also tried to get the exact date the account had been opened, but he would not give me that information either. So at that point I had at least established that the funds from my father's account were transferred to the Schaffhausen bank.

"I then went on to Germany to see if I could find this so-called cousin. Due to the horrors of the war, our family has very few relatives left but I persisted in looking up every last one of them. It took me several weeks traveling around Bavaria to Augsburg and Munich and a number of small towns, but I am now absolutely convinced that there is no cousin or nephew or any other distant relative who could possibly fit the description I gave Mr. Meier." Elsa paused before she went on, and then looking straight at me, she said, "But that description does fit one person, it fits Mr. Wenner here."

Dr. Hofbeck sat up in his chair as if he had been physically struck, and said, "Mrs. Wilhelm, you're making a terrible accusation."

She looked more determined and more vengeful than ever, as she said, "Yes, I know, but everything fits. Mr. Wenner visited my father, he got him to sign that form, maybe he had my father sign it in blank and told him he would fill it in later. The money was not transferred until well after my father died so that Mr. Wenner had plenty of time to open that account in Schaffhausen. And that is the point—timing is everything! All I'm asking you to do is to check and see if the account that received the money was opened after my father died. If it was opened before, if it was opened before Mr. Wenner visited my father, then I will have to give up. I am sure, however, that you will find that it was opened after my father died and after Mr. Wenner returned to Switzerland from Argentina."

Everyone sat in stunned silence for several minutes, and I realized immediately that I was lost—totally and completely lost. Once they started checking with the Schaffhausen bank, there would be no question as to who had opened that account. I stared at Elsa for a minute feeling defeated by this bitch. She didn't need the money, and had only pursued this matter out of her own sense of self-importance. As my feeling of defeat turned to intense dislike for her, I roused myself to go on the attack. "Mrs. Wilhelm, I cannot tell you how offended I am by your allegations against me—your totally baseless allegations. Since you began questioning this transfer several months ago, I have tried to spare your feelings, but I can see now that I was wrong to have done so. I was a guest in your father's home in Argentina for a period covering two days, and I had several long talks with him. He was very explicit in telling me, and let me emphasize this, that he had no intention of leaving you anything, not a single mark, not a single franc, not one kopeck, not one pfennig. He told me how you had treated him when he came back from the Russian prison camp. He told me how you blamed him for the deaths of your mother and brother. He told me that you and he were virtual strangers, never seeing each other, and never corresponding with each other. Yes, you sent him a Christmas card every year, but there were no presents, there were no birthday cards. The father/daughter relationship had been destroyed.

"And he told me how you had behaved when you did come to Argentina to visit that one time—how you had refused to permit Maria and Toni, his housekeeper and her son, to sit at the dining room table with you and your father. These people were his family for almost fifteen years, and he could not forgive you for treating them as you did. You continued to make slighting comments about them, but your father told me that Toni was like a son to him, and had replaced your dead brother, Hans, in your father's affections. These people meant everything to your father, whereas you had abandoned him and now try to blacken their names. I have to tell you that he felt very, very strongly about this, and I hate to say it, but he referred to you as 'that bitch.'"

Both Dr. Hofbeck and Dr. Schnabel seemed about to intervene, but I was not to be stopped. "You think that your father was going to leave you something because there was that statement in the will that he had made some other provision for you. Do you know why that statement was there? Well, your father told me that the lawyer had put it there so that if you challenged the will in Argentina, they could tell the court that you had been provided for elsewhere. It was strictly a pro-forma statement that meant nothing. He did not intend to leave you anything!

"Now let's talk about the fact that the person that opened the account in Schaffhausen may have looked like me. Has it never occurred to you that I have a very strong resemblance to your late brother? Your father saw that instantly, and even showed me pictures of your brother taken in about 1944 when he would have been in his late twenties. And he also showed me pictures of this cousin that you deny exists, a cousin that also has the same family resemblance. You say that you went to Argentina after your father died. Didn't you take your father's personal belongings? Didn't you take the old family pictures? You must have them. Look through them, and you will find the picture and the letters from this cousin or nephew or whatever he was. And you will see that there is a resemblance: we both have a very typical German look. But I deeply resent your making these very serious allegations against me on the basis of your totally superficial investigation."

Everyone sat in stunned silence for several minutes until I again spoke up, this time much more quietly. "I'm sorry, Mrs. Wilhelm, to have spoken to you so sharply, but I felt that I had to tell you the truth as I know it to be."

After another couple of minutes of silence, Dr. Hofbeck said, "Mrs. Wilhelm, I must tell you that I have the utmost confidence in Mr. Wenner. It is inconceivable to me that Kurt would have done what you accuse him of. It would make no sense to jeopardize his entire career—and a very, very promising career—for a mere 250,000 francs. Even if it were ten times that amount, I know that Kurt is too principled a person to consider such action for even one second. As to your suggestion that he may have some resemblance to the person who opened the account in Schaffhausen, this is too speculative a suggestion for us to entertain for one minute. Your description was entirely too superficial. I would think that hundreds of young men would fit that description. The money may have gone to that bank in Schaffhausen, but there is nothing to indicate—not one single thing—that your father intended you to have it.

"And I must add, Mrs. Wilhelm, that it seems to me most improper for the account officer at the Schaffhausen bank to have talked with you about another account, even if it was for one of your relatives. If that were to happen here at Schleswigbank, the account officer would be fired."

Mrs. Wilhelm had not expected my counter-attack and was clearly shocked by the vehemence of it, and she may not have expected that Dr. Hofbeck would support me as he was doing. She said in a lower and calmer tone than she had used in her original accusation, "Perhaps I was wrong in making an accusation against Mr. Wenner. I should not have let my imagination run away with me. But there still is the question of the timing of the account opening. I continue to feel that you should look into that. If the account was opened after my father died, then there is no way that he could have filled in that number on the form that he signed."

Dr. Schnabel, who had remained quiet up to this point, finally spoke up. "I know that this is a most distressing situation for you, Mrs. Wilhelm. You had been estranged from your father, and I am sure that it is important to you to find that he had remembered you before he died. However, everything that we know at this point would indicate that he did not do so. And clearly Mr. Wenner cannot stand accused of anything on the basis of your suppositions alone. It also seems very odd to me that anyone would go into the bank, claiming to be a relative and thereby draw attention to himself, if he were not what he said he was.

"But I think that you do have a point about the timing of the account opening, and I would be happy to look into that in the morning. I would do it now, but it is after four o'clock, and the bank in Schaffhausen will be closed, so I will do it first thing in the morning. We have the account number, and I will merely ask the chief legal counsel of the bank to let me know the date on which that account was opened. I'm sure there will be no problem in getting that information. I must insist, however, that if we find that the account there was opened in a timely manner, as I expect we will, then you will agree to let this matter rest."

Elsa responded, "Obviously I will have no choice at that point. All possible avenues of investigation will then be closed to me."

Everyone stood as Mrs. Wilhelm moved toward the door. She then turned to me and said, "Mr. Wenner, I am truly sorry if I offended you. I have been trying to find the truth, and my theory seemed to me to be the most logical one, and it still does. However, what you said about my father, and his attitude toward me—it was hard hearing it as brutally as you put it to me, but I am sure that I would not have faced those facts otherwise. Perhaps I may still be proven wrong about the account in Schaffhausen. For your sake, I hope so."

When she left the room, Dr. Hofbeck sat shaking his head. "She's a woman possessed. She's prepared to do anything to try to get that money."

Shaken as I was, I roused myself to say, "I have to apologize to both of you for speaking to her as I did. It seemed so outrageous and so unjust, I simply could not contain myself. That's not the way a banker ought to act, I guess."

Dr. Hofbeck also looked shaken, and said, "I was going to try to stop you, but perhaps that was the only approach that could get through to her. What do you think, Rudolph?"

Dr. Schnabel said, "I think that it was wonderful to see Kurt's outrage. We could have been reasoning with her in bankerly fashion for hours, instead of having her stopped dead in her tracks, the way Kurt did it."

Dr. Hofbeck said, "Is there really any necessity, Rudolph, for checking with the Schaffhausen bank? I'll just call her in the morning and tell her that the account was opened before her father's death."

But the bank's chief counsel said, "Let's remove the last possible doubt. I'll check in the morning and then you can call her."

This answer made it absolutely clear to me that everything was lost—there was now absolutely no hope that I could escape—and I knew that I had to get back to my office before I broke down completely. I also saw that Dr. Hofbeck really did have doubts about what would be revealed at the Schaffhausen bank, and that he would prefer not to know the truth, particularly if it implicated me. I realized then how much I had betrayed this man by doing what I had done, but I also realized that the cloud was there in Dr. Hofbeck's mind, and that it would never go away unless they did check with the Schaffhausen bank. When Dr. Hofbeck finally asked me what I thought ought to be done, I looked him straight in the eye, and said, "Dr. Schnabel must do what he thinks is right."

CHAPTER XIV

I stood as Dr. Schnabel and Dr. Hofbeck left the conference room and then, exercising every ounce of self-control that I possessed in order to appear as calm and normal as possible, I made my way back to my office. I stopped at the desk of the secretary that I shared with Steiner and told her that I had an important report that I had to work on for the rest of the afternoon and that I was not to be disturbed by anyone. I closed the door to my office and sat down at my desk, head bowed, realizing that the entire world, as I had known it, had just collapsed. I knew instantly and conclusively that my career at Schleswigbank, my freedom, perhaps even my marriage—everything that I valued had been destroyed by what had just happened in that conference room.

I spent a long time—I can't even recall how long it was—trying to think of some way out of the trap that I had created for myself. They would know tomorrow morning that the account had been opened after Herr Reinsdorf had died, and after I had returned to Switzerland. And there was no way that I could keep the bank from finding out a day or two later that I was the one that had opened that account. The account officer at the Schaffhausen bank would identify me, and my fingerprints would be on the account opening forms. How could I explain that? Obviously, I could not. I thought of going to Dr. Hofbeck and telling him that Herr Reinsdorf had decided to give the money to me because I had reminded the old man of his son. But no one would believe that. I thought of arguing that there really was a Johannes Reinsdorf and that he was to have given me an account number, but since he did not do so, I had opened an account for him. Again, no one would believe that, particularly since the money had all been withdrawn.

My mood swung from depression to giddiness. I almost laughed aloud as I thought of my verbal assault on Elsa, and the way I had used every scrap of information I knew about the Reinsdorf household in Argentina. I had twisted some facts, invented others, and attributed things to Herr Reinsdorf that were, in fact, said by Toni. But it had certainly worked. If only I could have diverted Dr. Schnabel from his determination to check with the Schaffhausen bank.

Thinking about Dr. Hofbeck again dropped me back into depressed reality. This reserved and austere man had opened up to me and taken me on as his protégé; now I had betrayed him. I had seen the fear in Dr. Hofbeck's eyes, the fear of finding out that I had committed this crime. I wished I could go to him tonight to confess and to beg his understanding, and I sat debating with myself for what seemed like hours as to whether or not I should do this. I thought of telling him that I had not wanted to do this; that it was entirely my wife's idea. She was the one that wanted the money, and I had foolishly given in to her insistence. But even if he believed me, I would still be fired for what I had done and my career at the bank would be finished. My concentration was broken, however, when my secretary knocked at the office door, and came in to tell me that it was 5:30 p.m. and that she was leaving. She also wanted to tell me that Dr. Hofbeck's secretary had called and asked her to remind me that there would be a meeting in Dr. Hofbeck's office at eleven in the morning.

When the secretary left, I realized that I would have to start planning for tomorrow. I spent another hour thinking about what I would do—what I had to do—and I then emptied my attaché case and took the empty case with me as I left the office. When I reached the street, my thoughts turned to Ingrid—a meeting that I had not wanted to think about—and the terrible trauma that I would have to face when I told her what had happened. As I stood waiting for a streetcar to take me home, I remembered what I had told her when we were arguing about taking the money: "If we're caught, it's the end of everything for us. You do know that, don't you?" Well, now we had been caught, and it was, in fact, the end of everything for us.

When I came into the apartment, Ingrid was in the kitchen preparing dinner. I walked in slowly and went to her, taking her quickly into my arms. I merely held her for a minute without saying anything, until she pulled away. "Is something wrong, Kurt? You look terrible. What's happened?"

"Let's go in the other room where we can talk." Before leaving the kitchen, I went over to the stove to turn off the burners. I realized that we were unlikely to eat that night.

With my arm around Ingrid, I guided her to the sofa, and then, taking both of her hands into mine, I began to tell her. "Mrs. Wilhelm came back today. She had found out about the Schaffhausen bank, and she accused me of taking her father's money."

"But how could she? Who would have told her?"

"It was my own fault, my own stupid mistake. When I opened the account, I gave the name of Johannes Reinsdorf. I did that because I thought that the government authorities might check, and if they saw that a relative from Germany had gotten the money, they would check no further. It also made it easier to open the account as long as I had references. It never occurred to me that some idiot was going to tell her that her cousin had been in to open an account. We never would have done that at Schleswigbank—only in a small country bank like Schaffhausen would something like this happen. I feel so stupid. If I had used any other name, nothing would have been said to her, and she could never have made the accusation."

"What made her accuse you? Why did she think of you?"

"She's absolutely convinced that her father wanted her to have the money, and she figured out that I was the most likely one to have done something to prevent that. And she described me to the account officer at the bank, and he agreed that that was what Johannes Reinsdorf looked like."

"Oh, god, Kurt, what did you do?"

As I continued to hold her, I said, "Well, I really laid into her, and attacked her every way I could think of. Maybe I overdid it since I think Hofbeck began to suspect something. But I'll tell you it made me feel good, particularly when I said her father had called her a bitch."

Ingrid was almost crying as she said, "They didn't believe her, did they?"

"No, I'll give Hofbeck credit; he really stuck up for me. But Schnabel agreed with her that they should determine when the account was opened in Schaffhausen, and they are going to do that tomorrow morning."

"Tomorrow?"

"Yes, as soon as the bank opens. You understand what this means, don't you?"

Ingrid now began to cry and I tightened my arm around her and drew her to me. We were silent for a very long time as we sat there holding each other, trying to gauge the depth of the disaster that had overtaken us. I finally roused myself and went to the sideboard and mixed a whisky and soda for each of us. Since this was a late February evening, I decided that there was no need for ice in our drinks, something that we had become accustomed to when we were in Sicily. I returned to the sofa, and again put my arm around Ingrid while we sat sipping our drinks.

After a time, Ingrid said, "There's no way out, is there Kurt?"

I replied, "I certainly can't think of one. And I've been wracking my brain for hours trying to come up with a story that Hofbeck might believe. But they'll have an air-tight case. The important thing now is to keep you out of it. No matter what happens, no matter what anyone says or what they accuse you of, you have to keep insisting that you knew nothing about this whole thing. You must tell them that you never heard of the bank in Schaffhausen and that I had never said a word to you about taking any money from the bank or anyone else."

She protested, "But that would put it all on you. I can't do that. We were in this whole thing together."

"Look, tonight I don't know what's going to happen to me. I do know that I am going to be blamed for this—there's no way I can escape it. But you don't have to shoulder any of the blame. That doesn't mean you won't have to suffer because the next few months will be tough, and maybe the hardest part will be taking the sympathy, the terribly phony sympathy that so many people will offer. Just maintain complete ignorance of the whole thing and be strong, and you will get through, you will survive. You absolutely have to do this, Ingrid."

She shook her head, saying, "I feel as if I would be betraying you if I denied my part in the whole thing."

However, I insisted. "As long as you and I agree on this, as long as we understand what we're doing and why we're doing it, and as long as we love each other, there can be no question of betrayal. We both wanted the money, we talked about it, we knew what the risks were, and what we would lose if we were discovered. Now we have the opportunity to keep you out of it, and there is no reason at all for you to do anything but to deny all knowledge of what I did. Promise me that."

Ingrid said nothing, but she held me tightly and kissed me quickly on my cheek. We again sat together silently for a very long time, until I realized that Ingrid had fallen asleep. It had long since grown dark in our apartment, and I must have dozed off for a short time since I now heard a church bell strike one o'clock. As Ingrid slept, I began to focus more intently on what I had to do in the morning. I had developed the rough outline of a plan as I sat in my office immediately after the confrontation with Elsa, and I now began to rehearse this plan in my mind and to elaborate on all of its details.

I slowly disengaged myself from Ingrid and got up to make myself another drink. The only light in the room came from the street-lamp outside, and I had to feel for the things I needed for the drink. As I was doing that, Ingrid awoke and said, "What are you doing?"

"Making a drink. Would you like one?"

"I think so, yes. What time is it?"

"It's after midnight."

She yawned and finally said, "I must have slept. . . We didn't eat. Are you hungry?"

"No, I'm afraid not. The whiskey is all I can take. What about you?"

"The thought of food is terrible."

We again sat together and clung to each other, each hoping to draw strength from the other. The bell in the church tower soon struck two o'clock, but Ingrid was sleeping again. Tears ran down my cheeks as I realized that I might never be able to hold Ingrid like this again. She meant everything to me—she always had, and she always would. I could not imagine the road ahead without her.

I awoke with a start, trying to remember where I was and why I was sitting here in the dark on the sofa with Ingrid. A crushing weight descended upon me as I remembered the events of the previous day. I sat clearing the cobwebs from my mind and heard the church bell began to toll again. I counted each stroke and held my breath as it stopped at five. I knew that I had to get up and I had to put my plan into effect. I felt that leaving Ingrid was the hardest thing I had ever done in my life or could ever conceive of doing in the future, but I knew that there was no other way.

CHAPTER XV

Zürich/Genéve –1966

Since the meeting with Elsa, I had thought about what I probably faced now that the embezzlement was discovered, and I realized that it would be almost impossible for me to avoid a fairly long jail sentence. I knew that I would be convicted of embezzling the 250,000 Swiss francs—I could not imagine any possible way of preventing that from happening—and although I did not know what the penalty was under Swiss law for this crime, I was sure that it would involve several years in jail. I had decided as I sat in my office after the meeting with Elsa that I was going to make every possible effort to avoid a jail term at all costs, and the only way I could do that would be to get out of Switzerland as fast as possible. And I had to face the fact that, if caught, I would also be required to return the money that I had taken. Again, this was something that I definitely did not want to do. Having to abandon my wife, my career at the bank, my life in Switzerland—this was penalty enough. I would do everything I could to avoid having to return the money also.

So as I awoke after the night on the sofa with Ingrid, I got up and went into our bedroom. I showered and dressed as quickly as I could, then I brought out the largest suitcase that I owned. I began to pack, carefully choosing both business suits and casual clothes, since I had thought about what clothes I might need over the next several days, or however long it took me to get out of Switzerland. I went through my entire wardrobe, but since I could only allow myself one suitcase, I had to make innumerable decisions as to what I would take and what I would leave behind. I knew that I needed enough clothes for at least a week, and I wanted to be able to appear both as a businessman and as an American tourist, making the selection of clothes very important. When I finished packing, I carried the suitcase and the empty attaché case I had taken from my office and went downstairs to the garage, putting both in the trunk of our Mercedes.

Back upstairs in the apartment, I made a pot of coffee and several slices of toast, and then went into the living room and woke Ingrid who was still sleeping on the couch. I said to her, "It's six-thirty, Ingrid, you've got to get up. We have to talk." Her mood this morning was much more subdued than the previous evening. Sometime during the night, she had accepted what had befallen us, and I could see that she was steeling herself to deal with it. We went into the kitchen, and I gave her a cup of coffee and urged her to eat something.

I had never seen her look so defeated as she said, "What will happen today? What are you going to do?"

I reached across the small table at which we were sitting and took her hand, "Darling, I hope you understand, but I have to leave. I can't face being arrested. I couldn't face a trial, and I could never face going to jail. And that's almost certainly what will happen if I stay here in Switzerland."

"Where will you go?"

"I'm not going to tell you anything. It's really much better that you do not know. You'll be much more convincing telling the police that you have no idea where I've gone. I will call you though in three or four days. Today is Wednesday; maybe you could go to your mother's on Friday evening and I'll call you there. It sounds ridiculous, but the phone here might be tapped."

Ingrid nodded, but said nothing.

I felt it was necessary that she understands what lay ahead, so I said, "Let me tell you what I think will happen today. I would guess that you will get a phone call at about eleven-thirty or twelve o'clock. There is a meeting in Hofbeck's office at eleven, and when I'm not there, they will start checking around to try to find me. When they realize that I'm not in the bank, the first place they will check is here. You've got to act surprised that they would ask since, of course, your response will be that your husband has gone to work and they must know where he is. Later in the day, probably at around four o'clock, someone from the bank will come to see you. That is when you have to do your best job of acting. You have no idea where I am—you can't believe that I would ever take any money, and you simply dissolve in tears. It will be hard for you, but you must continue to deny any knowledge of the Schaffhausen bank or that there was any stolen money. Tell them that because of my promotion you thought that I was getting a much larger salary, and that that was how I had explained everything to you. Do you think you can do it?"

Ingrid looked at me for a long time, showing no emotion; and in a flat voice said, "Yes, I can do it."

I added, "One more thing: don't go to the bank in Küsnacht for two or three months. You have enough money in our account here in Zürich so that you should have no need to go there. And when you do go, be careful that you're not followed. After all that we went through to get that money, and all the suffering we will still have to endure, let's be sure that at least one of us gets a chance to enjoy some of it."

She said, "You're not planning to return the money?"

"No, I have no intention of returning it. Having the use of some of that money from time to time may ease the pain for both of us, particularly until we can get our lives straightened out again."

We sat together over our coffee and toast for a few more minutes, until I finally said, "Ingrid, I have to go now. I'm going to take the car, but I'll let you know where I left it so that you can get it back in a few days."

We walked to the back door of our apartment, and held each other for several minutes, saying nothing. We kissed quickly and without passion, and then I turned and ran down the backstairs to the garage and our car.

I drove into the center of Zürich, and parked the Mercedes in a small garage just off the Bahnhofstraße. Then, trying to appear as if this was just another working day, I walked over to Schleswigbank and went up to my fourth floor office. I wanted to delay any suspicions on the part of Dr. Hofbeck for as long as possible, and I was confident that by my coming to work that morning I would accomplish that. I sat at my desk and deliberately took out several files so that I would appear to be busy. My secretary arrived at about eight-thirty and came in to say good morning. "Did you finish that report last night, Mr. Wenner?"

I replied, "No, I'm afraid not; I'm still working on it. And I have a client coming in at about ten, so I won't get to it until this afternoon. Incidentally, I'll be with that customer in one of the conference rooms downstairs from about ten to eleven, so I shouldn't be more than a few minutes late for Dr. Hofbeck's meeting."

I kept looking at my watch as the minutes ticked away, until about ten minutes to nine, when, as I had expected she would do, Mrs. Jendricks called. I picked up the phone, and she said, "Dr. Hofbeck wanted to be sure that you would be available for the meeting this morning with Dr. Schnabel."

"Of course I will. It's a very important meeting."

I knew that Hofbeck was really checking to see if I had come in that morning, and the managing director would now be able to relax until that meeting. As soon as I finished talking with Mrs. Jendricks, I got up and went to the men's room. To get there, I had to walk past the reception desk and through the elevator lobby, then turn right down a short corridor. When I got into the men's room, I found Steiner washing his hands at one of the washbasins, and my heart sank out of fear that I might get into a long conversation with him. I went beyond the partition that separated the washbasins from the urinals, and stood at a urinal until I heard Steiner leave. I then came back to the door, and waited there for a minute until I was sure that Steiner was out of sight. I stepped back into the corridor, and walked a few steps to the fire escape stairs, hurried through that door, and rushed down the four flights of stairs to the ground floor. When I got to the lobby, my heart was pounding, but I did not hesitate as I opened the door into the lobby. No one was in the ground floor corridor and I hurried around through the elevator lobby and out the front door of the bank building, not having been recognized by anyone.

By 9:20 a.m., I had retrieved my car from the garage and was on the road to Küsnacht. The bank there opened at 10:00 a.m., and I had to have a fair amount of money to help me get out of the country and to get established in the

United States or wherever I ended up. I had plenty of time and drove slowly for the twenty-kilometer trip. The road ran along the Zürichsee, and it was a trip that I always enjoyed. I wondered when I might make this drive again. I arrived in Küsnacht about fifteen minutes before the bank opened, and I thought of looking for a restaurant and getting something to eat, but decided against it. I waited in the car until a few minutes after 10:00 a.m. and then entered the bank and went down to the safe deposit vaults. I had no problem getting access to the box in which I kept the cash, and I was given a private room to examine its contents—the remaining 200,000 francs of Herr Reinsdorf's money. I decided to take 50,000 francs, stuffing this money into the empty attaché case that I had taken from my office the previous evening. The 50,000 francs were the equivalent of about 40,000 US dollars, and I knew that I would need at least that much for airfare and to get settled in the US or wherever my new home turned out to be. This left 150,000 francs for Ingrid or for myself, if I could ever find an occasion to return to Switzerland.

Back in the Mercedes, I continued on the road heading southeast. I was now in a tremendous hurry since I had decided to head south to Lugano and my plan required that I be there by the late afternoon. I needed one more day in Switzerland to do something with the cash, since I did not want to travel with 50,000 Swiss francs in a briefcase, and I felt that dealing with large amounts of cash was most easily done in Switzerland. By heading to Lugano first, I wanted the police to think that I had fled south across the border to Italy, when, in fact, I planned to head west to Geneva.

Küsnacht was on the east side of the Zürichsee, and the Zürichsee ran to the southeast, forcing me to drive farther east than I would have liked before I could turn back south and west toward Lugano. About 25 kilometers from Küsnacht at the town of Rapperswil, there was a causeway across the lake, and taking the causeway enabled me to begin heading almost straight south to Lugano. The entire trip from Zürich to Lugano was only about 250 kilometers, but it was mountainous driving a good part of the way. I knew that I had to average at least 50 kilometers an hour to reach Lugano by three o'clock in the afternoon, and with the mountainous two-lane roads, this would not be easy.

Once over the causeway, I picked up Route 8 heading to Schwyz, the town that gave its name to the whole country of Switzerland. The road bypassed Schwyz and I continued to follow the two-lane road in flat country along the Urnersee to the town of Altdorf. Continuing south toward Andermatt, the road remained in the valley, but I could then begin to see the mountains ahead. After Andermatt, the slow climb began toward the St. Gotthard pass, with innumerable hairpin bends. Traffic was heavy, with a number of trucks literally crawling up the steep inclines and forcing me to do the same. From time to time, there was a passing lane, and my Mercedes had a great deal of power and was able to zoom by a number of slow-moving vehicles, but there were always more in front of me. I was becoming increasingly exasperated with the slow traffic, and I started to worry about reaching Lugano at the time I had planned.

I began cursing the government officials: they kept talking about building a tunnel through the mountains here to eliminate this bottleneck, but no one ever did anything about it.

As I was crawling along in traffic, I was trying to figure out exactly what I would do in Lugano. I wanted to leave the car where it would be found in the next day or two so that the police would know I had been in Lugano, and would have to deduce that I had gone from there to Italy. But I also did not want to do anything that would cause anyone to remember me as I headed for the airport in Lugano. I thought of parking the car on a street next to the lake, but did not like the idea of getting out of the car with my suitcase and attaché case and hailing a taxi—the driver would almost certainly remember me. I also thought of going to a hotel such as the Splendide, but there was no way I could park the car where I wanted and get the luggage into the hotel, and then out again, without attracting a great deal of attention.

I was still considering this problem, as I crept up the St. Gotthard pass in a long line of traffic, finally reaching the summit. The descent from the summit was a little faster, but there were an enormous number of sharp bends on the way down, and it remained impossible to pass all the slow-moving traffic. At one o'clock, it was still fifty kilometers to Bellinzona and another fifty-five to Lugano, and my frustration and fury at the traffic grew by the minute. Gradually, however, the road descended into the valley of the Ticino and the flow of traffic improved. After Bellinzona, the road became a four-lane highway for the first time since leaving Zürich, and I was able to make up much of the time I had lost crossing the St. Gotthard pass.

As the traffic moved more rapidly, I again concentrated upon the problem that I would face when I get to Lugano: what to do with the luggage. What I needed to do was to get rid of it as quickly as possible. So as I drove into Lugano at a little before 2:30 in the afternoon, I headed straight to the airport. What better way to solve the luggage problem than to check it with the airline? I parked just outside of the tiny terminal at the Lugano airport, and carried my suitcase in to the Swissair counter. I knew I was pretty early for the 4:30 p.m. flight to Geneva, but airline personnel were used to seeing people check in quite a bit ahead of time for a flight. I quickly bought my ticket, paying for it in cash and using the pseudonym under which I had made the reservation from my office in Schleswigbank that morning. I then walked out to the car, keeping the attaché case containing the money with me, and drove back into Lugano.

Once in town, I drove down to the shore of Lake Lugano and found a spot to park along the Riva Albertoli. I knew that cars were not permitted to park there overnight, and that my car would be found by the local police sometime in the morning. It would probably be a day or two after that before the Zürich police were informed, and they would then almost certainly think that I had fled to Italy, since Lugano was virtually right on the Italian border. After parking the car, I walked up to the elegant, old Hotel Splendide, which was a few short blocks away and overlooked Lake Lugano. I walked up the semi-circular front drive, and went into the impressive white and gilt lobby of the hotel. I went straight to the very ornate bar just off the lobby and ordered a whiskey and soda. I had some time to kill and I also felt that I needed a drink after what I had been through so far that day.

As I finished my drink, I checked my watch and saw that time was getting short, so I paid for the drink and went to the concierge desk, asking the concierge for information as to the next bus to Milan. The concierge suggested taking one of the bank limousines, but I indicated that I would prefer the bus. There was a bus at four that afternoon, so I walked out and told the doorman that I needed a taxi to take me to the bus depot in town. As we were waiting for the taxi to pull up, I mentioned to the doorman that I had to get to Milan immediately, and was anxious to catch the four-o'clock bus.

Once in the taxi, I made a point of talking with the driver, telling him that I was in a hurry to get to Milan, hoping that the driver would remember me if he were questioned by the police. When we arrived at the bus depot, I paid the driver and walked into the depot and then waited a few minutes before going back out and taking another taxi to the airport. It was only a few minutes' drive to the small Lugano airport, and I arrived in plenty of time for the flight to Geneva. I hoped that I had left enough clues pointing to Milan so that if the police were actively looking for me, they would focus on Italy.

As I walked into the airport, I suddenly saw that there were three police officers in the terminal. They had not been there when I checked my suitcase a few hours previously, and they were standing right next to the gate with the sign indicating that this was the departure gate for the flight to Geneva. I literally froze, and for a minute I simply stood staring at the police. But, with a great effort, I pulled myself together and headed into the men's room. It was a small room that could only be used by one person at a time, so I felt that I could stay there for just a few minutes, since someone else might want to use the facilities at any moment. To try to calm myself, I splashed water on my face, and then wiped my hands and face with a couple of paper towels. Still unsure of what the police were there for, or what I should do, I ventured out of the men's room, and quickly sat on one of the old wooden benches in the waiting room facing the departure gate. The policemen were now talking with the airline agent at the gate, and it was clear that the flight would be announced momentarily. I debated heading back into Lugano and getting the car to try to drive out of Switzerland. But my luggage had already been checked and, while I still had the brief case with the 50,000 francs, all my clothes and everything that I needed were in the suitcase that was now on that plane.

As I sat debating with myself as to what I should do, an announcement was made that the flight was boarding, and I continued to sit there almost paralyzed with indecision and fear. The three policemen stood to one side of the departure gate and simply watched as the passengers handed their tickets to the agent at the gate. They seemed intent on checking each of the passengers, but they stopped no one and only glanced at each other from time to time.

I finally decided that I would be too obvious if I waited until everyone had boarded, so I picked up my attaché case and, with pounding heart and afraid that I might lose control of my bowels at any moment, I approached the gate. I thought that all three policemen looked intently at me as I handed my ticket to the gate agent, but they quickly and almost routinely turned their gaze to the passenger behind me and the next thing I knew I was outside the small terminal, walking toward the steps leading up to the Swissair DC-3.

I almost staggered as I walked toward the plane, and the attendant at the bottom of the steps asked if I was all right. I smiled and thanked him, quickly climbing the steps and boarding the plane. As I sat on this DC-3 I remembered walking out to a DC-3 just over a year earlier in Buenos Aires for the trip to Tucamán. The differences this time were ironic. On the one hand, the Swissair DC-3, painted white and with the red cross of Switzerland on its tail, was in perfect condition, as opposed to the battered, leaking Areoliñeas Argentinas DC-3 on which I had flown to Tucamán. On the other hand, I had been an up-and-coming young bank executive when I boarded that plane in Buenos Aires, while I boarded this plane in Lugano, only thirteen months later, as a fugitive. And my fugitive status would never be more sharply impressed on me than it had been by those three police officers at the departure gate at the Lugano airport. As I sat on the plane, I wondered if I would be facing other crises similar to this in the days and months ahead.

After takeoff, I embarked on one of the most spectacular flights that I had ever experienced. I had thought that this flight to Geneva was to be over the Alps, but it turned out to be a flight right through the Alps, something I had not thought possible. It was a beautifully clear day, and the DC-3 headed almost due west toward Geneva. The plane flew just barely above most of the mountain peaks, but actually below the tallest ones. The pilot would head directly toward a snow-covered mountain top, only banking one way or the other just seconds before reaching it. The passengers, most of whom were Italian or Swiss Italian, were exhilarated by the seemingly unending thrills of the flight, yelling their delight as the pilot maneuvered between the peaks. I had hoped to relax on the plane after the traumatic events of the past two days, but was caught up both by the excitement of the flight and by the awe-inspiring beauty of the Alps. The scenery was so spectacular that it was almost impossible to take my eyes away from it. I did look away for a minute when the stewardess came around serving coffee, and I asked her if the flight was like this every day.

She said, "Yes, it's quite exciting, isn't it? We never fly any higher than this."

"But what do you do in bad weather?"

"We have radar, you know, and the pilots know this route very well, although if the weather is too bad why then the flight is cancelled."

I was glad that this was a clear day and that the flight had not been cancelled. There seemed to be an unending succession of mountains and of thrills, before the plane finally emerged into the valley in which Geneva was situated. The pilot pointed out Mont Blanc to the left of the plane, and it was one of those rare days on which one could see that magnificent snow-covered peak very clearly. The plane now descended over Lake Geneva, and headed toward the airport. From my window seat, I was able to see the Jet d'Eau shooting skyward from the lake near the center of town. I took this to be a good sign since the jet was only turned on in good weather, and I offered a silent prayer to some unknown God that I would soon re-enter a period of good weather for myself.

Chapter XVI

Genéve/Paris – February 1966

After landing in Geneva, I had to decide where to spend the night. If I went to any of the well-known hotels, such as Le Rhone, the Des Bergues, or Le Richemond there was always the chance that I might be recognized. These were the hotels frequented by the wealthy tourists, and the lobbies of these hotels were usually crowded both with the tourists and with Swiss bankers waiting to meet their clients. I had too many clients who stayed at these hotels, and I had also met quite a few bankers from Geneva who might very well be visiting someone at one of these hotels. So I knew that I had to spend the night at a hotel that attracted a different class of people. I decided to try the Arbalète in the old part of town. This hotel was also somewhat touristy, but it would be highly unlikely that one of my wealthy private banking clients would be staying there. This was February and, although it was not the tourist season, the hotel could still be pretty fully booked since its rates were relatively low. But I decided to take a chance and to go directly to the hotel, rather than phoning ahead.

My luck held one more time since the Arbalète had one room left. It was a tiny room, on the top floor of the small hotel, with a slanting roofline and a dormer window overlooking the street. I took most of the clothes out of my suitcase and hung up my suits to let some of the wrinkles hang out, and then I simply dropped on the bed. It was only a little after 7:00 p.m., but I had slept only fitfully the night before and today I had fled from Zürich on that roundabout trip here to Geneva. The extraordinary tension of the past two days had really worn me out. As I lay in bed and thought back on the day, the whole experience seemed incredible to me. Starting out by having to leave Ingrid, and then forcing myself to go into the office at Schleswigbank, followed by the drive to Küsnacht to get the money, and then the frustrating rush to Lugano—I wondered how I had done it. And to top it off, those policemen scaring me half to death just before that incredible flight from Lugano! The flight was certainly exhilarating and the scenery was awe-inspiring, but it was the last thing I needed on this day of all days.

At one-thirty in the morning I awoke, still fully clothed, and could hear the noise of tourists walking the streets of the old town and making their way back to their hotels as the night-spots in the neighborhood closed down. I was famished and wanted to get something to eat, but I was still too tired to even think of going out, so I simply undressed and returned to bed. I went back to sleep immediately and slept soundly until close to six in the morning. When I awoke my first thought was of Ingrid and how she had made out when they had come to question her. I felt guilty about leaving her, but the alternative would have meant branding her as a criminal too, and I simply could not do that. She had certainly pushed me to take the money, and I don't think I would have done it without her urgings, but I still felt that I had to protect her if I could.

My intention in coming to Geneva was to do something with the 50,000 Swiss francs that I was carrying in my attaché case. I did not think that it was a good idea for me to carry that much cash while traveling internationally. Going through customs, particularly in the United States, I would run the risk of having my luggage opened, and I would have difficulty explaining why I was carrying so much cash. Most of the major US banks had branches in Geneva, and I was thinking of claiming, when I talked with them, that I was an American citizen returning to the States and wanted to open an account that I could access when I got to New York. I could show them my US passport to support my claim that I was going home. Almost from the moment that Elsa began accusing me in the conference room at Schleswigbank, I had begun thinking of heading to New York and I had not seriously considered any other possibility. As a result, I was hoping to find a bank here in Geneva at which I could open an account.

The banks would not open until ten o'clock, so I had plenty of time to shower and dress and then find a restaurant for that long-awaited meal. I put on one of my business suits—a dark blue suit such as all bankers wear—and walked over to the nearby hotel Les Armures to have breakfast in the hotel dining room. I treated myself to a full breakfast—eggs, ham, croissants, and a great deal of coffee. I felt much better as I finished, having had a full night's sleep and a good breakfast. As I thought back on the previous two days, I began to congratulate myself on the way in which I had gotten out of Zürich. Rather than feeling depressed, which is what I thought I ought to feel, I had a sense of accomplishment, bordering on elation, at my escape up to this point. The police would almost certainly find the car in Lugano today, and any search for me would probably be concentrated in the south and in Italy.

I'm sure that when Elsa heard that she was right, that it had been me who had opened that account and taken the money, she would expect me to be crushed and already in jail. And I had been distraught that first night as I sat in the dark with Ingrid contemplating the disaster that had overtaken us. But as I sat having another cup of coffee at the Hotel Les Armures, I had a feeling that was close to being proud of the fact that, so far at least, I had gotten away, particularly since the money was still there in the bank in Küsnacht. I knew that it was premature to be congratulating myself since I was not yet out of

Switzerland. But I would be out later in the day, needing only this one morning in Geneva to do something with the 50,000 francs that I was carrying. As soon as that matter was taken care of, I would head to France as fast as I could.

Shortly after the banks opened, I went to the office of the First National Bank of New York, which was on the Quai Général Guisan overlooking the Pont du Mont Blanc. When I indicated that I wanted to open an account, I was referred to a very pleasant young woman in what was apparently the new business area. I explained that I was an American citizen and was returning to the United States and that I wanted to open a checking account with the New York bank so that I could draw on it after I arrived back in New York. The woman was very helpful, explaining that it would probably be necessary for me to give the bank wire transfer instructions to move the money to the States since normal checks could take a very long time to clear. However, when she found out that the account would only be for 50,000 francs, she smiled very pleasantly as she said, "I'm really very sorry, but we do require considerably larger minimum balances for our accounts here in Switzerland. However, when you arrive in New York, please go to one of our retail branches in the city since they have much lower minimums there than we do here in Geneva."

As I walked back out on to the street, all I could think about was those damn banks. They have no interest in serving the small customer—all they want are the super-rich. You would think that a US bank that prides itself on catering to small accounts back in New York would be eager to handle a 50,000 francs or a $40,000-customer here in Switzerland. I had to confess to myself that my feelings were somewhat ironic since getting rid of Herr Reinsdorf's small account on behalf of Schleswigbank was what had brought me to my present situation. Realizing that all large New York banks would probably have the same account opening requirements, I decided to try one of the smaller, and presumably hungrier, American banks and went to the Chicago National Bank on the Place des Eaux Vives. But the story was the same there, except that a very self-important German Swiss was almost rude in turning me away.

After being turned down by the two banks, I stopped at a small café and had an espresso. I now realized that it would not be possible to open a checking account with one of the American banks, and it suddenly hit me that it would have been a really dumb thing to do. I had thought that I could open an account in my own name by using my US passport to establish American citizenship, and that the Swiss bank secrecy laws would have protected me. However, the more I thought about it, the less attractive that option seemed. I had been burned once by relying on Swiss bank secrecy laws, and I decided that it would not make sense to rely on those laws again.

Therefore, I came up with another plan, and spent the rest of the morning visiting several of the large Swiss banks, buying a total of $30,000 in traveler's checks at two of the banks and converting 6,250 Swiss francs into $5,000 of American money at two others. I decided that I would have to hide the rest of the francs in my suitcase and convert those to dollars once I got to the US.

By the time I finished running around to all the banks, it was early afternoon, and I had to get back to the Arbalète to change my clothes and check out. At the hotel, I changed into a pair of old jeans and a sport shirt and was pretty confident that I would pass for an American tourist. I knew that my shoes were too European and not as casual as most Americans wore, but I doubted if anyone would be checking my footwear. I repacked my suitcase, checked out of the hotel, and took a taxi to the railroad station, the Gare de Cornavin. To look more like a tourist, I had left my attaché case at the hotel and had bought a small canvas bag where I had put most of my shirts and underwear, together with some of the cash. The rest of the money and my Swiss passport were hidden in my suitcase.

Once at the station I bought a ticket for Paris on the train leaving Geneva at 4:45 p.m., and then headed for passport control. I was carrying the American passport that had been re-issued two years previously by the American embassy in Berne. My parents had regularly renewed this passport for me after they returned to Switzerland when I was two years old, and I kept it current after I became 18. I had always felt that I might need it someday if war ever again engulfed Europe, and I knew that I was only able to flee Switzerland now because I had that passport. The memory of the police at the airport in Lugano was fresh in my mind as I approached the passport control booth, but the guard merely glanced at the passport and at my picture and handed it back to me, waiving me through. The French immigration officials would check the passport again on the train, and I was confident that they would be no more curious about me than the Swiss official had been.

The train was not crowded and I found a compartment to settle into. As with so many European trains, the passenger cars were divided into smaller compartments with seats facing each other. There was only one other passenger in this compartment—an elderly man who appeared to be a French farmer. He clearly had no intention of talking to me, which was fine with me, and I settled down for the trip to Paris. About an hour into the train trip, the French immigration officers came into my compartment and began checking passports. After checking the French farmer they asked for my passport, which I handed to them, trying to appear as calm as possible while the two officers turned the pages. One of them finally said to me, "But there are no stamps in this passport. The passport is several years old and you have never used it to travel?"

I took a deep breath and said in French, "As you can see, the passport was issued by the American embassy in Berne, and I have been resident in Switzerland—my parents live in Lucerne and I like to stay in Switzerland to be near them. I work in Zürich and I have not traveled much in the last few years. Sometimes when I drive to France or to Austria I go by the back roads, and the passport does not get stamped. You know how the guards are at those small crossings. Sometimes there is no one there. I don't recall but I think the passport that you have there is only about two years old, so there are no stamps in it. I should have brought my old passport to show you—it had many stamps from France, from England and from America."

My voice trailed off as the two immigration officers alternately stared at me and then at my passport. Finally, one of them said, "We will take the passport and check back with you in a little while."

The next hour was absolute hell for me. I had no idea where the immigration officers had gone or what they were doing. I knew that I had babbled on with my explanation too long, and I imagined that they were sending a report back to the Swiss police. I became convinced that at any minute, I would be arrested. This was an express train to Paris, but the next thing I knew the train began to slow down and soon came to a stop. I peered anxiously out the window trying to figure out where we were and why the train had stopped, but all I could see was a group of men in uniform standing on the platform up ahead apparently talking to each other. The uniformed men could have been the immigration officers or they could simply have been some of the conductors on the train. After about fifteen minutes, the train started up again and as the train left the station. I finally noticed a sign that identified the town as Dijon.

It was at least a half hour later when one of the immigration officers came back into my compartment. He reached in his inside coat pocket and took out my passport. The officer merely handed it to me, saying, "Your passport, monsieur." I tried to force a smile and managed to croak in response, "Merci!" As the immigration officer walked away, I turned back to the window and closed my eyes, as waves of relief washed over me. For the rest of the trip to Paris, I remained seated, staring out the window, almost too exhausted from fright to even consider moving. I never understood why the train had stopped at Dijon, but I was too afraid to even consider asking anyone.

The train trip to Paris had taken a little over four hours so it was almost nine o'clock when I disembarked at the Gare de l'Est. As in Geneva, I had no hotel reservation and I had to decide where to spend the next two nights. Ideally, I should have gone to some small hotel on the Left Bank, but I had only been to Paris a few times and had always stayed in one of the better hotels on the Right Bank. I was able to remember the name of a small hotel called the Lotti, which was on the Rue de Castiglione near the Place Vendôme. It was in a good location, but I could be fairly confident that none of my private banking customers would be staying there. The Meurice across the street and the Continental next door were more likely places for the wealthy to be staying.

I phoned the hotel from the station, trying to decide whether to speak English or French. My credibility as an American tourist would be undermined if I spoke French too well, but I was sure that I could not make myself understood at the hotel if I spoke English to them. Proceeding in French, I was relieved to find that the Lotti did have a room, and, after booking it, I immediately went out and took a taxi to the hotel. There was a good deal of comment at the reception desk that an American could speak French so well, but I explained that I had gone to school in Geneva and had perfected my French there. I smiled to myself as I realized what an accomplished liar I was becoming, making up whatever stories were required to get myself through a given situation. The clerk at the reception desk took my passport, the usual practice in many European cities so that it could be reviewed by the police overnight. She assured me that it would be returned to me in the morning. Obviously, after the events on the train, this made me nervous, but it was standard practice and there was nothing I could do about it.

I had booked the room at the Lotti for two nights, Thursday and Friday. This would give me time on Friday to buy a plane ticket to New York, and then Friday night I could call Ingrid at her parents' home, as I had told her I would do before leaving Zürich. My room at the Lotti was not as small as the one at the Arbalète, but this one did not have a private bath. The toilet was at the far end of the corridor, and I also had to arrange with the chambermaid to get access to the bathroom. I had to wait almost forty-five minutes in the morning for my turn to use the bath, and then found that there was a large tub, but no shower. I loved the shower that Ingrid and I had had installed in our apartment in Zürich, but European hotels rarely had them, so I had to make do with a quick bath.

I asked the concierge for the address of the Pan American Airways ticket office and found that it was on the Champs Elysées at number 138. The concierge also gave me the phone number, BAL 88-00. I phoned ahead to find out if there was space on Saturday's flight to New York, and what the fare would be. After getting that information, I asked the airline to reserve a seat for me. Since it was a pleasant morning, I decided to walk over through the Place de la Concorde and along the Champs Elysées to the ticket office. The city was surprisingly quiet for a Friday morning; but since it was February, there were few tourists and it was probably a little too cold for the French to be strolling the boulevard. I found the ticket office quite easily, but before going in I stopped at a Bureau de Change and changed enough Swiss francs into French francs to cover the cost of the ticket. Remembering the Lufthansa flight to Buenos Aires and the crowded conditions in coach, I would have loved to buy a first class ticket to New York but I decided that my guise as an American tourist was better served if I suffered in coach and I also realized that, as a fugitive, I would have to be careful how I spent my remaining money.

After purchasing the ticket, I spent the rest of the day wandering around Paris. Although it was rather cold, walking around that beautiful city was very restful, and I tried simply to enjoy the beauty of the city and to forget everything else. However, try as I might, my mind kept coming back to what had happened in Zürich and to my present status as a fugitive. I continued to have very mixed feelings about these events—fury at myself for having been so stupid as to pretend to be Elsa's cousin when I opened the account at the Schaffhausen bank, something akin to depression at the price I was being forced to pay for my own stupidity, and a certain amount of elation as the ingenuity I had shown in getting away from Switzerland.

My mind kept wrestling with these conflicting ideas, as I walked over to the Left Bank and found a little café where I enjoyed an omelet and a half bottle of wine. There were tables outside, but I decided that it would be more comfortable sitting indoors. I finished my lunch more quickly than I would have liked, so I resumed walking along the Seine, crossing over to the Ile de la Cité to see Notre Dame and Sainte-Chapelle. I did not go into Notre Dame, but I did go into Sainte-Chapelle. I had seen the glorious stained glass windows there on my first trip to Paris many years earlier. Seeing them again now I realized that they were still beautiful, but for some reason I did not feel the emotional impact that I had felt the first time. My emotions were in such turmoil from the events of the last two days that nothing could have a meaningful effect on me.

I went on to the Ile St. Louis, a charming old residential area, with narrow streets, looking much as it did three hundred years ago. I spent about an hour on the Ile St. Louis, exploring as many of the old streets as I could, and then crossed over to the Right Bank. I followed the Seine back up to the Louvre, walking through the courtyard and on into the Tuileries. I stayed there for another hour before crossing over the Rue de Rivoli and heading back to the Lotti.

Time passed slowly as I waited in my room for evening to come so I could place my call to Ingrid. Looking out of the small window from my room at the Lotti, I could see the white dome of Sacré Coeur off in the distance. The setting sun striking the dome had turned it a vivid orange, and I was again struck by the beauty of Paris. I had seen so much beauty on this trip—along the Zürichsee; going through the St. Gotthard pass; along the lake in Lugano; flying over the spectacular Alps; and now Paris. It occurred to me that here I was fleeing from certain conviction and imprisonment and my route had taken me through some of the most beautiful scenery in Europe. A few months ago, I would have been overwhelmed by what I had seen these past three days, but now I was beginning to understand what it was to be a fugitive, when the connections with the world around me had been virtually severed. I wondered if I would ever again be able to travel as an ordinary man, and feel that I was a part of my surroundings, a part of society.

I had planned to call Ingrid at eight o'clock, but about twenty minutes before eight, I decided that I couldn't wait any longer and I asked the hotel operator to place the call. Ingrid answered at once and I was enormously relieved to hear her voice.

"Ingrid, I've been dying to talk to you. Is everything all right?"

I could tell that she was nervous as she replied, "Yes . . . yes, but where are you?"

"We can talk about that in a minute, but first tell me what happened."

She said, "Well, it was as you said it would be. At a little before noon, Dr. Hofbeck's secretary called and asked if you were at home. I told her that of course you weren't at home since you had gone to work. I asked her why she was calling—hadn't you arrived at work that morning? She assured me that you had, but that you must have stepped out and that Dr. Hofbeck was anxious to talk with you. It was a brief conversation, and she clearly did not want to upset me."

"I knew they would check with you. What happened next?"

"Then at about four-thirty, two men came to the apartment. I had been out most of the afternoon walking—the apartment was driving me crazy, and I had to get out and walk. I had only been back about a half-hour and had just begun to re-heat the meal from the night before to show anyone who came that I expected you home. One of the men said he was from bank security and the other was from the personnel department."

"Do you remember their names?"

She said, "I wrote them down somewhere, but I must have left them back in our apartment. At any rate, they told me that you seemed to have disappeared and that they were investigating the possible embezzlement of a large sum of money. I told them that it was impossible, my husband could not possibly have had anything to do with any embezzlement. And I asked them why they were here. But they persisted. They wanted to know how we had suddenly gotten so much money. I told them that we did not have very much, and I asked them what they meant by saying we had suddenly gotten a great deal of money. They mentioned the fact that we had moved to a new apartment and bought a new car. I told them that I did not understand what they were talking about, and the fact that we had been able to do these things was due to your promotion and the fact that the bank had given you a substantial raise."

I asked, "Did they say how much was missing?"

"No, they just kept talking about a large sum of money. I said to them, 'Don't keep trying to tell me that my husband is a criminal or that he has stolen a lot of money. Tell me where he is, or if you don't know, we should call the police and have them look for him.'

"They finally asked about how you went to work in the morning, did you take the streetcar, or did you drive. I told them that usually you took the streetcar, but that this morning you had driven because you had an appointment to meet a customer. It just went on and on and on."

Even though I had anticipated everything that had happened, I was still upset to hear it. I said, "I'm really sorry; maybe you should have come with me."

Ingrid did not respond to my suggestion, but said, "They finally got up to leave and the security man said, 'We hate to tell you this, Mrs. Wenner, but it would appear that your husband has fled Zürich and may be trying to flee Switzerland with a large amount of money. We will have to report this to the police.' I was crying when they left, but I think I did everything just as you told me."

"Darling, I'm so sorry that you had to go through this. I only wish that you were here with me now. Has anything else happened?"

"Yes. . . Yes, today the police came. They told me that our car had been found in Lugano, and they had talked with people there who told them that you were going to Italy—to Milan. They asked the same things that the men from the bank had asked, and I just kept telling them I could not believe it. I seem to be able to cry very easily, and that seems to get the conversation over with rather quickly."

"Ingrid, I'm so sorry that you have to go through this."

"I'm afraid it's the way it has to be, but Kurt, where are you? Are you still in Switzerland?"

"No, I'm out of the country and I don't want to tell you where I am now or where I will be going tomorrow. But as soon as I'm settled, I'll call again and I pray that in another six months or so you can come and join me."

"Kurt, I'm at my mother's house now, and I think I should stay here for a while."

"That's probably a good idea."

"It's going to be necessary. I found out today—I went to the doctor this afternoon after the police left—he confirmed what I had suspected. I'm pregnant, Kurt."

The news hit me like a bombshell. We had been hoping that Ingrid would become pregnant for the past several months and I had stopped using condoms during our intercourse. To have it happen now though was a cruel blow after all that had happened in the past three days.

I couldn't say anything for a minute or more, and Ingrid said, "Kurt, did you hear what I said?"

"Yes, I heard. I should be so happy, but I feel so horrible. Leaving you was hard enough, but with a child coming it makes everything that much more impossible. I can't be there to help you, and the child will have to know that his father was a criminal. Ingrid, I don't know what to say."

"We'll think of something, darling. We can't decide everything tonight."

"Ingrid, I will tell you after all. I'm going to the United States. You know I have a US passport. Follow me there in a month or two while you're still able to travel. We'll start over in the US and the child will never know about what happened in Switzerland. We can make a go of it in the US. I know we can."

"I'm too exhausted tonight to make any decision. I'm even thinking of having an abortion. But you and I can't decide anything tonight. Call me after you get to the States—I'll be here at my parents'. We have to think, we have to have time to plan."

"You're right, we can't decide everything tonight."

"You know I love you, Kurt, and we will find some way out of this."

"I love you too, darling, and I do so want us to be together again."

The phone call ended and I sat staring at the faded wallpaper, with questions teeming in my mind. How could this have happened to me? I never wanted to be a criminal. I never set out deliberately to steal anything. That money just seemed to fall from the sky in front of us, and all we did was pick it up. I had a career that was just taking off; I had a wonderful wife; I even had a child on the way that I didn't know about. There was no reason to risk anything. I'm not a criminal! If only the bank had paid me a decent salary, there would have been no need to take the money. If only Ingrid had not been so insistent, I would never have done it. How can I be blamed for what happened? If only I had it to do over again, I would never take that money. If only . . . .

And, much as I tried to repress the thought, it kept coming back to me that it had mainly been Ingrid's prodding that had finally caused me to do it. It had all seemed so easy, but what I had told her at the time also kept coming back: "If we're caught, it's the end of everything for us. You do know that, don't you?" "The end of everything for us"—the phrase would not get out of my mind.

I sat there on the bed most of the night, trying to decide what to do. Thoughts of suicide passed through my mind, thoughts of returning to Zürich and facing the charges, thoughts of staying here in Paris until Ingrid could join me. As the first rays of daylight crept into my room, however, I knew that I would go out to Orly Airport in a few hours, and I would take that Pan Am flight to New York. What would happen once I got there, I had no idea.

The following article appeared in the Züricher Neuzeitung on November 20, 1966:

Banker Convicted of Embezzlement;

Sentenced to Long Prison Term

Kurt Wenner, formerly a Vice President and account administrator for Schleswigbank in Zürich, was today convicted *in absentia* of embezzling 250,000 francs from an account at the bank. Mr. Wenner was accused by Swiss federal prosecutors of illegally transferring that amount of money from the account of a recently deceased customer of Schleswigbank. Mr. Wenner opened an account in a fictitious name at another Swiss bank to receive the transfer. Upon discovery of his theft, Mr. Wenner fled Switzerland and has not yet been apprehended.

Judge Manfred Bloem, who heard the case in Zürich Federal Court, sentenced Mr. Wenner to six years in prison, the maximum sentence under Swiss law. Judge Bloem indicated that this was a very serious crime, and that Mr. Wenner had betrayed the trust that had been placed in him not only by the bank and its customers, but also by his wife and family. Judge Bloem commented, "A crime of this nature, if allowed to go unpunished, would serve to undermine the worldwide confidence that now exists in the Swiss banking system."

In a related action, Judge Bloem denied the request of the deceased's daughter for a judgment against Schleswigbank for 250,000 francs. The daughter had claimed that the bank had been negligent in permitting the embezzlement to take place. In making the ruling, Judge Bloem commented that there was no evidence to support the daughter's claim that her father had intended that she receive the money. The judge ruled that when Mr. Wenner is apprehended and the money recovered, it should be turned over to the deceased's executor in Argentina.

NEW YORK: PHASE I

CHAPTER XVII

New York – 1975

"Ladies and gentlemen, I'm only going to take a few minutes to tell you what an excellent meeting I think we've had over the past two days. I know that it is an imposition on you to ask you to give up a weekend to come to a meeting like this, but I do think it is important that we get together from time to time away from our offices so that we can take an objective look at our business, learn more about the strengths that we have today, and decide what it is that we need to do to be more competitive in the future. I am convinced that here at Morris, Brunner & Company, we have one of the best teams of equity analysts of any firm on Wall Street, and I am sure that you agree with me on that.

"We believe that we are unique in having the research capability to cover the common stock markets not only of the United States, but of Europe and the Far East as well. With the world economy becoming more integrated, we believe that it is imperative for US institutional investors to diversify their portfolios internationally. And this is something that we want our institutional sales representatives to be stressing in the months ahead.

"As President of Morris, Brunner, I can't tell you how exciting it has been to watch the development of our research department, particularly during the past two years. As many of you know, we added a new investment team leader for international investment about a year ago, right after our last conference, and this has expanded and deepened our international capabilities. However, since Kurt wasn't here a year ago, some of you—particularly from our offices in Chicago and San Francisco—may not have had the chance to meet him or to get to know him, so let me just briefly mention some of the facts from Kurt Wenner's impressive background.

"Kurt was educated in Bonn, Germany, at the Institute Polytechnique and subsequently received an advanced degree at the Sorbonne University in Paris. He worked for many years with a number of Swiss private banks in Berne and Lausanne, Switzerland, where he became an expert in both the European equity markets as well as the foreign exchange markets. He came to this country about ten years ago to continue his studies at New York University. For the past year, he has had the mandate of building our capabilities in international investing, so that we can provide our customers with a service that we have never had before, and that few of our competitors are capable of having. We believe that Kurt is a particularly valuable addition to our team since he is following not only the rapidly growing stock markets of Europe and Asia, but he also brings to his analytical work a tremendous amount of experience in the foreign exchange markets, and this, as you well know, is a major factor in making investments in overseas markets."

As I sat listening to Sam Brunner introducing me, I thought back over the last ten years and realized how easy it had been to develop a new identity in the United States. When I had first arrived in New York ten years previously in 1965, I had known that it would be hard to get a job comparable to what I had had back in Zürich. So I hit upon the idea of enrolling at NYU to work on a master's degree in business administration. I had brought enough money with me from Switzerland so that I did not need to work immediately, and I figured that, as a student, it would be much easier to get a part-time job in one of the Wall Street brokerage firms. Moving from one firm to another over a period of about two years, I built up a number of respectable references, so that I had finally felt secure in looking for a full-time job in an investment advisory firm. I worked as an analyst for several Wall Street firms, until June 1974 when I had joined Morris, Brunner & Company.

I smiled to myself as I sat at one of the tables toward the back of the dining room listening to Sam Brunner's introduction. Americans loved to fawn over foreigners, and particularly over Europeans. No one ever checked my background—and so Sam Brunner was now reading off names of schools that I was supposed to have attended and firms that I was supposed to have worked for—and no one had ever checked. The fact that I was extremely knowledgeable about foreign markets totally stopped anyone from even thinking that my credentials might be suspect. And now here I was, ten years after fleeing Switzerland to avoid prosecution as an embezzler, being introduced at the concluding dinner of the company's semi-annual planning meeting as the key employee who would provide the company's sales staff with this exciting new product—foreign investing.

I was proud of what I had accomplished during the past ten years. It had taken a tremendous amount of determination on my part to start over in New York, and to fabricate a new background while building upon the knowledge and experience I had gained at Schleswigbank. It had been lonely without Ingrid, and never being able to see my daughter, who was now almost ten years old. But after that night in the Lotti in Paris, I had never permitted myself to be despondent again, and, while there had not been much joy during these past ten years, I could now take satisfaction from the fact that I had fought my way back to a responsible and challenging position.

Sam Brunner's remarks had ended, and there was a general rush toward the exits. Most of those attending the conference had not been too happy that it had been held at the Scantikon Center in Princeton. This was very convenient for Sam Brunner who lived in Bernardsville, New Jersey, and Leonard Morris who lived just outside Princeton, and it was not too bad for the out-of-towners who flew in and out of Newark Airport. It was a real hassle though for everyone who lived in New York City, in Westchester, or out in Long Island. I lived on East Eighty-Second Street in Manhattan, but had no reason to hurry home, and as I slowly made my way out of the dining room, several of the customer's men stopped to introduce themselves and to welcome me to the team. I almost resented the familiarity and their apparently false camaraderie, feeling that the Schweitzer Deutsch in Zürich would never have acted this way. However, I was pleased by the recognition I had received from Sam Brunner, I was becoming more comfortable in my job, and I left Princeton to return to New York feeling a great deal of self-satisfaction.

As I sat in my office at 17 Broad Street the next morning, I was studying the Reuters monitor next to my desk to check on the European and Asian markets, and to see how the dollar had performed in Tokyo and London. I was in the investment advisory division of Morris, Brunner, rather than in the brokerage division, and my team managed about 150 large accounts, most of them for wealthy individuals. We were beginning to get more institutional business, but institutions usually wanted to see three-to-five-year performance numbers before they would select an investment advisor, so I had focused primarily on getting business from wealthy individuals, many of them foreigners who wanted to have some of their capital in the United States.

There were two other portfolio managers and two traders in my unit, together with four assistant portfolio managers. I know that they looked on me as a demanding manager, and I doubted if any of the people really liked me, but either because they respected me or were afraid of me they jumped when I asked for something. I know that I had been a lot easier to get along with back at Schleswigbank, but I knew that none of the people I worked with here in New York were as knowledgeable as I was about foreign investing, and I saw no reason to hide my feelings.

As I was considering my position here at Morris, Brunner, I was surprised to hear someone enter my office and when I looked away from the Reuters monitor I found that Sam Brunner had come in.

He made no greeting of any kind, simply starting off by saying, "I think the conference went pretty well, didn't you, Kurt?"

"It was my first one, but I thought it went well, yes. And thank you for mentioning me. I hadn't been expecting that."

"Well, Kurt, you know we're investing a lot in you and your group. As I said at the dinner last night, this international investing thing can set our company apart. Competition between advisory firms is becoming fierce, and we've got to have something unique to attract investors. And you know that it's not just having something unique, but we've got to have really good performance numbers in order to sell. That's why this European Stock Fund of yours is so important."

I could tell that he was needling me, and I answered, "I fully understand that, and I'm sure you know how hard we're trying. But the foreign markets aren't doing much right now."

"I know, but it's damned important that this Fund of yours show not just good performance numbers, but great performance during the next six months, or even a year. We can really capitalize on it to attract new business, and I don't need to tell you that it will have a big impact on your bonus if it works out. You know how Lenny can be. We're spending a lot of money on you and your staff, and he wants to start to see a return."

I tried to conceal my irritation, as I answered, "But, Sam, my group is profitable—we more than cover all our expenses."

"That's right, but we have pretty high profit margins in the rest of our business, and as of today the international group's margin is only about a third of everyone else's. If you get the performance of that Fund of yours up, I'm sure our sales staff can really push it, and bring in a tremendous amount of business."

I did not want to get into an argument with him, so I said something vague to indicate that I understood what he was saying.

After Sam left, I could only sit there with my head in my hands, feeling totally flattened by what I had just heard, and particularly by Sam's emphasis on the performance of the Fund—the Morris, Brunner European Stock Fund. I had been pushing the firm to start such a Fund for over a year ever since I started to work at the firm. It had taken several months to convince Sam both that there was a demand for such a Fund by American investors and that this would be a good time to start getting into the European stock markets. Even after Sam had been convinced, it took another four or five months to convince Leonard Morris. All the while that these delays were occurring, the European markets were going up, and in some cases quite sharply. This clearly helped my arguments for the Fund, but, when the Fund finally was introduced, it made it more difficult for me to find any stocks that still seemed to be at prices at which I wanted to buy them.

All through the period that the idea of having a European shares mutual fund was under consideration, I had been buying many of those stocks in the various individual accounts that I managed. The individual customers had made a lot of money, since the team that I had put together seemed to have a good deal of skill or luck in picking one winner after another. Right after the Fund was introduced, however, some of the foreign markets began to peak out, and finding new winners was proving to be much more difficult. And now everything was conspiring to make the performance of that fund the most important determinant of my professional future here at Morris Brunner.

I sat for a long time with my head buried in my hands, and it took me a while to realize that someone else had come into my office. I immediately heard a female voice saying, "I would have thought that you'd be celebrating this morning after the endorsement the boss gave you last night."

I looked up at Gina, my principal assistant, and had to smile. "I would have thought the same thing."

"Well, this doesn't look much like a celebration, Kurt."

"I know, but Brunner comes around this morning to tell me in a not too subtle way that I had better get the performance of the fund up, or else. Apparently old man Morris doesn't think we're making enough money, and that's because the fund's performance is lagging right now."

Gina shook her head and said, "Look, I'd forget it if I were you. That's the way they are—they like to talk tough, but everyone in this place recognizes that you're the only one with any brains around here."

She stood in front of my desk for a couple of minutes while I again bowed my head and looked down, staring at nothing. Finally she walked around and stood beside me, putting a number of papers down on my desk and indicating that they needed signing. She was a beautiful young woman, dark hair, a good figure, and great legs. As she stood next to me, I have to admit that I felt an almost irresistible urge to put my hand on her leg and up under her skirt, but I knew if she complained about any unwanted sexual approach from me, I would be out on my ear. You just couldn't have any fun in the office anymore.

Gina put a stack of orders on the desk for me to approve, and I mechanically signed each one without paying any attention to what they were. After I finished, I watched her go to the door, where she stopped and looked back at me. "Oh yes, one other thing. Remember when we bought all of those stocks about three months ago for the Galleni account—we invested about a million dollars. I found out this morning that he withdrew all the cash in his account, and all those stocks are going to be delivered tomorrow. We're going to have about a million dollar overdraft."

I was really surprised by what she had said. "They were bought three or four months ago, weren't they? Are you telling me that they're only being delivered now?"

"You know how those European markets are, particularly Spain and Italy. Deliveries can take months, if you ever get the stocks at all. We bought all those stocks through our affiliate in London, and the English back offices are more fouled up than anywhere else. They actually tried to deliver everything yesterday, but our delivery window saw that there was no cash or money market balances in the account and refused to accept the securities. But the Brits called later in the day and said they would deliver again today, so we're facing a nice million dollar overdraft."

"Christ. You know that's the one thing that bugs old man Morris. He's a nut on overdrafts. There's nothing in the account we can sell?"

"Not for cash settlement today or tomorrow. I thought you ought to know before the screaming starts."

As she walked out of his office, I was even more upset than when she had come in. That's all I need—having a one million dollar overdraft with no way to cover it for at least five business days. Leonard Morris would really be upset and, with the flap over the fund's performance, I could see the Chairman having another good excuse to criticize me. I kept thinking that I ought to have Gina bring me the Galleni account so I could decide what to sell, but I was too depressed to do even that. The phone rang several times, but I shook my head when Gina looked in to indicate that I did not want to take any calls.

A few minutes later, Gina came back to the door of my office to say that the trading desk was calling, and I would have to take that call. She connected Chuck Lindsay, the trader, who said to me, "Mr. Wenner, you've got $2 million of commercial paper that matures this morning in the European Stock Fund. You want me to roll it for another thirty days?"

I said, "Yes, go ahead for thirty days and try to get the best rate you can." I put down the phone and a second later it hit me. I immediately called the trader back and said, "Chuck, let that paper mature. I will need most of that cash today. We can roll some of it, but I probably can't tell you the exact amount until later on. OK?"

I then called Gina and told her to come into my office. "I've solved the Galleni overdraft. Put those stocks in the European Stock Fund. We have $2 million of commercial paper coming due there today, so just change the account numbers on those orders."

She did not seem to like my idea, and said, "Well that's great for the overdraft, but those stocks were bought months ago at much lower prices. I mean it's hardly fair to poor Mr. Galleni to put them in the fund now."

I had made up my mind and did not want to hear an argument from her. "It can't be helped. He took the money out, and there's no reason that Morris, Brunner should have to have a million dollar overdraft for a week or so when it wasn't our fault. Anyway, Galleni doesn't know that we bought those stocks for him. This is a discretionary account so he'll never know that we moved them to the fund. It's a perfect solution."

As Gina left the room, I smiled to myself, knowing that it was not just a solution for the overdraft problem, but would have a big effect on the performance of the fund—at least for one week. The Fund was still fairly small, and the gains on the $1 million of stocks that had been bought for Mr. Galleni's account would have an effect on the performance of the fund. It would be a fairly small effect, but getting positive results when all the markets in which the fund invested were essentially flat had to have some effect on the fund's overall performance.

Chapter XVIII

When the mutual fund performance figures were reported for the third quarter of 1975, the small Morris, Brunner European Stock Fund was among the top five performers. Most European markets had declined during the quarter, but the Morris, Brunner Fund showed a small positive result—it was just a small fraction, but positive nevertheless. A number of the financial publications commented on the Fund's surprisingly good record, and my name was mentioned in both *The Wall Street Transcript* and *Barrons* as the manager of the Fund.

Sam Brunner phoned me as soon as the reports came out to congratulate me. "That's really great, Kurt. I knew if you really put your mind to it that we'd start to see this kind of performance. Lenny's started bragging already about how smart he was to start this whole European research effort, so you'd better keep those numbers going up."

I shook my head when Sam hung up. *Don't these idiots know that you don't suddenly get good investment performance just by working hard. The markets have to be going your way, and your strategy and timing both have to be right. If anyone really studied that Fund,* I thought to myself, *they would see that it would have been impossible to get that kind of performance.* However, performance numbers were the name of the game now and no one really looked behind the numbers. We'll probably start attracting a lot of money to the Fund in the next couple of months, and getting decent performance will become all but impossible, at least until the European markets turn.

I got up from my desk and walked out of the office. As I passed Gina's desk, she said, "You sure look unhappy. I would have thought that you'd be walking on air after all the newspaper publicity."

"Well, our friend Mr. Morris is taking all the credit for that. After all, it was his idea to start our group, wasn't it?"

I stood next to Gina and as I looked down on Gina's desk I saw that she was working on the pending-trades report. The thought suddenly struck me that there were probably a good many more stocks that had been bought several months ago for individual accounts that had not yet been delivered. If it had happened in the Galleni account, it must be happening in other accounts as well.

I decided that it would be a good idea to talk with Gina outside the office, so I said, "How about dinner tonight, Gina? I really need to discuss a few things with you." Gina and I had had dinner on a number of occasions, primarily when we were working late or when there was some business problem that we needed to discuss.

She raised her eyebrows as she looked up and asked, "Any particular reason—or are you just dying for my company?"

"Well, obviously, your company, but there are some things I'd like to talk to you about."

"OK, fine, but I need to be home by about nine o'clock."

With our date settled, I turned and went back into my office and stood looking out the window. I realized that I should have remembered that pending-trades report before. I thought that I probably only needed to get through the next three months, since as we get into the last quarter of the year, the European markets would start to discount 1976 earnings. I was sure that next year was going to be a better year and those markets would start to rise. So I decided that if I could just transfer a few more profits from those individual accounts into the Fund, I should have it made. It's just like at Schleswigbank and the other Swiss banks—they allocated their gains and losses on bonds and F/X between the bank and individual accounts in whatever way it did the bank the most good. What I used to do at Schleswigbank might have been a little shady, but moving profits from the individual accounts to the Fund doesn't bring any profits to the company directly, as was the case in Switzerland— there's only an indirect benefit here since Morris, Brunner would benefit indirectly from having a fund with excellent performance.

This whole prospect of improving the fund's performance really excited me. I decided that I wanted to see the pending trades report myself, but I did not want to ask Gina for it. Instead, I called Susan Maleska, who was one of my assistant portfolio managers. She was an attractive young woman, about twenty-five, who had graduated from Columbia University with honors. I always suspected that she had a slight crush on me—and maybe it wasn't even all that slight—and I decided to phone her now and ask her for the report.

"Susan, could you bring me an updated pending-trades report. I'm checking on something, and I need to look at one of those reports. And Susan, don't mention to anyone that I wanted this report. This is an audit procedure that needs to be done quietly."

Susan indicated that she was only too happy to be doing something for Mr. Wenner, and she quickly got the computer printout of the report and brought it to me. I thanked her for it and as soon as she left, I started to total all the purchases for the individual accounts that had not yet settled. I went through the list and picked out those transactions where there were significant gains since the purchase date, and then added them up. There were about $9.5

million of unsettled purchases, with gains of close to $900,000, or just under 10 percent since the dates of purchase. Transferring those transactions into the Fund would help, but $900,000 was still a very small amount relative to the size of the Fund.

I made a list of the transactions that I wanted to divert to the Fund, and decided I would talk with Gina about them at dinner that night. When 6:00 p.m. finally rolled around, Gina and I walked over to Delmonico's, which was just a block away, and we got a table in the back, as far away as possible from the crowd and the noise at the bar. We had a drink and I would have preferred to wait before ordering, and probably have a second drink, but Gina wanted to order immediately, and rather than argue with her, I agreed. We made small talk all through dinner, mainly about the office, until finally over coffee I brought up the subject I really wanted to talk about.

"I guess we both know that transferring those trades from the Galleni account to the Fund really helped the performance of the Fund."

Gina nodded and said, "Well, there was quite a gain on those shares—I think it was over $250,000—maybe up to half a million."

"I know you thought it was unfair to poor Mr. Galleni, but that transfer helped the shareholders of the Fund do pretty well. It's not as if we stole the money ourselves."

"No, but I thought it was immoral, if not illegal, to allocate trades like that, particularly months after the transaction."

"But Gina, he didn't have any money to pay for them at the time the shares were delivered. What else could we do? There would have been hell to pay if we had carried that big an overdraft until we could sell something else."

"I know, but I still felt sorry for him."

I tried not to look impatient with her, and replied, "You know doing something like that is really almost standard operating procedure where I come from. Swiss banks routinely underwrite corporate bond issues and then turn around and stuff the bonds into accounts that they manage, particularly if it's not a very successful underwriting. And I really think practices like that are a lot more common here in New York than maybe you realize yourself."

She looked directly at me as she said, "What are you trying to tell me?"

"I just don't think that you should make a big deal out of something like this. It happens more than you think. You know that the Fund is of extreme importance to Morris, Brunner right now, and I think that we maybe have to stretch a point here and there to insure that its good performance continues. By the fall I would expect that the European markets will be picking up, but in the meantime we may have to, let's say, subsidize the Fund a little bit."

"Are you telling me that you're planning to do more of what you did with the Galleni account?"

I'm sure that I made my intention perfectly clear as I said to her, "Yes, I think so."

"Well, it just doesn't sound ethical to me."

"Gina, don't go getting all moralistic. We all have to do things in our jobs from time to time that we may not like or we may find disagreeable. But we have to do them if we want to keep our job, and I can assure you that if you work with me on this—and keep it quiet—you'll have a better bonus than you ever dreamed of at year-end."

"Look, Kurt, my parents came here from Mexico eight years ago, and I really am afraid of doing anything that would get me or them into trouble. This whole thing sounds wrong to me, and I don't think I want to be involved in it. OK?"

I did not want to show my irritation with her at this answer, so I merely replied "That's OK by me. You've got to do what you think is right."

"The more I think of it, why don't you ask Susan to handle whatever transfers you need to make? You know she would do just about anything you asked."

I laughed and said, "That sounds like a catty remark, Gina. But if you don't want to be involved in this, there's no reason you have to know anything about it. And you're right—Susan probably will do just about anything I want."

CHAPTER XIX

Over the next few days a typical August heat wave enveloped New York City. Temperatures each day were in the nineties, but what made it particularly unbearable was the humidity that also reached extraordinarily high levels. I had to walk every morning over to Lexington Avenue subway station at 86th Street, and then descend into the subway, which was like a steam bath. When the graffiti-covered trains arrived, I had to push my way into a hot, crowded car and had to endure the heat and the odors all the way downtown. By the time I arrived at work, I really needed another shower and a change of clothes, and I was usually in a foul mood. Even though I had been making this commute for years, as all of the different firms that I had worked for since I arrived in the States were all in downtown Manhattan, I despised every day that I had to do it, and I constantly compared it to Switzerland and to Zürich. How could the United States consider itself a great country when it had a horrible subway system like this one, jammed with dreadful, dirty, smelly people? I knew that it would be beyond the comprehension of anyone in Switzerland to imagine anything like the Lexington Avenue subway in 1975.

Following my conversation with Gina, I knew that I could not count on her to help me transfer any more unsettled trades into the European Shares Fund. My first inclination was to ask Susan to make the transfers, but I decided that I had better prepare the ground before doing so. Therefore, I decided to write out the revised purchase orders myself, and to ask Susan only to co-sign them. All purchase and sale orders had to have two signatures, and I frequently had to initial the orders that were prepared by one of the portfolio managers or one of the assistants. What I finally decided to do was to type up the orders and to have Susan sign them as the portfolio manager who had initiated the orders, and I would merely initial them as the approving officer. This was the normal procedure that was followed all the time in my division.

That night I stayed late at the office waiting for everyone to leave, and while I waited I selected those trades from the unsettled pending trades report that would help the Fund the most. Since there was not $9 1/2 million cash in the Fund, I could only use about one-half of the trades right away, and I made up new order forms covering those. My typing was not very good, and it took me several hours to get the new forms filled out. I had all the details of the trades, and I went to the files to get copies of the broker confirmations, which I attached to the new purchase orders for the Fund. I also made up the necessary forms to cancel the old orders for the individual accounts, and in the morning I planned to have Susan sign all of them and have them put through into the computer.

Reports on the individual accounts that were sent to the clients were prepared on a cash basis so that transactions were only reported on the customer's statements after the settlement of a transaction—after cash had been received on a sale or paid out on a purchase. In the Fund, however, it was necessary that all transactions be reported on an accrual basis, so that once a purchase was made, whether that purchase had actually settled or not, the security was treated as being owned by the Fund, and the value of the Fund was adjusted up or down depending upon the market price of the security. Therefore, as soon as I had the new transactions put into the computer, the accountants for the Fund would recognize the gains involved, and this would cause the unit value of the Fund to rise. As I finished up everything at the office, I was really pleased with myself both for the thinking up this way of subsidizing the Fund's performance and for executing it myself.

The next morning I asked Susan to come to my office. "Susan, I've been wanting to have a talk with you for some time now. You've been working as an assistant portfolio manager for about two years now, isn't that right?"

Susan merely nodded, and I went on, "Well, I was wondering how you liked your job."

"I really like it very much. I studied investments, you know, at Columbia, and so I really enjoy working on the portfolios."

"I assume that you would like to manage your own accounts one of these days."

"Well, what I really want to do is to run an international stock fund, like you do."

"You mean be a fund manager?"

"Yes, exactly. But I think this kind of fund ought to be run from overseas— probably from London or Zürich. And I would love to live in either place."

I laughed as I realized that getting Susan's cooperation was going to be fairly easy. "I agree with you one hundred percent. And I too would love to live in Switzerland again, but you have to admit that New York is still the major money center in the world."

"I know, but don't you find it hard getting the information you need on European stocks when you're here in New York?"

"I'm sure I couldn't do it if it weren't for the connections I developed when I was working in Switzerland."

"Well, you're an exception, Mr. Wenner. You've had all that training in Switzerland so you've been able to get really great performance in your accounts.

I just feel for myself that I would have to live over there to try to understand those markets if I were to be at all successful in managing European equities."

"What I've been thinking, Susan, is that maybe we should give you a new challenge. You've had your present job since before I got here, and I would like to give you a chance to take on some additional responsibility. If you are planning to manage an international fund someday, I would like to transfer you to be my assistant for the next year or so. We could give the job a title of something like 'assistant fund manager.' What would you think of that?"

Susan was clearly surprised and turned beet red at the suggestion. After a minute, however, she recovered and said, "I'd really love that. It's exactly what I hoped I could do, and why I came to work here."

"Great. Let's consider it settled. Don't say anything to Gina or anyone else for a day or two—I haven't talked to her yet, but as soon as I do, I'll put out an announcement."

Susan stood up and said, "And thanks again, Mr. Wenner, I really appreciate it."

"Oh, and Susan, while you're here, would you initial these orders for the Fund and have them entered. I've already signed them. We bought a lot of these stocks using the numbers of the individual accounts some time ago, but we had to do that because we didn't have enough cash in the Fund. I knew these stocks wouldn't be delivered for months. Now that we've got cash in the Fund, I'm switching them over so they'll be paid for out of the Fund."

"That was a great idea, Mr. Wenner—planning ahead like that."

I couldn't decide if she was naïve or gullible, but I winked at her, and said, "You've got to do things like that every once in a while if you're going to have a successful fund, but some people around here feel that we're breaking some rule or other. So I wouldn't mention it to too many people if I were you."

She assured me that I could count on her, and she left my office almost walking on air.

The next day I called Gina into my office and told her that I wanted Gina to take a new job as a portfolio manager. She would be given accounts that did not require much investment expertise, since the accounts were primarily invested in short-term securities. "You've wanted to become a portfolio manager, Gina, and this is a step in that direction. You'll be dealing with customers directly, and I'll gradually try to give you a number of, what I'd guess you'd call, more demanding accounts."

Gina was actually pleased at the change, but she could not resist saying, "And I suppose that Susan will take my place."

"Yes. Does that bother you?"

"No. After our discussion the other night, I thought you would probably make some kind of change."

"And you're not happy with the new job?"

"As a matter of fact, I really like the idea, and I guess I should say thank you."

I was relieved when Gina left my office. I was never comfortable with her since there was an aloofness about her, an almost condescending attitude that irritated me. Most of the other employees, and Susan most of all, showed some kind of respect for me or at least for my position, but Gina always seemed to want to show that she was not in awe of me, that she was not taken in. I was convinced that this was probably the attitude she showed to everyone—the tough, smart, cynical woman who could see through all the phoniness around her. Going from that attitude to Susan's wide-eyed naïveté would be quite a change for me, and I looked forward to working with Susan from now on, rather than crossing swords with Gina every day.

Chapter XX

For the next couple of weeks, things were fairly quiet. The European stock markets had been declining, thereby wiping out most of the gains that had existed on the stocks I had been planning to transfer into the Fund. Cash kept pouring in, but I kept it in short-term commercial paper rather than put it into any of the markets. Doing nothing proved to be the right thing, and the Morris, Brunner European Stock Fund continued to show relatively good performance. Its unit value declined as the markets went down, but the large cash component kept the decline fairly small, and all of the transfers from the individual accounts helped to some extent.

I was quite satisfied with the way things were going as the third quarter of 1975 came to a close. I knew that the Fund would show up well when the performance numbers came out three or four weeks later, in mid-October. Therefore, when Naomi, Sam Brunner's secretary called, I expected that Sam was calling to congratulate me on what was shaping up as another good quarter. Without any preamble, Naomi said, "Kurt, Sam would like to see you. Would you come down to his office."

"Yes, of course. Does he want to see me right now?"

"Yes, he said right now."

"OK. I'll be there in a minute."

Morris, Brunner had two floors at 17 Broad Street, the fifth and sixth, with Sam Brunner's and Leonard Morris's offices being on the fifth floor. When I walked into his office, Sam said rather abruptly, "Close the door, Kurt." I could immediately sense that something was wrong, but before I had a chance to think about it, Sam almost shouted at me, "What the fuck you been doing in that Fund of yours?"

I was so surprised by the attack, that the only thing I could say was, "What do you mean?"

"You know goddamn well what I mean. This whole thing's been a phony. All that great performance crap—it was all phony. You got it by screwing our other accounts. Isn't that right?"

I thought to myself, *Shit, how did he ever find that out?* But after hesitating a minute, I merely said, "You're talking about those pending trades?"

Continuing on the attack, Sam said, "You're fucking right I'm talking about those pending trades—those trades that you stole from other accounts and put into that damn Fund of yours. I can't believe it—I can't believe what you've done."

"Sam, let's talk about it."

"Talk? What the hell do you think you can say? Do you realize what you've done? You've put the very existence of this company into jeopardy, that's what you've done. And just to make yourself some kind of hero. If the SEC or the NASD gets hold of this, our reputation won't be worth shit—that's what you've done."

I wanted to reason with him, and said, "Sam, look no one got hurt."

"No one got hurt? You don't see what you've done? You literally stole those profits out of the individual accounts and put them into your fuckin' Fund just to make yourself look better. We could be faced with all kinds of penalties, and maybe even banned from the securities industry."

I was having trouble keeping my emotions under control and replied, "Well, if worse comes to worse, maybe I could be banned, but the firm wouldn't be."

Still almost shouting at me, he went on, "Don't give me that shit. When something like this goes on, everyone takes a hit. And how many millions it's going to cost, I can't even guess."

"Sam, listen, there were about $10 million of those trades that I transferred—I admit that—and if you had to make it good to everyone, it would cost you about a million bucks, more or less."

He was clearly vindictive as he said, "And every penny of that is coming out of your hide, Kurt baby."

"But why do you have to do anything about it? Who knows that they got hurt? The investors in the Fund are all happy, and the individual investors don't have a clue that we ever bought those stocks for them. So who's ever going to complain?"

Sam seemed to calm down a little as he said, "Jeez, Kurt, you gotta realize that we can't run a business where we're screwing our customers every day and expect to stay in business very long. Maybe that's the way you did things in Switzerland—screw the customers all the time—but even if we wanted to do that here, there are too many of those damn accountants and auditors and government regulators so that we'd never get away with it."

I think that I stayed pretty calm as I answered, "I happen to think that the Swiss banks do a great job—they're probably the only ones in the world who know how to manage tremendous amounts of money—but that's neither here nor there. I just wish you'd let me convince you that the problem is not as great as you think it is. In fact, I don't see it as a problem at all."

I had been shocked when Sam had launched into his attack, but I felt that I had recovered pretty well and had made a couple of good points. I almost smiled as I thought back to the scene in Dr. Hofbeck's office ten years previously when Elsa Wilhelm had accused me of the theft of her father's money, and I remembered very clearly how I had risen to that occasion. This conversation with Sam was different, since I was not trying to deny what I had done—I was only trying to convince Sam that it was the best thing that I could have done for Morris, Brunner & Company.

Sam's fury seemed to have abated somewhat, and in the brief silence that followed our exchange, I began to wonder how Sam had found out. Could Gina have been the one to tell me? So I said, "Can I ask how you found out about this?"

He rather scornfully replied, "Don't you know anything about the way this place works? All those transfers you put through on the pending trades had to go through the Operations Department. And one of the guys in the department, Joe Keckisen, began to wonder about all those corrected orders, so he started to look at them. Joe's no dummy. He caught on pretty quick that all those transactions had big profits on them, and they were all being put into your goddamn Fund to make your Fund look good. I bet the whole Operations Department knows about it now."

There was another long silence, and Sam finally said, "Well, I sure as hell am not going to cover up for you." With that he buzzed on the intercom, and said, "Naomi, ask Lenny if we can come in to see him. Tell him it's a real emergency." Sam flipped off the intercom switch and sat staring ahead, without saying anything. In a minute she rang back, "Mr. Morris said he'll see you in about ten minutes."

The two of us sat silently for a few minutes. Sam Brunner used both hands to rub his face, and then the top of his balding head, before leaning back and locking his hands behind his neck, looking up at the ceiling. I knew that Sam was fifty-five now, and I realized that Sam must have been a good-looking man when he was younger. Sam's dark hair was now thinning and beginning to turn gray; he was starting to get a double chin, and lines were starting to show in his face. But I knew that Sam played tennis or handball regularly at a midtown club since he frequently asked me to play with him, and Sam had kept himself in pretty good shape. Sam frequently talked with me about his boyhood in Brooklyn, where his father had been a tailor in a heavily Jewish neighborhood. Living in Bernardsville, New Jersey, now with a wife and three children seemed light years away from his Brooklyn upbringing, but Sam had always impressed me with the fact that he had not forgotten his parents or his background. I had been glad to report to Sam at Morris, Brunner since I felt that Sam was an honest, practical guy.

I sat looking around Sam's office. I was never comfortable in this office because of the incredible clutter. My office was half the size of Sam's, but I was almost obsessive about keeping everything in its place. I shook my head as I looked at a coffee table piled with back issues of the *Institutional Investor, Barrons, The Wall Street Transcript* and other investment-oriented publications. There was a foot-high pile of old *Wall Street Journals* in one corner and a big box in another corner that was open with packing material sticking out of the top.

The credenza behind Sam's desk had several pictures of his wife and children, but they were practically hidden by all kinds of sports trophies, coffee mugs, and just plain junk.

Finally Sam broke the silence by asking, "Why did you do it, Kurt? Were you that desperate to show performance? Did you think for one minute that we wouldn't find out? Jesus Christ, I still can't believe that you did this."

I replied in as firm a voice as I could muster, "I was doing it for the firm. You and Len wanted good performance, and the markets weren't moving. So here was a way to get that performance, and no one would be hurt."

"And you don't see that the individual accounts were hurt?"

"Yes, but they don't know it. None of those customers were told that we had bought those stocks for their accounts, so how are they going to complain?"

Sam irritated me as he said, "Maybe they don't have the same words in Switzerland where you come from, but around here we have something we call 'fiduciary responsibility.' I know it sounds corny, but when we're managing an account for someone, we have to act in their best interests, and screwing them out of stocks that we bought for them because the stocks went up and we want to put those profits someplace else, is a complete violation of that fiduciary responsibility."

"Sam, aren't we supposed to do well for the company too? I took a little something away from the customers to make the flagship Fund of the company look a little better. I don't see that that's a crime."

"Yeah, well at your trial you can tell that to the judge. He'll read you the law."

I was relieved when Naomi buzzed on the intercom and told Sam that Mr. Morris would see us now.

I felt remarkably calm as Sam and I walked the few steps to Leonard Morris's corner office. I just could not take Sam's threats seriously. I knew all along that what I was doing in the Fund violated a number of rules, but I had looked upon those as technicalities and not as things that would get me into real trouble.

The Chairman was on the phone when Sam and I reached his office, but he waved us in and pointed to the two chairs in front of his desk. As often as I had been in Sam's office, being in Leonard Morris's office was something of a rarity for me. The office itself was in striking contrast to Sam Brunner's. The Chairman's wife was interested in modern art, and she had seen to it that her husband's office had a number of abstract paintings on the walls. She had also decorated it with very modern furniture, everything being glass, chrome, or black lacquer. Morris was as fastidious as I was in keeping the office in perfect condition, so that it really seemed to be a model of what a very prosperous chief executive's office should look like. The only discordant note was a half-smoked cigar smoldering in an ashtray, filling the office with the rather unpleasant smell of a stale cigar.

Morris soon finished his phone conversation, and said to Sam, "OK, what's all this about an emergency?"

"Lenny, we're in real trouble. This asshole here has been screwing around with that Fund of his, and trying to get performance by actually stealing from the individual accounts."

Morris leaned forward, "Come again."

"You heard me. That performance of his was totally phony; the only way he got it was by transferring trades from the individual accounts."

"I still don't understand what you're talking about."

Sam then explained in detail what I had been doing and how the individual accounts had been hurt.

"OK, I see what's been done. Now where does this leave us?"

"It leaves us up the creek. If the SEC, the NASD, the SIA—if any of these people or the state or federal governments find out about this, we're sunk. We're going to have to come clean right away."

Morris looked at me, and said, "What a goddamn stupid schlemiel! How could you do something like this?"

I said, "Could I say something? I know Sam is really upset about this, but let's try to put things in perspective. The Fund is supposed to represent the investment performance of Morris, Brunner & Company. Well, that's all I was trying to do. I was trying to put the stocks in there that we had been buying earlier in the year, when we'd had great success and big gains. We didn't have the Fund early in the year, but we had bought those stocks in our other accounts. If you want to show the world how well we're doing, you've got to put those stocks in the Fund, and you've got to put them in at the prices we paid for them earlier in the year. Now I know that it breaks some rules or regulations to take the profits away from the other accounts, but I still don't think that we're in any kind of danger."

"We're not in any danger? Why not?"

"Who's going to complain? No one. No one can feel that they were screwed or that they had some profits taken from them because none of the accounts that had the trades taken away knows anything about it. We had complete discretion in those accounts and only reported to those people at the end of the quarter. It may be unethical as Sam says it is, and I guess someone might think that it's illegal, but I don't think I've put the firm in any danger."

Lenny Morris thought about it for a minute, and then said, "OK, let's look at our options. If we say that what hotshot here did was wrong and we go to correct it—and that's what you want to do, isn't it Sam?" Sam nodded. "Then what happens?"

"We'll have to go to our lawyers and have them notify whatever agencies need to be involved."

"So we have to go public, right? And take some bad publicity."

Sam said, "Yeah, there will probably be some. And we'll have to fire our Swiss friend here and probably get him banned from the investment business for life."

Morris asked, "Will there be any penalties on us?"

"I don't think so, not as long as we reported it and turned him in."

"They won't try to claim that we were negligent in supervising him?"

"Oh, some government agency or other might make that claim, but we can show that our own Operations Department discovered the scheme, and we reported it immediately."

Morris persisted, "And what other costs will there be?"

"Well, we can't take those stocks away from the fund—it's too late to do that—so we'll have to reimburse the individual accounts that were screwed, and Kurt here says that that will amount to about $1 million, which is the amount of profits he skimmed into his fund."

"And what happens to the fund?"

Sam sounded almost pleased as he said, "I think it's dead. The record will be shown to be phony, the manager will have been fired, and we'll have no credibility at all in trying to sell any kind of international investment product for years to come. The only thing I can see is to sell everything that's in the Fund now and give the money back to the investors."

Morris thought for a while, and reached over for his dead cigar, spending several minutes trying to light it. "And what happens if we don't do anything now?"

"You're not serious. You're not going to let this jerk get away with this whole scam, are you?"

"I want to know what our alternatives are, Sam."

"I don't know what happens. I don't know how we can keep a lid on the whole thing."

I then felt that I had to interject myself, and said, "You may not want my opinion, but as far as I can see, if you don't do anything, then nothing happens. There's no million dollar payment, there's no problem with the government, there's no scandal, we keep selling the fund, and we don't lose our individual accounts."

Looking directly at me, Morris said, "But Sam thinks that we won't be able to keep a lid on the whole affair."

I replied, "Well, that's a danger, but there are probably only a handful of people in operations who know about this, and you could certainly give them a big song and dance about putting new procedures in place to keep this from ever happening again, and all that kind of stuff. They may realize that the old transactions were not reversed, but if you make a big enough commotion about seeing to it that this never happens again, the old transactions will be forgotten. And then give Joe Keckisen a big bonus for bringing it to Sam's attention. No one will think you're sweeping it under the rug. And if you want a scapegoat, you could always fire Gina. She was my assistant who entered the orders when this whole thing started."

The Chairman sat for several minutes, chewing on his cigar, and finally turned to me and said, "OK, you get out of here and I'll let you know what I decide. But in the meantime, don't you enter one fuckin' order or do anything else—nothing at all. Got it? Just sit in your office and try to look intelligent." As I got up to leave, he added, "Sam, you stay here."

I left Morris's office and returned to my own. It was three o'clock in the afternoon, and I was hoping that the chairman would get back to me before the end of the day. I thought back about the discussion we had had and felt that I had done a good job of defending myself. I grimaced a little as I thought of my own suggestion that we blame Gina and fire her. I realized that it was pretty obvious that I was trying to use Gina as a scapegoat, and I was surprised that Sam Brunner had not jumped all over me for suggesting it.

Time passed incredibly slowly, and nothing of importance happened, although occasionally one of the members of my staff would come in to ask me about a particular account or about one of the stocks the group had been buying. The phone rang several times and I jumped to answer it every time, but none of the calls were from Sam or Morris. I had not been particularly upset when I was at the meetings being accused of all the illegal trading, but as the time dragged on, the uncertainty began to get to me.

John Grey, one of the portfolio managers who worked for me, came in to my office and said he had some questions about an account. Grey was one of the people on my staff who always irritated me, and I could tell that he did not care very much for me either. This time he had a question about an account: "Kurt, could you look at this account for me. It's a new account that just came in—$5 million, all cash, and it's supposed to be a growth account. I was wondering whether I should buy any stocks now or if I should wait. What do you think?"

I did not look at the papers that John held; I merely stared at John for a minute, and then said, "Do you want me to do your job for you? You're getting paid—probably too much—but you're getting paid. Why do you come to me with questions like that?"

John was clearly stunned and finally stammered, "Well, you're the boss. I mean this is a policy matter and you set the policy."

"OK, well then read the policy that I set."

John glowered at me for a minute, and then shook his head, saying, "As far as I know, you've never put out a policy on new accounts, so I guess I'm free to do whatever I want in this account." He got up and walked to the door, saying over his shoulder, "Thanks a lot."

As John left, I regretted having treated him that way, but this young guy, who had a master's degrees in business administration and economics, always gave the impression that he knew at least as much as I did, if not more. In fact, this was a rather rare occasion for John to come in and ask me for advice. He usually went his own way in the accounts he managed, and then argued with me that there were good reasons for doing what he had done.

At about 5:30 p.m., Susan came into my office and said, "What's wrong?"

"Is it so obvious that something is wrong?"

"John has warned everyone to stay away from your office, unless they want to have their heads handed to them on a platter."

Welcoming the chance to talk about the confrontation with Sam, I said, "All right, sit down—but close the door first. It seems that management is not at all happy about the orders that we transferred into the Fund. They think that we broke a number of laws."

"You mean they didn't know about it?"

"I don't know. At any rate, Sam is in an uproar and is threatening all kinds of things—like firing me and calling in the SEC."

"Kurt, he's not. You must be kidding. What does Mr. Morris say?"

"He's thinking about it. Look Susan, how about having dinner with me tonight. I think I'd feel better with someone to talk to."

Susan readily agreed and we decided to meet about an hour later. I suggested that we go to Firenze, a small Italian restaurant on the Upper East Side, not far from my apartment. Rather than take the subway, we got a taxi for the long trip from downtown Manhattan to the Upper East Side. We sat in a booth toward the back of the dimly lit restaurant, and I immediately ordered a bottle of wine. "Let's not talk about the office tonight, Susan, I'd rather try to forget it." After we decided on our orders, there were long silences, and I soon put my hand over Susan's. She did not move away, and we remained that way until dinner was served. Neither of us seemed very interested in our food, however, and as we sat together over coffee, I moved my chair closer to hers so that I could put my arm around her. Judging that the moment was right, I asked her if she would come back to my apartment with me, and Susan, trying to contain her emotions, could only nod in agreement.

As we lay together in bed the next morning, I felt a surprising sense of well-being. I knew I should be concerned about what might happen at the office, but having Susan's young body pressed close to my own seemed quite wonderful. I used to love to lay this way in the morning after a night of lovemaking with Ingrid, and while this morning reminded me of that time back in Zürich, I really felt that in some ways Susan was a better sex partner than Ingrid. Considering that this was the first time that Susan and I had been together, I thought that things had gone remarkably well, and the affair had been a tremendous release for me.

After a while, Susan awoke and lay rubbing her hand over my chest. Nothing was said until I finally asked her, "How are you doing this morning? Are you OK?"

She smiled and said, "I'm still trying to believe that this happened. I used to fantasize about how I might get you into bed."

"Well, you better watch it, because if you keep rubbing on me like that, we'll never get to work today."

"But you have such a nice body, Kurt. Your stomach, your chest, everything is in such great shape. You must exercise a lot to keep everything so firm. It's hard for me to keep my hands off you."

I tried to think of a similar compliment for her, but was afraid that anything I might say would sound phony. Susan did have a good body—she was just a little heavy. The word that came to my mind was "voluptuous" but I decided I had better not use that one. After lying together for several more minutes, I realized that we would have to start getting ready for work.

I finally said, "You've got a beautiful figure, Susan, but you should wear clothes that show it off more. Those business suits you wear all the time hide everything. Why don't you come into the office today wearing something really daring—low cut and very tight—show them everything."

"That'll be the day. But I do have to figure out what I am going to wear today, and I have to get home to change. It wouldn't do for me to come into the office wearing the same thing two days in a row. The other girls would know immediately what had happened."

I said to her, "I never even asked you where you lived."

"Down on 10th Street, near Washington Square."

"We could take the Lexington subway down—I take it to work anyway, and you could get off at Astor Street—but with our luck, someone would probably see us. I think you'd better take a taxi, unless you'd rather not come into the office at all today."

"Absolutely not. I have to be there to see how this whole thing comes out. If you're out of a job, I'm probably fired too."

Susan dressed quickly and headed for the door. I did not dress in order to avoid having to go down to the street with her, and I kissed her quickly at the door as she went out to get the elevator down to the lobby. When the door closed, I felt relieved that she was gone. The night had been what I needed. But as I stood with a bath towel around my waist looking down on to 82nd Street, I wondered where things went from here. Is it smart for me to get involved with a woman at work, and one who is almost twenty years younger than me? All of the arguments about having an affair with Susan went through my mind: she had certainly been useful in handling the trades that Gina had refused to put through, and she would probably be useful in the future. And as long as I'm taking her to bed, I probably ensure that cooperation, although there is always a chance that she could become a problem if I don't keep her in line. But what the hell, the sex was great, and I know I'll have to see her again.

CHAPTER XXI

There was nothing to do at work the next day but to sit and wait for the call from Leonard Morris. Time passed excruciatingly slowly as it had the previous afternoon, and I tried to go through the motions of at least looking as if I were busy. I tried to read the *Wall Street Journal*, I checked with the trading desk to find out what the foreign exchange markets were doing, I sorted through all the papers on my desk, but nothing worked. Time seemed to drag by, and I sat for minutes on end looking at the second hand on my Movado watch as it made the complete circuit around the dial. The Swiss watch reminded me of Zürich and what had happened there, and I almost wished for something as conclusive as the events ten years previously back at Schleswigbank. That had been a black and white situation, and I had known that once management found out what had happened, I would have been arrested and ended up in jail, and therefore I had had no choice but to flee.

Here at Morris, Brunner the situation was less clear, at least in my mind. The transfers may have been illegal and were certainly unethical, but I had not profited from them myself. I felt that what I had done was very similar to what Swiss banks did every day in allocating bonds between the bank's own account and customer's accounts, depending upon how the bank would benefit the most. I wondered how Dr. Hofbeck would have responded to this situation, and I felt sure that there would have been none of the moral posturing that I had been forced to endure from Sam Brunner.

Finally, at about 4:00 p.m., I got a call from Naomi, telling me to come down to Leonard Morris's office. I put on my suit coat and, looking at my reflection in the glass of one of the pictures on the wall, I straightened my tie and quickly combed my hair. I winked at Susan as I went past her desk, and she held up her crossed fingers in response. Her hand shook, whether voluntarily or not I couldn't tell, but I knew that she was praying for me.

When I walked into the Morris's office, Sam Brunner was slouched down on the modern sofa against the wall to the left of Leonard Morris's desk. Both men were in shirtsleeves, but Morris still looked fairly sharp, while Brunner, with tie askew, looked exhausted.

Morris motioned to one of the chairs in front of his desk and said, "Sit down. As you can imagine, I've spent the last twenty-four hours thinking about the problem that you created for us. I've not only been thinking about it, but I have also talked with a number of people—I just discussed this kind of a problem hypothetically. You get different advice from everyone. Even my lawyer tells me what I should do legally, but then tries to give me some BS about how we're friends, so he'll give me some advice as a friend, and not as a lawyer.

"Sam, here, is 100 percent straightforward. He wants to fire you and to report the whole thing to the SEC—come clean 100 percent. But I've finally decided that we're not going to do that. The penalty for all of us—for Sam, for me, for the company—would be just too great. We're going to put procedures in place to see to it that something like this can never happen again, and we're going to give Joe what's-his-name, back in operations a fat bonus for bringing this whole scam to our attention. That's the easy part.

"The hard part is what to do with you. We could fire you. You couldn't go running off and tell anyone about what happened here or why you were fired— you'd be in deep shit if you did anything as stupid as that. And let me be 100 percent honest, about three or four times today Sam and I had agreed to do just that—fire you. But it's in our interest to keep you here. We've just started to push this whole international thing, and you were the point man of that whole operation, so it would look bad for us if you were to leave right now. So you luck out, and get to keep you job.

"Now from your point of view, I'm sure you can see that this is the best possible outcome. You're still the manager of the goddamn Fund, and the record of the Fund has been good. So you get the credit for managing a successful Fund—even though you and I both know that the record was phonier than hell. Obviously, there won't be any bonus for you this year, and obviously there won't be any raise for you at the end of the year. But you get to keep your job at least for a year. So what we want from you, buddy boy, is an agreement that you will stay here working on that Fund of yours for the next twelve months at least, and an absolute promise that there'll be no more of those shenanigans in trying to phony up the performance. Also, I think it's pretty obvious that not a word of what's been said here in this office today gets repeated to anyone."

I could not keep from being a little sarcastic when I had a chance to answer Lenny Morris. "Obviously" and I stressed that word. "I have mixed feelings about your decision. I'm glad that you've decided to keep from blowing this into an unnecessary crisis. And I think your way of handling it will keep it from going any further than this room, as I suggested the other day. And while I'm not happy that you feel that I have to be punished for what happened, I have to accept your decision and I will agree to the conditions you have laid out."

I knew that my response had sounded stilted and maybe somewhat phony, but there was no possibility that I was going to show enthusiasm for what Lenny Morris had just said. There was a silence and a very icy atmosphere in the room when I finished. It seemed clear to me that there was nothing further to be said, so I said to Morris, "Is that it?" and when he nodded, I quickly got up and left his office.

Back in my own office, I felt more depressed than anything else. This was the second time in my life that I had had to face a situation in which I was being accused of doing something illegal. I knew that in both cases I had done something that would benefit myself—taking money at Schleswigbank and juggling the books at Morris, Brunner to enhance my professional reputation and ultimately my salary—but I refused to accept the fact that I had been wrong in either case. I remembered that terrible night in Paris after I had fled Switzerland, and thinking at the time, "I never wanted to be a criminal. I never set out deliberately to steal anything. That money just seemed to fall from the sky in front of us, and all we did was pick it up." Now, ten years later, I was more convinced than ever that I was not to blame for what had happened back in Zürich. Maybe Ingrid was to blame, maybe no one was, but more than anything else, I had come to the conclusion that what had happened then was simply not a crime. I had merely done what anyone would have done to take advantage of the circumstances—it seemed to me it was like picking up a roll of bills that someone had dropped on the street. The punishment, and that ludicrous six-year prison sentence, seemed totally unjust.

And now, not only was I not going to be rewarded for having good performance in my Fund, I was actually going to be punished for it. I knew that I had cut a few corners to get that performance, but Morris, Brunner should be happy about what I had achieved. They would benefit; they would continue to get new business and their profits would grow. I, however, was going to suffer another punishment—another unjust punishment. If they had done what I wanted, when I wanted, it wouldn't have been necessary to move those trades around. They stalled for almost a year and the markets finally turned against me, so I had to be a little creative to show everyone just how good our performance had been. And I end up being punished. Well, I still have this job, and I hope they don't think that I'm just going to roll over like a trained poodle and not try to get even with them for this.

Susan came into his office as these thoughts went through my head, and I really wished that she would just go away. The only thing I wanted at that point was to put my head down and cry—cry for the bad luck that kept dogging me; cry for the success that kept eluding me; cry for what might have been. But, taking a deep breath, I looked up at her and tried to smile, saying, "I think I won."

She sounded hopeful as she said, "What do you mean, you won?"

"They are going to do exactly what I told them to do. They're going to let all the trades stay in the Fund, and they'll try to square everything with the Operations Department. And, oh yes, they will let me keep my job."

"Kurt, that's great. Then they're not blaming you at all."

"Well, not exactly. There's no raise, no bonus, and I maybe get to keep the job for only a year. As soon as they can get rid of me without any commotion, they'll do it."

"They didn't say that, did they?"

"Well, not directly, but that's what they meant. They certainly said the no-raise, no-bonus bit, and they added that they wanted me to stay for a year, but there are no promises after that. So it doesn't take much imagination to figure out what will happen then."

Susan walked around the desk and put her hand on my shoulder. "They need you, Kurt. Don't ever forget that—they need you. If they wouldn't fire you today and they're going to try to cover the whole thing up, why then you've won. You've got to know that you've won. They won't admit it and they may try to make it difficult for you, but I don't think that they can touch you."

I looked up, surprised by what Susan had just said. "Maybe you're right. I'm starting to feel better already, and I will really feel better when we get out of here. Have dinner with me again, OK?" When Susan nodded, I said, "Only this time, let's just order in at my place."

Lying together in bed the next morning, I said, "I can't thank you enough for being with me last night, and being tough about those idiots at the office. I was feeling sorry for myself when you came in yesterday afternoon, but you really helped me put this whole thing in perspective." I reached over to kiss her, and went on, "Let's go away together, Susan. You must have some vacation coming, and it would be tremendous just to get away from New York and Morris, Brunner & Company for a few weeks. And being with you would make it perfect."

Susan turned on her side, saying, "Kurt, are you serious?"

"Of course. We could go to Italy. It's my favorite country; it has everything—art, history, charming little towns, great food, wonderful wine, and the people are the nicest people you can find anywhere. We could rent a car in Rome, and just drive up through Orvieto and Assissi and Sienna until we get to Florence. And then we could go to Venice or even, come to think of it, we could drive up to Lugano in Switzerland."

"It sounds wonderful, but it would take so much planning, we couldn't possibly do it until next year."

"No. No, not at all. It's already October, and it would be perfect to go the last two weeks of this month. Yes, and going up into Switzerland as well, I'm sure you would enjoy that."

"It's too fantastic. My vacation is actually scheduled for those two weeks, and I was going to go out to Indiana to be with my parents. But how could you get away at the same time that I'm gone?"

"Oh, I'll make up some excuse that there's a family emergency, and I have to go back to Switzerland. I'll do it right at the last minute, but we'll have everything planned. And at work, I'll just have Gina and that idiot Gray look after things while I'm gone."

"I won't be able to think for the next two weeks until we leave, so please don't tease me. If you're not serious, please tell me now so I don't get all excited and then have a terrible let down."

"Susan, I'm really serious. It will be great showing you Italy, and just being with you for a couple of weeks. And the more that I think of it, the more that I like the idea of our spending one week in Italy and then another week in Switzerland. You know that I'm from Zürich, and I'd love to go back there for a few days. We could go to Lugano and then drive up through the Alps to the Zürichsee, which is a beautiful lake with the city of Zürich at the northern end. There might even be a few things that I could do in Switzerland." Rising up on one elbow and taking hold of her hand, I said, "I'm going to make our reservations today, Susan. This is a trip that we've just got to take."

CHAPTER XXII

It had been ten years previously, in October 1965, that I had flown to New York on a Pan Am flight from Paris. At that time, my whole world had just crashed down on me as the embezzlement from Schleswigbank was about to be discovered, and I had been forced to become a fugitive. Now, in October 1975, I was flying back over the Atlantic on another Pan Am jet, this time from New York to Rome, and while my world had not crashed down on me this time, it clearly seemed to be teetering. I was fleeing now, not from the law, but simply from a very unpleasant situation—a situation that had been created at Morris, Brunner & Company when some relatively minor, as I saw it, juggling of the records had been discovered. But now I had none of the depression or self-doubt that I had experienced ten years previously. Being with Susan, knowing that I would return to New York in two weeks, and believing that what I had done at Morris, Brunner was completely justified, gave me a support and a feeling of self-justification that was totally lacking in 1965. I had thought then that I had done wrong—I refused to acknowledge that now.

At age forty-three, my belief in myself had grown enormously. I knew that I was smarter than most other money managers in New York as to the international markets. I felt a certain sense of superiority vis-à-vis my co-workers at Morris, Brunner. I even felt a certain ethnic superiority, believing that the Swiss, and particularly the Schweizer Deutsch, were more intelligent, more disciplined and more civilized than the polyglot Americans who I saw every day in New York City. And I knew that I remained a man with a great deal of attraction, having kept myself in great shape and having retained the clean-cut, blond Germanic look that I had always had. That a woman almost twenty years my junior was traveling with me bolstered my ego on this score. With the plane descending into Rome, and with Susan's head resting on my shoulder, I could not help feeling a certain amount of self-satisfaction despite the troubles I was leaving behind in New York. It was early morning in Rome as the plane landed, and I felt that the fact that it was a bright, sunny morning was a good omen for the start of our vacation.

I had made reservations at the Hotel Cardinal on the Via Giulia, which was in one of the oldest parts of Rome. It was just a block from the Tiber River, and within walking distance of many of the most famous attractions in Rome. The hotel itself was quite old and had not been kept up all that well, but there was a certain elegance about it, although a faded elegance, that both Susan and I found charming. I had remembered hearing about the hotel years earlier when I was living in Switzerland, and I was glad that we had decided to come here. Since it was late October, and the city was not crowded, we were shown to our room as soon as we arrived, even thought it was not yet ten o'clock in the morning. I felt that we should rest for a few hours before setting out to see Rome, and we both collapsed on the big, old double bed. The mattress had seen better days, and we laughed as we rolled together into the soft center of the bed.

Later that day, I got up and discovered that there was a hand-held shower in the bathroom, and I quickly made us of it. After Susan had also finished bathing, I led her out for our first walking trip around Rome. The Via Giulia— old, unchanged for several hundred years, and certainly a little grimy—was still one of the most impressive streets in the city, and it was a great place to start our tour. The afternoon sun in the late fall, low in the western sky, struck the old stone buildings on one side of the Via Giulia giving those buildings a warmth and brightness that belied the years of accumulated history embedded in their facades. It was a memorable picture, and Susan and I walked slowly to the end of the street, before wandering off into the Piazza Navonna. We looked for an outdoor café on the sunny side of the Piazza, and ordered cappuccinos as we sat simply enjoying our relaxation, and watching the people and the bustle around us.

This was one of the most relaxing moments of the entire trip, since the next day we started upon the arduous sightseeing schedule that I had laid out. After two days in Rome, we rented a car and began driving north, with Orvieto, Assissi, Perugia, and Arezzo following one upon the other in quick succession. In Tuscany, I made a special effort to see the paintings of Pierro della Francesca. Years earlier when I was still in Zürich, Ingrid and I had planned to take the so-called "Pierro tour" that covered a great many towns in Tuscany, including Arezzo, Perugia, Sansepolcro, and Florence. I had brought along a book that described the tour, and I gave it to Susan after we left Rome. Although our time was short, particularly if we were to spend a week in Switzerland, she found the idea of the tour exciting, and agreed with me that we should see as many of Pierro's paintings as we could before leaving Tuscany.

We started in Sansepolcro where we went to the old town hall to see Pierro's *Resurrection*. We next went to Monterchi, not much more than a dot in the road between Arezzo and Sansepolcro, to see the artist's *Madonna and Child* in the chapel of a small cemetery. We walked through the cemetery, admiring the flowers on the well-tended graves, and were surprised to see how tiny the chapel was in which the faded masterpiece had survived. And finally we stopped at the Church of San Francesco in Arezzo to see Pierro's famous frescos, and almost froze from the cold in the church, even though it was a sunny fall day. The frescos were truly impressive for both of us, and we spent almost an hour studying the powerfully human images of the guards watching over the tomb of Christ and of a very human Christ rising from the dead. Neither Susan nor I was particularly religious, but, like so many others who visited this spot, we could not help being moved by what we had seen.

We rushed through the next three days—lunching in the incredible town of San Gimignano and marveling at its ancient towers; enjoying cappuccino in the Piazza del Campo in Sienna—probably our favorite spot in all of Italy, and fighting the hordes of tourists from all over the world who had flocked to Florence, even though it was supposedly out of season. We were soon exhausted after fighting our way through the Uffizi, jostling with the throngs trying to see the gold doors of the Duomo, and straining to see the David over the heads of the crowds in front of us. We decided that the crush of tourists was too much, and began walking away from the Ponte Vecchio along the banks of the Arno. It was another beautiful October day, and again, as our first day in the Via Giulia, the low sun in the clear sky flooded the buildings on the north side of the river with sunlight, only here a mirror image of those buildings was created in the sparkling waters of the Arno. We found a spot to sit along the banks of Lungarno, and watched in silence as the light on the buildings slowly faded from bright yellow, to orange, and then to red as the sun dropped below the horizon.

The next day we began driving north to Switzerland, heading to Lugano. I could not help but remember my last drive to Lugano ten years previously, although this one was completely different. I was now able to speed along the Italian autostradas from Florence, to Bologna, to Milan to Lugano, which was a totally different approach to Lugano from the south as opposed to that frustratingly slow drive coming down through the Alps in 1965. At the Italian-Swiss border, we stopped briefly at the Italian checkpoint and simply held up our passports to show the guards that we were Americans. But it was a nerve-wracking time for me at the Swiss checkpoint, since the Swiss border police took our passports from us and spent several minutes looking through them. The fact that I was under a prison sentence in Switzerland had never been brought home to me more forcefully than during those minutes at the border crossing.

When we arrived in Lugano, I could not resist going back to the Hotel Splendide, and Susan and I soon found ourselves in one of the hotel's old, ornate rooms, overlooking the lake.

Susan came up to me and put her arms around me, saying, "Kurt, I'm beat. After all we've seen in the past week, and the drive from Florence today, I don't know if I ever want to leave this room."

"I think you might be suggesting that you don't want to go out for dinner tonight."

"Would you mind? When we get to Zürich I promise to go wherever you want."

"Of course, I don't mind. I'll order dinner here in the room—that will certainly be more romantic."

I immediately ordered two gin and tonics, and after they came, we sat together drinking. We were sitting very close together as Susan said, "We've hardly thought about New York during the past week, and everything that happened back there before we left."

I agreed. "But that was at least one of the reasons for the trip, wasn't it? To get away from that company which shall remain nameless, and to forget about all that craziness."

"Yes, it was certainly one of the reasons, but what they did to you still bothers me. And it was so pointless."

"Well, it wasn't pointless from their viewpoint."

Susan shook her head and said, "No, I mean it could have been avoided—you didn't have to put the orders through the Operations Department."

I said, "What do you mean? How can the Operations Department be avoided?"

"Well, when I took over from Gina, she told me that she had worked out an arrangement to transfer funds in or out of accounts, without going through Operations. She had direct access to the computer and she showed me how to do the same thing, because quite often we have to transfer money very quickly out of a client's account, maybe to his checking account or something like that. And if I can go directly into the computer to transfer money, I'm sure I could have done the same thing for transferring those securities that you wanted to move into the Fund."

I was really surprised. "I can't believe it. You mean that you can transfer money out of a customer's account, let's say to a bank or some other broker, without having to go through Operations or get someone's approval? The place must be out of control."

As only Susan could do, she very sweetly replied, "Well, we're supposed to get someone to co-sign the transfer, but if I'm in a hurry because a customer wants to have the money right away, I can put the transfer through on my own."

I was really amazed to get this information and said, "We're going to have to change that when we get back to New York. I trust you, of course, but Gina might decide to transfer a bundle off to her grandparents in Mexico, and you're telling me that she could do that on her own, by inputting it directly into the computer. That's bizarre. But look, that's water over the dam now, so let's not talk about New York anymore. I want to enjoy this vacation, and I want to enjoy being here with you." With that, I put my arm around her as we sat on a love seat drinking our gin and tonics.

Chapter XXIII

Susan and I spent a day in Lugano, simply resting and doing some sightseeing. It was a beautiful day, and we enjoyed walking hand in hand along the lakeshore, stopping for a cappuccino at a little café, and returning to the hotel for a rest before dinner. From my viewpoint, it had been a great time to relax and forget all about New York. We set out the following morning, driving north again toward Bellinzona and the St. Gotthard Pass. The road was much improved compared to the way I remembered it from ten years previously, since it was now four-lanes all the way to Airolo. Here the newly opened St. Gotthard Tunnel now took automobiles for ten miles straight through the mountains, coming out on the other side of the St. Gotthard massif north of Andermatt, near Göschenen. I knew that the Tunnel was now open, and I thought back to my frustration in fighting the traffic going over the Pass as I was hurrying to Lugano in 1965. But I was certainly in no hurry this time, and I said to Susan, "What would you like to do? We can go through the Tunnel, which will be fast and very easy driving, or we can take the old road over the Pass, which will be very scenic, but it could be fairly slow, difficult driving."

"Have you ever driven over the pass?"

"Yes, many years ago, but the traffic was very heavy then since the tunnel was not open, so I would expect that there would not be too much traffic now. But it's up to you."

She answered as I expected her to, "Of course I want to go over the Pass, and I'm pretty sure that you do too."

"You're right, if you had said the Tunnel, I would have been disappointed."

This time I was really able to enjoy the stark, majestic scenery of the Alps, as I navigated the sharp hairpin turns going up to the summit. There was, of course, much less traffic now than there had been in 1965, since most of the traffic now used the Tunnel. As a result, I found that I was able to drive at my own pace, and I actually found the drive surprisingly enjoyable as we wound our way to the summit. There was a scenic viewpoint at the top of the Pass, and I stopped there so that Susan and I could get out to enjoy the scenery. It was extremely cold at 12,000 feet, and I put my arm around Susan and held her close to me for warmth as we looked out over the austere scene before us. Mountains that were black, rugged and rocky rose up from valleys in which small icy lakes shone with their cold, reflected light. In some places in Switzerland, the snow-covered Alps, gleaming white in the sun, appeared majestic and beautiful, filling the eye of the beholder with joy at the beauty of the spot. The top of the St. Gotthard Pass was not one of those places; rather, it seemed to be a place that had been designed both to awe and depress the viewer, making him understand that everything in the world was not beautiful, even in Switzerland. Susan and I hurried back to our car, shivering from the cold and from the bleak, yet impressive, austerity of the spot.

After descending from the Pass, we drove on to Altdorf, and I suggested that we stop there for lunch. This was the spot where William Tell was supposed to have shot the apple off of his son's head, and there were many curio shops in town with various Tell-related souvenirs. We tried to avoid the tourist spots, and found a small restaurant that seemed to be patronized mainly by locals, and had a leisurely lunch there. After wandering around the town for about thirty or forty minutes, we set off toward Zürich again.

I hoped that it was not too obvious to Susan that I had been deliberately trying to waste time since leaving Lugano—driving slowly through the Pass, and taking a long lunch break in Altdorf—and that I did not want to get to Zürich that night. I had made up my mind that I had to spend the night in Küsnacht. It was not possible for me to drive through Küsnacht without stopping at the bank and checking on the safe deposit box. Not having seen it for ten years, it now became very important to me that I get to see the money that Ingrid and I had embezzled ten years ago. But I knew that if Susan and I had arrived in Küsnacht in the afternoon when the bank was still open, I would have found it hard to explain to Susan why I was going into the bank, and, since I was planning to take some of the money with me, why I was bringing out a small package. It seemed to me that if we stayed overnight, I would be able to get away in the morning and go to the bank alone. Staying overnight in Küsnacht seemed to be the best way to accomplish my objective.

The money had been sitting in the safe deposit box in Küsnacht for ten years. Ingrid had told me when we talked about it shortly after I fled Switzerland that she was afraid to touch the money. Since that was Ingrid's attitude, I decided that I could definitely make use of some of that money now. I knew that I was not going to get either a bonus or a raise at Morris, Brunner this year, and my living expenses were not going to go down. I had always sent some money to Ingrid for her expenses and for my daughter, Petra, and I now had to think about my relationship with Susan and where that might lead. The 150,000 Swiss francs in the safety deposit box, equal to well over $150,000 at current exchange rates, would be a tremendous help if the situation at Morris, Brunner resulted in my being out of a job for any period of time.

And I also felt very strongly that I should have the money. I was the one who had been forced to sacrifice because of what had happened ten years ago, and I was still being forced to do so. I had been branded a criminal and been forced to flee Switzerland. I had had to give up my wife and had never been able to be a father to my daughter. Even if Ingrid did not feel as she said she did, I was convinced that I had every right to the money. When the idea of a trip to Europe had first come up with Susan, I had immediately started to think of that money sitting in the bank in Küsnacht, and my anticipation of getting back into that safe deposit box had been growing since we left New York. That anticipation began to flare up as Susan and I crossed the Zürichsee at Rapperswil, and began driving the last 35 kilometers to Küsnacht.

As we drove into the small town, it was about four in the afternoon, and I said to Susan, "If you don't mind, I think I'd really like to stay here in Küsnacht tonight. There's a little inn just off the highway, and I think you'd like it."

Susan seemed to me to be a little surprised when she responded to my suggestion. "Kurt, you're not only my boss but my tour leader too, so I don't think I dare argue with you. And I don't really want to. You haven't led us astray on this trip yet, and after all that rushing around in Italy, I think I would enjoy a more relaxed pace here in Switzerland."

I reached over and took one of her hands in mine and said, "Well, in Italy there were so many things I wanted us to see—it was just endless—and trying to cover all those places really forced us to follow a pretty rough schedule. I think we were both getting totally exhausted by the time we got to Florence. But here in Switzerland, it's the beautiful scenery and the charming villages that are the things we should see, and I think that this requires a much slower pace. We'll go on to Zürich tomorrow, but I bet you'll think back and remember Küsnacht as a more romantic place."

Susan smiled at me, disengaging her hand from mine and instead placing her hand on my knee. She smiled her most winning smile, as she said, "If you're thinking of romance, then I'm all for Küsnacht."

It took a little searching, but Küsnacht is a small town and I soon found the inn. After we checked in and got settled, we went for a walk along the Zürichsee. It was another beautiful day, and we found a bench where we could sit and watch the ducks and geese swimming in the water. After we had been settled there for some time, I took Susan's hand and said, "There's something I want to tell you that I maybe should have told you before. It's hard for me to talk about this, and I don't think I've ever told anyone else in the United States. But you should know that I was married about fourteen years ago, when I was just twenty-nine, to a woman who is now in Zürich. When our marriage broke up back in 1965, I decided that I had to leave Switzerland and start over someplace else. The bank that I was working at did not like the idea of marital problems for their young officers, and I knew that my career there would be badly hurt if Ingrid and I separated or divorced. Even so, I tried to convince her to give me a divorce, but she's Catholic and absolutely refused to discuss it then, and still refuses to.

"So I felt I had no alternative—I had to leave Switzerland, and I really felt defeated when I came to the States ten years ago. But now, with a good job—I think I still have that job—and with you, things have started to look up for me.

And I don't want you to feel upset when we're in Zürich tomorrow if I go and see Ingrid for an hour or so."

I could feel Susan pull back when I told her this and she looked away toward the water. I felt I had to continue my explanation to her: "Now don't go getting all uptight about this. That marriage has been over for ten years. But there was a child—a daughter. When I left Zürich I had no idea that my wife was pregnant, and she never told me until the child was born. Even then, it was her mother who let me know. I've only seen the child twice in those ten years, and I really would like to see her again while we're in Zürich. I'm sure you can understand that. I don't want to hide anything from you—I want to be completely honest— and I know I should have told you this before. You've been so great to me, and so supportive through everything, so I know that I can tell you that I may have to be away from you for a few hours tomorrow or the next day."

She immediately asked the question that I had expected her to ask: "Does your wife know you're coming?"

"No, she has no idea. Virtually the only time we ever communicate is when I send her money—I send a check every month for child support, but there are no letters or anything like that."

I thought that she was a little sullen as she asked, "Was that the idea behind this trip—so that you could see your daughter again, and your wife?"

"No, the idea was to be with you, and to see all those marvelous places in Italy that I'd always wanted to see, and that I knew you would love. And I also wanted to bring you to Switzerland, since this was my home, and I wanted you to know it and to love it as I do. Seeing Ingrid and the little girl—her name's Petra—is an obligation, but it's more than that. I don't think I would be normal if I didn't want to see my child. How can I come here without at least trying to see her?"

Susan squeezed my hand and held it for a few minutes. Finally she said, "Oh Kurt, I really do love you. Everyone at work thinks you're so aloof and so cold, but to me you're like a vulnerable little boy. I won't make tomorrow any more difficult for you than it will be anyway."

I put my arm around her and pulled her closer to me. "The main reason I wanted to stop here in Küsnacht was so that we could have this talk, and I wouldn't have to spring something on you tomorrow in Zürich."

We walked back to the inn, going directly to our room to make love, and I am sure that we both enjoyed that lovemaking more than ever before. We found it hard to get dressed to go to dinner since we kept teasing each other, and we barely got to the dining room before its nine o'clock closing. As we sat having dinner, I was really in a very good mood since Susan had so easily accepted the story I had told her about Ingrid and about why I had left Switzerland. I knew that I had lied to Susan, but I really did not think that there was anything wrong in having lied to her. It would have been impossible to tell her the truth about being an embezzler and having to escape as the law closed in. The story I had given her about having to leave because my marriage was breaking up seemed to me to be quite plausible, and one that I hoped Susan would repeat to others in the office when we got back to New York.

The next morning, we had a late breakfast in our room. I took a long time having a shower and dressing, and then spent some time reading the newspaper. About 9:30 a.m., I told Susan that I would have to go out for a few minutes. "I need to get one of the tires checked; I think we may have a slow leak."

She surprised me by saying, "I could come with you if you'd like."

"No, why don't you finish packing up, and be ready to leave. I should be back in about a half hour or so."

I then went down and got the car and drove first of all to a service station. I managed to kill about twenty minutes by having the gas and oil checked, and even having the attendant check the tires. It was now close to ten o'clock, and I drove to the bank and parked across the street. When the doors opened, I was one of the first customers in, and I went straight downstairs to the vaults. I had rehearsed this whole procedure in my mind any number of times, but I was still more nervous than I could ever remember being as I descended the stairs into the vault. When I had crossed the border into Switzerland three days previously, I had been using my American passport and there had been little chance of my being recognized as a fugitive from ten years previous. Here in the Küsnacht bank, however, I was going to be required to identify myself as Kurt Wenner of Zürich. Was it possible that the Swiss authorities had discovered this hiding place, and were just waiting for me to try to get access to the safe deposit box?

I went to the counter and filled in the form that was required by the bank, printing my name, address, date of birth, my mother's maiden name, and signing the bottom line, as required. I took the form up to the bank guard at the desk just outside the vault entrance. The guard would check the records and then escort me back to the safe deposit box so that it could be opened with my key and with the guard's key. I had, of course, taken the vault key with me when I left New York. I handed the guard the completed form and the guard went over to the files and looked for the corresponding signature card. The guard spent several minutes looking through the files and finally came back to me and said, "Would you wait just one minute, Mr. Wenner?"

I literally froze as the guard turned and walked over to talk with a man seated at a desk in the back of the room. I became convinced that the records had been marked just as I had feared, and that the bank would alert the police momentarily. A wave of panic swept over me, and I thought of running out of the bank. But where could I run? If the police would be alerted, there would be no way that I could make it out of the country. I gripped the edge of the counter to steady myself, and decided that there was nothing to do but to wait and see what the bankers did.

After a few minutes, during which the two men had carried on a conversation that I could not hear, the second man rose from his desk and came up to me. "Mr. Wenner, I am Jürgen Reiter and am responsible for the vault area here at the bank. I think that there has been some misunderstanding. This safety deposit box of yours was one that had two authorized signatures. Either party could have access to the box. Isn't that right, Mr. Wenner?"

This line of conversation was so unexpected that I had to focus my thoughts for a minute to understand what was being said to me. As I continued to hesitate, the banker said, "Did you understand what I said, Mr. Wenner."

I took a deep breath, and said, "I'm sorry, I did understand, and you are correct, Mr. Reiter, there are two signatures that are authorized for our box, and either party may have access to it."

"Well, Mr. Wenner, I must tell you that our records indicate that Mrs. Wenner was here this past December, and she terminated the lease on the box. She must, of course, have removed all its contents at that time."

Ingrid had taken all the money! I could not believe it. All I could do was to stammer, "But she couldn't have—that was not our agreement."

Mr. Reiter appeared somewhat flustered by what I had said, and replied, "I do hope, Mr. Wenner, that you don't think that the bank was at fault in any way. We had no way of knowing about any agreement between the two of you. As you said, the signature card permitted either party to have access to the box."

I calmed down a little bit and said, "Oh, no Mr. Reiter, no, no. It's not your fault." There was a long pause as I continued to try to pull myself together, and I finally said, "Mrs. Wenner and I have been separated for a number of years, and it was part of our separation agreement that the items in the box were not to be disposed of by either of us individually. I was merely checking today to see if that agreement was being followed, and, as you can see, I'm rather stunned to find that it has not been."

Mr. Reiter, seeing that I was quite upset by the news that he had just given me, offered to let me sit in one of the rooms that the bank's clients used when looking at the contents of their safe deposit boxes. He suggested that I might like to have a cup of coffee or even tea. However, I thanked him and declined the offer.

I left the bank virtually in a state of shock. I crossed back over to the car, got in, and sat gripping the steering wheel with my head bowed as the realization overwhelmed me that the money was really gone. For the past ten years I had always known, deep inside myself, that the money I had embezzled from Schleswigbank was waiting in that safe deposit box in Küsnacht. If there was any justification for all that I had endured during those years, I had found that justification in the fact that I had gotten away with it—the money was still there and someday I would reclaim it. It was like a trophy to me symbolizing my success in taking the money and in getting away from Switzerland.

When I had first left Switzerland, I had thought that Ingrid would go to Küsnacht from time to time to get whatever money she might need, but my attitude about the money quickly changed. As soon as I had a regular job in the United States, I had made a particular effort to send Ingrid money on a monthly basis, so that she would have no need to take any of the embezzled funds. I wanted to know that it was still there as kind of a symbol of the success of the entire embezzlement. And now it was gone! The feeling of loss, of being stripped of one of my most important psychological underpinnings—this feeling of emptiness was absolutely overwhelming.

And on top of the feeling of loss was the sense of betrayal. How could Ingrid possibly have done this without telling me? She had assured me that she never went to Küsnacht, and that she did not want anything to do with that money. Our relationship had clearly gone downhill during the past ten years, but I had sent her money regularly to help support our daughter, and we had never divorced. Our "temporary" separation had simply gone on over the years, and we had become much more independent of each other. But together with the money in the safe deposit box, Ingrid had always been the other justification—the other psychological underpinning—for what I had done. She had not been forced to flee; she had not been branded a criminal as I had been; and the fact that I had protected her was another fact that I could always hold on to and always take satisfaction from. I really felt that it was her fault that the embezzlement took place, and the fact that I had taken the blame and protected her provided me with a strong sense of the sacrifice that I had endured for her. And now, with one fell swoop, Ingrid's taking the money—both of my justifications were pulled from beneath me and I felt shattered.

I really did not know how long I had been sitting in the car with my eyes closed, gripping the steering wheel, when I looked up and saw a local policeman standing a short way down the street watching me. I had a momentary fright since I was afraid that the policeman might be getting suspicious. The last thing I wanted was to end up being questioned by the police. As a result, I quickly decided to take the initiative before the policeman did anything, and I picked up the road map that was on the seat next to me, and got out of the car, going directly over to the policeman. Speaking English, I explained that I was an American tourist and that I had been studying the map to see if there was a way to get to Winterthur, without going through Zürich, explaining that I had reservations at a hotel in Winterthur. The policeman spoke very little English and had some difficulty understanding me, as I made no effort to speak German. Finally, however, the policeman was able to understand what I was asking him, and he explained that at this point I would have to drive into Zürich before I could turn east to Winterthur. I thanked him and got back into the car feeling that I had assuaged any suspicions that the policeman might have had. I then drove slowly back to the inn where I would have to face Susan.

When I got back to our room, Susan seemed a little upset, as I had expected she might be. "Kurt, it's after eleven o'clock, where have you been?"

I was still upset about the money, but tried to appear contrite in my response to her. "I'm sorry, Susan. Everything just took longer than I thought it would. Have you ever had a tire fixed? It can take forever. I was going to call, but there was no phone at the garage, and I was just stuck." I went over to her and took her in my arms, pulling her close to me. "I really am sorry but you shouldn't be upset just because I'm away for a few minutes. Let's get the bags down to the car and get going and we can talk about it while we're driving."

As we drove out of Küsnacht, my emotions were still in turmoil. I was reeling from the discovery that the money was gone from the safe deposit box, and from what I perceived as Ingrid's betrayal. Ironically, however, just when I felt the most upset and insecure, I should have been giving reassurance to Susan who must have imagined all sorts of things after what I had told her the previous day about my Swiss wife and now during my two-hour absence. I really wanted to comfort Susan and make her feel that she had nothing to worry about, but it was totally impossible for me to concentrate on anything but the money and Ingrid. Since I could not begin to think of anything to say to Susan, and since she was still apparently upset by my being out for two hours that morning, the drive into Zürich passed in silence—a cold, tense silence that was really rather uncomfortable. The short trip into Zürich seemed interminable, but we eventually arrived in the city and made our way wordlessly to our hotel.

Chapter XXIV

It had changed so little since I had last been there over ten years ago. The buildings in the neighborhood still looked the same. The people on the streets still seemed to dress the same. The same streetcar still ran on nearby Dufourstraße—the streetcar I had taken to and from work at Schleswigbank. And our apartment building looked almost exactly the same, just as I remembered it had looked when I had driven away that early morning back in 1965. Maybe some of the trees or some of the shrubs were a little bigger, but it seemed to me that the good burghers of Zürich had even managed to control them, so that it was hard to see any change in the neighborhood at all—the neighborhood that I used to call home.

I had not called Ingrid to let her know that I was coming, and I sat in the car now wondering if that was a mistake; wondering how she would react to seeing me; and wondering above all what excuse she would give for taking the money from the bank. Ever since I had decided to come to Switzerland with Susan, I had debated with myself the question of whether or not I should see Ingrid. When I had told Susan about Ingrid and Petra in Küsnacht, I was fairly certain that I would see them. But in the morning, as I went to the bank in Küsnacht, I had pretty well decided that it would be better—better for myself and probably better for Ingrid as well—if I did not see her. It would be better if she did not know that I had been there and taken the money, and it would be better for Petra not to face a father that she had never known. However, that all changed again when I discovered that the money was gone, and I now walked into the entrance foyer of the apartment building and rang the bell for what I knew could only be a serious confrontation with my wife.

After a very short wait, I heard her voice, that very familiar voice: "Yes, who is it?"

"Ingrid, it's Kurt. I'd like to come up."

"Kurt . . .? What are you doing here?"

"As I said, I'd like to come up. I'd like to talk with you."

"But Kurt, I don't know whether . . ."

"Ingrid, just buzz me up so we can talk."

There was a silence of about thirty seconds, although it seemed much longer to me, until I finally heard the buzzer releasing the entry door. I went in quickly and walked up the two flights of stairs to the second floor and waited for her to open it. When she did, and stood there facing me, all my anger left me for a moment and I could only stare at her and say nothing. The thought went through my mind that this was the woman I had once loved; this was the woman I had been married to; this was the mother of my child; and this was the woman for whom I had made such incredible sacrifices. And only this morning I had discovered that this was the woman who had, for whatever reason, betrayed me.

As I got to the door of the apartment, she quickly said, "You'd better come in, Kurt. Someone might see you."

I went in, closing the door behind me. "I doubt if anyone would remember. There can't still be the same neighbors here after ten years."

She looked very upset at my being there and said, "You don't think so? Remember, this is Zürich." She quickly started to turn her back on me and walk into the living room, but I stopped her by saying, "And I don't even get a kiss after all this time."

She turned toward me again and let me kiss her on each cheek, and I began to recognize that I had never seen her so agitated. I really had not known what to expect when I met Ingrid again, and I realized that I had not thought enough about this problem. I had known that we could not go back to our old relationship, but I really had not known what to expect, and I could see that she was finding this meeting even more difficult than I was.

As we sat down in the living room, she said, "Kurt, I can't believe that you've come here. It's incredibly dangerous for you. I really don't understand it."

"I travel on my American passport, and there has been absolutely no problem."

"But what if someone recognized you. I'm sure you know that you haven't changed very much in the past ten years."

"I'm being very careful. This is actually the riskiest thing that I will do on the entire trip—coming here to see you and perhaps Petra."

"Why would you want to see Petra?"

"Ingrid, she is my daughter, and I think she should know that her father has a real interest in her and in her future."

Ingrid shook her head several times, and said, "Kurt, please don't do that. Petra is doing just fine, and for you to appear on the scene now would only upset her. And I can't believe that you've come here to Zürich just to see Petra, or primarily to see Petra."

"Well, I'm sorry that you don't believe it, but I wanted to see her and I wanted to see you again."

"You should have let me know that you were coming, and we could have met in Lugano or Geneva, or someplace near the border. It would have been less risky."

I could not resist saying rather sarcastically, "Someplace like Schaffhausen perhaps. It's right on the German border. Wouldn't that be appropriate—a really fitting place for the Wenner family to get together?"

Ingrid was clearly not pleased by my referring to Schaffhausen and said, "Do you have to bring that up—I've been trying to forget that for ten years."

"Well, you may try to forget it, Ingrid, but you shouldn't forget that I was branded a criminal because of Schaffhausen while you've been able to sit here and play your part as the aggrieved wife, relatively unscathed by the whole thing."

"How dare you say to me that I haven't had to suffer because of what happened. Raising a daughter alone and being looked upon as the wife of a criminal—do you think that that has been easy? Let me tell you that I would have changed places with you any day. You were able to start a new life in America, and no one there is constantly reminding you of the shame that was brought on our family by that embezzlement."

"Don't forget, it was your choice, Ingrid. I wanted you to come to the States, and we could have started our new life there together, and we could have raised our daughter together. But for whatever reason, you chose to stay here and to play the part of the innocent wife, and you've played it very well, haven't you?"

Ingrid was silent for a few moments, and finally said in a much quieter voice, "Sometimes I think that I made the wrong choice. Maybe I should have gone with you, but I felt that it would be branding me—and particularly Petra—with being criminals. And I really could not do that."

"But you are willing to enjoy all the fruits of that embezzlement."

"What do you mean by that?"

"I was at the bank in Küsnacht this morning, and I found that the box had been given up last December. You seem to have taken all the money."

Ingrid was clearly surprised that I knew about the money, and I wondered if that was why she had been so agitated when I first arrived. After a minute of silence, she drew back in her chair and, staring directly at me, said, "And what were you doing in Küsnacht? I can only imagine that you were trying to get the money for yourself. You probably never would have come here if the money had still been there."

"You don't think that I had a right to at least some of that money?"

Ingrid waved her hand to the side in a dismissive gesture, and said, "How can we talk about what's right and what's wrong in a situation like this, or who had a right to something? Maybe neither of us had a right to it. At any rate, yes, I did take the money out last December, and I don't think that there's much that you can do about it now."

A real feeling of betrayal was boiling inside me, and I hardly knew how to answer her. In desperation, I finally said, "I could go to the police."

She laughed and said, "You? Go to the police? You don't think I'm going to be impressed by that threat, do you? Let me see, what would the complaint be? A convicted criminal complains that his loot—what he stole from a small-town bank—has been stolen from him. I think that means you'd be giving yourself up, and I doubt if you have any intention of doing that."

I seemed to regain a certain amount of confidence as Ingrid talked. "You don't think so? Of course, I wouldn't do it until I was out of Switzerland and could send the police a letter. But I think it would be pretty clear what had been in that safe deposit box in Küsnacht. Wouldn't the bank still have records showing that I went there the day that I fled from Zürich? And why would I do that unless I had gone there to put some money in or take some money out? Those same records will show that you were a co-signer on the box and, as the gentleman at the bank told me just this morning, it was Mrs. Wenner that came to the bank and terminated the lease on the box in December. So, yes, I could contact the police, and I think that you might have more to fear from them than I do."

"You fled Switzerland when our little escapade was discovered in order to avoid that pending jail sentence. Do you think I'm going to believe that you're willing to run the risk of having to face that jail sentence now? Don't be silly. There are extradition treaties with the United States, after all, so I don't believe that you will put yourself in danger of going to jail."

We sat looking at each other for several minutes, as we both must have been thinking about the impossibility of my contacting the police. I ultimately broke the silence by saying, "But what I don't understand is what you did with the money. After ten years—and I've been sending you money monthly all that time—why did you need 150,000 francs now? The Swiss franc keeps rising from what it was ten years ago, and so that's over $150,000."

"I have things that I want, I have things that I need. I don't know if you can understand what it's like to be a woman alone, trying to raise a child. You've been good about sending money—I don't deny that—but there are so many expenses that keep coming up that I finally decided that it was stupid not to use that money that was lying there in Küsnacht."

"Ingrid, you couldn't have spent 150,000 francs in ten months, unless you made some tremendous purchase, or unless you made a big investment. You're clearly living here in the same style, and I'm sure with expenses that are only a little higher than we had ten years ago. So if you haven't spent it, there still must be a great deal of that money in an account someplace else." I began to hope that if Ingrid had not spent all the money, I might be able to persuade her to turn part of it over to me.

"But what difference does it make to you, Kurt? You've said in your letters that you have a big job in New York now and you must be making very good money. Let me ask you the same question: why now, after ten years when things must have been much worse for you financially, why do you now suddenly feel that you have to have that money?"

Lying to Ingrid was not something that came easily to me, not as easy as it had been to lie to Susan the previous day. While Ingrid and I were married and living together here in Zürich, I would never have dreamed of lying to her.

There was no way, however, that I was going to tell her about the problems at Morris, Brunner, and I felt that I could not tell her about Susan. "I had to start over in New York ten years ago with nothing. I had no furniture, no clothes, nothing. You're right, I do have a good job now, but I have to live in Manhattan, and that's horribly expensive. Because of my job, I really have to get a larger apartment—just as you felt that we had to get a larger apartment when I was promoted at Schleswigbank. And when I get that apartment, I will have to furnish it. It's ironic: the first thing that you and I used that money for was furnishing this apartment and buying our Mercedes. And now I want to use some of it to do about the same thing in New York."

Ingrid looked down and shook her head. "I'm sorry Kurt, the money's gone. It's all gone. I made a bad investment, and it's lost."

I looked directly at her for a minute, while she kept her eyes averted, and I finally said, "I don't believe you. There was no investment. You did something else with it, but there was no investment."

Ingrid was about to reply when the telephone rang, and she immediately rose to answer it. Instead of using the phone in the living room, she went into the kitchen to use the wall phone there. When she had left the room, I got up and walked over to the sideboard near the kitchen door. The crystal decanters with the various liquors were still there, and I wondered if Ingrid had made herself another drink since that terrible night ten years previously. As I stood by the sideboard, I could hear snatches of Ingrid's conversation, and I heard her say at one point, "Yes, he's here" and "No, it's all right. Don't you come here. I can handle it." I wondered who she was talking to and who she could possibly be on such good terms with that she could tell the person that her fugitive husband was there.

I was determined to ask her about this as soon as she came back into the room, but before I returned to my chair, I noticed a framed picture at the end of the sideboard. It was a picture approximately four by five inches in size, in a heavy wooden frame. The picture was of a dark-haired young man standing in front of a large trailer truck. He was dressed in blue jeans and a tight-fitting T-shirt, showing that he had a very well-developed muscular body. He stood with one foot up on the front bumper of the truck, and his whole attitude seemed to indicate that this was his property. I stood holding the picture as Ingrid came back into the living room and I said, "Someone I know?"

"You mean on the phone?"

"You seemed to have confided in whoever it was about my being here, so it must either be someone I know or someone you have a great deal of confidence in."

"Well, you have changed, Kurt. I didn't know that you were into eavesdropping ten years ago."

"It wasn't deliberate. I actually came over here to look at this picture, and rather accidentally heard part of your conversation. But the question can apply to either the phone call or the picture. I assume it was the same person."

"If you must know, that picture you're holding is Paulo. He's a friend of mine, and, yes, it was Paulo on the phone."

"I suppose I shouldn't ask what your relationship is."

"I think it would be better if we didn't discuss it."

I continued standing by the sideboard, still holding the picture. "Maybe we should discuss it, Ingrid, because maybe it was for Paulo that you took the money. Am I right?"

"Kurt, I told you. I don't see any reason to discuss this with you."

"Well, unless you can give me a plausible story as to what you did with 150,000 francs, I'm going to have to assume that Paulo had something to do with it."

"And what if he did? I've already told you, it has nothing to do with you."

"I'm willing to bet that you bought him this truck with part of the money. A truck and trailer like that have to cost a great deal of money." It was a shot in the dark on my part, and I could barely conceal my surprise when it hit home.

"If you already knew about that before you came here, then why have we been verbally fencing for the last half hour?"

"Ingrid, are you telling me that you're sleeping with this guy?"

"I hope that you're not trying to tell me that you've been celibate for the last ten years. Knowing you, you've probably never been without a woman even for one week. Well, I went as long as I could, but when Paulo came along, I decided that there was no reason to deny myself any longer. A woman has to have sex too, or didn't you ever think of that?"

"So you paid this stud Paulo here 150,000 francs so you could get fucked."

With that Ingrid stepped up to me and slapped me in my face as hard as she could. I was so surprised that I fell backwards against the wall and, as I righted myself, my first thought was to hit back at her. But that thought quickly passed and I finally set the picture down on the sideboard and went over and sat down in the chair I had been sitting in before.

Rubbing my cheek that continued to smart from the slap, I shook my head and almost smiled. "You're right, I shouldn't have said that. I'm sorry. I don't blame you for taking a lover—although maybe I'm a little jealous. And you may be right about the money too; losing that is a real blow. After all we've suffered because of that money—both you and I—it's hard to accept that neither one of us is going to benefit from it."

Ingrid came over and sat down opposite me, curling her legs under her and crossing her arms across her chest as she apparently tried to control her emotions. There was another long silence, before I said, "I can't be a hypocrite about this, and I can't blame you for taking a lover." Realizing that telling Ingrid about Susan might hurt her, at least slightly, I went on, "You haven't asked, but I have someone too, and she's traveling with me now. In fact, she's right here in Zürich. Maybe we should all get together."

Ingrid merely raised her eyebrows slightly and showed by her expression that she was not amused by the suggestion. This time it was Ingrid that broke the long silence. "Well, if this is true confession time, then I should tell you that Paulo lives here with me now. Yes, he is younger, as you can see from the picture—he's just thirty-two and he's a truck driver. My parents are horrified, all the more so because he's from the working class, and Italian to boot, rather than because I'm living with someone. But we've been together almost two years now, and he's been wonderful with me and wonderful with Petra. Buying him the truck gave him a chance to go into business for himself, and I can't tell you how amazed I've been at how hard he's been working and how successful he's been. So I'm sorry you found out about the money, but I'm not sorry that I gave it to him. I really should say that I lent it to him, but I have no idea when he might pay it back."

I sat leaning forward, elbows on my knees looking down at the floor. This interview with Ingrid had been a catharsis for both of us, and I now knew that the money was gone and that she and I had really gone far down very separate roads. There was no fury; there was no feeling of betrayal anymore; there was just a feeling of emptiness. I looked around the apartment and tried to remember that night ten years ago when disaster had overtaken us, but those emotions seemed to have died too. Until now, it had always been painful to think of that night as Ingrid and I had sat together on the sofa trying to absorb what had befallen us. But those memories now seemed to be robbed of emotion, and, again, emptiness was all that remained.

"I guess then that there's nothing left, is there?"

Ingrid shook her head, and said, "Maybe there's nothing left between us, but I think we've both made new lives for ourselves. Isn't that the way it always is?"

"Yes, I guess you're right. And that means, doesn't it, that we ought to get a divorce?"

"Well, let's think about that." Ingrid laughed a little for the first time since I arrived. "It's funny, but being married—even to you—seems to make my relationship with Paulo a little easier. I've thought of asking you for a divorce, but I've been afraid of making him think that I was, you know, clearing the decks for him."

"You mean that marriage may not be on his mind. In my case, though, I think that Susan would be elated and would want to drag me down the aisle the second I was divorced. That is funny—we both have relationships with younger people, but divorce would probably not be helpful in either case. You might scare your friend away, while staying married is a defense against my friend. So what do we do, just go on as we have for the past ten years?"

Ingrid smiled again. "If you don't mind, I think that it would be best for me if we did. But if things change, Kurt, for you or for me, we should talk about it again. Maybe someday divorce will make sense."

I realized that our conversation was at an end, and I stood up and said, "You may not think so, Ingrid, but I think that it was good that we had this meeting. It was good that the whole situation that each of us faces finally came out. We now know more about where each of us stands, and hopefully we can talk from time to time in the future. I think I ought to go now. You're right again, I probably should not see Petra, and I do have to get back to the hotel."

Ingrid came up to me and this time she took the initiative to kiss me on both cheeks, saying, "I agree. Let's try to talk more, and maybe in another year or so you can visit with Petra somewhere here in Europe—but not in Switzerland." As I started down the stairs, Ingrid called after me, "Oh and Kurt, you will keep on sending the checks for Petra every month, won't you?"

CHAPTER XXV

I had gotten into the office quite early on my first day back from Europe. It was a gray, dreary day in New York, and I was still a little jet-lagged after the return flight across the Atlantic. I had mixed feelings about being back at Morris, Brunner—glad to be at work again after all the trauma with Ingrid in Switzerland, but still resentful at what I considered the unjust treatment I was receiving from Morris, Brunner. There was a certain amount of mail and other papers that had accumulated while I was away, and I was going through them when Gina came in.

She seemed glad to see me, and sat down in the chair in front of my desk. "Welcome back. How were things in Switzerland?"

I looked up and smiled at her as I said, "Not good, I'm afraid. I guess it was a good idea that I went there, but I don't think I solved anything. In fact, the trip was pretty disillusioning."

Not expecting anything other than the usual pleasantries, Gina was a little surprised and for once was somewhat at a loss for words. "Oh, sorry. I had thought that you might be able to get some vacation in, and would come back feeling all refreshed."

I decided not to pursue the discussion of my trip and changed the subject to the office. "How have things been here? I guess the place didn't fall apart while I was away, did it?"

"No, it was pretty quiet actually. Did you get to follow the markets at all? They really didn't do much, although I guess that in Switzerland you would have been able to follow the currency markets almost daily."

"There's no way that you can avoid it over there. But the dollar didn't seem to move much during the last two weeks, and the stock and bond markets didn't seem to do anything either."

Gina came up to the desk with a pile of order forms, and said, "Since you're back, and with Susan not here . . ."

"Susan's not here? I thought she was due back today."

"No, she called from Indiana this morning and said she wasn't feeling well. She hopes to get back to New York tomorrow or the next day. I thought I'd charge her with a couple of sick days."

"Yeah, I guess you'd better. Incidentally, you can put me down for two weeks of vacation. I'm afraid Sam Brunner would dock me for two weeks' pay if I tried to claim personal business."

"If that's what you want."

"You want me to initial all these order forms?"

Gina nodded, and I went through them quickly until I got to the last one. It was a form that I did not immediately recognize, and I asked, "What's this?"

"That's a cash transfer to the client's checking account at First City."

"I've never seen a form like that before."

"You probably just haven't noticed since I've had you sign quite a few of them. I can go right into the computer with that form, and don't have to wait for Operations to process it."

"Oh yes, Susan told me about that, but it does bother me that anyone could transfer money without some kind of control."

"We don't use it very often, only when there's some real rush to get money to a client. But we could put some restrictions on it if you think that they're necessary."

"I think we'd better. After all the brouhaha about the transfers between accounts, I don't want to give Sam Brunner anything else to yell about. I think you should put out a memo that I have to initial any of those transfers from now on. I guess if Susan had been here, you would have had her initial it."

"Or John Grey."

"Oh yes, dear John. How's he doing?"

"Pontificating on everything as usual, but he's out to a client meeting this morning."

I merely grimaced at the thought of Grey, but I then looked up at Gina and asked, "Incidentally, who is that young kid that I saw sitting at the trading desk this morning?"

Gina smiled at me in what seemed to be her most condescending way. "Oh, I guess you haven't heard. He's our new trader. Sam Brunner transferred him up here a few days after you left. He seems to be a nice enough young guy."

Transferring someone into my department without telling me was a slap in the face, and I made no effort to hide my displeasure from Gina, even though I knew that she was enjoying my discomfort. "Without asking me, he transfers someone into my unit—someone I've never met? I was going to say that I can't believe it, but I suppose, after what's been going on around here, I probably can. Does this kid know anything?"

"If you ask me, no. He's pleasant enough, but he really doesn't know anything about the stock or bond markets, and I don't think he's ever heard of the FX markets."

I thought for a minute, and then asked, "What was he doing downstairs?"

"He worked for Brunner as some kind of clerk."

"Well then it's pretty certain that he was sent up here as Brunner's spy. And you'd better tell everyone to be careful as to what they say when our little spy is around. Shit, I can't believe it. I'm away for two weeks and the bastards send a spy into the unit." I shook my head in disbelief, and as Gina was leaving said, "Oh, by the way, what's the kid's name?"

"Tom Quinn—I think he went to college out in Ohio with one of Brunner's sons."

When Gina left, I got up from my desk and walked over to the window. It had begun to drizzle, making the day even gloomier than it had been. As I stood looking out at the gray November day, I thought about the conversation with Gina. Susan had carried out our plan and had called in saying that she was sick, pretending to be in Indiana. We had decided that people might get suspicious if we both came back to the office on the same day, and our plan seemed to have worked.

I was also interested in this money transfer system that Susan had told me about in Lugano and that Gina was utilizing this morning. I felt that I would have to learn more about it, and smiled to myself as I wondered if there was any way that I could make use of it in the future.

It was the Quinn thing that really bothered me though. As far as I was concerned, there could be no doubt at all as to Sam Brunner's motivation in transferring Quinn up to the trading desk. Brunner had a number of so-called bright young men working for him, and it occurred to me that maybe Brunner had some kind of a thing going for handsome young guys. But I immediately dismissed that thought—at fifty-five and with three children, Brunner was simply not the type. No, without having met Quinn, I was pretty sure that Brunner was primarily interested in having someone in the investment management unit that would keep Brunner advised as to what was going on. So telling Gina that the young man was a "spy" was almost literally true.

The more I thought about it though, the more I became convinced that I should not make an issue of the transfer. Brunner probably expected me to do that, but I realized that I would not get the decision reversed. No, I thought, it would be better for me to try to use the young man—to get him to pass on to Brunner what I wanted Brunner to hear. And maybe I could even find a way to set the kid up and make him the fall guy for some problem—preferably a problem that costs the firm some money. What I did in transferring securities into the Fund was done entirely to help the company, and if Brunner hadn't been such a hard nose, Lenny Morris probably would have let the whole thing pass. So I'm going to have to see if there isn't a way to use this guy Quinn to try to even the scales with Brunner. I hated to admit it to myself, but getting even had become an important motivating factor for me.

As I continued to stand looking down on the street, and watching the people hurrying along trying to protect themselves with their umbrellas, my mind turned back to Gina and to Susan. I couldn't imagine two more different young women. Gina was dark-haired, had a great figure, knew that she was very attractive, and almost exuded self-confidence and even a certain defiance. She knew exactly who she was and what she was willing to do, and she would never compromise just to try to please her boss.

Susan, on the other hand, just missed being a truly beautiful blonde. She had all the right features, but she was someone who would always have a weight problem. She fought it constantly, and when she was winning the battle, she looked great, but too often she appeared to be losing the battle and the weight showed, particularly in her hips. As opposed to Gina, I knew that Susan would do just about anything that I wanted. She had shown that at work, and she was clearly the most satisfying sex partner that I ever had.

But I had to admit to myself that I was getting somewhat bored with our affair. As the drizzle turned into a more steady rain and wind whipped it against the windowpane, I wondered where my relationship with Susan would go now. I had understood for many years that what always attracted me in women was the unattainable, the chase. Gina was unattainable, and the thought of going after her was exciting; Susan was all too attainable, and I knew that was the reason our relationship was starting to bore me. I also knew that that had been, and perhaps still was, the fascination with Ingrid—even when we were married, I never felt that we were as united as a man and wife should be; she was always there, just beyond my reach.

What had disturbed me the most about the meeting with Ingrid in Zürich was the fact that she was now farther away than ever. She had Paulo now, and I could no longer dream that one day we might be together again. I probably should not have used the f-word when I accused her of paying Paulo for sex, but the more I thought about it, the more convinced I became that I was right, and she had done exactly that. As I turned away from the window, I grimaced as I thought of the three women in my life and the rather bleak prospect that I might end up spending most of the rest of my life with the one that I found the least exciting.

Back at my desk, I called Chuck Lindsay, the head trader, and asked Chuck to come into my office. When the young man arrived, he asked about my vacation and after we had talked about that for a couple of minutes, I asked, "What have you got this young guy Quinn doing?"

"Well, not much. I'm not sure that he knows very much, so I just want him to sit at the desk and kind of listen to what's going on until he gets the hang of things."

"I'm sure you're right, Chuck, and if it were up to me I'd want to go pretty slow too. But Sam Brunner seems to want to give Quinn some responsibility right away, so I think maybe we should make him responsible for trading Government bonds."

"Mr. Wenner, I really don't think we should do that. I mean there's usually no big price swings in Govvies, but we trade in pretty big blocks, and if Tom makes a mistake, it could be a big one. Y'know, I guess maybe before you got here, one of the guys at the desk bought some bonds he should of been selling, and it cost the company a real bundle."

"I know . . . I know. But if you give him pretty strict rules he won't be able to screw up too badly. And Chuck, we really don't have much choice—this is really Brunner's decision."

"Well, I'm the head trader, and if something goes wrong, I don't want people blaming me for it."

"OK, and I don't want to be blamed either, so write out some rules as to how the guy is supposed to trade, and then if he makes a mistake neither one of us will be blamed. I'm also going to make sure that Brunner specifically approves the whole arrangement." As Lindsay got up to leave the office, I added, "But one more thing—you're still the trader for the Fund, and we sometimes hold our cash reserves in Government bonds or T-Bills. I don't want Quinn messing up the Fund, so you still do all the trades on the Fund, and that includes Govvies. OK?"

Chapter XXVI

Several days later, I was at my desk when I became aware of the phone ringing on Susan's desk, just outside my office. If Susan were away from her desk, someone else would usually pick it up, but this time the phone just went on ringing. Since my phone had access to Susan's phone lines, all I had to do was to punch the flashing button on the phone on my desk to answer the call.

When I answered, a very rough voice asked, "Is this Morris, Brunner?"

"Yes."

"Well, this is the Operations Department at R.W. Pressprich. I been tryin' to get someone to talk to at your place all morning, 'n I keep gettin' a run-around."

I was inclined either to hang up or to try to transfer him to our own Operations Department, but finally asked, "What seems to be the problem?"

"You guys took over an account for some foreigner named Antonelli, or something like that. You know anything about that?"

I knew that this was a very wealthy Italian, now living in Switzerland, and he had been someone that I had been trying to get as a client. "Yes, I know Mr. Antonelli. What about it?"

"Well, he had his account here at Pressprich, y'know, and we got instructions to transfer all his securities to you, guys."

I immediately realized that instead of opening an investment management account, Antonelli must have opened a brokerage account with Morris, Brunner. There was always internal fighting between the two groups at the firm, as each group tried to convince the client either to have a discretionary investment management account on the one hand, or a simple trading account with the brokerage unit on the other. I was irritated to learn that he had opened a brokerage account and asked, "Was there any problem with the instructions?"

"Yeah, the guy only told us to transfer all the stocks, but he didn't say nothin' about the cash."

"But if he's transferring the account, he must have wanted the cash transferred too."

"That's the trouble. The instructions say to transfer the stocks, 'n then he lists all the stocks. But he don't say nothin' about any cash."

"How much cash is there."

"Well, there was about $95,000 when he transferred the stocks, but you guys gotta be pretty slow about gettin' all those stocks re-registered, 'cause we keep on gettin' more dividends in, so we got over $100,000 now."

I was impressed with the amount, and glad to get the news about the oversight. It was nice to know that the Operations Department was not always perfect, and it was also interesting that $100,000 was sitting there unclaimed. "I tell you what. Give me your name and phone number, and I'll get back to you in the next day or so with instructions."

"OK, good, but they gotta be signed by this guy Antonelli himself."

I got up from my desk and walked over to the window, which was my favorite place to go when I wanted to think about something. New York was having one of those prolonged rainy periods that settle in so often in the fall, and the day was again dark and gloomy, as it had been almost every day since I had returned from Switzerland. I stood at the window looking down on all the umbrellas hiding the people hurrying along on the street below, and I could not help being intrigued by the thought of all that money sitting there unclaimed. This seemed to me to be very similar to the situation that Ingrid and I confronted at Schleswigbank; the money had again suddenly fallen in front of me and all I had to do was to stake a claim for it, and it would be mine. I would not be going out of my way to embezzle money; I was merely responding to a situation that had presented itself.

I spent the rest of the day trying to decide whether or not it would be worth it to go down the road of another escapade such as the one in Switzerland ten years before. It had seemed a momentous decision when Ingrid had convinced me to take that money ten years ago at Schleswigbank; and my deliberations about the new opportunity continued all through the night. I thought long and hard, as I sat in my apartment alone with a scotch on the rocks, as to whether or not I should try another embezzlement. But sometime during the night, I decided to take the first steps. I couldn't help feeling that there was a certain challenge and a certain thrill associated with doing something as daring as this. And, of course, I had every confidence that I was smarter than the people at Morris, Brunner, and there was no question that I could pull it off successfully.

Therefore, the next day I asked Susan to see if there was an Antonelli file in the brokerage group. Susan had been involved when we had originally made a presentation to Signor Antonelli, and as soon as I asked her to get that file, she told me she understood why I wanted it—to see if I could find out how the brokerage group had gotten the account away from investment management. Susan had no problem going over to the brokerage area and getting the file, and she brought it to me right away. After Susan left, I looked through the file to find something that had been signed by the client so that I could get a sample of his handwriting. That evening, after everyone had left, I went over to the brokerage department to use a typewriter and wrote out a letter to R. W. Pressprich instructing them to continue to hold the cash that was left in the Antonelli account. The letter said that they should hold all statements for the next couple of months until permanent mailing instructions could be decided upon. Forging Antonelli's name was not hard, and I was really pleased with myself when I went home that evening after mailing the letter.

I again sat for a long time that night thinking of what I was now going to be engaged in, slowly sipping a glass of Chevas Regal. I remembered the agonizing that had accompanied the decision that Ingrid and I had made to start the embezzlement ten years previously in Zürich, and I wondered why the move this time had seemed so much easier. Were the chances of getting caught so much less this time than they had been at Schleswigbank? As far as I could tell, the chances were not much different. If it hadn't been for Herr Reinsdorf's daughter and the stupid mistake I had made at the bank in Schaffhausen in claiming to be a relative, Ingrid and I almost certainly would have gotten away with it. In this case, no one seemed to notice that almost $100,000 had been left at the brokerage firm, and as more time passed, it would become less and less likely that anyone would. Signor Antonelli was clearly a very wealthy man, and he apparently did not have an accountant or anyone else keeping records of things like this for him, or if he did, the accountant was not very competent.

Still, I wondered why I felt absolutely no guilt at again trying to embezzle funds from one of my employer's clients, and I had to face the fact that that was exactly what I was doing in sending that letter to Pressprich. I thought that maybe the soul searching that I had endured ten years previously in Zürich, in Paris, and later in New York had been due to the fact that the act that I was contemplating then was at total variance with everything I had been taught and everything that I had believed in up to that point. And then I had been risking what was clearly a very bright future at Schleswigbank, while this time, in middle age, I was only risking a job -- a job that I might lose anyway.

Now, sitting in my apartment in New York, I could see that, consciously or not, when Ingrid and I elected to take the money from Schleswigbank, I had deviated from what had been my established career path—a path that would change only rarely for me at that conservative, tradition-bound bank. But for me, once I had embezzled funds from Schleswigbank and had ultimately been exposed, my life had followed an entirely different path. But even though I had been exposed, I could never think of myself as being at fault. I remembered that night in Paris when I kept repeating that phrase to myself—"I am not a criminal". And if Ingrid and I had not made that decision ten years ago, I might still be at Schleswigbank in Zürich, and I might have had a brilliant career in that organization, perhaps even taking Dr. Hofbeck's place as managing director. That was what I had given up when I decided to go down what looked like the easy path to quick riches; that was what my mistake of ten years ago had cost me.

But I could not think of that now; there were too many other things that impelled me to try another embezzlement. The loss of the money from the bank at Küsnacht and Ingrid's part in that whole fiasco still rankled. And my feeling of being wronged by Morris, Brunner, and particularly by Sam Brunner, remained strong. In a strange way, I was able to convince myself that trying to take this money now was merely some form of compensation for the losses I had suffered in the past few weeks. It was even compensation for the life that I had been forced to live since the original embezzlement went awry ten years ago.

And I had to smile to myself as I thought of the excitement of the whole challenge right now. I remembered the excitement I had felt when I had opened the account at Schaffhausen and the 250,000 francs had been transferred to my new account at that bank. It had even been exhilarating when I had had that final argument with Elsa Wilhelm—the argument that had led to my exposure. If I had made mistakes at Schleswigbank, I felt sure that I could avoid those mistakes now. It was almost sexual, as my whole nervous system seemed to tingle with the thought of this new challenge. And together with the excitement, there was a feeling of real superiority. I knew that I was smarter than anyone else at Morris, Brunner, and I felt confident that I could outwit them.

There were so many elements that merged at this point that helped me rationalize what I was doing: the sense of having been wronged; the desire to get even with Morris, Brunner; the challenge of trying to commit a better embezzlement than the first time; and the sincere belief that I was smarter than anyone else at the company and that I could get away with it. As I continued to sit thinking about this new challenge and sipping my Chevas Regal, I realized that I was getting an erection. I thought of calling Susan to see if we could get together, but I knew that she would just be a distraction at that moment. As I opened my fly and reached in to take hold of my hard penis, I decided that I could take care of myself.

For the next several weeks, much of the excitement began to ebb. I thought that the money was still sitting at the Pressprich brokerage firm, but I had no way of knowing if that was, in fact, the case. I knew that I had to let some time pass before taking any further action in order to see if anyone would realize that there was a substantial amount of cash that had not been transferred to Morris, Brunner. But the waiting was becoming more and more difficult, so one day I simply called the man at Pressprich who had originally phoned me. I asked if they had as yet received instructions as to mailing the monthly statements.

The man immediately said, "Yeah, I'm really glad ya called. Our auditing department's been givin' me a hard time 'cause I ain't been mailin' out these statements. I hope ya got an address for this guy."

I assured him that I did have one, and would send it to him in the next day or two.

Choosing an address for the statements was a difficult decision for me. The statements would be addressed to Mr. Antonelli, but I could not have them sent to Morris, Brunner. I had to choose a mailing address that would permit me to pick up the statements from time to time, but an address that could not be traced back to me if anyone ever checked. It occurred to me that it was almost like giving the name and address back in Schaffhausen when I had claimed to be Herr Reinsdorf's nephew, the action that had proved to be my undoing. Having learned from that mistake, this time I would definitely be more careful. I would also see to it that the blame was pinned on someone else, if the mailing address were ever traced. My candidate for the blame was, of course, Tom Quinn. Sam Brunner had sent Quinn into my department to spy on me. What better way to get even than to use Quinn as the fall guy if something should go wrong with my plan? But what I had to get was something that I could use to identify myself as Quinn when I set up the mailing address, wherever that might be. I knew that I would have to present some identification at that time, and I finally hit upon the idea of calling the Human Resources Department, identifying myself as Quinn's boss, and asking for a new employee identification card for Quinn. I indicated that Quinn had lost his, and asked that the replacement card be sent to me so that I could give it to my employee.

A few days after receiving the card, on a Saturday morning, I tried to disguise myself by wearing the oldest clothes that I had, and I also found in my closet a New York Yankees baseball cap. I left my apartment with the cap in my pocket and walked over through Central Park to the West Side of Manhattan. The rain from earlier in the week had passed offshore, and it was a clear, crisp early December day. I enjoyed the walk through the park and, as I watched all the joggers and bicyclists, I resolved that I would have to get more exercise myself if I was going to stay in shape. I did not come to the West Side too often since, like most New Yorkers, I stayed pretty much in my own neighborhood, so I was not 100 percent sure where I should go as I reached Central Park West. But I continued west for a couple of blocks, and began to walk up and down Columbus Avenue and Amsterdam Avenue. I soon found what I was looking for—one of those stores called Mail Boxes Etc. that takes care of mailing packages and that also has mail boxes for rent.

Before going in to the store, I found a drugstore on Amsterdam and 67th Street and was able to buy a pair of glasses that had a heavy, dark frame. With the old clothes, the baseball cap, which I put on with the peak to the back, the way the "cool" young people did, and the glasses, I felt pretty sure that no one would be able to identify me if that question ever came up later. I went back to the store, and filled out the application for a mailbox, using Tom Quinn's name and a fictitious address. I showed Quinn's identification card and paid cash for the first three months rental fee. To insure that my fingerprints did not get on the application, I kept a glove on my left hand and held the application with that hand. I also tried to disguise my handwriting by printing everything and by trying to imitate Quinn's printing style as much as possible.

When I left the store with a key to the mailbox and an address for the statements from Pressprich, I felt a great sense of accomplishment. As I added the mailbox key to my key chain, I was sure that this time I had avoided any possible mistakes, such as those I had made ten years previously. I knew that I could have simply directed Pressprich to transfer the $100,000 to an account in Switzerland or some other tax haven, but I wanted more. I was convinced that I could get more money out of Morris, Brunner, and perhaps over time it might be two or three times the amount that was in the account now. But, more importantly, there was also the challenge of getting away with a complex, multi-faceted embezzlement, and the account at Pressprich would be a vehicle for taking up that challenge.

Now I only had one more thing to do, and that was to open an account in one of the Caribbean tax havens. The idea of opening an account in my own name was out of the question, even though places like the Cayman Islands and the Turks and Caicos Islands had bank secrecy laws similar to Switzerland's. I decided that one of the best approaches would be to create a holding company in one of the islands—and I decided upon the Turks and Caicos Islands for this—and have that holding company, in turn, create a checking account on Grand Cayman Island. That way, when the time came to get some of the money, all I would have to do would be to travel to Grand Cayman to withdraw or transfer funds since air connections to Grand Cayman were relatively good, compared to Turks and Caicos.

Rather than travel down to the Caribbean, I decided to handle the whole matter by phone. When I was in my office the next Monday, I closed the door to ensure complete privacy, and then looked through my collection of calling cards for a woman whom I had met two or three years previously. There had been an international estate planning conference at the New York Hilton, and I had bought a couple of drinks for her one evening. I finally found her card— Louise Bowles, who worked as a paralegal in the International Tax Planning Department of Baker, McKenzie, one of the largest law firms in the world. I immediately called, and after renewing acquaintances with her, I asked her which firm Baker, McKenzie used when setting up holding companies in the Turks and Caicos Islands. She told me that they used the Terra Nova Bank and Trust Company, and particularly a Mr. Nigel Dunster. Louise said, "You'll love working with Nigel. I think he took early retirement from some bank in London about seven or eight years ago, but he does everything you ask him to do, and does it quickly and brilliantly."

I thanked her for the information, but then said, "Louise, I can't tell you how often I've thought of calling you, but I really haven't been free to do so. Things seem to be changing, however, and I wonder if we might get together for dinner in the near future."

Louise laughed and said, "Well, I guess I'm glad you asked. For a time after that conference I wondered what I had done wrong since I never heard from you. But if things have changed for you, I would certainly love to get together."

After I hung up, I thought that Louise was one helluva lot more interesting than Susan ever was or could be. I had completely forgotten her after our meeting since I was quite involved with Susan at that time. But starting some kind of relationship with Louise would be a real added bonus to the whole embezzlement project in which I was now engaged. I would definitely plan to call her in the very near future.

I then proceeded to dial the Terra Nova Bank and Trust Company, and was quickly connected to Mr. Dunster. "Mr. Dunster, this is Samuel Brunner, of Morris, Brunner & Company in New York. As you may know, we are a brokerage firm and a member of the New York Stock Exchange."

"Yes, I have heard of your firm. How may I help you?"

"Well, I understand that one of the services your bank offers is to form holding companies for investors."

"Yes, that's one of our services."

"Good, one of our clients needs a holding company right away, so could you immediately form one—perhaps just use a shelf company, since the name doesn't make any difference."

"Of course."

"And I understand that the bank will provide the officers and directors of the company."

"That's correct."

"The owner of the company will be a Signor Giovanni Antonelli, and you should send the stock certificate to Mr. Antonelli at his address here in New York."

"There should be no problem with that, as long as I get the correct spelling of his name."

I provided the spelling, and then added, "Would you also open a checking account at a bank on Grand Cayman Island? Mr. Antonelli goes there from time to time, and wants to be able to draw cash out when he's gambling at the Casino."

"We will have to send you the signature cards for Mr. Antonelli to sign. To what address should those be sent?"

I then gave him the address of the post office box I had opened at Mail Boxes Etc. on the West Side and then asked, "Do you need any further information on Mr. Antonelli?"

"It would be helpful if we could get a copy of his passport. We have to be certain that he's not an American citizen, since the American tax authorities are always on us about opening accounts for Americans who are trying to avoid US taxes. I've never understood why the United States can't be more like England—if English people earn money offshore, the tax authorities couldn't be less interested."

"Well, we all hope that the US will become that sophisticated at some time in the future. But let me assure you that this is an Italian citizen, and my understanding is that while there might be tax laws in Italy, no Italian would ever consider paying taxes, particularly on money he earned overseas."

"It's a lovely approach that the Italians take. I think when I retire from here in a few years, I may go to live in Tuscany myself. Now is there anything else we can do for you?"

"We will need the name of the company and all of the information on the account in Grand Cayman. We will also need appropriate resolutions of the

Board of the new holding company permitting Mr. Antonelli to withdraw funds from the Grand Cayman account."

"He will have signature authority on the account, so that should be no problem."

"But assume that he goes to the bank, won't he have to show them something if he were to withdraw cash?"

"That's possible, yes. I'll have some resolutions prepared and be sure that the Grand Cayman bank will accept them. Mr. Antonelli can sign them when he signs the signature cards."

"Well, that seems to be everything. When might he expect to receive all these papers?"

"I should have everything for him in the next two or three days."

"Great. Oh, yes. Include your invoice when you send all the papers, and I will take care of the charges right away. And I believe it would be preferable if you sent everything to the address that I gave you for Mr. Antonelli, rather to us here at Morris, Brunner. He very much likes to feel that he is in control of everything."

"I understand perfectly. And one more thing, Mr. Brunner. Could you tell me who referred you to Terra Nova?"

I almost blurted out Louise Bowles's name, but checked myself and finally said, "I'm afraid I don't know offhand, since one of my associates got the information for me. If you really need to know I can find out and get back to you."

"No, it's not necessary. We sometimes like to give credit for referrals."

The conversation ended with the usual pleasantries, and I sat back in my chair extraordinarily pleased with myself. There would now be a Turks and Caicos company owned by Mr. Antonelli; there would be a checking account in Grand Cayman from which only Mr. Antonelli could make withdrawals; the signature cards and resolutions would be sent to the account I had established for him, and signed by me forging Antonelli's name; and in the very near future, I could begin transferring money out of the Pressprich account to Grand Cayman. And, more importantly, I could also start transferring additional money out of other accounts at Morris, Brunner to the Pressprich account en route to Grand Cayman.

Chapter XXVII

The plan that I had decided upon was to use the money transfer system that Gina and Susan had told me about, and to transfer money from clients' accounts to the Antonelli account at R. W. Pressprich. And over the next couple of months I found a number of opportunities to do just that. I simply typed out tickets indicating that a transfer was being made to a brokerage account, either to settle a dividend claim or to correct a trading error. I did this only at night and I was particularly careful to use a typewriter in some other department. And while I knew that neither the Operations Department nor the internal auditors were likely to question these transfers, I also wanted to have a cover story available if they were questioned. Therefore, I would usually wait until most of the staff was at lunch and would then ask Tom Quinn to sign the forms, as if Quinn were the person initiating the transfer. I would then sign to approve the transfer. If anyone asked, I was fully prepared to say that Quinn had explained that a mistake needed to be corrected, and I had taken his word for it. I would have to explain why I did not fire him or move him off the trading desk if he were coming to me with all of these mistakes that needed correction. But I could easily say that Sam Brunner had moved him into my department, and there was nothing I could do about it.

Most of the transfers were relatively small, but within the next few months, as the spring of 1976 came to New York, I had managed to build the Pressprich account up to over $150,000. I knew that this was still a relatively small amount, but I could see now that the system worked, and that the transfers were not being questioned. With growing confidence, I decided that I had been fooling around with these $5,000 and $10,000 transfers long enough, and I would have to start looking for opportunities to transfer significantly bigger amounts.

An opportunity seemed to present itself in early June when Gina came into my office to tell me that one of her largest accounts, for a Mexican client, was being transferred to the Second National Bank of New York's trust company in Nassau. The Mexican was worried about confidentiality, and was concerned that the Mexican tax authorities might find out about his account in New York. The U.S. tax authorities had begun to cooperate with Mexico in identifying Mexican nationals who had accounts in the United States. The account was worth $700 million dollars, and I decided that, as with the Antonelli account, $100,000 probably would not be missed when the transfer was made. The prospects looked even better when Gina reminded me that she was taking two weeks' vacation in June, and she asked if John Grey should follow through on the transfer of the Mexican's account while she was away. I said, "Gina, there's not really very much to follow up. Operations will handle the transfer, so I don't see any need for Grey to be involved. If any questions come up, I can handle them myself. As you know, I'm not terribly busy these days since I'm buying very few stocks in the Fund with the European markets as high as they are."

"I know, Kurt, but we're still going to be giving them investment advice, since the guy's just transferring custody down to Nassau, and I don't want anything to get messed up while I'm away."

"Don't worry about it, Gina. I'll make sure that everything goes OK."

After Gina left, I got all the records on the Mexican's account and studied the transactions for the past year. I found a series of transactions that had occurred three months previously, on March 10, and that involved the purchase of a $25,000,000 time deposit, using the proceeds from some stock sales that the client had directed. I therefore prepared a form transferring $104,763.37 to the Pressprich account, describing the transfer as the correction of a trading error that occurred on the March 10 date. In this case, I simply traced Quinn's initials onto the form since I was sure that Quinn would question such a large transfer. Tracing the young man's initials was clearly the simplest way to accomplish the transfer.

The transfer went through and, since I kept the Mexican's account on my desk while Gina was away, a few days later I saw the transfer recorded in the latest computerized account update. I could not believe how simple it had been, and I had to congratulate myself on my ability to get around the controls at Morris, Brunner. In point of fact, I came to the conclusion that there were no controls in the entire company; money comes and goes and no one has the least idea what's going on. However, I decided that I should not do anything further, at least for the time being, since I did not want anyone who might question this transfer to begin looking for some kind of pattern.

But while I waited, I started to think about transferring some of the money from the Pressprich account to the account in Grand Cayman. Several months earlier I had received at Mail Boxes Etc. the information from Nigel Dunster as to the checking account for the Turks and Caicos company that the Terra Nova Bank and Trust Company had established in Grand Cayman. I had signed the signature cards, forging Mr. Antonelli's signature, and returned them to Mr. Dunster, for forwarding on to the Grand Cayman bank. So, since everything was in order, I decided that it would be well to fund that account right away. Accordingly, I prepared a letter of instructions from Mr. Antonelli to Pressprich, ordering them to transfer $100,000 to the Grand Cayman account. I then sat back and waited for all the confirming statements to come to the post office box showing that the transfer had actually taken place.

What I ultimately wanted to do was to get the money out of the Grand Cayman account in the form of cash, and then deposit the cash in a safe deposit box. My experience with the embezzlement from Schleswigbank convinced me that having cash in a safe deposit box was the safest approach. I would have left for Grand Cayman shortly after the initial transfer was made, but it was now getting into July and, while the weather in New York was almost unbearable, I knew that it would also be hot and humid in the Caribbean. However, I did not think that there was any hurry in getting the transfer done, even though I would like to begin using some of the cash as soon as possible. I started to think of getting a car, perhaps a bigger apartment, and definitely trying to follow up with Louise Bowles. Waiting until September or October to transfer the money and to begin to enjoy it was a minor inconvenience and one that did not bother me to any extent.

When Gina returned from her vacation she had asked to see the Mexican's account and I had given her those files. Several days later, she came into my office and sat down in the chair in front of my desk. I could see that she was holding a file, and I guessed that it was for the Mexican's account. Gina said, "I have a question for you."

I could tell by the tone of her voice that she was being somewhat confrontational, but I merely said, "Shoot."

"What was the transfer out of the Mexican's account for over $100,000 that took place while I was away."

I said, "I assume you read the ledger entry. Doesn't that explain it?"

"Well, it says that there was a trading error back in March."

There was a pause while I looked directly at her, and I finally said, "OK, so what's your question?"

"It's my account, you know, and I sure didn't know that there was any kind of error when all those trades took place."

"Gina, no one's blaming you for anything. All those trades went through the trading desk, and somehow Quinn was the guy that entered the orders and he screwed up. When Operations and the auditors or someone checked up on the entries, they discovered the error—or maybe the brokerage firm discovered it—I don't really remember. Anyway, the customer's account got over a hundred thousand dollars that it shouldn't have had. So we had to put through the correcting entry. Quinn filled the thing out and I approved it."

"Why do we keep that idiot around? I'd hate to lose the investment management of this account now that the custody is being transferred down to Nassau, and it really looks bad for us to make mistakes like this. In fact, if it was our mistake, shouldn't the company eat the loss, instead of sticking it to the client?"

"Can you imagine what would happen if I put in a loss ticket for over $100,000? Brunner would be all over us, and after what we've been through in the last year, I don't think I need that kind of problem right now."

Gina was clearly getting more and more upset, and she shot back at me, "Well, tell Brunner that it was his boy that made the mistake. If he hadn't sent that kid up here, and if it had been one of the other guys at the trading desk that handled the trades, the mistake would never have happened."

"You're probably right, Gina, but what's done is done, so let's just leave it for now. If it happens again, then we'll have to stick it to Brunner."

Gina got up and walked toward the door, turning again to me to say, "I'm going to go and tell that little jerk Quinn what I think of him. My client loses over $100,000 because of him, and he doesn't even get a slap on the wrist."

"Gina, come back here and sit down." I waited while she did so. "Look, in the first place our client was not entitled to the $100,000. The mistake was in giving his account more sale proceeds than his account should have received. So don't go around screaming that our client was somehow screwed because that just isn't true. The correction was a proper correction, and the account got what it should have had and the broker got what it deserved. And no puns, Gina, we all know what the brokers deserve—they usually rape us so they deserve nothing, but that's not the point. The point is that everything is now in balance. As to Quinn please don't—in fact I'm ordering you—don't say anything to him about this. We had it all out while you were away, and he's not a bad kid. I think Brunner's trying to make use of him, but I don't want to make it any worse for him than it already is. So let's just forget it, OK?"

Gina said nothing for a couple of minutes and sat looking out the window, avoiding my eyes. She finally turned back to me and said, "You really surprise me at times. Here you could really ream that kid and probably show up Brunner at the same time, but you go all soft and decide to take pity on him. I always tell Susan that she's wrong when she tells me what a soft-hearted guy you are. I keep telling her you have no more emotions than a piece of cold steel—and probably German steel at that. But maybe I'm wrong,. I sure hope so. OK, I won't say anything to anybody about this. But it better not happen again."

As soon as Gina left my office, I had to get up and walk over to the window. I felt absolutely great. I knew that my handling of Gina's questions had been masterful, and I felt that I had boxed her in with logic and emotion so that there was no chance that she would express her doubts about the transfer to anyone else. I crossed my arms across my chest and almost hugged myself, trying to suppress my elation at this confrontation. I felt that this one had been child's play compared to the final fight with Elsa Wilhelm back in Zürich, but it had been a challenge and I knew that I had surmounted that challenge. This time there would be no Dr. Schnabel who would follow up on Gina's suspicions and undermine my story. I felt totally secure; I knew that I was safe.

The coming weekend was the Fourth of July, and Susan and I had planned to go away together. Susan wanted to go to Cape Cod, or at least get a place in the Hamptons, but I decided that we should go to Atlantic City. With all the money sitting in the account at Pressprich, I could afford to risk a fair amount of my savings at the gaming tables. Susan was not happy about the decision, but

I really gave her no choice. As a result, we spent three days in Atlantic City, and I was at the crap tables practically the whole time. Susan was amazed that I would risk literally thousands of dollars on a couple of throws of the dice, but I did that repeatedly throughout the weekend. At times, I was thousands of dollars ahead, and at other times I was behind by the same amount. But when the weekend was finally over, I had won close to $3,000, and I was almost walking on air as we left the casino. Everything was going my way, and I couldn't even lose at the crap tables. I could only think that the gods were finally smiling on me.

A few days after returning to work, Gina came into my office. "Excuse me, Kurt, but maybe you could help me." I was working on an investment report and was not pleased at the interruption. "The bank down in Nassau is on the phone, and they can't understand that $100,000 charge to the Mexican's account. I tried to tell them that there had been some mistakes on the stock trades that took place back in March, but this guy from Nassau says that they have checked all the trades, and the original entries were correct. So I don't know what to tell them."

I looked down and thought for a moment, realizing that I should have anticipated questions coming from the trust company in Nassau. They probably had a bunch of clerks down there who had nothing better to do than to go back over new accounts trying to find some kind of error by the previous custodian. "Let me speak to the guy, Gina. Transfer his call in here. I can probably straighten him out."

When the call was transferred, I asked, "What seems to be the problem?" The trust officer explained that they had reviewed all the transactions, and had checked the market prices on that day, and they could not understand why there had been the need for a correction. I said, "Well, I don't know why you were checking the market prices. The error had nothing to do with the stock sales. I can't believe that someone told you that." The trust officer replied that that was precisely what he had been told by Gina.

I laughed and said, "Well, I'm afraid that she just didn't understand. You know Gina was my secretary, and I'm not sure that she really understands investments all that well. No, the error was in the purchase of the $25,000,000 time deposit. There was about $104,000 of accrued interest that should have been paid when that TD was bought, and the selling institution claimed the back interest. Our Operations Department should have computed that interest when the TD was purchased, but it apparently failed to do so. I hope that this explains what happened."

The trust officer appeared to accept my explanation, and I then said, "But I am glad to hear that you checked all the stock transactions, and that they all fell within the trading range for the day. I'm confident that our trading desk does a good job, but it's nice to get outside confirmation of that fact. Actually, if you could send me a copy of your study, I'd like to give it to my boss to show him just how good a job out traders are doing."

When that conversation was over, I felt a little shaken, but continued to feel that the situation was under control, and really felt proud of myself for asking for a copy of that report. I thought that that had been a nice touch. However, I received another blow a minute later when Gina came back in.

Looking at me with little attempt to conceal her irritation, she said, "First of all, thanks for stabbing me in the back. But more importantly, when did we start buying TD's from a brokerage firm? You know perfectly well that we only buy them from banks. To give Nassau a totally different explanation than you gave me before—that sounds like you're trying to cover something up. I think there's gotta be something fishy about that whole transfer and I think it's about time that you started to level with me."

I realized at once that she had been listening in on the other line while I talked to Nassau—the bitch. This was getting serious. I looked at her for a long time trying to decide what to say to her, and finally said, "Close the door and sit down." When she had done that, I said, "Now you listen to me. I told you before that you were to forget about this thing, and that you were not to talk about it with anyone. Here you are listening in on my phone conversations, questioning my judgment, arguing with my decisions. Who the hell do you think you are? You work for me; you do what I tell you to do; it's not up to you to make decisions about what goes on in this department."

There was another long pause, during which time Gina remained silent, but was clearly irritated by what I had said. So I then leaned forward and said to her slowly and deliberately, "Now I want you to listen to me and to listen to me good. I don't want to hear another word from you about that transfer. It's none of your fucking business. Ya got that? It's none of your fucking business. If you so much as think about this again, you're going to find yourself out on the street without a job, and with no hope of getting a job. I'll see to it that you're blackballed from every possible job on the Eastern seaboard of the United States. The only thing you'll be able to do is to take your wetback parents and go back to Mexico. Ya got that now?"

When Gina said nothing, I continued, "I want you to tell me that you're going to forget this whole thing and that I'm not going to hear any more about it."

She looked at me, and if looks could have killed, I would have died on the spot. But I could see that she was shaken by what I had said. My comment about her parents had been a shot in the dark, but looking at her reaction I realized that I was right—her parents were in the U.S. illegally. And I was able to convince myself that if it came to my word against hers, very few people would believe her. On top of everything else, I could see that I had actually frightened her; she must have been afraid that if she kept arguing with me, I might resort to violence.

She finally broke the silence by saying, "OK, I'm sorry; I guess my imagination was running away with things. I won't say another word to anyone."

I replied, "OK and if Nassau calls again, all calls come to me."

When Gina left my office, I got up and closed the door behind her. I leaned against the door for several minutes, trying to get my nerves under control, and then walked over to my favorite position by the window from which I could watch the traffic on the street below. I had never expected that I would have to resort to blatant threats to keep those illegal transfers hidden, and I immediately realized that such threats could only keep a lid on things in the short term. Hopefully, I had scared Gina enough so that she would not talk to anyone about her suspicions, but I could not be sure of that. At some point, I was going to have to get her out of the office, and I would have to do that without causing her to tell anyone what she knew or what she suspected. I did not know how I was going to do that, but I would have to think of something. In the meantime, I realized that I needed to consider a fallback position, and I began to think that it might be best to move all of that money out of the Pressprich account to the Grand Cayman bank account. Therefore, that night I prepared another letter of instructions to Pressprich, directing them to transfer all but $10,000 to the Turks and Caicos account, so that I could subsequently transfer everything in that account to Grand Cayman.

While everything appeared outwardly calm, there was an unnatural tension in the office for the next few days. Gina completely avoided speaking to me, and I noticed that virtually everyone else, except Susan, stopped talking and turned away whenever I walked by. My concern grew that Gina had told people about the transfer, but I had no way of finding out what the situation actually was. I asked Susan, as casually as I could, if everything in the office was OK, and she indicated that, as far as she knew, everything was fine. I realized that I was becoming almost paranoid, and I felt that the pressure of the situation was becoming unbearable. The situation finally became so difficult for me that I went to my doctor and obtained a prescription for tranquilizers so that I could appear under control as I tried to get through the day.

But the situation in the office continued to go downhill and two days later there was another blow. Sam Brunner called me to his office, and after a few preliminaries said, "Kurt, I hear that things aren't going too well in your department. I don't really know what the problem might be, but I'm told that a number of people who work for you are thinking of quitting. I know that you and I have had our differences, and I'm not trying to undermine your authority in any way. All I want to do is to find out what's going on and why there seems to be this dissatisfaction. You know, we're pretty proud of the way we treat people here at Morris, Brunner and I feel I have an obligation to look into things when there seems to be problems. So what I'm planning to do is to talk with each one of your people individually to see if I can find out what's going on. I assume you have no objection to my doing that."

I held my breath for a second, and then forced a smile. Although it killed me to do it, I said, "Sam, I have no objection at all. I can assure you that the people in my department are as happy as clams. If there is a problem, I don't know anything about it. Certainly, no one has said anything to me. So if you can find out anything, particularly if I'm somehow at fault, please let me know."

After exchanging a few pleasantries with Sam, I got up to go, but at the door I turned and said, "I'm only guessing, but I assume that Quinn is the one that's complaining to you, and I can only tell you that his work has not been at all satisfactory, and you may want to consider the source of the complaints." I know that that remark did not go over very well with Brunner and I probably should not have said it. Brunner replied rather coldly, "I'll do just that."

When I got back to my office, I closed the door and took my usual position at the window to stand staring at the crowds on the street below. It was a hot, August day, and the crowds moved more slowly. I could tell that everyone was dressed very casually, and I watched the people on the street, trying not to think of what had just happened. For several minutes I tried to concentrate on the skimpy, tight-fitting outfits worn by so many of the women. I thought of going down to the street just so I could get a better view of all these attractive New York women who were passing by. One of the things I loved about New York was the fact that during the summer practically every young woman who had attractive breasts wore a tight-fitting top of some kind to show them to their best advantage. I permitted myself to gaze down on the street thinking about this for the next several minutes.

But I had to consider what Brunner had just said, and in view of that discussion I realized that things were getting serious. I had no idea what Gina might say to Brunner, but there was certainly a good chance that she would tell Brunner about her suspicions concerning the money transfer. Under the circumstances, I knew that I had to do whatever was necessary so that I could hold on to the money that I had embezzled. And that meant that I would have to start transferring all that money out of the Grand Cayman account and into a safe deposit box as soon as possible. And the only way I could do that was to go down to Grand Cayman and take the risk that was involved of going into the bank and pretending to be Signor Antonelli. I had all the necessary papers; I had signed and returned the signature cards for the bank account; the Terra Nova Bank and Trust Company had provided me with the necessary resolutions authorizing Signor Antonelli to withdraw money from the corporate account; there might be the need for some article of personal identification; but the details had all been taken care of. All that I had to do now was to get there.

I realized that I could not fly to Grand Cayman, since flying under an assumed name would be difficult if not impossible, and even flying to Florida could be dangerous. If the police started to investigate, the first thing they would do would be to check airline passenger lists. I briefly considered taking the train or even driving down to Florida myself, but since I did not own a car, I would have to rent one and could only do that with a valid driver's license and a credit card, so there would be no way that such a trip could be hidden. Driving also ran the risk of my getting a speeding ticket somewhere along the way, and that was not a risk that I was willing to take.

So I finally decided that the best way of getting to Florida would be to take the bus. It was completely anonymous—I wouldn't have to give my name when I bought the ticket—and it would probably even be faster than driving since I was sure that they changed drivers and the bus kept going day and night. I could wear my oldest, shabbiest clothes for the bus ride, but change into my best and most fashionable suit to appear as Signor Antonelli at the Grand Cayman bank. And so the bus ride was it. This was Thursday and I decided that I had to leave Friday morning to get to southern Florida by Saturday evening. That would give me all day Sunday to find a charter service to fly me over to Grand Cayman on Monday morning.

I then called Susan and asked her to come into my office. When she sat down, I said, "Susan, I'm sure you know that I haven't really been myself lately. I don't know what the problem is, but my nerves seem to be shot. I really think that it must be this place—I keep having the feeling that Sam Brunner is out to get me, and I seem to be getting paranoid, or something. I really felt so great when you and I were in Europe last year, but I feel that I've been going downhill ever since we got back."

I paused, and Susan said, "I'm glad you're finally facing up to it, because it seems to me that something's been bothering you for quite some time."

"I know it. I talked with my doctor the other day, and he thinks that I just ought to stay home and rest for a few days, so that's what I'm going to do. I would really appreciate it if you would cover for me—just tell anyone who asks that I'm at home resting, but hope to be back in a day or two. I'll call in and check my messages here, and, since I'm not going to be answering my phone at home either, I'll check my messages a couple of times each day. Do you think you could do that?"

"Of course I could. I think it's a great idea. You've got to get back in shape pretty quick before Brunner finds an excuse to start making changes."

"I'm sure he's looking for an excuse. You've heard about his decision to start talking with everyone in our division?"

"Yes, I really thinks it's terrible, but I can imagine why he's doing it—he's just jealous of you and he's trying to get something on you so he can undermine you. It's all politics, and he's got people like Quinn and maybe even Gina feeding him anything they can think up."

I smiled and said, "I think you're probably right, and thanks for being so supportive. But he does have the right to talk to anyone he wants to, so let's just hope that they're not too hard on me. In any event, I think it's better if I stay away while those interviews are taking place. I can't do anything about what Gina and Quinn are going to say, so all I can do is sit back and see what happens. If Brunner decides that he doesn't like the way I'm running the division, he might let me go, but I really don't worry about that anymore.

Susan was almost in tears as she answered, "This whole place will fall apart if they let you go."

I got up and, with my arm around her; I led Susan to the door. "I'll call you at home—probably not this weekend—but I will call next week and we can get together, and you can tell me all the dirt from the office. But I don't want to hear any of that for the next few days."

After Susan left my office I called Nigel Dunster at the Terra Nova Bank and Trust Company in the Turks and Caicos Islands. "Mr. Dunster, this is Sam Brunner from Morris, Brunner in New York."

"Yes, Mr. Brunner, what can I do for you?"

"I just wanted to alert you that Mr. Antonelli will be in Grand Cayman in the next few days, and I imagine that on Monday he is going to want to withdraw some cash from the company account."

"That should be no problem."

"You're right, it shouldn't be, particularly since he has all the papers you prepared. However, Mr. Antonelli speaks very little English and I'm concerned that if the people at the Grand Cayman bank start asking questions, he might have difficulty answering them. I don't think we could count on finding someone at the bank who speaks Italian. So I was wondering, if a problem should arise, can Mr. Antonelli call you to verify everything?"

"Absolutely, that's what we're here for. And I think I can help with the Italian, since I've been taking lessons to prepare for when I retire there."

"Oh that's right, I'd forgotten that you were going to retire to Tuscany. Well, that should be perfect then—if there is any kind of misunderstanding, I will have Mr. Antonelli, or someone from the bank, phone you.

The next morning I was at the Port Authority Bus Terminal at 42nd Street and 8th Avenue to get the 8:00 a.m. bus to Washington, D.C. In talking with Greyhound the previous day, I had discovered that there was not one bus all the way to Florida, but I would have to change in Washington, again in Charlotte, North Carolina and again in Jacksonville in order to get down to the Miami area. Dressed in faded and torn jeans and a T-shirt, I found a seat at the back of the bus that I had all to myself. As the bus headed down the New Jersey Turnpike, I was able to stretch out and actually sleep for most of the way to Philadelphia. But the bus filled up in Philly with a lot of people who were heading for Baltimore and Washington and I had to share my seat with a big, heavy woman. She and I nodded to each other, but did not speak all the way to Charlotte.

It was almost noon on Saturday when I finally arrived in Jacksonville, where there was an hour and a half wait for the bus that would take me to West Palm Beach, Ft. Lauderdale and Miami. About ten o'clock Saturday night, as the bus pulled into West Palm Beach I had had enough and I decided to get off. I knew there was an airport in West Palm Beach, and I felt that my chance of finding a charter flight at this airport was at least as good as it would be if I tried at Miami International. So I hailed a taxi at the bus depot and had the driver take me to a nearby motel. There were plenty of motels in the area and, since it was August, most of them were virtually empty. The taxi driver probably had some kind of arrangement with the one he took me to, but it had a Best Western sign on it and it looked perfectly OK.

The first thing that I did when I got to my room was to take a shower. Two full days on the bus were not only tiring, but I couldn't remember when I felt dirtier. After the shower, I sat on the bed with nothing on but a towel across my lap while I looked through the yellow pages for charter airlines. There were several listed in West Palm Beach and I decided to wait until morning to check with them. There was a restaurant adjacent to the motel and I went over to it and had a hamburger, before going back to my room and going to bed.

When I called one of the charter airlines in the morning, I pretended to be at the concierge desk of a Palm Beach hotel, calling on behalf of one of their guests. "One of our guests, a Signor Antonelli is very anxious to fly to Grand Cayman the first thing Monday morning. Would you be able to do that for him?" When I got an affirmative answer, I said, "Now Signor Antonelli is Italian and speaks very little English. He will pay you cash for the trip, which I understand will be $10,000, and you will undertake to get him there by noon. Is that agreed?" Again getting an affirmative response, I added, "And Mr. Antonelli wants to return to Palm Beach Wednesday afternoon. So you will pick him up in Grand Cayman around noon on Wednesday and bring him back to Palm Beach. He will again pay you another $10,000 fee in cash. OK?" After another agreement, I added, "I think you will find that he's a very nice guy, and you will have no problem with him. So good luck."

The next morning I went to the front desk at the motel and settled my bill and then went back to my room. I put on a new light gray, double-breasted suit that I had only recently bought in New York, and also put on the brightest and most garish tie that I owned (something I had ordered out of a catalogue by mistake). I also had large dark glasses, together with a very big white hat. I had found the hat at the bus terminal in Charleston and it looked like something that an old Southern plantation owner might have worn. There was a black band around the crown of the hat, and the entire brim was rolled up. When I put the hat and the glasses on and looked at myself in the mirror, I could not recognize myself. It was a really effective disguise.

The flight went remarkably smoothly. I was still fluent in Italian even though I had been away from Switzerland for so many years, and I made an effort to talk with the pilot as we were boarding. I used very elementary English phrases, and kept resorting to Italian that the pilot, of course, did not understand. As a result, I sat alone several seats behind the pilot for the entire trip, and there was almost no conversation between us. When the plane landed at Grand Cayman, I immediately phoned the bank, asking for the manager and telling him that I—Signor Antonelli -- would stop by within the hour.

As I walked into the bank I felt pretty confident that Sam Brunner could not know yet about the embezzlement. Even if he talked with Gina the first thing Monday morning, it would take time for them to check with Pressprich to find out where the money had gone. So I felt I was still fairly safe. Now all that

I had to do was to convince the bank to let me withdraw some of the money. Approaching the information desk, and again speaking in very broken English, I asked to see an account officer. I was referred to a Mr. Joseph Osborne, who was a very English looking young man. Osborne was quite thin, rather tall, and had a thatch of blond hair that kept falling over his forehead. Again, in a mixture of English and Italian, I tried to explain that I wanted to withdraw $150,000 in cash from the company account. I showed Osborne the papers that had been prepared by Terra Nova Bank and Trust Company that gave me signature authority on the account and authorized me to withdraw funds from the account.

As I had anticipated, the bank wanted some additional identification, but I continued to indicate that I did not understand what they wanted, and would rattle on in Italian whenever Osborne would push for Signor Antonelli's passport, or something equally specific. Finally, I gave him the name and phone number of Nigel Dunster at Terra Nova Bank and Trust Company and using mostly sign language—pointing to the phone and making a dialing motion— suggested that Osborne call him. Osborne went and consulted with the bank manager, but finally agreed to call Dunster. He spoke with Dunster for a couple of minutes, but then asked me to talk with him. Our conversation was entirely in Italian, and I could tell after a minute or two that I had completely impressed Dunster. I gave the phone back to Osborne and, as soon as the conversation was concluded, Osborne approved my withdrawal request. As I walked out of the bank with $150,000 in U.S. currency in my brief case, I realized that I had not been so elated since I had opened the account at the bank in Schaffhausen. The success of the embezzlement was now assured; all I had to do was to avoid getting caught.

I went back to the bank on both Tuesday and Wednesday and withdrew the rest of the money. I had called Susan on Tuesday night to find out how Brunner's investigation was going. Susan had reported that Brunner was only planning to start on Wednesday morning so I knew that I was safe as I visited the bank for the final time on Wednesday. Immediately after withdrawing the money, I headed for the airport and found my private plane waiting for me. Within minutes we were in the air, and I sat with a bag containing $300,000 between my legs for the flight back to West Palm Beach.

Chapter XXVIII

When I came into the office on Monday morning I knew that a major crisis would be facing me. Susan had warned me that there had been long, and apparently serious, discussions involving Gina and Quinn on Thursday and again on Friday. I immediately noticed that neither Gina, Quinn, nor Grey were at their desks on Monday morning, adding to my sense of foreboding. I had not gotten into my own office more than a few minutes when Sam Brunner's secretary called and asked me to come down to Sam's office.

When I walked into Brunner's office, I saw that another man was there, in addition to Sam. Brunner said, "Sit down. I want you to meet David Rosenberg whose law firm represents Morris, Brunner. I asked David to be here because we discovered quite a problem last week. Incidentally where were you last week?"

"I was at home. I wasn't feeling well."

"Can you prove that?"

"I beg your pardon. Do you want me to prove that I was at home or that I wasn't feeling well?"

"It's gonna be necessary that we know where you were."

"Well, I'm afraid all I can tell you is that I was at home."

"We'll get back to that. But first of all, I have to tell you that we discovered that there have been a series of illegal transfers taking place in your department."

"What are you talking about? You're not referring to those transfers between accounts that we discussed last year, are you?"

"No, I'm not talking about those. I'm talking about transfers of money out of accounts that we manage and out of the company to a brokerage firm."

I could see that Brunner was blustering and probably did not know too much about the transfers, so I simply stared at him, looking puzzled.

Brunner went on, "Well, what have you got to say about that?"

"Since I don't really understand what you're talking about, there's nothing much that I can say."

"Let me refresh your memory. We've just begun to examine all of our accounts but we've discovered a whole series of transfers to an account at R.W. Pressprich. And the transfer tickets in each case were initialed by you."

"I still don't understand what you're trying to say. Are you implying that that was my account at Pressprich and that I was stealing money from our clients? Because if that's what you're implying you're going to have a lawsuit on your hands very fast. It's a good thing you've got your lawyer here. Maybe he can keep you from getting into more trouble than you're already in."

At this point David Rosenberg spoke up and said, "Mr. Wenner, I can understand why you are upset with what Mr. Brunner has said, and I'm sure that what Sam is trying to do is to discover what exactly has gone on with these transfers."

"That's fine. But since he doesn't seem to know what has gone on with these transfers, he shouldn't be making accusations until he does know."

Getting more visibly irritated, Brunner said, "I already told you that you initialed all the fuckin' tickets."

"Sam, you know perfectly well that I initial piles of tickets every day. The tickets are brought to me by the account officer or by Gina, and I sign them. There are buy tickets, sell tickets, transfer tickets—they cover all the activities of my department. Somebody else has to originate the tickets—I only approve them. So who originated them?"

"Tom Quinn signed as the originating account officer."

"Tom Quinn? He's got no right to do that. Did you ask him what he was doing in writing up those tickets?"

"Of course we did. And he says that he only signed them when you told him to do it."

"So it's his word against mine. I have no doubt whose word you will take."

"What's that supposed to mean?"

"Quinn's been your boy from Day 1. You're not going to deny that you put him into my department without consulting me, actually doing it while I was on vacation last year. I've never understood what he was supposed to be doing there, other than to act as a spy for you."

"I'll agree with you that he's not the brightest kid around, but all the more reason that this whole scheme couldn't have been his doing—it's far too complicated or sophisticated for him."

"We don't have to assume that he was acting alone. Someone like Gina could have been helping him. And anyway, what's so complicated about transferring money to a brokerage account?"

"The money didn't stop there obviously. Pressprich tells us that the money was transferred on to a company account in the Cayman Islands."

"You never told me whose account it was at Pressprich."

"The account was in the name of Giovanni Antonelli."

"Antonelli. Well, I'm sure you know that Antonelli is a client of the firm. We tried to get him in investment management, but he opened an account in the brokerage division, which I assume is still there. Are you saying that he was a party to this whole scheme?"

"No, we're trying to figure out why the account was in his name, and who authorized the transfers to the Cayman Islands. It's gonna take us a while before we can figure this whole thing out."

"But you've already leapt to the conclusion that I'm at fault, and you're only too happy to start accusing me." Turning to the lawyer, I said, "Mr. Rosenberg, as I said before, I think you ought to caution your client before he gets himself—and his firm—into really serious trouble."

Before Rosenberg could say anything, Brunner said, "I haven't accused you of anything yet. You gotta admit that it looks pretty fishy when your initials are on all the tickets, and the only other initials are those of a fairly junior clerk. So if you know anything about this, you ought to tell us about it right now."

"I'm sorry to disappoint you, Sam, but I don't know anything about this at all."

"Well, Gina thinks you do. She pointed out a big transfer from a Mexican's account, and said that you had given a couple of different explanations for it. And you also threatened her with all kinds of stuff if she ever talked about it. So you must have known that something funny was going on."

"I have to admit that I couldn't figure out how or why that transfer was made out of the Mexican's account. It was over $100,000 and I first thought that it was to correct some trading errors. Gina was all set to go off on a rampage, yelling at Quinn on the trading desk, and causing all hell to break loose. I tried to calm her down, and was going to look into it, but actually forgot all about it, until that call came in from Nassau saying that there was no trading error. I realized then that I should have checked into it more carefully, but tried to cover up by telling Nassau it was accrued interest. The last thing I wanted was to put in a loss ticket for $100,000—you and Lenny would have had fits.

"However, it turned out that Gina was listening in to my phone call—and that got me pissed off—and then when she accused me of lying, I really got furious with her and told her to keep her nose out of the whole fuckin' business. I admit I didn't handle this right. I should have had someone check into that transfer in more detail. I guess that's all I can say. But was that transfer part of this whole scheme that you're talking about?"

"That's a nice explanation, but I don't know if I buy it. One hundred thousand dollars gets transferred out of a client's account, and you found out about it, and then instead of trying to do anything about, you try to invent explanations to cover it up. You can't tell me that that doesn't sound fishy."

David Rosenberg now spoke up and said, "Sam, at this point I think it would be a good idea if you told Kurt what's been decided."

"Yeah, I guess it is. We're not going to learn anything arguing back and forth the way we've been doing. So what we want to let you know, Kurt, is that we are going to have to carry out a complete investigation of this whole matter, and we're going to have to report it to the Government. Under the circumstances, we're going to have to put you on leave—we'll keep paying you, at least until we find out who was responsible for this whole mess. But you won't be able to come into the office."

"I assume you will be treating Quinn and Gina the same way."

"Quinn is gonna be on leave too. But why should we do that to Gina? Her name is not on any of the transfer tickets."

"If you agree that Quinn wouldn't have the brains to pull this whole thing off, the only logical person to help him would be Gina. She's always telling me how she can transfer money without going through Operations. And she's the one that brings all those tickets in for me to sign every day. And if that money is gone out of the account at—where did you say, the Cayman Islands?—I'd suggest that you look for it in Mexico."

"I'm not going to argue about that now. You and Quinn will be on leave and unless something concrete points to Gina, she's going to keep coming to work."

I actually felt relieved at the outcome of this conversation. I had always been afraid that the transfers to the Pressprich account could be discovered, and they had also traced the subsequent transfers to the Grand Cayman Bank. But so far, they hadn't been able to go any further. They still had no idea if the money was still at the Grand Cayman Bank or, if it had been withdrawn, where it had gone. I thought that my defenses were still holding. As I got up to leave, Brunner said, "You still haven't told us where you were last week."

"What do you want me to say, that I was off spending all the money I embezzled? And, by the way, how much was it anyway? Since you're accusing me of taking it, I ought to know how much I have to spend."

Rosenberg interrupted at this point and said, "I don't think that this kind of discussion gets us very far. I'll go with you to your office so you can take out any personal effects, but I'm sure you understand that you can't remove any papers belonging to the firm."

I did not bother to reply to the lawyer and, without even glancing at Brunner again, I got up and left Brunner's office. Rosenberg followed me as we took the elevator back up to the sixth floor. I felt humiliated as I walked past my staff and into my own office, followed by this middle-aged, very serious-looking man in a dark blue suit. Once inside my office, the door was closed and I picked up my attaché case, putting it on top of the desk. This was the very attaché case that I had used to take the money from the Küsnacht bank after the embezzlement from Schleswigbank over eleven years earlier. Rosenberg said, "I'm going to have to check everything that you put into the case, since we can only permit you to take your own personal papers." I was seething inwardly, but merely nodded, and took a number of papers from different drawers in the desk, showing them to Rosenberg, and then putting them into the case. Rosenberg looked around the office and commented, "There seems to be a number of personal mementos—awards, and things like that. Don't you want to take them?" I shook my head and said, "No, I have no desire for any of that crap. I don't want anything that reminds me of this place. The only thing I'm ever going to want from these people is a settlement for my libel action." Rosenberg smiled faintly, but said nothing.

I then picked up my attaché case and said, "Well, let's get it over with and get out of here." I opened the door and walked down the aisle between the desks where the staff was sitting. No one had been around in the morning, but they were all there now. Every eye was on me, as I knew that they would be, and I stopped and slowly looked at Grey, at Gina, at Susan, at the trading desk.

I then announced, "I know that many of you will be happy to hear that I have been fired and am in the process of being summarily evicted from the office. Unfortunately, I hate to disappoint you, but I have to say that I'm only too happy to get out of this place."

As I started to walk away, Rosenberg said, "I would like to say, on behalf of Morris, Brunner & Company, that Mr. Wenner has not been fired—he is merely on leave until a number of matters have been cleared up. We are conducting an investigation of some irregularities that were discovered in a number of accounts, and until that investigation is completed, Mr. Wenner and one or two other people will be asked to be on leave, but they will be fully paid during that period."

I had kept walking toward the elevators while Rosenberg talked, and I never looked back as the elevator came and I entered it for my last ride out of Morris, Brunner & Company.

I sat alone in my apartment that evening, slowly sipping a scotch on the rocks as I usually did. I remembered the night back in Zürich when my world had fallen apart and Ingrid and I had sat all night in a darkening apartment, unable to eat and unable to face the disaster that had befallen us. But eleven years had made a great deal of difference in me, and I could not conjure up the same feeling of disaster tonight, after the events at Morris, Brunner, such as Ingrid and I had felt back in Zürich. Tonight, all I could think about was how I might take advantage of the situation—how should I play my cards to get the best possible financial deal for myself. As I sat sipping my drink and thinking about the problem, the phone rang occasionally and I knew that it must be Susan, but I did not want to talk to her, so I let it go on ringing. It never occurred to me that she might be terribly upset by what had happened and really needed to talk to me. My primary concern was to extricate myself from this problem and to do so with the best monetary settlement I could arrange. I kept fantasizing about a libel suit against Sam Brunner and Morris, Brunner & Company, and I imagined that they might have to pay me millions for their false accusations. But the fantasies crashed to earth when I finally faced the fact that the accusations were not false, and I was in fact guilty of another failed embezzlement.

For the next few days I was somewhat at a loss. I had virtually nothing to do and I heard from no one. The phone had stopped ringing since Susan had apparently realized that I was not going to talk to her. I heard nothing more from either Morris, Brunner, or from their lawyer, Rosenberg. And, having nothing to do, time passed very slowly for me. I finally decided that I had to get out of my apartment and not just sit there waiting for something to happen. So I began to take walks in Central Park.

Fall was a wonderful time of the year in New York, and Central Park looked especially beautiful as the leaves turned to red, brown, and gold. Perhaps only in the spring was the Park lovelier when all the flowering trees come into bloom. But I really liked the fall—there was a coolness in the air that was tremendously welcome after the heat and humidity of the summer. And there was a certain sadness as leaves fell, flowers faded, and nature prepared for the coming winter. I had never been particularly aware of Central Park during all the years that I had lived in New York City since I had always been too busy working to take strolls in the nearby park. But now, as week followed week and nothing happened, I found Central Park a place of real solitude for me. There were very few people in the park from Monday through Friday and I soon discovered what a truly fabulous place the park was. I found that I could spend hours exploring different parts of the park and be continually amazed at the diversity and beauty of the place. I often sat by the Belvedere Fountain at the center of the park, sometimes reading, sometimes merely thinking, but always enjoying the peace that I found there. That this island of beauty and solitude could exist in the center of Manhattan constantly amazed me.

I was still taking daily walks in Central Park as November ended. It was colder now and my walks were, of necessity, faster and shorter. The Belvedere Fountain had been turned off and I no longer found it comforting to sit there. But Morris, Brunner continued to pay my salary, and I heard absolutely nothing from them or anyone else. That finally ended on the Monday after Thanksgiving, however, when I found that there was a message on my answering machine when I returned from my walk. The message was from the District Attorney's office for New York, and it requested that I come to their office in Downtown Manhattan for a meeting. They did not say what the meeting was about, and it was worded as a request, but I knew that I had no alternative but to comply with their request. And so a week later, during the first week of December 1976, I took the Lexington Avenue subway down to the Brooklyn Bridge station and walked over to the office of the U.S. Attorney for the Southern District of New York.

I had never before had a direct confrontation with law enforcement officials. I had fled Switzerland to avoid just such a confrontation and, as I entered the U.S. Courthouse on St. Anthony's Plaza, I realized that this was to be a unique experience for me. I announced myself to the security officer at the front desk and was taken to a small conference room on the third floor. A few minutes later, I was joined by two men who introduced themselves as investigators for the U.S. Attorney's Office. They sat across the table from me and one of the investigators, John Malone, started the conversation by saying, "I believe that you know about the embezzlement that took place at Morris, Brunner & Company."

I merely nodded, and the man continued. "Morris, Brunner has now filed a formal report about that embezzlement, and we have been assigned to look into it. So we would like to ask you a few questions this morning, if you have no objection. You do understand that you can have an attorney present if you wish, and I am sure you also understand that anything you say to us this morning can be used against you if you were ever to be charged in connection with this case." I replied, "Yes, I understand, but at this point I see no need for me to go to the expense of having an attorney."

The second investigator, Carl Hess, now said, "I wonder if you can explain how it happened that all of the tickets that authorized the illegal transfers of money out of Morris, Brunner were signed by you."

I said, "Well, I think that's rather obvious. People on my staff brought me tickets to initial and if they had already signed them I automatically signed them as well." I thought of expanding on that statement, but decided not to say anything else.

Hess said, "But wasn't it your job to know what was involved in the transfers that you were approving, and particularly when money was being transferred out of the company?"

"Yes, I suppose that was my job, and if I am guilty of something I am certainly guilty of negligence in trusting people like Gina and Susan and the others. Gina was the one who always brought all those tickets to me for signature and I assumed—apparently mistakenly—that she had examined them and understood what was in them and where the money was going and why it was being transferred."

Hess continued, "But it never occurred to you to question the fact that so many tickets were being originated by Tom Quinn?"

"Quite frankly I never realized that any tickets were being originated by Quinn. There were a great many tickets that were given to me every day and they represented buy orders, sells, money transfers, and I initialed all of them as a routine matter. I have to confess that I never examined any of them, and perhaps I should have, but I really didn't have the time, and I felt that Gina was handling these kinds of routine administrative matters."

Malone now said, "You live on the East Side of Manhattan, right?" I nodded agreement.

"Do you ever go over to the West Side?"

I smiled and said, "It's really quite an adventure to go over there. My routine is to go back and forth from my apartment to my office, and that's it."

"A mailing address was set up over on the West Side, at a place called Mail Boxes, Etc. Do you know anything about that?"

I shook my head to indicate that I did not.

"I think you know—Sam Brunner says he told you—that when the money was transferred out of Morris, Brunner, it went to an account at R. W. Pressprich. They had to have an address for statements and they were given this mail box number over on Amsterdam Avenue."

There was a pause, and I felt that it would be better if I said nothing, so I waited for Malone to go on.

"The people at Pressprich say that they talked with someone at Morris, Brunner asking for instructions, and they finally got them. Do you know anything about that?"

I said, "I'm afraid I don't understand. Someone at Morris, Brunner gave Pressprich instructions as to where they should send statements, and Pressprich accepted those instructions?"

"They were apparently forged instructions, purporting to come from the registered owner of the account. But getting back to that Mail Boxes place. Have you ever been there?"

"A Mail Boxes on Amsterdam Avenue? I can't remember the last time I was on Amsterdam Avenue."

"Well, we've shown the staff pictures of you and Quinn and just about everyone else in your office, and you're the only one that anyone can ever remember seeing."

I thought Malone was bluffing so I again shook my head and said, "I really don't know what to say. All I can tell you is that I have never been to one of those places on the East Side, the West Side, or Downtown. Maybe if we . . . No, I don't even want to speculate as to why the staff might have picked my picture out as looking like someone who was in their store once."

The questioning went on for about an hour, covering virtually every detail of the embezzlement. It was clear to me that the investigators knew how it was done and where the money had gone before it disappeared, but they still did not have anything concrete to pin on me. I was feeling reassured as the meeting came to an end, until Hess said, "We will definitely want to talk with you again, Mr. Wenner, so we hope you're not planning to leave New York."

I answered, "No, I have no plans to go away. With the cold weather, of course, I might like to go to Florida sometime, but there's nothing definite now." The thought of all that money in a safe deposit box in West Palm Beach passed through my mind when I thought of Florida.

Hess went on, "There are just a few more pieces of information that we're waiting for from the two banks in the Caribbean that were involved in these transfers, and as soon as we get them we will want to talk with you again. In the meantime, we would strongly advise you to retain an attorney and as soon as you do, please have him contact us."

The suggestion that I should have an attorney clearly meant that they expected to take some action against me. I had never before in my life felt so trapped as I did now, walking out of the U. S. Attorney's office on that December morning.

While the meeting with the investigators was terribly unsettling for me, another prolonged period of silence followed which was equally unsettling. Christmas was approaching and I realized that nothing would happen until after the first of the year. But this delay at least gave me time to find an attorney, as the investigators suggested, and I turned my mind to that problem. I realized that I needed a criminal lawyer but I had no idea how to find one, and there was really no one I could ask. So I simply turned to the Yellow Pages of the phone directory and found a list of criminal lawyers. I continued to believe that I had been smart enough so that the Government would never be able to pin the embezzlement on me. I might be their prime suspect, but I still felt that I had been able to outsmart them. Therefore, I did not feel that I needed a high-powered lawyer; all I needed was someone who knew the basics of criminal law. The thought of fleeing the US as I had fled Switzerland eleven years previously also crossed my mind, but I really could not think where I might go this time and I still felt that I would be able to get away.

I called a number of law offices and discovered that many of them were unable to give me an appointment until after the first of the year. But I did find one lawyer with an office down on Union Square who was able to see me, and I set up an appointment for December 15. The lawyer, Alan Greenberg, was a young man who had only recently been admitted to the bar and he was clearly eager to have me as a client. I spent an entire morning with him, giving him my version of what had transpired at Morris, Brunner. Greenberg accepted my claim of innocence and seemed very upbeat about the case. He assured me that there was really nothing for me to worry about and suggested that I enjoy the holidays since nothing would happen until January. Greenberg took the name of the two investigators and said he would contact them in the next few days.

The rest of December passed very slowly for me. I decided to call Ingrid on Christmas Eve just to have someone to talk to. She was clearly surprised at the call and our conversation ended up being very brief and very cool. I realized that Paulo, Ingrid's truck driver friend, was probably there when she got the call, and that made it difficult for her to talk. I thought of trying to arrange a dinner with Susan, but decided that that would really be too much trouble. Susan had been useful when we worked together, but I really did not feel that I wanted to go through all the explanations about why I had not returned her calls when this problem began to escalate. That would have been difficult for me, and I decided not to face that problem.

It had seemed an interminable time, but 1976 finally ended and 1977 arrived, and now I began to hope that the Morris, Brunner embezzlement would soon be settled. I started to make plans for spending some of the money by taking trips to Europe and South America, and thought about other things that I might buy for myself. I even began to think about what kind of a job I would look for once this issue was settled. I could not wait to hear from my attorney, but again several weeks passed with no news, until finally during the last week of January, Greenberg called and asked me to come down to his office. As soon as I came into the office I could see that Greenberg was a good deal more somber than when I had seen him the first time.

The lawyer started the conversation by saying, "I'm not going to beat around the bush, since I have to tell you that I have some rather bad news.

The Government has gone before a grand jury and has had you indicted for embezzlement, attempted embezzlement, and a bunch of other things."

I was visibly shaken and tried to compose myself as I said, "I thought you felt that I had nothing to worry about."

"I have not seen all the evidence that they presented to the grand jury, but there must have been more than what you told me about."

After a minute, I asked, "Will you find out what they know, or what they claim to know?"

"Oh, yes. The Government has to let me know what evidence they will be presenting if this were to go to trial."

I sighed and said, "Well, this is really a blow. What do I do next?"

"You will have to appear at an arraignment before a judge and bail will be set at that time. We will also try to decide on a trial date as well."

"Do you think that the bail will be very big? I'm not a wealthy man, despite all these allegations."

"I imagine that it should be reasonable, but as a formality they will ask that you surrender your passport."

"When will this arraignment take place?"

"As a matter of fact, it's scheduled for this afternoon. I really think it's better that we get it over with, so we can begin to concentrate on the next steps."

After agreeing to meet Greenberg at the U.S. Courthouse at 2:30 p.m., I left his office and took the subway back up to the 86th Street station. I was absolutely stunned by the indictment, since I had been confident that I would get away with the whole thing. I again thought that I should immediately flee New York, just as I had run from Zürich when the embezzlement was discovered there. But this time I could not think of any place to run to. Switzerland was out of the question, and I did not like the idea of going to Brazil or one of the countries that did not have an extradition treaty with the US. And it also occurred to me that there really was no hurry. They were going to take my US passport, but I still had the Swiss one. I had needed the US passport to get out of Switzerland, and it was ironic that now I might need the Swiss passport to flee the US, if that should ever be necessary.

The arraignment that afternoon took place fairly quickly but it was still humiliating for me. Having to be fingerprinted, having to surrender my US passport, having to listen to all the allegations against me—I hated every minute of that afternoon. But it was soon over and I was again back in my apartment alone and with nothing to do. The next two weeks were really terrible since nothing happened and the weather in New York was so bad that I was forced to stay indoors most of the time. I watched television and read to try to kill time. I discovered Trollope at the time since those long, meandering novels of his were a great way to pass hours. They were almost like soap operas— they just went on and on, without getting the reader involved. But finally my attorney called and asked that I come to his office.

Greenberg again started out with bad news. "I'm afraid that I have to tell you that the evidence that the Government has is pretty convincing. They know that you opened the account at the Terra Nova Bank in the Turks and Caicos Islands, and, what is worse, they found your fingerprints on the forms purportedly signed by Signor Antonelli in Grand Cayman."

I merely looked down for a long time and did not respond. Finally, Greenberg said, "As your lawyer, I have to recommend that I negotiate a plea agreement for you."

I looked up and said, "What would that involve."

"I think we could work a deal where you agree to plead guilty to a lesser charge—maybe attempted embezzlement—the $300,000 is returned, and you are put on probation for a year or two. There's no jail time, there's no fine, and you will be able to resume your life again in a fairly reasonable period of time."

I stood up and walked to the window—my usual escape route when I wanted to think about something. There was a rather bleak view of an areaway between two buildings, but I was still able to see the cold rain coming down. As I stood there looking out the window I knew that I had failed again. This time there would be no escape as there was from Zürich; this time I would have to take the best deal I could get. And what Alan Greenberg was suggesting was probably the best deal possible, under the circumstances.

I turned back to face the attorney, saying "Have you talked to the U. S. Attorney's Office about such a deal?"

Greenberg nodded.

"And is it something they will accept?"

"They have assured me that this case is too insignificant for them to pursue. They are going after poor Leona Helmsley at the present time, and Giuliani just dragged all those poor brokers out of their offices in handcuffs. Those are the cases that get all the publicity. So they're happy to get this one off the docket. But they need to get the money back, and you have to get at least a slap on the wrist."

I came back to my chair and sat down again facing Greenberg. I rubbed my forehead and tried to smile as I said, "I guess I'm a rotten crook. I'm not going to try to tell you why I did it, but you might as well know that I did. And since the Feds seem to know too, I guess the deal you outlined is the best we can do, so let's go with it."

As I stood up to leave, I shook hands with Greenberg and thanked him for everything and turned and left his office. I took the subway back uptown and went back to my apartment, where I immediately fixed myself another scotch on the rocks. At that point, there was nothing I could do but sit and wait until the judge passed sentence.

Pleading guilty to attempted embezzlement caused me to feel as if my life had come to an end. I had never before felt so depressed; I had never before considered myself to be such a complete failure. When the embezzlement at Schleswigbank had been discovered, it had been a terrible blow, but there was still a sense of elation at having successfully embezzled all that money which was still hidden in that safe deposit box, and there was the challenge of fleeing Switzerland and starting anew in the United States. But this time here in New York, I felt completely cut off and was convinced that I faced nothing but a totally bleak future. It was hard for me to go to sleep at night, since all I could think about was my stupidity in executing the details of both embezzlements. I kept swearing at myself for making such idiotic mistakes in both cases, mistakes that caused me to be convicted in each case. And I sat there in my apartment night after night trying to reconcile my firm conviction that I was not a criminal with the harsh reality that I had been convicted in both Swiss and American courts of being an embezzler. This was a blow to my self-esteem from which I thought I would never recover.

The following article appeared at the bottom of the seventh page of the Business Section of the <ins>New York Times</ins> on February 20, 1977

Broker Pleads Guilty to Embezzlement
Barred from Securities Business

The former head of international research at Morris, Brunner & Company pleaded guilty yesterday in Federal District Court to a charge of attempted embezzlement. Kurt Wenner of New York City was accused of trying to transfer over $300,000 from accounts at Morris, Brunner to an account at a tax haven in the Caribbean. As a first offender, Mr. Wenner was sentenced to two years of probation and required to perform 200 hours of community service. In addition, the New York State Attorney General's Office informed the Court that Mr. Wenner's license to serve as a broker in New York State had been revoked and that he would be barred from the securities business for life. All of the embezzled funds were recovered in connection with the settlement.

LOS ANGELES: THE TRANQUIL PERIOD

Chapter XXIX

I pleaded guilty to attempted embezzlement at my trial in the New York State Court in Brooklyn. Fortunately neither the prosecuting attorney nor the judge knew anything about my conviction back in Switzerland, so I was considered to be a first-time offender. As a result, I avoided any jail time but was banned from the securities business for life and had to return the embezzled funds. In addition, my sentence required that I meet with a probation officer once a week, and I was required to do this for two years. I also had to put in 200 hours of community service, so, in many respects, I felt that I had gotten off rather easily since there was no jail time. I did the community service as quickly as possible by working at a homeless shelter in Brooklyn. And I hated every minute of it since I had no sympathy for the homeless. I know I should have felt some compassion for them, but I always had the feeling that most of them were either drug addicts, alcoholics, or simply lazy. I tried to hide my feelings as much as I could and was tremendously relieved when that part of my sentence was completed.

But I still had to deal with the requirement that I report to a probation officer once a week. I particularly disliked the probation officer to whom I was assigned, and she apparently disliked me as much as I disliked her. She was a very aggressive black woman who was always complaining to me that I was on probation solely because I was white, and if I had been black, I would have been sentenced to jail. This may have been true, but I felt that she should have been complaining to the judge rather than to me. After only two visits to the probation office, which was far out in Brooklyn, I decided that it would be impossible for me to continue with these visits. Taking everything into consideration, I came to the conclusion that I would have to leave New York. I had left Switzerland rather than face a term in jail, and I could not tolerate being treated as a common criminal by the probation department in New York City.

I considered a great many different possibilities about where to go and what to do, but realized that as long as I had to get out of New York, it would also make sense to get out of the US entirely. I had no idea where I might go and, not having any money to speak of, my options were limited. However, one day in February, I saw a cruise ship slowly sailing down the Hudson and decided that working on one of those ships would be a great option. I was still blond and considered myself to be fairly good-looking. And I also thought of myself as a relatively young man, even though I was now forty-five years old, so I felt it would be easy for me to get a job on a cruise ship. I started scanning the newspapers every day to learn about ship sailings, and discovered that Holland-America had a ship that was leaving New York in a couple of weeks. The MS Maasdam, one of Holland-America's older ships, was hiring staff and I went down to their office and filled out an application for a job. I told the man who interviewed me that I had been a waiter at several premier hotels in Switzerland, knowing that the cruise line would almost certainly not be able to check those references. I was actually surprised that my application was accepted immediately. This was to be a leisurely cruise through the Caribbean and down the east coast of South America, then past Tierra del Fuego and Cape Horn, and back up the west coast, stopping in the Galapagos Islands, Peru, and Acapulco before ending up in Los Angeles. It was planned as a month-long cruise, but I was not sure when or if I would return to New York, so I gave up my apartment, put everything into storage, and tried to sever all of my connections with the city that had been my home since 1965.

I reported for work a few days before the ship was due to sail, and I really enjoyed it as we sailed out of New York harbor since it had gotten me away from that extraordinarily unpleasant situation in New York. And I found that it was not hard for me to adapt to the role of a waiter. I knew that ever since I had left Zürich, I had actually been playing a part in whatever job I had had in the States—I had never been able simply to be myself—and so playing a part as a waiter now was not all that difficult. I enjoyed conversing with the passengers, most of whom were wealthy Americans or Europeans, and I liked to impress them with my urbanity—my fluency in foreign languages and knowledge of things like wine. I went ashore at each of the ports where the cruise ship stopped at the islands in the Caribbean and at Rio, and at several of them I was able to find a young woman whom I could pick up and pay for sex. I really disliked paying for sex but there was never time to pick someone up and get to know her before taking her to bed. I usually felt after the fact that the event had been a waste of money since to me sex had to be something more than just the simple physical act. But women who were available at the ports at which the ship stopped were far too experienced in the world's oldest profession to worry about anything other than getting paid for the act itself.

Despite the fact that I was working as a waiter, I was really enjoying the trip and I had really started to relax. However, I had a major disappointment when the ship docked in Montevideo. I decided to call Tony to try to renew that old relationship, since I was hoping that he might invite me to visit him at what was now his ranch. So I called the old phone number that I still carried in my address book—the number I had called when I had discovered that Gus had died. A woman answered the phone and I asked to speak with Tony. A half-minute later, Tony came on the line.

"Tony, I hope you still remember me. This is Kurt."

There was a pause for a short time until Tony said, "Kurt, from Zürich—from Schleswigbank?"

"Yes, I'm glad you remember after all these years. I've thought of you often and have always wanted to get back to visit you and to experience again that marvelous place where you live."

There was a fairly long pause before Tony said, "Well, I'm afraid, Kurt, that I have thought of you pretty often too, but I have to tell you that my thoughts have not been very kind."

"Not very kind? But why? I've done nothing to offend you."

"You don't call stealing 250,000 Swiss francs from me nothing?"

I was momentarily staggered by Tony's accusation, but finally said, "Yes, all right, I did take that money, or more precisely my wife and I did, but we didn't take it from you. Gus wanted that money to go to his daughter and, after what you had told me about her, I didn't want that to happen. So if anyone has a right to be mad at me it is Elsa, but I would never have done anything to hurt you."

Tony waited a few seconds and then said, "Kurt, there are some people who are simply born liars—and I can see now that you are one of them. Elsa was not going to get that money—I was. The court in Zürich ruled that there was no evidence at all that Gus ever intended that Elsa get anything, and the court also ruled that that money should come to me when it was recovered. You were the one that stole it, and you stole it from me. So I am really stunned that you would have the nerve to call me and try to pretend that we were somehow still friends."

"Tony, if only I could explain to you what happened and why it happened. I would really love to have you understand."

Tony cut me off, saying, "Well if you want to explain what you did, first send me the 250,000 Swiss francs and then I'll listen to what you have to say. But for now I don't have time to listen to any more of your lies." With that, Tony hung up, and I was left listening to the buzz of a dead phone line.

I was totally shocked by what Tony had said and felt really depressed after talking to him. What I had tried to tell Tony was definitely true—Gus had wanted Elsa to have that money, not Tony, so to the extent that Ingrid and I had cheated anyone it had been Elsa. But ironically I was that only one who knew what Gus wanted, and the court in Zürich had found no evidence that Elsa was supposed to get the money, so the court awarded it to Tony. I wonder if Ingrid and I would have taken the money if we knew that it was going to Tony. I really think that I wouldn't have done it in that situation, but I wonder what Ingrid would have done.

Contacting Tony was one of the rare times that I had tried to go back and re-open an old relationship out of the past—out of one of my previous lives. I had done it once before with Ingrid on that trip to Zürich with Susan—a trip that had really ended up finally closing the door on my relationship with

Ingrid. As I sat at the bar at a hotel in Montevideo that night, I realized that if I was going to be able to rebuild my life again going forward, I would have to forget about all of my old friends and relations from past lives, and would again have to create another new persona with no reference and no connection to any person or any incident from the past. I had liked Tony and I had loved that ranch in the foothills of the Andes. But all of that belonged to a life that was long gone, and I vowed never to make a mistake again such as I had just made in trying to talk with Tony. It also occurred to me that if Tony was as vindictive as he sounded on the phone, he might let the police know that I was in the area. Fortunately, I did not say that I was in Montevideo and he might have thought that I was in Buenos Aires, but I decided that I better get back on the ship while I was still able to do so.

The ship left Montevideo the next morning and, for the first time since leaving New York, I felt terribly depressed. If my conversation with Tony had gone well, I had hoped to stay at Tony's ranch for a while, and perhaps remain in Argentina for several years since I knew that checking one's background was not considered a requirement in that country. So many Germans had come to Buenos Aires after World War II that it had become socially incorrect for anyone to ask questions about a person's background. But the hope of staying in BA had now been shattered, and I simply could not think what my future might hold. Back on board ship, I went through the ritual of serving both lunch and dinner to the same guests that I had been serving since the ship left New York, but I found it difficult to engage in any repartee with the regular guests at my tables, as I had done at the beginning of the cruise.

That night, after the main dining room had been cleared, I went back to my cabin and changed into khaki slacks and a t-shirt and went out on one of the lower decks for a cigarette. I stood for a long time in the darkness, with only a half moon overhead, thinking what a mess I had made of my life. The thought even occurred to me that jumping overboard might be an easy way out. Suicide, however, was not a serious consideration, and I'm sure that I only thought about it since I was feeling sorry for myself. It seemed very peaceful as I stood smoking with the moon overhead reflecting off a fairly calm ocean. However, as I lit my second cigarette I was startled when someone, just a few feet away, said, "I do hope you're not considering jumping. Things would become so inconvenient if you did." It was a woman's voice, but in the darkness I could not immediately recognize her.

I turned and walked slowly toward the woman, who was dressed in a long, flowing white dress that was shimmering in the moonlight and a rather strong breeze. As I got closer to her, I recognized her, and said, "Ah, Mrs. Bernstein. Now, why would you think I was going to jump?" She was one of the diners whom I had been serving every day since the boat had left New York.

"Well, I must say that you intrigue me, and seeing you here alone looking over the side so intently, I really didn't know what to expect."

Her comment about being intrigued immediately caused me to enter into the spirit of the conversational exchange, and I said, "Now why should someone like you be intrigued by a ship-board waiter?"

"Because you know, and I know, that you are not simply a ship-board waiter. Someone your age, which I guess to be in the mid-40s, who is able to speak several languages—I have watched you talk to guests at other tables—and who seems to know exactly the right wine to suggest for every occasion—that person is not simply a waiter. Now I have nothing against waiters—I have had some simply marvelous encounters with waiters on other cruises—but you are a cut above the common, ordinary waiter that one runs into on these ships."

I hesitated a minute and finally said, "Mrs. Bernstein, you flatter me, and I really don't know what to say."

"Well, honey, you could simply tell me who you are, and what you are doing masquerading as a waiter on this ship."

I again waited a long time before responding. At last I said, "Well, you are at least partly right. I needed to get away from New York and the anonymity of being a waiter on this ship seemed to be an ideal way out. But I don't consider myself to be a cut above the common, as you put it. Quite the contrary."

"Dear boy, you were smoking a minute ago, so you must have a lighter. Would you light my cigarette?"

After I had done so, I also lit another for myself, and there was a long silence as we stood next to each other looking at the vast darkness of the ocean, with only the faint light of the moon reflecting on the water. Finally, she said, "I suppose you don't want to tell me what you're running away from."

I considered telling her about Morris, Brunner, but decided that I needed a story that would elicit sympathy from her, and the Morris, Brunner story certainly would not do that. So I turned directly toward her and said, "To some extent you might be right, I suppose I'm not what might be called an ordinary waiter. I guess I have to confess—if that's the word—that I come from what at one time was a fairly well off family in Zürich. I was sent to all the right schools in Germany and Switzerland, and worked for several years at one of the principal banks in Zürich. Then, several years ago, my family sent me to New York to handle their investments in the U.S. I had never felt, and I hate to say it, but I never felt as important as I did after arriving in New York with a great deal of money to invest. But I failed—that's all I can say—I failed, since I incurred very large losses on the investments that I made. My father died while I was in New York and before all the losses had become apparent, but my brothers and sisters have now found out and they seem incapable of forgiving me for what I have done. And, of course, my wife has left me and is filing for divorce back in Switzerland. Everything that could possibly go wrong seemed to hit me all at once, and so I decided that I just had to get away. And I had no money—I had lost just about everything that my family had given me. So being a waiter on this ship was a great escape for me."

I could sense that Mrs. Bernstein was looking at me for a minute, and she finally said, "Honey, that's certainly one of the most heart-rending stories that I have ever heard. But don't worry; I don't think I'm going to cry. Whether I believe your story or not, I can't decide right at this minute. But I'll give you the consolation of saying that I believe that you come from a pretty good family and have been educated well—that much is obvious. And being Swiss makes sense, since you speak all those languages. Let me think about the rest."

"I'm sorry if you don't believe me, and I know that I should not have said all that I said. I probably rambled on too much. I'm not looking for sympathy, but I haven't been able to talk with anyone about the problems back in New York until now, and you did ask. So I guess all I can say is that I hope you will simply forget what I just said."

"Kurt—and I assume that is your right name—don't be an ass. All I wanted to establish is that you're a pretty cultivated guy and are several cuts above the average. Now, why don't we go up to my cabin and have a drink and let me see if I can find some other way of consoling you."

It suddenly occurred to me that she was planning to have sex with me. She was a woman in her late fifties—maybe even sixty—and the thought of having sex with her was a complete turn-off for me. But as she walked away, all I could do was follow her to her cabin and see if I could find some way of getting out of it after I got there. However, once in her cabin I discovered that she had prepared to bring me—or someone—back with her. There was a bottle of champagne on ice, with two glasses, on the cocktail table, and she asked me to open the bottle. The lights had been turned down low when we came in and we sat drinking champagne for some time with neither one saying a word. The pressure kept building on me since I knew what was expected of me, and, without really knowing why, I finally moved over and sat next to her on the small love seat. And then it just happened, as we came together and had sex right there where we had been sitting. It was not all that comfortable on the cramped love seat, and dealing with clothes was a problem, but I felt that it was better to get it over with right where we were, rather than having to go through the ritual of heading for the bedroom and attaching any romantic aspect to the whole thing. When it was over, she got up and went into the washroom, while I straightened my clothes and took another glass of champagne. When she came back, she said, "Well, that wasn't so bad, was it?"

I hesitated for a minute and then stammered, "No, no, it wasn't bad at all."

She laughed and said, "Now that shows honesty, if nothing else. It has been so awful when I have had an event like this with less sophisticated young men who feel that they have to profess love or try to rhapsodize over what just happened. Thank you for sparing me that."

"Well, Mrs. Bernstein, I really don't know what to say."

"I would think that since we've just had sex that you could at least call me by my first name, which is Naomi."

I merely nodded, and she went on, "But you were great. I can't wait to tell all the girls at my table in the dining room."

"You're kidding! I would think that we would both want to keep anyone else from finding out about this."

"Kurt, darling, you must know that you are the absolute Number One male heartthrob on this trip. All of the old bags are simply drooling over you. There is no one else who comes close. Some of the waiters are so young that they probably haven't reached puberty yet, and the others are so old that they couldn't even remember the last time they were able to get it up. But now I can tell them about that fantastic body of yours, and they will simply die when I tell them about your thing, which is terribly impressive. How long should I say it is?"

"Naomi, you aren't serious. You can't be serious."

"Of course I'm serious. Maybe I'm exaggerating a bit, but you have to be aware that every woman in that dining room is either a widow or a divorcée and would give anything—including money—if you would take her to bed."

I said nothing for several minutes as I poured myself another glass of champagne. I finally turned to her and rather sullenly said, "You really make me sound like a male prostitute."

"Darling, don't be a baby—I didn't mean to offend you. I was simply trying to tell you how desirable you appear to be to all the old bags on this ship. Of course you're not going to try to get paid for having sex with them—and I don't intend to insult you by offering you payment for our little interlude. But sex, or at least the faint hope that something sexual might occur, is one of the main reasons that so many women like me go on these cruises. We love the food, we love our cocktails, we love being waited on, and there is always the chance, no matter how remote, that some Adonis like you will come along and we can lure him into our bed. And when I tell them what happened tonight—and about your glorious body—they will get as much vicarious pleasure out of hearing about it as if it had happened to them. So it is not demeaning at all. Just remember that you're Adonis, and from now on you have to play that part to the hilt."

I continued to stand and look her, not knowing what to say as I finished my glass of champagne. I then reached over and took Naomi's hand, saying, "Thank you, I guess what you say does make sense. It seems I'm always playing a part wherever I go, but I had never thought that I would be cast as Adonis. It's hard for me to think of myself in those terms, and I wonder what my soon-to-be ex-wife and daughter back in Zürich would think. But I will take your advice, and tomorrow you and your friends will be served by the best Adonis any of you have ever seen." I walked to the door of Naomi's cabin and as I left I turned and said with a smile, "And you can tell them that it's the biggest thing you've ever seen."

But as I left the room, Naomi called after me, "I wouldn't go that far, honey. You're really overestimating yourself."

When I got back to the tiny cabin that had been assigned to me in the bowels of the ship, I simply collapsed on the one small chair that was jammed in between the bed and the door. For as long as I could remember, both in Zürich and New York, it had been my brains that had mattered—the fact that I was smarter than my competitors at Schleswigbank had led to my rapid advancement there, and my knowledge of all the global markets had been the reason I headed up the foreign investment group at Morris, Brunner in New York. I certainly considered myself to be good-looking and I had never hesitated to use my looks to impress both business associates and any woman that interested me. But my German good looks had never been the primary thing that I had relied upon to get ahead or to build my own self-esteem. So I found it terribly ironic that Naomi was now telling me that all I had to do was to play the part of Adonis and let the women on board the ship enjoy looking at me and let them fantasize about getting to bed with me. It was both ironic and somewhat troubling, but I had to admit to myself that it was also rather flattering. And since there were only about three weeks left on the cruise, I decided that all I could do was to try to make the most of the situation—and I became determined to be the most desirable Adonis imaginable.

Chapter XXX

Los Angeles – 1977

The final three weeks of the cruise were uneventful—nothing remotely as interesting as my first encounter with Naomi happened again—and the ship sailed into the port of Los Angeles. It took some time before the ship was finally docked, and many passengers crowded the deck waiting to debark. I stood near the gangplank down which the passengers would be leaving the ship, and many of the women pressed little envelopes into my hand as they left. I felt a little depressed at the thought that I had been reduced to taking tips, but at the same time I appreciated the fact that I had made the trip enjoyable for these women. I had expected that some of them would give me something, but I was surprised at how generous they were. Those that I had waited on most frequently gave me between $200 and $300 each, but one woman that I had hardly dealt with at all gave me $500. As she pressed her envelope into my hand, she said, "Naomi told me about what happened between the two of you a couple weeks ago. Just tell me one thing, was she exaggerating?"

I smiled and said, "Knowing Naomi, I would guess that she was exaggerating—at least a little bit."

The woman said, "Oh, I hope not. It sounded so wonderful." And with that she proceeded down the gangplank.

So with a couple thousand dollars from tips, plus the salary that I had had no occasion to spend, I had managed to accumulate close to $8,000. Since legal fees from my indictment back in New York and living expenses while I was performing community service had eaten up what little savings I had previously had, this $8,000 would have to support me, at least until I could get another job.

It did not take me long to get my things together since I had brought very little with me on the ship, and I was ready to walk off the ship along with the last passengers who were debarking. I had no clear idea of where I would go but had planned to look for a hotel in Long Beach near the port since I thought that in a week or two, I might take a job on another cruise ship. When I got out to the street, I stood looking around trying to decide which way to go, when I heard a woman's husky voice say, "C'mon, buster, don't stand there like a dumb schmuck. Get in—we're going to my place." It was Naomi, of course, who was seated in the back of a large Lincoln Continental, driven by a chauffeur.

I walked over to her car and said, "Oh, thanks, Naomi, but I don't think I can go with you right now. I have to find a hotel."

"Honey, the accommodations at my place are infinitely better than anything you're going to find in this god-forsaken neighborhood, and they're a heck of a lot cheaper. So just get in and stop screwin' around. I'm anxious to get home."

The driver got out and took my bag without giving me a chance to protest, although I was not very inclined to protest. He put the bag in the trunk of the car and then opened the door so that I could get in the back seat with Naomi.

I had just seated myself next to her, when Naomi said, "Honey, I'm sure you're going to find that Beverly Hills is much better than Long Beach, any day of the week, particularly for a man with your talents."

"I imagine it is, and I appreciate your offer, but I do feel a little awkward about this."

"There's nothing for you to feel awkward about, honey. You should know me by know, and know that I'm a realist above all. I think you're an interesting guy and some of my friends in Beverly Hills are going to think you're an interesting guy too. And some of them are even going to think that you're sexy. In Hollywood, as you can imagine, both sexes will probably find you very sexy. All I'm doing is introducing you to some people—what you make of it is entirely up to you. And just to put you at your ease, I won't be looking for a repeat of that passionately romantic scene that we went through several weeks ago on the ship. Once was probably enough for both of us. At my age you learn to live on memories."

It did not take me long to get settled into Naomi's home. It was, of course, one of the more beautiful houses in Beverly Hills, and she put me up in a suite at the back of the second floor. Her bedroom was in the front, and it quickly became clear that she really did not expect a repeat of our sexual encounter from the ship. She tried to make it clear that I was free to come and go as I pleased, but she did want me to appear with her at various social functions. And as we were having breakfast together on the first morning that I stayed at her home, she told me that I had to go down to Rodeo Drive and spend a few thousand dollars getting a new wardrobe.

As Naomi handed me a credit card she said, "Try to forget that you're Swiss and that you were in investments, or whatever it was that you did back in New York. You're in California now and you have to have a totally different way of thinking about yourself. You played the part of Adonis on the ship pretty well, so now you've got a new part. Think of yourself as the Playboy of the Western World—you would look the part if you dressed right; all you've got to do is to act it. You're in your forties now, so you should still be able to pull it off."

Since I had brought very few clothes with me from New York, I really needed to buy quite a few things, particularly if I was going to accompany Naomi to social events that were important to her. I asked her to come along, but she replied, "Baby, you're a big boy. I don't need to dress you. If you go to the right stores, they'll see to it that you get the right things. Just tell them you'll be accompanying me and that while you don't want to look like a 'boy toy,' you do want to look like you're really with it—like I said, a Playboy."

I did as Naomi suggested and, after spending several thousand dollars of her money, I returned to her house and wanted to show her what I had bought. She turned me down flat, saying, "Lover boy, I am not your mommy. I will see what you bought when the occasion arises and we go out together. Now go take a nap, or whatever it is you do in the afternoon, since I want to be alone. If you haven't noticed, I'm playing Greta Garbo today." This was the way Naomi was—absolutely genuine, and it is the Naomi that I will always remember and always love.

With Naomi's backing and advice, I began to be introduced to a great many wealthy people in Los Angeles, and particularly to a very wealthy Jewish crowd, all of whom were Naomi's friends. I told all of them the same story that I had told Naomi on the ship—that I came from a well-to-do Swiss family and that I had been handling my family's investments in New York. But I did not tell them anything about my actual career in New York or how it ended. I was surprised what a great conversational gambit it was to talk about investments, since virtually everyone I met—men and women—were interested in investments, and particularly the stock markets, and wanted to talk about them. Since I had really been an investment advisor all my professional life, I was able to talk very knowledgeable about the subject and I guess that I must have really impressed many of the people that I met.

One night Naomi said to me, "You remember Rachel Goodwin, don't you? She's Myron Goodwin's wife. Well, she was asking if she could hire you."

"She thinks I'm available for hire?"

"Well, she may have at one time. She told me that she had thought at first that you were my 'boy toy'—even though you're clearly not a boy. But she said that she and Myron had decided, after talking to you, that you were a pretty impressive guy and knew a lot about investments. I guess that they were impressed when we were at that cocktail party at the country club and you were talking about the dollar and currencies and all that kind of stuff. I certainly didn't understand what you were talking about, and I'm pretty sure that Myron didn't either. But last weekend Myron repeated to his golfing buddies what you had told him, and Myron was pretty pleased with himself since the group agreed that what he said sounded pretty good. They were all probably having martinis on the nineteenth hole, or whatever they call it, and none of them would know if what Myron said made any sense of not. But they said it did, and Myron is such a twit that any time he can feel like he knows something, he almost has an orgasm. So Rachel would like to talk with you to see if she and Myron can hire you somehow and maybe advise them about their investments.

"Now honey don't think I'm trying to push you, but it has been close to six weeks since we got back from that cruise, and you do have a great tan, but you don't have very much else to show for the last six weeks, do you? Aside from the fact that I think you've put on a little weight."

I realized, of course, that she was telling the truth, as usual, and I tried to smile as I replied, "I guess I haven't accomplished very much, aside from the fact that I've been enjoying myself enormously, and that's probably why I've gained weight. But of course I'd be happy to talk to Rachel."

I had really enjoyed living in Naomi's house—sleeping as late as I wanted in the morning; spending the day at the pool; using the exercise equipment in the little gym she had above the garage; escorting Naomi to a dinner at someone's home or going to some charitable event in the evening, where I was introduced to some of the wealthiest people in Beverly Hills. This was such an easy life and, after the trauma of New York and the pressure that built up on the cruise ship, I felt that I could have gone on this way almost indefinitely. But I had to acknowledge to myself that I was getting a little bored, and the idea of talking to Rachel Goodwin about being hired by her and her husband as an investment advisor was somewhat intriguing.

A few days later I met with Rachel and Myron Goodwin and, after a fairly brief discussion, it was agreed that they wanted to hire me. This was a very preliminary plan, with Myron suggesting that I should form some kind of investment counseling firm, and I agreeing to explore the idea. With their backing and with Naomi's introductions, I was also able to secure promises from most of Myron Goodwin's golfing partners that they would be interested in hiring me as well. So within only a little more than two weeks, I had eight potential clients ready to sign up. But there was one problem—how was I, as a convicted criminal back in New York, one that had been banned from the investment business, going to be able to start an investment advisory business in California?

The law in California required that investment advisors be licensed by the state, and I knew that there was no possibility of my getting approved by California. As I thought about the problem, I decided that I had to find a way to work with the Goodwin's, and Rachel was clearly the key to obtaining their cooperation. Rachel was in her early fifties and looked several years younger. She was dark, with sharp features, had a good figure and always looked as if she had just walked out of the beauty parlor. While she was fairly old compared to my usual preferences, she was certainly an improvement physically over Naomi. So I called her one morning and asked her to have lunch with me, which she quickly accepted. I had read her correctly, as I'm sure Naomi had also, and it was pretty clear that she was interested in getting me into bed. As a result, as I had done with Naomi, I let her guide me back to her home and into her bed.

This was a pretty uninspiring sexual event for me, since I had planned to have sex with her in order to enlist her help in getting what had become a prime objective for me—the formation of an investment-counseling firm. But for Rachel, on the other hand, going to bed with me was an epic event—it was the first time she had slept with anyone other than her husband since they were married over twenty years previously. As a result, she attached a great deal of significance to the fact that we had slept together and it also added to her fantasies about me. I had the feeling that she had been interested in me when we first met, but taking her to bed clearly increased that interest.

I knew that it would be a mistake to ask for her help immediately after we had sex for the first time, and I realized that it would probably take several weeks and several more sessions in bed before I could even begin to hint that I might want something from Rachel and her husband. However, I found that our relationship advanced more quickly than I had originally expected it to, so after only our third time together, as we sat having a drink on the terrace outside the Goodwin's living room, I said, as wistfully as I possibly could, "I hate to tell you this Rachel, but I may have to go back to New York."

"Darling, you must be kidding."

"I wish I were, but one can only be unemployed so long, and I do feel guilty living like some poor relative sponging off Naomi."

"Well, I'm sure she's only too happy having you there. She does take advantage of you something awful, dragging you around to all those dreadful charity events that she likes to be seen at. And she wants everyone to think that there's some great romantic interest between you. It's really awful."

"I thought that you and Naomi were friends."

"Darling, I love Naomi as if she were my sister—my closest friend. But that doesn't stop me from commenting on some of her—what should I say—her little idiosyncrasies. No, all I'm trying to say is that she would love to have you stay there as long as you like."

"Yeah, I guess you're right. I think I could stay there almost indefinitely, but she is starting to hint that I ought to get to work. And Rachel, don't you think it would be better if I had a place of my own?"

"Now that you mention it, yes, I'm sure it would be. And darling, let me get an apartment for you; I'd love to do that."

"I'm sure you would, but I do have some pride and I really think I should get back to work so I can become independent again."

"Why can't you get work here in Los Angeles? There must be something you can do. You don't have to go back to New York just to find work."

"The fact is I think I could get a job in New York, while here in LA I would have to start my own company."

"Of course, darling, form a company—an investment counseling firm or something like that, whatever they call it, that's exactly what you should have."

"Well, what I would really like is to have a company just like the one I worked for back in Zürich, or it could even be like the private investment office our family had in New York."

"So start one—it would be an immediate success. I think all of our friends already want to hire you as their advisor. Isn't that right?"

"Yes, there are about eight of them, but I doubt if I have the resources to start one."

"Darling, if by resources you mean money, that is really the most trivial problem. I'm sure I could convince Myron to lend you what you need."

"Rachel, you're too much. Let me think about it. I hate to borrow money, so maybe we can talk about some kind of partnership. But I'll think about it and we can talk about it again next week."

Later that afternoon, as I was on my way back to Naomi's, I had to congratulate myself on the progress I had made with Rachel. I realized that I was, in effect, using her to advance my own business objectives, but I felt that she was getting a great deal of satisfaction out of our relationship, and so I had no reason to feel guilty about what I was doing.

When we next met a week later I was able to convince Rachel that she and her husband should form an investment advisory firm. I had come up with the name Good Win Investments and Rachel loved the name. Rachel told me that Myron was not too excited by the idea when Rachel first came to him with it, but he finally agreed that he would at least meet with me to discuss it. He and I had several meetings without Rachel being present, and initially Myron only wanted to make a loan to me. A loan was of no use to me as far as starting an investment advisory business was concerned, so I used two arguments to get Myron to consider a partnership. First, I emphasized that since the Goodwins had introduced me to so many of their friends, they should share in any profits that the firm might make. And secondly, I told Myron that I really liked the name Good Win Investments, but felt that the only way that I could use that name would be if Myron were a full partner. It was Rachel, however, who finally convinced Myron to form the partnership by pointing out the prestige he would gain by having his name on an investment-counseling firm that catered to their wealthy friends.

Once we had agreed on the concept of forming a partnership, I had no trouble convincing Myron that he would have to be the one to actually form the advisory company and get all the necessary approvals, and that I would be hired to run it and would only be an employee. I obtained the required papers from the California Secretary of State's office and had them filled out so that all Myron had to do was to sign them. He and I drew up an agreement that provided that I would get a base salary of $100,000 per year, and that any net profits over that amount would be split 33 percent to the Goodwins and the remaining 67 percent to me. Myron also agreed to underwrite the expenses during the first two years after the company was formed, including the expense of opening an office just off Wilshire Boulevard in Beverly Hills.

So within four months of arriving in Los Angeles, I found myself with an office in Beverly Hills and with access to some of the wealthiest families in the city. As I sat in my new office, I could only congratulate myself that I had once again overcome the bad luck that always seemed to haunt me. Having to leave Switzerland because I had made a silly little mistake when opening that account at the Schaffhausen bank, and then getting arrested in New York because I had decided to take a little money that a wealthy Italian had apparently forgotten—in my opinion these were not criminal matters and the punishment that I had had to endure in both cases was totally unfair. But as I had proven in New York, I had made a successful comeback after the Zürich debacle, and I was well on my way to making another comeback here in Los Angeles after the New York setback. And I knew that it was my talent, my intelligence, and perhaps my good looks as well that enabled me to overcome all of these obstacles. My only concern was that age seemed to be creeping up on me, with the dreaded fiftieth birthday getting closer and closer every day.

I thought of that dark night on the deck of the ship as it sailed from Montevideo, and I knew that Naomi had helped me recover from the depression that had hit me at that time. And I appreciated what Naomi had done for me, not just on the ship, but in helping me get established here in Beverly Hills. I knew that I could not have done it without her, but I also felt that in the final analysis I was the one that had made it all happen and I really did not need to thank anyone else for my new success.

And I also appreciated what Rachel had done for me, but I really felt no debt to her. I suppose that I felt a little guilty about having used Rachel, but I was convinced that she had been thrilled by the sex—I am sure that every woman I have ever had sex with was thrilled, at least to some extent, since I considered myself to be pretty good at it. And I knew that she would want me to carry on with her for the foreseeable future and I was resigned to doing that. I would have to disentangle myself from her gradually over the next few months, and while it was possible that she might not be happy about that, there was no way that she could complain to her husband. I would be seeing a great deal of the Goodwins going forward, and I knew that it would be much easier if I could end my involvement with Rachel as soon as possible. I immediately started to look for my own apartment now that I had a salary again, and I began to consider where that apartment should be. I decided that once I was established on my own, one of the first things I would do would be to look for some stunning young thing that would fit the image that I now wished to convey in Lala land.

Naomi was, of course, fully aware of my negotiations with the Goodwins and seemed very supportive of what I was doing. However, she could not help making a few comments about my relationship with Rachel. "Honey, I know you're not a newborn innocent, much as you might like to have people think that you are, but I have to tell you that I don't know if you know what you're getting into with that one. Rachel is a very dear friend of mine, but she can also be a real bitch if she doesn't get her way. Right now she's probably got some cockamamie idea in her head that she simply swept you off your feet and that you're really hot for her, but one of these days she's going to wake up and realize that you might have been using her, and you better watch out for her when that happens."

"Naomi, Rachel is a big girl and the two of us have not carried on as if we were great lovers. I'm sure she doesn't think for one minute any of the things that you suggest—either that I'm hot for her or that I've been using her. And she can't really think that the fact that we had a little sex is any kind of big deal."

"Well, you keep thinking that, buster, but one of these days when you want to get away from her, she's going to pull that leash real tight."

This was one of the very few times that Naomi was wrong; Rachel never tried to pull that leash.

Chapter XXXI

Looking back on it now, it's hard to realize that I stayed in Los Angeles—or, I should say, Beverly Hills—for almost thirteen years. This was one of the most stable periods of my life, even though one doesn't usually think of Los Angeles as being a stable place. I worked with Good Win Investments for almost the entire time I was in LA, and my personal and social life always centered on Naomi and her friends. For some reason, I had seemed to get along really great with Naomi and I truly enjoyed being with her. She became my main confidante all the while I was in California.

I had been worried at one time as to how things would work out with Rachel, but that relationship wound down rather easily. I gradually cut down on the frequency with which we got together, and also moved our relationship out of the bedroom and into a more businesslike setting. I found that Rachel was a very intelligent woman and was very interested in the world of investments. She liked to hear what I was doing in the accounts that I was managing at Good Win Investments, and seemed particularly interested in my currency trading. I think she was a little miffed when I started showing up at various social functions with a very attractive young woman who, like every other young woman in Lala land, was hoping to become a Hollywood starlet. But I pointed out that I did not have a serious relationship with the woman—who, depending upon the occasion, called herself either Gloria or Glory—and it was much better for Myron to see me with another woman, rather than for me to show up at these functions alone or with Naomi. She replied in a rather catty way that she could see my point since if I kept coming to events with Naomi, Myron would probably think that I was gay.

Good Win Investments was even more successful than I had expected. It always amazes me the way people make decisions as to how their money is invested or who invests it for them. Because I was, in effect, sponsored by the Goodwins, and because the Goodwins belonged to a number of the right clubs in Los Angeles, including the most important Jewish clubs in the area, people came to me imploring me to manage their money, asking only a few rather superficial questions. I really had expected Myron or one of the investors to ask for references or for some indication of my investment record either with respect to what I had done for my "family" in New York or even for the banks I was supposed to have worked for in Europe. And I had been thinking of ways that I could phony something up to answer their questions. But fortunately, there were no serious questions, and I never had to make up any answers.

The amount of assets that I was managing grew rather dramatically and it soon came to about $350 million. I had to hire an assistant very quickly to help me deal with all the clients and the paperwork involved with their accounts. I think that running Good Win Investments was both one of the most challenging but also one of the most satisfying jobs that I ever had. And I was determined not to spoil it by making the kind of mistakes that I had made both in Zürich and New York. I know that I considered this my company, even though Myron owned most of it, and I took great pride in the success of the company. I wanted everything with Good Win Investments to be 100 percent honest, with every transaction being totally above board. I hired an outside auditing firm to come in every year to check on every transaction and make sure that all the client reports were accurate and that the clients got every penny to which they were entitled. Myron did not like having to pay those big auditing fees, but it gave me a great deal of satisfaction to send the audited reports to the clients every year, and I think that most of the investors liked them too.

My only possible complaint during all these years was my own compensation. I had started with a salary of $100,000 plus the percentage of profits that we had agreed upon. But the fees that I charged at Good Win Investments were not all that great and, with the rent and other expenses, there simply were not very many profits to divide. However, at the end of each year Myron and the Board of Directors (Myron had the right to name two of the principal investors to the Board) would decide on a bonus for me. I suppose that they felt that a 20 percent bonus was pretty generous for an employee, but I felt that I was more than an employee—I was the brains of the entire organization.

As opposed to the little profits that Good Win Investments was making by charging the investors a modest fee, the real big potential for me lay in getting a share of the returns that I was earning for the investors. It took several years to accomplish, but the combination of my urgings and the fact that I had provided them with outstanding investment returns finally convinced Myron and the other directors to adopt what is called a hurdle rate, or the base rate above which I would get a percentage return. In other words, the directors and I agreed on a base annual rate of 12 percent, which was defined as the hurdle rate. I would get 15 percent of any return above that amount plus my basic $100,000 salary. So if I produced a return of 14 percent for the clients, that was 2 percent above the hurdle rate and I would get 15 percent of that 2 percent. Now that does not sound like very much, but since that percentage would apply to the hundreds of millions of dollars of assets that I was managing, it really amounted to something quite significant. As a result, my total compensation really escalated. Of course, there were years when the markets went down or I had misjudged the currency markets and there was no bonus, but overall I was pretty satisfied with what I was making.

The other good thing about having a much larger income is that it enabled me to resume making payments to Ingrid. After my conviction in New York, I had stopped sending her anything, and I assumed that she believed that I had simply disappeared. I now wrote to her and told her that I had run into a problem that had kept me from sending her and Petra anything for close to five years, but was now able to start making payments for child support again. She wrote back thanking me but insisting that I make up for the payments I had missed, which I started to do. She also told me that an old friend of ours had been in New York when my conviction was reported in the newspapers and had told her about it. I guess Ingrid was the one person in the world that I could not fool.

Naomi, of course, continued to be a very good friend, and I felt that I had grown closer to her the longer that I knew her. I really liked her and liked being with her. I could see that the years were taking a toll on her and that she was not aging as well as I had hoped she would. But I still accompanied her to two or three major charitable events each year, and the two of us would have dinner together once a week. More and more often those dinners were at her home, since she found it easier to stay in, rather than to go out to a restaurant.

One night when we had just finished dinner at her home and we were still sitting at the dining room table finishing a final glass of champagne, she turned to me and said, "Honey, how long have you been in Los Angeles now?"

"It's been about twelve years. That cruise when we met was in 1977 and here it is 1989. Why do you ask?"

"Well, honey, I was just thinking that you've been a pretty good boy all these years, a really good boy, and I'm proud of you for what you've done."

I could immediately sense in saying I had been a "good boy" that she must be referring to my past, so I said, "Did you think I wouldn't be—a good boy, that is."

"C'mon, buster, you don't think I ever bought that song and dance story you gave me on the ship about why you left New York. It didn't take my attorneys more than a couple of days to find out everything that had happened back there in New York at whatever that company was called. And what a schlemiel—you didn't even change your name."

"So you've known all along."

She nodded but said nothing.

"But how could you . . ."

"How could I what?"

"Recommend me to the Goodwins?"

"Honey, give me some credit. I think I'm a pretty good judge of a person's character and, like I told you on the ship, you intrigued me. And I've been right—look at the success you've been."

I knew it would irritate her, but I had to ask, so I said, "Do the Goodwins know?"

"Buster, sometimes you're a real idiot. Maybe Rachel would think it was exciting getting laid by an ex-con from New York, but that Myron is one of the most uptight jerks I ever met. He walks around like he's got a red hot poker up his rear end. If he had any idea at all about your record in New York, there would be no Good Win Investments. You're just damn lucky that he wasn't smart enough to have someone check your background, and that none of the other investors did either."

"Naomi, give me some credit. I never told Myron or any of the other investors that I ever worked for anyone that they could check with in New York. You're the only one here in LA who ever found that out. The investors all thought that I worked for the family office in New York, an office that is now closed. If any of them were going to check on me, they'd have to check in Europe and that would have been impossible since the banks that I told them about have all merged or gone out of business. You're the only one who checked out everything."

"OK, maybe you're not as dumb as I thought. But if I was able to find out about your past, those other schlemiels should have been able to do the same. And I still think you should have changed your name. You could have had a lot more business if your name had been something like Weinstein instead of Wenner."

"Maybe, although I think I've done pretty well with the name Wenner. But Naomi, why bring this up now?"

"Well, honey, you're the only one I'm going to tell this to, but I'm probably not going to be around too much longer. They just found that I have lung cancer—I guess I should have listened when they kept saying that cigarettes were bad for you. It's too late now, though, so we'll just have to see how long we can keep things going."

I did not know what to say and I was hit by the greatest feeling of sadness that I ever experienced in my life. I really cared for Naomi and started to choke up, when she immediately said, "If you start to cry, buster, you better duck because I'm going to slug you over the head with this champagne bottle."

As I was trying to control my emotions and decide what to say, she must have rung for her houseboy, Ramon, because he suddenly appeared. In her usual pseudo-tough manner, she said, "Sorry to wake you up, Ramon baby, but go open another bottle of champagne. I don't think I'll be able to get rid of my guest here without giving him some more of that stuff."

So we sat talking for well over an hour, and she told me all about the discovery of the cancer—it was a very serious Stage 3—and all about the chemotherapy and radiation that awaited her. She had never told me her age before, but this night she told me that she was now seventy-two, so she had been sixty when I had met her on the ship. That was when we had had that one sexual encounter, and she had been in great shape then. I kept thinking while we talked that she was going to conquer this since she still had the spirit and determination of a very young woman. We finished off the second bottle of champagne—or maybe I finished most of it—and I finally went back to my apartment having had way too much champagne and bringing with me a very heavy heart.

The chemotherapy and radiation were extremely hard on her, but Naomi always seemed to be putting up a great fight. I'm sure that she never had any illusions about fully recovering from the cancer, but she seemed determined to prolong her life as long as possible. She had private nurses around the clock, and was taken to the hospital for the chemotherapy and, after that was finished, for the radiation. She lost her hair and the treatments were very hard on her, but she got several wigs and whenever I saw her, she made herself look as good as possible. When the treatments were over, she began to recover her strength, and she started to talk about having a nurse only at night. We began to have weekly dinners again, and even though she did not eat very much, I was becoming hopeful that she would be around for at least a few more years.

But one day while I was at my office, I received a call from her nurse that Naomi had had a seizure and had been rushed to Cedars-Sinai Medical Center. I jumped in my car and rushed to the hospital as quickly as I could, but I was too late. She had actually died in the ambulance en route to the hospital. They did an autopsy and discovered that the cancer had metastasized and a very small spot had appeared on the brain, and the doctors thought that this had caused the seizure. It was sad to think of all the suffering that she had had to endure with the chemotherapy and radiation only to die shortly after those treatments were finished. And it was a shock to have her death come so quickly; but knowing Naomi as I did, I think that this is the way that she would have wanted it. I contacted Rachel and she was, of course, as shocked as I was, but she offered to arrange for the funeral. Although Naomi had not attended synagogue regularly, Rachel felt that she would have wanted a funeral according to traditional Jewish practice, and therefore she arranged for the funeral to be held the following day.

The suddenness of Naomi's death and the speed of her burial made it difficult for me to really understand that she was gone. When things finally settled down, I began to realize how important Naomi had been to me. Not only did our relationship span many years, but she was also one of the most important guiding lights that I can ever recall having. I had been orphaned at a very early age, so I had no parents who set goals or standards that I was supposed to meet. Ingrid could have filled that role, but we were only married for a little over three years; and rather than act as a mentor keeping me on the straight and narrow path, she actually encouraged me to carry out the embezzlement from Schleswigbank. And in New York, I never really had anyone that I could look to. Even though I had turned to Susan from time to time, I did that more to have someone to talk to or have sex with, rather than to have someone who might give me advice. But Naomi had certainly filled the role of advisor, counselor, guide—whatever name you might want to give it—and she had done so successfully since my entire stay in Los Angeles was without any of the problems such as I had experienced in Zürich and New York. There was no question but that I would miss her a great deal.

Naomi died in March and about a month after her funeral I decided to take a vacation. I had not been out of Southern California since I stepped off the MS Maasdam twelve years previously. And for some reason, I suddenly wanted to see New York City again. It was 1977 when I sailed away from New York and here it was 1989, and I felt that I had become a totally different person in the intervening years. I had no fear of going back to New York since Morris, Brunner had been acquired by another brokerage firm and my old European Shares fund had been closed and liquidated long ago. I had to assume that all my old co-workers were now working for other firms in Wall Street, if they were still in New York, but I planned to avoid that part of town and did not worry about running into any of them. I don't think I would have recognized them, and I was fairly sure that they would not recognize me after twelve years had elapsed. I had worked at Morris, Brunner in the 1970s when I was in my forties, leaving New York when I was forty-five, and I would be coming back twelve years later and could no longer claim that I was the epitome of the young German youth. I also had to consider the fact that I was technically a fugitive of one kind or another as far as New York was concerned, since I had left the state and had not carried out the terms of my sentence that required me to meet regularly with my probation officer for the weekly meetings over a period of two years. But I also assumed that the New York City police had far more important matters to worry about than trying to find a very minor parole violator.

I spent almost two weeks in New York, staying at the St. Regis on 55th Street. I had a beautiful suite and did all the things that I had wanted to do but never seemed to have time to do when I lived in the city previously. I took in museums during the day, and there are so many great museums in New York, or simply renewed my acquaintance with Central Park. Spring is a great time in that city and walking through the Park with all the trees and bushes in bloom was an experience that one can never get in Los Angeles. And in the evening, I was always able to meet some really quite beautiful young woman who would join me for dinner, perhaps a play, and sometimes ending up with a night in my suite. It was truly exciting to be in New York again—the energy, the drive, the pace, whatever you wanted to call it, was exhilarating. I decided that I could not let such a long time elapse before visiting the city again.

It was really different returning to Los Angeles after my two weeks in New York. I'm sure that the reason that I found everything in LA to be rather flat and uninteresting was due to the fact that Naomi was no longer there to make things interesting for me. But I could not bring myself to think seriously about leaving Good Win Investments and going back to New York. I felt that I had too much of myself invested in that company to even think of leaving it, and I also realized that I would have to start all over again were I to go to New York. So I kept going through the paces and making the necessary investment decisions at Good Win Investments, even though I knew that my heart was not really in the job anymore.

I'm sure that I should have recognized that the savings and loan crisis that engulfed the US economy in 1989 was going to have a devastating effect on the markets. Everything was affected—stocks, bonds, real estate—all of them being severely depressed by the crisis in the economy. Unfortunately, I had not moved the accounts that I managed into defensive positions and our losses were admittedly quite significant. All of Myron's worst personality traits came out as a result of these losses. He really must have felt that his acceptance and standing with his friends in Beverly Hills depended upon the unfailing success of Good Win Investments. The fact that we were having a relatively bad period in late '89 completely wiped out for Myron our outstanding performance record for the previous ten years. More and more we spent our time arguing, or my listening to him bitching about our performance. In the past, I could have turned to Naomi and she would have talked to both Rachel and Myron and calmed things down. But now there was no Naomi to turn to and my relationship with Myron just kept going inexorably downhill. And I could not turn to Rachel either since I was pretty sure that she had found someone else to take care of those functions that I had previously performed for her. So I finally decided that the only thing to do was to go to the Board, all of whom, of course, were Myron's friends, and indicate that I wanted to resign.

Fortunately, there were a few businessmen on the Board, and I was asked to stay on until a successor could be named and put in place. As a result, I remained with Good Win Investments until the end of March 1990, bringing to a close what has to be considered one of the most satisfying and least controversial periods of my life. The only problem was that I did not get a bonus for 1989 and there were no profits in which I might share, so my basic salary was all that I was paid for that year and the first quarter of 1990. I have to confess that I had become accustomed to those bonuses and the profit shares and had not built up any substantial savings. So I quickly realized that I was not going to be able to stay unemployed for any prolonged period of time

It didn't take me long to realize that I would have to leave Los Angeles, and the only alternative that I could consider was to go back to New York. I had been bitten by the New York bug when I visited Manhattan after Naomi's death, and I quickly looked forward to moving back there again. So in one sense it could be looked upon as a defeat for me in having to give up Good Win Investments and everyone that I knew and had loved in Los Angeles. But I had to recognize that that phase of my life was over, and that I should look forward to the opportunity of going back to New York and again rebuilding my life there.

NEW YORK: PHASE II

Chapter XXXII

New York – 1990

After leaving the Second National Bank's office, I walked back down Broadway toward the harbor, still carrying the envelope I had taken from Irmane's office in which I had put my fingerprinting records. I crossed Battery Place and went back into the park and quickly found a bench where I could sit. I had not realized how tense I had become until I sat down and I could feel the tightness in my stomach and the back of my neck. It was a beautiful late afternoon and it seemed quite peaceful as I watched the ferries taking people home to Jersey City or Staten Island. I closed my eyes and sat there for maybe fifteen minutes, enjoying this solitude in the midst of turbulent Manhattan, and then decided that I wanted nothing more than a gin and tonic. So I walked over to Delmonico's, which was a few blocks away, and sat at the bar trying to decide what I would do next.

As I sat slowly sipping my second gin and tonic, I recalled that Irmane had said that I could start my new job immediately, if I wanted to, and I decided to do just that. I could not sit around waiting to hear whether or not my past had been discovered and whether or not I was going to be employed by the Second National Bank. I would call Ana Maria Ortega, the head of the New York office for International Private Banking, and tell her that I was planning to arrive at their office on Park Avenue the next morning to start my new job. I would be reporting to Ana Maria and to the head of investments for IPB, a man named Eric Petersen. I had been interviewed by both of them, but I really think that it was Ana Maria who was responsible for getting me hired, since she and I had hit it off very well, and I spoke Spanish as, of course, she did too.

As I got up to leave the bar, I realized that I was still carrying the envelope with my fingerprinting records. I sat down again and carefully ripped up all the papers, putting the scraps back in the envelope. I then walked out onto the street and dropped the envelope into the first trash basket that I found, hoping that that would be the last I would ever hear about the matter.

When I had returned from Los Angeles, I had originally taken a furnished apartment on the Upper East Side of Manhattan. This was great, as it was an easy commute to midtown where most of the investment-counseling firms had their offices. It was also expensive, however, and it turned out to be much more difficult to find a job than I had thought it would be when I left LA. As a result, my savings, which were not too great anyway, began to get eaten up rather quickly. After six months in New York and still unemployed, I decided that I would have to give up the Manhattan apartment, and after much searching, I decided to take another furnished apartment on Boulevard East in West New York, New Jersey, across the Hudson River from Manhattan. It was not in any sense a fashionable neighborhood, but the rents were much lower than on the Upper East Side of Manhattan, and the views of the city from across the river were really spectacular. There was a nice park in front of my building overlooking the Hudson and the park gave me a great view of the skyscrapers that crowded the sky in midtown Manhattan. I could also see the city skyline all the way down to the World Trade Center, which loomed up at the far tip of Manhattan, and those two towers, while not beautiful architecturally, were still very impressive. And since I had been forced to look for something with relatively low rent, I really felt that West New York was as good a place as I was likely to find.

Another advantage of the location was that there were little privately owned buses that ran down Boulevard East and into the Lincoln Tunnel, dropping passengers off at the Port Authority Bus Terminal at 42nd Street and 8th Avenue. The buses—called jitneys—were primarily for the Hispanic workers who were going into the city each morning from New Jersey for the various jobs that they had in Manhattan, and the fare was only $2. This was a cheaper and actually more reliable way to get into the city than the buses run by New Jersey Transit.

And so the next morning, without knowing what might happen as a result of my little foray into Irmane's office, I took the jitney to the Port Authority terminal and then walked from there to the Second National Bank's Private Banking office on Park Avenue at Fifty-First Street. I have to say that I was again tremendously enervated by the dynamism of New York City. Los Angeles had been wonderful, and it had been one of the more productive and peaceful periods of my life. But just walking the streets of New York again immediately brought back to me the unique spirit and the remarkable vigor of this town. I was glad to be back and I was looking forward to my new job and my new challenges at the Second National Bank.

The Second National Bank was in many ways a unique place. The First National Bank of New York was much bigger and seemed to have everything going for it. But the Second National was working hard to catch up and, because it had a great history and some new, young management, it was realizing some of its goals. Since the Vanderbilt family had been major investors in the bank for many years and still retained a position on the Board of Directors, the Second National was a particularly favorite bank for wealthy foreigners. Johan Vanderbilt loved to travel overseas, and he had met a great many of the most socially prominent and wealthiest people in whatever country he went to, and he had made a real effort to cultivate them. So when economic or political reasons caused those people to decide to invest in the United States, many of them came to the Second National Bank of New York without considering anyone else. This fact was, of course, a great advantage for the International Private Banking (IPB) Department of the bank. Since IPB was expanding, they needed people like me to handle their sophisticated and multilingual clients and prospects—someone who spoke at least English, French, German, and Spanish, all of which I did.

When I arrived at the bank's office that morning—the first day of April 1990—Ana Maria Ortega was not there, but a young woman who was from that dreadfully named department, Human Resources, took me to what was to be my new office. This was Karen Rogers, who was a very self-important person, but who really knew very little about how to deal with people. To say that I was disappointed when I saw my office was perhaps an understatement since it turned out to be more of a cubicle than anything else. But I had no choice, so I thanked Karen and tried to figure out how I could make this spot into something that would provide me with a new professional challenge. I was now in my late fifties and I knew that this would be my last chance to really amount to something professionally.

When I was in Beverly Hills, my large, comfortably furnished office had a TV set on which I could watch the stock market, and this permitted me to watch all the trades on both the New York Stock Exchange and NASDAQ as they occurred, or at least with only a short time delay. Therefore, before Karen walked away, I asked her if the bank would install a TV set in my office, but she merely laughed and acted as if my request was totally bizarre. In a sense it was bizarre, since the office was so small—perhaps being eighteen feet by twelve feet. So I decided to take matters into my own hands, and over the next two weeks—without getting anyone's approval—I bought some lumber so I could install a shelf on the wall high up in front of my desk. The office was too small for the set to be placed on any kind of table, so building the shelf was the only way to get it in. I worked nights and one weekend to get the shelf in place and then bought a small TV set that I placed on the shelf myself. It took quite a bit of ingenuity and a lot of hard work on my part, but I finally had the TV set installed and operational.

I had not realized that by putting in that TV set everyone else in the office would look upon me as being a really unique character. I was, of course, considerably older than any of the other investment officers in the department, with only the manager of the New York investment group being at all close to my age. I think I fairly quickly developed quite a reputation with the younger account officers and the young guys on the trading desk. I was not only older,

I was also far more experienced than any of them and, above all, I was Swiss. Swiss private bankers had an aura about them as being at the top of any ranking of this profession. Putting in that TV set myself—probably breaking many bank rules in doing so—was the final touch in stamping me as a truly unique character—one that would be allowed quite a bit of latitude when it came to bank rules.

My immediate boss—the one to whom all the investment account officers in the New York office reported—was Dick Engel. Dick had been pretty successful working for a big investment advisory firm before he joined the Second National Bank, but his emphasis had been entirely on the US common stock market, and I could immediately tell that he knew virtually nothing about the bond or currency markets. He wanted to have a meeting every morning to discuss the markets and after only a month or six weeks, everyone—including Dick—was looking to me to find out what they should be telling their clients as to bonds and currencies. And the clients from overseas were primarily interested in bonds and currencies, not in common stocks. I tried very hard not to embarrass Dick and, since he was not a very ambitious person, he seemed perfectly willing to cede all authority with respect to bonds and currencies to me. As a result, I felt that we had developed a very good working relationship.

However, the organization of International Private Banking at the Second National Bank was rather complicated. Each client who had an account with IPB had a primary relationship officer, and also had an investment account officer. And to add to the confusion, the investment account officers not only reported to Dick Engle, but we also reported to Ana Maria Ortega, as the head of the New York private banking office. I really liked her and felt that she was a tremendously impressive person, who knew exactly how wealthy foreigners should be handled. My only concern about her was that she seemed very driven to advance her own career and did not seem to care who was hurt as she rose in the organization.

I not only reported to Ana Maria, but also reported, at least indirectly, to Eric Petersen. He was responsible for the investment activity in all of IPB's offices worldwide, including, of course, New York. How this person ever got that job, I will never understand since he did not seem to me to know anything about currencies, or much else, for that matter. He was supposed to have had a great reputation in the stock market before he joined the Second National Bank because there had been articles about him in *Business Week*, the *Wall Street Journal*, and in many of the investment publications. But I felt that I was far more qualified than he was to be the CIO of the department. Fortunately, I only had to deal with him once a month when there was an Investment Committee meeting to review all of our accounts, and most of the time these meetings occurred without anything noteworthy happening. In fact, Petersen travelled a great deal to the other offices around the world for which he was responsible, so he frequently missed the monthly Investment Committee meetings in New York.

After I had been settled in my office for a couple of weeks, Dick Engle came in to see me one day and asked how everything was going. We exchanged pleasantries for a few minutes until Dick said, "I see that you've been buying some Australian dollars for your accounts. Were those directed purchases, or was that your idea?"

"No, that was my idea. At these levels, the Aussie dollar looks pretty cheap to me."

Dick then handed me a paper, saying, "Well, I thought I had given you this before, but the Investment Committee has a policy governing what currencies we can recommend to our clients, and the Australian dollar is not one of them."

I had remembered getting that policy statement, but since it did not make much sense to me, and since the Aussie dollar seemed so cheap, I had ignored the policy that Dick had given me. So I said, "I really am sorry but I guess the policy didn't register on me. But can I ask, who is it that sets the policy as to currencies?"

"The Investment Committee discusses it, of course, but Petersen pretty much has the final say on something like this."

I couldn't help saying, "I didn't realize that he was an expert on currencies."

Engle smiled and said, "Well he usually doesn't pretend to be, but he has this young guy working for him, Joshua Brown, who came up from the bank's treasury department downtown, and I'm pretty sure that Josh tells him what he ought to think—at least about currencies."

I had seen Joshua Brown a few times and he looked to me as if he were still in his twenties. Having policy set by a young kid like that, and having to follow that policy, really irritated me. Before I could say anything, Engle went on, "You should talk with Josh; he's a nice guy, and you could probably teach him a thing or two."

All I could reply was, "Good idea; I'll do just that."

In point of fact, I did make an attempt to discuss currencies with Brown, and we had several fairly long discussions. Those discussions always seemed to me to be positive, and Brown went away saying that he would talk with Petersen about my ideas.

Shortly after this, the department had its regular Investment Committee meeting, which was attended by about 10 people. Petersen acted as Chairman, of course, but Engle, Brown and the other investment officers were all there. I was surprised that Ana Maria Ortega also attended, and while she clearly had no investment experience, she did not hesitate to express her opinion on virtually any subject throughout the meeting.

There were the usual discussions about stock/bond ratios and about whether the European or US stock markets were more attractive. Petersen made it clear that he had much more confidence in the US market, and Ana Maria emphasized that most of the bank's clients had brought their money to New York to have it invested in the US. It was agreed, therefore, that the policy would continue to emphasize US equities.

We then got around to a discussion of currencies and Josh Brown passed around a policy paper showing the percentages that the bank would recommend for the US dollar, the British pound, the Swiss franc and the deutschmark. There was no mention whatsoever of the Aussie dollar. So I asked, "Was any consideration given to the Australian dollar?"

Petersen replied, "Yes, Josh gave me some information on it, but I don't think it's appropriate for the bank to be suggesting secondary currencies, like those of Australia and New Zealand. I'm sure you can make money in them from time to time, but I think that they are probably too speculative for our clients. Don't you agree, Ana Maria?"

She immediately said, "Oh yes, I would not want to speculate with our clients' money." She made it quite clear in the tone of her voice that no speculation was to be tolerated.

That quickly closed the discussion and I felt that all I could do was to sit quietly and accept the Committee's decision. I was not happy, but felt that I would have to adjust to working for a big institution. I had to realize that I no longer had my own investment-counseling firm, so all I could do was to try to smile and accept the Committee's decision.

Chapter XXXIII

After I had gotten into a routine of going to work in the morning and heading back home on the jitney in the evening, I felt that I should try to bring some excitement into my life. And that led me to want to talk with Susan. It had been twelve years since I had left New York, and I had not really thought about her very much since that time. But it was rather lonely going home to West New York every night and I remembered how accommodating Susan had been when we used to get together back in the late '70s. I thought it would be nice to have her available again for dinner and perhaps a little sex from time to time. So I took a chance and called her old phone number, thinking that she had probably moved, but I hoped that her number had stayed the same. I was actually quite surprised when she answered the phone with a very curt "hello". I immediately recognized her voice, but I hardly knew what to say, so I started by saying, "This is Susan, isn't it?"

Again a very brief, "Yes."

"Susan, this is Kurt."

"Kurt? You're not trying to tell me that this is Kurt Wenner?"

"I knew you'd remember."

Susan rather icily said, "How could I possibly forget?"

"Susan, I wanted to let you know that I've moved back to New York now, and I was hoping that we could get together and renew an old friendship."

There was a long pause before Susan replied, and she finally said, "What has it been Kurt, twelve or thirteen years since we last saw each other, and in all those years I never heard a single word from you. And now you want to get together to renew an old friendship?"

"You must know how difficult it was for me when my world fell apart at Morris, Brunner, and I really had no option but to flee New York. I finally ended up in LA and it took me years to put my life back together. But I'm still trying to do that now, and seeing you, talking with you, and trying to explain everything to you is an important part of that process."

"It may have been difficult for you, but did you ever think just how terrible it was for me? My life fell apart too, but I couldn't afford to flee, so I had to stay here and try to endure everything that happened."

I waited a long time before responding. "Susan, why don't we get together for dinner in the next week or so, and I can explain to you what I had to do after Morris, Brunner fell apart, and you can tell me about what you had to go through. I think we would both feel better if we could do that."

"Let me think about it, Kurt. There were times after you deserted me—and you know that that is what you did—there were times that I wanted to kill you. So I need to be sure that I'm not going to carry a knife when we do meet. Call me again in another week or so and I hope I can answer you then."

While I was surprised at the way she responded to my attempt at a reconciliation, I was pretty confident that Susan would relent and that we would be able to get together again. So I decided to wait not just a week, but for nine or ten days before calling her again. I was sure that having to wait that long would make her somewhat more anxious for us to get together again.

A couple of days later Imad El Kasim stopped by my office. Imad was one of the other investment officers in the department and had been at the Investment Committee meeting when currencies had been discussed. Imad said, "Kurt, you and I have not really had a chance to talk since you started, and I wonder if you would like to have a drink after work."

Imad was Egyptian and from the little that I had seen of him, he seemed to be a pretty smart investment professional. At the Committee meeting he had discussed his accounts in some detail, and clearly had a good understanding both of the markets and of his clients. I was happy to accept the invitation since I hoped it would give me a chance to learn more about the politics of the department and the bank.

That evening Imad and I went to the Bull and Bear at the Waldorf Astoria Hotel, which was just a couple of blocks from our office. The bar was packed, as it always is on a Friday evening, and we stood in the crowd of men—mostly guys in the investment business—who were jammed in trying to get the attention of a bartender so they could get a drink. It was hard talking in what was a rather noisy crowd, so Imad and I just exchanged pleasantries as we sipped our drinks. But when it came time for us to either order a second drink or to head home, Imad suggested that we move into the dining room for dinner. The dining room at the Bull and Bear was a rather formal place—paneled in dark wood, with white tablecloths on every table, and it never seemed to be very crowded. Since I had nothing else to do that night, I was completely agreeable to his suggestion.

After we were settled at a table and had ordered dinner, Imad said, "So Kurt, what do you think of the Second National Bank?"

I thought I ought to be somewhat careful as to how I replied since I did not know Imad all that well, so I said, "Well, I think it will take some time to get used to."

"With your Swiss background, the approach taken here must seem pretty parochial."

I laughed and said, "I suppose that that word might apply."

He then started to ask me about where I had worked in the past and what my experience had been. I had to be careful in answering his questions and also had to remember what I had told Bill Hoffman during my interview. When I got questions about my past, the story that I told people changed from time to time, and I had to be careful not to say things that would be inconsistent with other stories that I had told. So I dwelt at some length on my time in Los Angeles, and my own investment-counseling firm there, and then skipped over my last time in New York in order to talk about banks that I was supposed to have worked at in Switzerland and France.

In order to turn the subject away from my background, I managed to get him to start talking about himself. He had been born in Egypt and had gone to school in England, but came to New York about twelve years ago to study at NYU. After receiving a master's degree in finance there, he had started work at the Second National Bank in the Business and Economic Research Department. He had done very well, but the theoretical work did not appeal to him, so he asked for a transfer to the investment group in International Private Banking. Imad finally commented, "With my background and your background, we should be running the department." It was a thought that I frequently had, at least as to myself, so I only smiled and nodded.

As we finished dinner, Imad suggested that we have a brandy, and since that is something that I always enjoy, I quickly agreed. When the brandy was served, he held up his glass to me and as we clinked glasses he said, "To us!" I was a little surprised at what might be considered a rather personal toast, so again I merely nodded in acknowledgement. He then said, "It's too bad that we won't be able to end up running the department." I did not know how to respond to that remark so I said nothing, smiling at the remark. But he then stunned me as he went on, "Your past record, of course, would keep you from ever getting a position such as the head of a bank's investment department."

As soon as he said that, I realized that he knew something about my past and probably knew about what had happened at Morris, Brunner. A thousand thoughts ran through my head as I wondered what he knew and what his motive was in telling me this—and to do it in this way. I tried to stay calm and answered, "That's a rather provocative statement—that my record would keep me from heading up the department."

Imad said, "Well, you did live here in New York back in the late '70s and worked at a firm that's now gone out of business, Morris, Brunner & Company. I should explain that I met a guy at a party that I was at, and we got to talking. It turns out that he used to work at Morris, Brunner and told me about the head of research, someone named Kurt Wenner. I have to assume that that was you."

All I could say at this point was, "And who was it from Morris, Brunner that you were talking to?"

"A guy named John Grey. He seemed like an OK guy."

I rather coldly replied, "What one seems and what one actually is can be two very different things."

There was a rather long pause after I said this, and we both just sat there sipping our brandies. Finally Imad said, "Look, I guess I should explain how all this came about. As I said, I was at this party—it was just a small party with some guys in the investment business—and Grey and I got to talking. I was telling him about someone at the bank I worked with who knew a lot more about currencies than those who were running the department did. And I happened to mention that he was Swiss. Grey told me that he used to work for a Swiss guy when he was at Morris, Brunner who seemed to know a lot about currencies too, but he said that it clearly could not be the same person. The Swiss guy that Grey had worked for had been banned from the securities business for life after being convicted of something or other. And obviously the Second National Bank would not hire anyone with that kind of record. Grey then mentioned that this guy's name was Kurt Wenner."

"So how long have you known this?"

"Since last weekend."

"And Grey now knows that I'm back in New York too."

"No. When he mentioned your name, I just shook my head and said that it was a coincidence that we both had worked with guys from Switzerland. There would be no reason for him to follow up on our conversation, and anyway he had had a lot to drink and probably doesn't even remember our discussion."

I still could not figure out what Imad's game was, so I said, "And you've waited a week to tell me that you know all this."

"Look, Kurt, I imagine that you're somewhat upset that anyone else knows about what happened eleven or twelve years ago, but I don't intend to tell anyone else what Grey told me. I happen to think that you're a pretty smart guy and I have the same opinion of myself. So maybe sometime in the future you and I can find a way to cooperate on something. I have no idea today as to what that might be, but I hope that we can be friends and be able to take advantage of any opportunity that might come along."

I closed my eyes with my head down for a minute or two, feeling that my world might be crashing down on me again. If there were only some way that I could strike out—slug someone or strangle someone or cause John Grey to disappear from the face of the earth—I really wanted to do it. But finally, gathering all the willpower I could muster, and feeling that I had no alternative, I looked Imad directly in his eyes, saying, "I think we ought to have another brandy to celebrate our newfound friendship."

When I got back to my apartment, I sat up half the night thinking about this new development. My first thought, of course, was the confrontation with Elsa back at Schleswigbank when my world had collapsed as she accused me of taking the money that her father had wanted her to have. Somehow that final confrontation with Elsa still seemed to haunt me, and it always came to mind whenever I was faced with a new problem. However, I realized that tonight was different: Imad was not accusing me of anything as Elsa had been. Tonight I did not have to plan to flee and start a new life somewhere else, as was the case after Elsa's accusation. But there was no question that Imad's knowledge of my past was a serious development.

Next I thought of Naomi and realized that she had been right—I should have changed my name either on the ship when I left New York or at least in Los Angeles. I remembered that she wanted me to take another name—I think she suggested Weinstein—and told me I was a real idiot for keeping the name Wenner. She had been right; I should have tried to escape the past. And it was a real blow to find that I could not escape it. I really thought that I had been able to do that with my foray into Irmane's office and the destruction of my fingerprinting records. Since I had never heard anything further from Human Resources after I started at the Second National Bank, I was convinced that I had been successful in preventing the bank from learning about my past in New York. For all the years that I lived in LA, my past had never been an issue, but it had certainly risen up pretty dramatically tonight.

I couldn't help feeling sorry for myself, going all the way back to that terrible mistake that Ingrid talked me into at Schleswigbank. I still felt that I was not a criminal in any sense of the word; all I had done, both in Zürich and New York, was to take advantage of opportunities that had fallen in front of me. I kept thinking that if it had not been for what Ingrid convinced me to do at Schleswigbank, I would almost certainly be one of the top officials of that bank today—if not actually having taken the place of Dr. Hofbeck. I sat there dreaming for quite some time, trying to imagine what it would have been like if I had been the managing director of Schleswigbank, and what a really marvelous life I could have had. Instead, here I was living in West New York and taking a cheap jitney into the city every morning. And now my very professional existence in New York was under threat. I'm sure I felt more depressed after the confrontation with Elsa, but having my cover blown by Imad was still very upsetting.

However, I had to concentrate on what had just happened, and the question that I had had at the Bull and Bear kept coming back—what was Imad's game? Why didn't he run immediately to Dick Engle or to Ana Maria Ortega and tell them what he had found out about me? And why didn't he even let on to Grey that the two of them had been talking about the same person? After wrestling with that question for a couple of hours, I finally decided that I would not be able to answer it that night. I would only be able to understand Imad if I got to know him a lot better and that would take time, probably a good deal of time. I got up, took a tranquillizer, and went to bed. My mind continued to whirl for an hour or so, but I finally went to sleep, not waking up until late Saturday morning.

While I was distressed by what Imad had said and felt that I had to think about that a great deal more, I was also looking forward to my next conversation with Susan. In fact, after Imad told me what he knew about my past, I became even more anxious to talk with Susan. But I still waited the full nine days that

I had planned before finally calling her. When she answered, I said, "Susan, this is Kurt."

"Oh, I thought you had forgotten me again."

"Susan, I never forgot you, but my life has been in turmoil since I got kicked out of Morris, Brunner."

She seemed almost impatient with what I had said, and responded, "Kurt, why are you calling?"

"Obviously, I want to get together with you."

There was a pause, until she said, "What did you have in mind?"

"How about dinner at the Four Seasons Restaurant on 52nd Street on Friday?"

"I could do that. What time?"

"Let's make it seven o'clock, and I'll have a reservation in the Pool Room."

"OK, I'll see you there."

I was going to suggest that I could pick her up, which would have been rather inconvenient for me if she still lived downtown as she did before and I had to come in from New Jersey to get her, but fortunately she never gave me the chance.

When Friday came, I got to the Four Seasons a little early and ordered a bottle of chardonnay since I remembered that that was a wine that she liked. She arrived only a minute or two later and I was struck by the change in her appearance. She may have been a young thirty when she worked for me at Morris, Brunner, so she would now be about forty-two. And she was clearly not the eager young woman who traveled with me to Italy and Switzerland. She was now far more mature and actually seemed to have a certain elegance about her.

After the usual greeting—I kissed her on both cheeks as one does—I then poured some wine for both of us and offered a toast, "To us." As I said it, it occurred to me that this was the toast that Imad had used just a few days before.

She shook her head slightly as I said that, but smiled and raised her glass. After a minute she said, "You must be doing very well, Kurt, to afford the Four Seasons."

"Since I'm only working at the Second National Bank, I can't say that I'm doing all that well."

"I'm surprised that you're at a bank. I thought you would not be able to work in the investment world again after what had happened at Morris, Brunner."

"Oh, that was twelve years ago, and I think it's all forgotten now."

All she said was, "Lucky you."

The rest of the dinner seemed somewhat strained and I was making every effort to be as friendly and upbeat as I could. I could not remember having to make such an effort with Susan before.

I finally said as we were having coffee, "Well, Susan, I hope . . ."

But before I could finish my thought, she jumped in to say, "I hope to God that you're not going to say that you hope we could resume our old relationship. You've got to know—but you probably don't since you've almost certainly never thought about it—that getting back together with you is the last thing in the world I would be willing to consider. You've never thought of me—you've probably never thought of anyone else in your whole life. The only thing you ever think of is yourself. The whole world revolves around you, doesn't it, Kurt? You're the best looking, you're the smartest, you're the greatest, and no one else matters. After the disaster at Morris, Brunner, I tried calling you I don't know how many times, but you wouldn't take my calls. It never occurred to you that I might be upset because of what had happened. You were too concerned with your own feelings to think of anyone else. And then you never, ever called me after your sentence appeared in the newspapers—you just disappeared from New York and, for all I knew, you were dead.

"You can't imagine how often I was hoping to read in the papers that your body had been found somewhere. But I did finally pull my life together—it took time—but I did it, and I now have a very good job—thanks to all that you taught me—and I'm married and have a beautiful young son who will be six next month. So the only reason I came here tonight is because I love the Dover sole at The Four Seasons and I wanted to tell you what a fucking bastard I think you are."

With that Susan quickly got up and walked out, leaving me sitting there somewhat stunned. Fortunately, the tables at the Four Seasons are far enough apart that I don't think anyone heard what she had said. There was still a fair amount of wine in the bottle so I slowly finished the wine and then ordered dessert and coffee. While I sat there, I thought about what Susan had said and acknowledged to myself that there might be some truth to it, but I also felt that she had not understood how traumatic it had been for me when my world had fallen apart twelve years previously. Seeing her at that time would have been a real distraction for me, so I could not blame myself today for what had happened then. However, what really irritated me the most right now was that I had been so weak as to give in and call Susan—that was the real mistake. I should have understood after my failed attempt to get together with Tony when I called him from Montevideo that I should never try to bring people from one of my past lives into the present. It did not work then and it certainly did not work now.

It took me a few days to get over the confrontation with Susan, but after that the next few months fell into a routine: I would take the jitney into New York in the morning and take it back to Jersey at night, spending rather uneventful days at the office. Since the only restaurants that were close to where I lived in West New York were on Bergenline Avenue, five or six blocks from where I lived, and they were all Hispanic of one kind or another, I never went out for dinner and would microwave a Stouffer's frozen meal almost every night that I spent in my little apartment.

The one thing that did occur during that summer of 1990 was that Imad and I got into the routine of having drinks and dinner every Friday night. This was usually at the Bull and Bear, but we occasionally tried other restaurants, such as Smith and Wollensky's or the Palm. But the Bull and Bear was convenient, the food was not bad, and the dining room was rarely crowded, so we ended up going there most of the time. At those dinners, I really was able to get very little specific information about Imad or his motivation, but I did get to realize that he was a very smart person and was driven to succeed. I also came to understand that Imad considered himself to have been discriminated against because of his Egyptian background, and that he felt that this was holding back his career.

When September came around, Ana Maria Ortega called me into her office and told me what a great job she thought I had been doing. She apparently had received some very positive feedback from my clients and, as a result, she told me that I would be getting a raise. In addition, she told me that she wanted me to start traveling to meet with my clients in their home countries. This was great news for me since I had clients in South America and the Far East and would be able to do a great deal of traveling. I could not think of anything I would rather do than to be able to travel first class at the bank's expense and stay at the best hotels wherever I went around the world. I remembered how it had been when I went to Buenos Aires for Schleswigbank, and I was anxious to repeat that experience for The Second National. So with the threat from Imad's discovery seeming to abate, and with a vote of confidence from Ana Maria, the rest of 1990 passed rather quickly and almost pleasantly.

At the end of January 1991, however, there was another Investment Committee meeting, and it turned out that everyone was there—Petersen, Ana Maria, Engle, Imad, and all the other investment officers. The minutes of the Committee meeting always started off with a detailed list of all the purchases and sales that had occurred in our clients' accounts during the preceding month. Usually no one paid any attention to these, but at this meeting Petersen started off by saying, "I'm afraid that I have some questions about some of these transactions. Kurt, could you tell me how it happened that during the past month you were selling a lot of Australian dollars out of your accounts."

I quickly responded, "Those had been directed purchases and since there were fairly substantial gains in all of their investments, the clients decided to sell."

Petersen stared at me for a minute, and then said, "Do you really expect me to believe that seven of our clients independently decided some time ago, completely on their own, that the Australian dollar was a good investment, and then they all decided in the same month to take profits in those investments? And none of our other clients, managed by other investment officers, were similarly motivated to buy or sell the Australian currency?"

I hesitated for a few seconds before responding, but finally said, "No, of course, I don't expect you to believe that. As you know, I have personally liked the Aussie dollar and have told that to my clients when they asked for my personal opinion. But I always tried to make it clear that it was my opinion and not the bank's, and that they would have to take responsibility for the purchases by directing them since buying Aussie dollars was not official bank policy."

Petersen shook his head and again looking directly at me said, "I guess I fail to see how we can have any kind of effective investment management organization if each of the investment officers is free to run off and tell our clients what he thinks, even though it is diametrically opposed to what the bank is recommending. Maybe you can explain that to me."

Before I could say anything, Ana Maria said, "I would also like to hear your explanation."

I was more than a little irritated by what seemed to me to be a deliberate attack on my professional capabilities, but I tried to restrain my response, saying, "It has always seemed to me that successful investment management was highly dependent on building trust between the advisor and the client. I thought that I was doing that by giving the client my personal opinion as to the Aussie dollar, but making it clear that my opinion was not the same as the bank's."

Petersen quickly said, "It seems to me, however, that what you're doing is to confuse the client and, at the same time, undermine the bank's credibility as their investment advisor. Wouldn't you agree with that, Ana Maria?"

"Absolutely. Nothing could be more confusing to a client than to receive conflicting advice from one of our investment officers. This just has to stop."

Petersen now said in a very authoritative tone of voice, "I know that you have spent many years at your own investment counseling firm, Kurt, and it may be hard for you to understand how necessary it is for our investment officers to adhere to the policies that are established here by this Committee. But that is a necessity, and I hope you understand that."

I would have loved to get up and walk out of that conference room, quitting right on the spot. I must have turned beet red since I was so mad. To think that this young guy, who came from Chicago or someplace out west, and who knew nothing whatsoever about currencies, was telling me that I had to adhere to his totally unimaginative ideas simply infuriated me. But I could never do anything as rash as quitting right on the spot, so I very coldly and in slow, measured tones said, "You should understand, Mr. Petersen, that I was in the Swiss Army many years ago, and while in the army I learned to take orders, to accept orders, and to follow orders. I can assure you that I can do the same thing here at the Second National Bank. There will be no more purchases or sales of any non-approved currency in any of my accounts."

Petersen looked almost cocky as he forced me to give in to his authority, and he merely smiled at my somewhat antagonistic statement, and responded, "Good. I'm glad we agree on that, so let's move on."

After that, I did not pay too much attention to what was being said for a good part of the rest of the Committee meeting. But I finally stopped seething internally and became aware that a very important account located in Lima, Peru, was being discussed. Ana Maria felt that the investment officer should go to Lima to meet with the client, who was considering moving his account to another bank. However, because the Shining Path guerilla movement in Peru had recently carried out some raids in and near Lima, the investment officer, Alberto Moreira, was reluctant to travel there. Ana Maria said, "We certainly can't require you to travel to Peru if you're concerned about your safety. But I hope that we don't lose this account—it's one of our biggest in Latin America."

At that point, I said, "I would have no problem in traveling to Lima. Those reports of raids by groups like the Shining Path are usually completely overblown. I wouldn't have any concern about going there."

Ana Maria said, "Well, let me think about it. You and Alberto come to my office after this meeting is done and we can discuss it."

I really don't know why I offered to go to Lima. I think it was partly just a desire to get away from the bank after my run-in with Petersen. But it was also a desire to show the young relationship officers that even though I was fifty-eight, I still had the nerve to do things that they were either afraid or unwilling to do. It ended up, of course, that Ana Maria not only agreed that I should go to Lima, but she transferred the Peruvian account to me. As a result, I became the investment manager for the Alvarado family, which was one of the largest accounts in the department. That committee meeting seemed to me to cut two ways—it helped my relationship with Ana Maria, but probably significantly hurt the relationship with Petersen.

Chapter XXXIV

The trip to Peru was perfectly routine, and I think I started to develop a good rapport with Señor Alvarado, the head of the family. The meeting included the entire family, which was rather large, including four sons and three daughters. However, since the father made all the important decisions, he was the only one that I needed to worry about.

But there was a more important development from my personal viewpoint: I also met a young woman in Lima who totally captivated me. Her name was Rosario Martinez, and I don't even want to think about what her profession might have been before I met her. One night when I came back to the hotel from dinner with the client and his family, I went into the bar to have a brandy before going to bed. I sat down at the bar and, as I looked up, I saw this really beautiful woman seated directly across from me. I just sat there—I could not stop staring at her, she was so beautiful. She had full, long, dark hair; from a distance it looked to me as if she had either very dark brown or black eyes; and she sat smoking a cigarette with an almost regal air, as if she were waiting for someone to pay her court. There was no way I could resist moving over next to her and trying to begin a conversation. For once in my life, I really did not know what to say, but after sitting next to her for a minute or two, I finally just blurted out, "I hope you don't mind my sitting here." I was sitting on the bar stool next to her, but as I turned toward her, my knee pushed against her thigh.

She did not move her leg, but turned her head toward me and said with total self-assurance, "I noticed that you seemed to be staring at me from across the bar so I expected that you might come over. Have we met sometime in the past?"

"No, I'm sure we haven't, but I could not help staring, and I hope you don't mind my saying it, but I couldn't help myself since you seem to me to be so beautiful." When she simply smiled and did not respond, I went on, "May I buy you a drink?"

"Of course, you may. That would be the conventional thing to do, since we are, after all, sitting at a bar."

After the drinks were served, and she did not bother to give an order since the bartender seemed to know what she was drinking, she said, "And what brings you to Lima? I cannot believe that you are here simply as a tourist."

"No, I work for a bank in New York."

"And your work brings you to Lima frequently?"

"I've only just started coming here, but I expect that I will be visiting Lima more frequently in the future."

I thought I felt her leg push slightly harder against my knee as she said, "You must be terribly important to the bank to come here frequently and to be staying at a hotel like the Basadre Suites."

I merely smiled at her remark, and made a gesture to indicate that this was not important. Since I said nothing, she then asked, "What bank is it?"

"The Second National Bank of New York."

"Oh, I've heard of that bank. I'm told it's one of the most important banks in the world."

"Well, yes I like to think that it is."

"And you're the president of the bank?" As she said this, her leg moved almost imperceptibly up and down against my knee.

I was only too happy to respond as I pushed my leg very slightly back against her, saying, "No, I'm afraid not. I'm just a humble little clerk."

She threw her head back and laughed at my remark. We kept on talking like this for ten or fifteen minutes longer, until I put my hand on her arm and said, "I really think that we should have another drink, but I'm sure it would be more comfortable in my suite. What do you think?"

"I think that bar stools can become very uncomfortable after a while."

With that we got up and walked toward the elevators and, as we left the bar, I noticed that she waved to the bartender. A few hours after we got to my suite, I had been totally hooked by her. The sex was good, of course, but I was amazed and flattered that a woman this young—she was probably in her late twenties—would have anything to do with someone as old as I. I know that I should have asked myself why this was so, but I really could not think clearly at that time.

As I lay in bed with her the next morning, I thought about the fact that I had not had a meaningful relationship with a woman since I was dating Susan about twelve years previously in New York. There had been the usual one-night stands both in New York and Los Angeles, but I had not felt really captivated by any woman in all that time, and really had never felt completely captivated by Susan. Ingrid was probably the only one that I had had that kind of feeling for, and then only at the start of our marriage. But I certainly felt captivated by Rosario that morning, and was determined that this would not be a one-night stand.

I was due to return to New York a few hours later, but I got out of bed and went into the other room in the suite to phone the airline and change my flight so I could stay in Lima for four more days. I then phoned the bank in New York and left a message with Dick Engle saying that I liked Lima so much I was taking a few days of vacation to get to know the place better. I went back into the bedroom and found that Rosario was awake. I told her that I was staying on for a few days so that I could see her more frequently. She seemed pleased, and said, "That's wonderful. But are you telling me that all you had to do was to call the bank and just tell them that you were staying here for a few more days, and that you didn't have to get anyone's approval?"

"No, I didn't need to get anyone's approval. I just told them that I was taking a few days' vacation."

"You must be very important if you can just call the bank and tell them that you won't be back for several days."

I simply shrugged my shoulders and laughed, saying, "It comes with the job."

We ordered breakfast and were sitting in the hotel bathrobes when room service arrived. As we were eating, she said, "I don't think you've really seen anything of Lima or Peru before, have you? In that case, it will be great fun for me to act as your tour guide. I know a wonderful driver who can take us around, and will make everything very easy for you."

My idea, of course, was never to leave the bedroom, but I knew that if I was going to build any kind of relationship with her, I had to agree to her suggestion. I also knew the limits of my own sexual prowess and realized that 100 percent of the time in the bedroom would not be a good idea. After breakfast, Rosario told me that she would go back to her suite to get dressed for the day. This surprised me since I had not known that she was staying at the hotel, but she explained that she did not live in Lima and only came into the city occasionally, always staying at this hotel.

When I learned this, I said, "Wouldn't it be better if you moved in here with me? We could be together more frequently, and I think it would save you a great deal of money."

"If you're sure that's what you want I'll have the bellboy bring my things here."

She then started to leave, just wearing a bathrobe, and I said, "But you can't go like that."

She laughed and said, "Why not? If I see anyone, they will think I'm going to the pool. This hotel has a lovely pool—you must try it or, better still, we will try it together."

A few hours later, we were seated in the back of a chauffeur-driven limousine as Rosario took me on the first of several tours of Lima. I can't begin to remember where we went as she led me through cathedrals, museums, and all kinds of historical sites in the city. I was totally focused on her all the while that we were in the car together on these trips, and I kept hoping that we could get back to the hotel and into bed as quickly as possible.

On my last full day in Lima, I went to the concierge at the hotel and asked him to recommend a jewelry shop since I wanted to buy something for Rosario. He recommended Casa Banchero, which was not far from the hotel, and without telling Rosario what I wanted to do, I suggested that we go for a walk rather than be chauffeured around in the limousine again. Although she may have had some idea as to what I had in mind, she readily agreed to the walk, and it only took about fifteen minutes for us to reach the jewelry store. Casa Banchero turned out to be a very elegant-looking store and I suggested to Rosario that we go in.

She shook her head, saying, "Why do you want to go in there? It's a horribly expensive store. If you want to buy something for a friend back in the States, I can take you to several other places that are much more reasonable."

I said, "Well, I like the looks of this place, and I'd like to take a look inside."

Rosario said, "If you're going to buy jewelry in Peru, you should at least buy authentic Incan jewelry, and I know a number of stores that specialize in that kind of thing."

I did not respond, but as she was holding my arm, I took hold of her hand and simply led her inside. A sales clerk came up to us right away and I told him that I was looking for a bracelet or a ring for my wife. He began showing me various pieces of jewelry and Rosario shook her head to show her disagreement with what I was doing. She actually stood several steps back from where I was talking with the clerk and began looking in another showcase. After a few minutes, I turned to show something to Rosario, but as I looked up I saw one of the Alvarado daughters several counters away. This put me in somewhat of a difficult situation since I was sure that she had seen me, and I felt that I had to recognize her. But it was also necessary to keep client relationships confidential, so I said to Rosario, "Excuse me, but I am going to have to go and say hello to that woman over there."

Rosario seemed stunned, saying, "Do you know her?"

"Yes . . . Yes, I do."

"But she's an Alvarado."

"Yes, I know. But excuse me for just a minute."

I then walked over to the woman—who looked as if she was in her mid to late forties. She was a fairly attractive woman, although I thought that she had a rather haughty air about her. I said, "Miss Alvarado, what a coincidence meeting you here."

"Yes, isn't it. I had thought, Mr. Wenner, that you had gone back to New York on Friday, after our meeting."

"I had planned to do that, but decided to stay on to see a few other people here in Lima and to get to know the city somewhat better."

"I do hope that you're finding your stay enjoyable."

"As a matter of fact, it has been quite enjoyable." I made a gesture toward Rosario as I said this.

Miss Alvarado then said, "I assume that Miss Martinez has been showing you around."

"Yes, she's been very helpful. Do you know her?"

"I do not personally, but I understand that one of my brothers has met her."

"May I introduce you?"

Miss Alvarado seemed to smile somewhat grimly as she said, almost accusingly, "You are an American, aren't you?" There was a pause until she added, "No, thank you, I really must be going. It was certainly nice running into you here."

I was going to say, "No, I am not an American, I am Swiss, and I understand class distinctions," but I did not want to offend her, so I half bowed and said, "Pease give my regards to your father."

As I turned to leave, she said, "Oh, Mr. Wenner, let me warn you of one thing—this is a terribly expensive store. You must be very careful what you agree to buy here."

"Yes, Miss Martinez has said the same thing, and has encouraged me to go elsewhere." I did not want her to think that I was buying something for Rosario, so I added, "I am looking for something for my niece back in New York, and Miss Martinez has suggested that I look at some native Incan jewelry."

Miss Alvarado's smile seemed rather forced as she said, "That's probably a very good suggestion."

I then went back to Rosario but since the sales clerk was there, we said very little to each other, and she announced that she would wait outside. As she left, the clerk said, "I had not realized that you were a friend of the Alvarados. In a special case like this, the management of Casa Banchero would be happy to offer you a 25 percent discount on anything you might decide to buy."

I wondered if the Alvarado family might be part owners of the store, which would explain why the daughter was shopping there, even though she thought its prices were very expensive. I did pick out a beautiful bracelet and had the store gift wrap it and send it to the hotel. Even with the 25 percent discount, the bracelet was still extraordinarily expensive, but I put it on my credit card, feeling that I could pay it off over the next several years, if necessary.

I then went outside and joined Rosario, who immediately attacked me by saying, "Are you trying to tell me that you know the Alvarado family?"

"Rosario, I'm not trying to tell you anything. I do know them, of course, but they are clients and we simply have a business relationship."

"You know them all?"

"Well, at least I've met them all."

"Even the head of the family, Señor Alvarado?"

"Of course, he's the most important one. He's the decision maker."

"Have you seen him alone or just with the whole family?"

"Yes, I did see him alone. There seems to be some things that he does not want to discuss in front of the entire family."

"But getting an appointment with him is like getting a private audience with the Pope."

I laughed and said, "I do not consider Señor Alvarado to be anything like the Pope. He's a businessman and we talk about investments and things like that. I can't say that we're great friends, but I think that we respect each other's opinions."

Rosario stood there looking at me for a minute or two and then said, "I have never known anyone else who could simply walk up to Alina Alvarado and begin talking to her. I had thought that you were important before, but this has totally blown away all of my ideas about you. I have to believe that what the chauffeur tells me about you is true—you are the president of the bank."

"Rosario, I am not the president of the Second National Bank. I have never told you that I was. I don't know where the chauffeur or anyone else would get that idea."

"Kurt, let's not argue. With the class distinctions here in Peru, no one— absolutely no one—can do what you just did. You walked up to a member of the Alvarado family and began talking to her, and she carried on a conversation with you, instead of demanding that the store have you thrown out. That puts you in a really unique class."

"Rosario, let's not argue about this. From my viewpoint, talking to Alina was no big deal."

She smiled beautifully at that point, and then said, "OK, have it your way. But what I really want to know is what she said about me."

"She said that one of her brothers knew you or may have met you."

"The bitch. She knows that I was going with her brother for a time, and the whole family was scared to death that he might ask me to marry him. Fortunately from their viewpoint, Jorge was a real rat and never carried through on all his promises."

"Well, one more thing—I did ask her if I could introduce you to her, and she accused me of being an American, implying that I would not understand the social structure in Peru."

"Thank you for making that offer. But it must have killed her to think that she might have been forced to meet me."

We then walked back to the hotel and, instead of going up to our suite, I led her into the bar, where I ordered a bottle of champagne. I thought that it would be better to sit in the bar for a time, have a drink, and relax, rather than go to the suite where there might be pressure to go into the bedroom. I am sure that she appreciated this and before we had finished even half of the bottle, we were both in much better spirits.

I had to leave the next morning and, as I looked back on the preceding four days, I realized just how wonderful they had been. Going to the airport and leaving Rosario was extraordinarily difficult, and I left Lima determined to return as quickly as I could.

Chapter XXXV

After I had been back in New York for a week, Imad and I had dinner and I filled him in on the details of the trip. He said, "That was a shrewd move on your part to volunteer for that trip. After your argument with Petersen, I was afraid that you might not be with us too much longer."

"I didn't argue with Petersen. I was trying to show that I would obey his orders in every respect."

"Well, all that business about taking orders while you were in the Swiss Army sounded kind of hostile."

"What did you want me to do—get down on my knees and beg forgiveness."

"At any rate, I think that by agreeing to go to Lima, despite all the dangers down there, you were able to show Ana Maria and maybe even Eric that you were a team player, after all."

I shook my head, and said, "There were no dangers. The Shining Path operates out in the jungle somewhere. I have to say that I really enjoyed Lima and, as you know, I took several days' vacation to get to know the place better."

Imad laughed and said, "When I heard that you were taking some vacation time while down there, I began to wonder if there wasn't some other attraction keeping you there."

I was constantly thinking about Rosario. These days she was, quite literally, always on my mind, so on an impulse I decided I would tell Imad about her now. "As a matter of fact, there was. I did meet a very attractive young woman, and she managed to keep me occupied for a few days. And I expect that I'm going to have to go back to Lima with some frequency from now on. I just keep on thinking about her and I have to see her again. I just can't get her out of my mind."

"Well, don't overdo it, because that's one sure way of getting into trouble—either with the bank or with the woman, or both."

I waited a minute or two while the busboy was clearing the table of our dinner dishes, and then, changing the subject, said, "It looks like I might be in trouble already."

Imad frowned and said, "Why?"

"I've been buying a lot of bonds from David Green, a broker down in Philadelphia with a very small, old-line bond-trading firm, Forgen and Company. I always like buying bonds that are part of a relatively small original issue and Forgen specializes in this type of thing. The yields are usually a lot better, although there might not be as much liquidity as in the big, actively traded issues. The problem is that Forgen is not on the bank's list of approved brokers. And some guy named Falcone—I forget his first name—who is in some Auditing Department, came around saying I shouldn't be trading with that firm."

"What's the problem? Just blame it on the trading desk."

"I really can't do that, because sometimes I've done the trade myself, and other times I have to twist some arms to get the trading desk to use Forgen."

"If that's the case then I do think that you have a problem. You know that you shouldn't be doing trades yourself."

"That's what Falcone tells me."

My dinner with Imad was on a Friday night, and I had to wait until the following Wednesday before I got summoned to Petersen's office. When I came in he was on the phone, so I had an opportunity to look around and get an impression as to the kind of office he had. This one could not have been decorated more differently than the office that Dr. Hofbeck had back in Zürich. Petersen's office was furnished with the very simple, very plain, and ultra-modern furniture that the Second National Bank used everywhere. And Petersen had not really added very much to the basics. There were two rather nice modern prints on the wall—the bank let senior executives pick the art for their office from the bank's rather extensive collection of modern art. But otherwise, the office was spotlessly clean, there was no disorder anywhere, and the whole place seemed to me to be rather cold.

When Petersen got off the phone, he said to me, "Roger Falcone has come to me to tell me about some of your trading activities. Roger is in the bank's control group and these people do not report to me. As you probably know, this is an independent group, like the Auditing Department, and they report to the head control guy downtown. So I have to listen to him. Maybe you can explain what it is that has gotten him so upset."

"I'm sure that I can, Mr. Petersen. I want to show you the trades that have bothered Falcone."

I then proceeded to show Petersen details on all of the trades that I had made with Forgen and Company, and explained why I thought that each one of them had been a good deal for our clients.

Petersen then asked, "And you know that Forgen is not a brokerage firm that is approved by the control group for use within the bank?"

"Yes, I know that, but they are a unique firm. They offer very interesting deals, such as the ones I've just shown you."

"What brokerage commissions do they charge?"

"They don't charge a commission. All the trades we do with them are net."

"So you're not getting any kickback from them?"

I was insulted by the question, but quickly answered, "Absolutely not."

Petersen then said, "Look, I'm sorry that I had to ask that question, but that's what Falcone is particularly worried about—that you, or someone at the trading desk, is getting a kickback."

"Mr. Petersen, I can assure you that nothing like that has occurred or will occur. I suggest that you send Falcone down to Philadelphia, Forgen's head office, and review all of their records, and I know that he will find everything is absolutely OK. When I had my own counseling firm in Los Angeles, everything was audited each year, and I know that everything will be audited here. So I can assure you that these are all absolutely legitimate transactions for our clients' accounts."

Petersen thought for a while before saying anything, but he finally said, "OK, you go and draft a memo for me to sign that permits the trading desk—not you, just the trading desk—to trade through Forgen. And it should be limited to the kind of corporate and municipal bond issues that you've been buying from them up till now. You have to understand that I'm taking a big risk in doing this, since if you screw up in any way and it costs the bank money, it will be your head and my head on the same platter."

I came away from that meeting feeling pretty good about the bank and about Petersen. He was not going to take my advice about currencies since I don't think that he really knew anything about that asset class. But he could understand that that there was lot of attraction in getting good investment-grade bonds with above average yields. So I was going to be permitted to go on with my trading activity.

This meeting with Petersen had taken place in June, and things settled down after that for the rest of the summer. I now had authority to trade the bond portfolios that I was managing pretty much as I wanted, as long as everything was reported to the Committee. From that point on, there were no further disagreements between Petersen and me. Nothing much was happening in my personal life either. It was impossible for me to schedule a trip to Lima during the summer and, while I talked with Rosario frequently on the phone, I was really upset that there was no way for the two of us to get together.

However, I did manage to secure an appointment with the Alvarado family for late September, and I then started to see if I could find other wealthy families or big institutions that I could call upon in Peru. Lima was much smaller than Sao Paulo or Buenos Aires and there simply was not the personal or institutional wealth in Peru that there was in Brazil or Argentina. As a result, there were only a limited number of new business calls I could make in Lima. So I went back to Ana Maria and suggested that starting in the fall, I be permitted to make new business calls in Brazil and Argentina whenever I went to Peru, since most of the airfare would be covered by the trip to Lima. Ana Maria thought that this was a great idea, and approved it right away. However, she insisted that I provide detailed call reports not only as to the meetings with the Alvarado family, but also as to all of the new business calls that I might make.

Getting the ability to travel to Sao Paulo and Buenos Aires at bank expense really helped my relationship with Rosario. She was a young woman who had never really travelled outside of Lima. While she was extraordinarily beautiful and had a certain refinement about her, I had come to learn that her family was quite poor, and she had not had much of an education. Everything that she had learned and her whole refined manner had been picked up through her experiences in meeting people at places like the bar where I met her. I never thought of her other than as an unfortunate young woman who had a great deal to offer. And in discussing her with Imad, I made sure that I never said anything that would let him get any other impression. But deep down I had to recognize what her past had really been. So being able to travel to Sao Paulo and Buenos Aires was tremendously exciting for her. I would always arrange for her to travel first class with me, and we stayed in suites at the best hotels in both cities. Fortunately, my expense accounts either were not checked very carefully back at the Second National Bank, or since I was considered to be a unique employee, no one felt that those expense accounts should be challenged.

Through the fall of 1991 and the first half of 1992, I made five trips to South America. I was always in the process of planning a trip, in the process of taking the trip or reporting on it when I got back. I am sure that Rosario was delighted as she entered into a whole new lifestyle. And my relationship with her caused me to be happier than I could ever recall being.

However, I always kept worrying that something was going to happen that would end this happiness, and I could not imagine with that might be. Unfortunately, that something happened far more quickly than I could ever have anticipated. When I got back to New York in late September from a trip to Lima, Sao Paulo, and Buenos Aires, Ana Maria asked me to come to her office. I was afraid that she would question my expense accounts or be upset that I had obtained only a few relatively small new accounts. What she told me, however, was totally unanticipated:

"Kurt, you have certainly been diligent in your travels to Peru and the other countries down there. I had hoped that we would have seen more new business by now, but I know that it takes time to build relationships and to convince potential clients to move their accounts to another institution. No, my concern right now is the Alvarado account. Since you have been calling on them, I see that they have been a lot more active and done a lot more trading, and that's all to the good. I assume all this trading is due to the fact that you have been seeing them with much greater frequency than anyone from the bank had seen them in the past.

"I have to tell you that I've been very pleased with what you have been doing, but going forward I've decided that we have to have a team approach to a major account like this. And I want to do this not just in Latin American, but in the Middle East as well. We have some very large accounts in the Middle

East, one of which is for a branch of the Saudi royal family. I think it makes a much better impression on the client if there are at least two people from the bank at every meeting with the client. Wouldn't you agree?"

I was not prepared for Ana Maria's suggestion, and all I could say was, "Perhaps you could explain in a little more detail exactly what you have in mind."

"It's really quite simple. I'm going to designate another investment officer to work with you on the Alvarado account, as well as other important accounts, so that he can join you when you meet with the client, either in Lima or here in New York. That way if you are on vacation or away if they were to call unexpectedly, someone will be fully familiar with their activity."

To gain time while I tried to think of a way to argue against this idea, I said, "And you would have this person travel with me to Lima as well as Sao Paulo and Buenos Aires?"

"Yes."

"But there would be much greater expense with two of us traveling."

"That's right, but I think it will help in the retention of the Alvarado account, and will make our new business presentations more effective."

This plan would destroy the arrangement that I had to see Rosario in Lima and to have her travel with me to Brazil and Argentina, but I could not think of any way to fight it. Ana Maria was the boss, and it was clear that we were not discussing her idea—she was simply informing me of her decision.

I did not say anything for a minute or two, so Ana Maria continued, "Kurt, I know that you are a real team player so working with someone like Jim Turner will not be a problem for you."

"Jim Turner is the one you've designated to work with me?"

"Yes, I think he is a very impressive young guy, and he is really looking forward to working with you. I think you know that he used to live in Brazil and speaks both Spanish and Portuguese, I'm told rather fluently."

"Yes, I've heard about his linguistic capabilities, but you know that I speak Spanish fluently myself—it's my second language."

"Of course I know that, Kurt, and I don't want you to think that adding Turner to your team will in any way lessen your importance in our Latin American marketing."

"Thank you. I guess you've already told Turner."

"I wanted to discuss this with you first, but you were in South America and I felt it was necessary to move ahead with this plan throughout the department."

"So Turner will go with me on the next trip."

"Of course, but you should start to familiarize him with your accounts starting right away."

There was clearly no room for argument, so I simply said, "OK, I'll get on it," and got up and left her office.

Back in my own office I felt crushed. How could I explain this to Rosario? She loved traveling with me, staying in the fancy hotels, and eating in all the best restaurants. All this would now end. If Turner were with me in Lima, it would be very difficult if not impossible to have Rosario stay with me at the hotel, and she clearly could not travel with me to Sao Paulo or Buenos Aires. I was really going to have to think up a way to explain this to her.

I decided that I would have to cancel the trip that I had planned for the following month. I knew that the Alvarados would not care since on this trip I was only going to see two of the sons and a couple of their local advisors. Señor Alvarado spent a great deal of time in Spain, and the other members of the family were only interested in meeting with me if they had nothing else to do or needed some more spending money. So I simply sent them a fax saying that something had come up and I would have to postpone my trip until later in the fall. Since I had not begun to make appointments for new business calls in Brazil or Argentina, there was nothing else to do to cancel the trip, other than to talk with Rosario.

The Peruvian winter season started in June and lasted through to late October. Temperatures did not go to extremes at any time of the year, so while it would be cloudy and rainy during the June to October period, there was no reason not to travel there at that time. When I was able to reach Rosario by phone, I told her that the trip had been postponed until October, and I tried to convince her how desolate I was by the cancellation. She was quite disappointed, but did not really buy my explanation, saying, "Kurt, you're the boss. You should decide these things. If you really wanted to come here, you would go ahead and do it, and not let other people order you about." I could not remember having to argue with Rosario before, but she had clearly been counting on my trip and everything that that implied. She was not at all happy that the trip was not going to take place. I had to face the fact that she had made it clear that she was more concerned about not staying at the best hotels and shopping at the fancy stores in Sao Paulo and Buenos Aires than she was about not seeing me.

I had never told her explicitly that I was the boss and ran the bank, but she had gotten that idea from the way I lived in Lima and the other cities, and from that chauffeur we had on our sightseeing trips around Lima, who kept insisting that I was El Presidenté. I simply did not know how to convince her that this was not the case. The conversation ended up being quite unsatisfactory, and all I could do was to promise her that I would try to reschedule for October. A few days later, I decided to send her some money so she could take a vacation, and suggested that she go to Cartagena in Colombia. She took the money, but did not go away.

The other question that I had after meeting with Ana Maria concerned why she had done this. My mind kept flipping back and forth between the blow that this decision has given to my relationship with Rosario and trying to figure out Ana Maria's motivation in doing it. She did not seem upset with anything I had done since I had begun handling the Alvarado account because I am sure that she would have made her concerns quite clear during our discussion. I decided that she was probably afraid that I was getting too close to the Alvarado family, and she was worried that I might again form my own investment counseling firm and take that account away from the bank. I decided that I would have to find a way to dissuade her from that idea since I had no thought at all of trying to take the Alvarado account away from the bank.

A few nights later I had dinner with Imad again, and he could tell right away that I was pretty depressed. I explained to him everything that was bothering me, and Imad said, "Kurt, I told you that that woman in Peru was going to be a problem for you."

"I don't know if it's that woman in Peru, as you call her, or that woman here in New York who's causing the problem."

"Well, I don't think it makes too much difference which woman you want to blame, but I'm pretty sure that you know that it all boils down to one pretty basic problem."

I was frowning as I looked at Imad, but did not say anything. He went on, "If you had a helluva lot more money, you could take care of Rosario and whatever Ana Maria did would be totally inconsequential."

"I'm sure that's right, but I just don't happen to have a hellluva lot more money, so I can't take care of Rosario as I have been doing, and I can't thumb my nose at Ana Maria."

Imad said, "I think it's really very simple. We just have to find a way to get a helluva lot more money."

I shook my head and said, "Thanks for that brilliant suggestion. How do you think I'm going to get enough money to do all that?"

"Kurt, we're working for an institution that manages billions of dollars for wealthy people all around the world. There ought to be a way to get a few paltry million for us without anyone being any wiser."

"Yeah, Imad, you just go on thinking that. But that's what I thought back at Morris, Brunner, and all I was trying to take was a crumby three or four hundred thousand. And look where it got me."

"But you were working alone. You and I have to put our minds together and come up with a plan so we can each walk away with several millions."

"Sorry, pal, but I'm not buying any more half-baked plans to try to steal money from whomever I happen to be working for at the time. It didn't work back in Zürich—you probably didn't know that I tried it back there too—and it didn't work at Morris, Brunner. I did pretty well in Los Angeles, and I stuck to the straight and narrow all the time I was there. And I intend to do the same thing here."

"OK. But there was a difference. You told me that in LA you had that woman Naomi taking care of you, so money was never a problem for you. But here you really need more money—and a lot more—or you're going to have to forget all about that Peruvian babe."

After Imad said that, we both sat at the table drinking the last of the wine that we had with our meal. It was an Italian brunello and I enjoyed the heavy full flavor of that deep red wine. After a several minutes I said to him, "I wasn't going to tell you this, but I sent Rosario money to try to placate her when this last trip was canceled. I told her to use the money to take a vacation someplace and suggested Cartagena in Colombia. She took the money, but hasn't gone anywhere."

"What do you want her to go to Cartagena for? Have her come here to New York."

"Are you kidding? She thinks I'm the president of the bank. What am I going to do—take her out to West New York so she can see where I live?"

"Rent a furnished apartment here in town and tell her this will be more convenient for her so she can go shopping and do other stuff while you're at work. If she were out at your estate in Jersey, she wouldn't be able to do any of that. She'll love being in town on her own all day."

"God, Imad, you do have some good ideas every once in a while. I've already sent her the money to take a trip, so all I have to do now is to tell her to use that money to come to New York. And she'll love the idea of coming to New York. She has said a couple of times how badly she wanted to come here, so I know she'll jump at the idea. The only thing I'll have to do is keep her from wanting to go out to Jersey to see that fantastic estate I'm supposed to live in out there."

Chapter XXXVI

As I expected, Rosario was delighted when I told her that she should come to New York, and I had to invent any number of excuses to keep her from getting on the next plane to the US. As Imad suggested, I told her that we would be living in town rather than at my country place in New Jersey. So the first thing I had to do was to find a furnished apartment on the Upper East Side in Manhattan and that took some time. I thought that the Upper East Side would be the best location for the apartment since it would be easy to commute to my office at 51st and Park, and I thought there were more places for Rosario to shop in the area—really expensive places on Madison Avenue and a wide variety of places on Lexington.

I finally found an apartment for rent in a coop building at 72nd Street and York, which was being rented by the owner of the apartment who had been transferred to Chicago. It was a one-bedroom apartment, very modern and very nicely furnished. It had been advertised as having one and a half baths, which meant that it had a full bathroom and a powder room. While it was a very nice apartment, it was also unbelievably expensive. I was so enthralled with Rosario at that point, however, that expense was only a very secondary consideration for me. I made sure that she understood that I had rented this apartment just for her, and that normally I would have returned to New Jersey each night. But I told her that as long as she was in the city, I would plan to stay at the apartment with her.

Rosario came up to New York in mid-July 1991 and, since she had to change planes in Miami, her flight from Miami came into LaGuardia Airport. I met her there on a Friday afternoon and I was elated to see her in New York. She seemed as happy as I did that we were together again, and we immediately went off to the new apartment. For the first couple of weeks, things worked out far better than I could have imagined. It seemed that our relationship became less stressful since I knew that she would be there waiting for me when I got home from work in the evening, and I think she felt more secure at the same time. Some of the urgency went out of our sexual relationship as well, although I continued to be captivated by how great we got along in bed.

Living with Rosario was, of course, different than seeing her from time to time on a business trip to Lima, and it was far different from our trips to Sao Paulo and Buenos Aires. Living together on a daily basis in a rather small apartment was not at all like travelling first class and staying in suites in posh hotels. I soon discovered that Rosario could not in any way be considered a housewife, nor did she do any of the things that a housewife would usually do. She expressed surprise that we did not have servants, and I had to tell her that it was impossible to get decent servants in New York. She accepted what I said, but I had the feeling that she did not really believe me.

She readily acknowledged that she knew nothing whatsoever about cooking, which meant that I had to make breakfast in the morning—usually just juice, coffee and toast—and we went out to dinner every night. (I never asked her what she did for lunch.) She clearly loved the most elegant restaurants, such as the Four Seasons or the dining room at the Carlyle Hotel. Other restaurants, such as Café Boulud, even though it might have a renowned chef, really did not interest her if the restaurant itself was not impressive. And while I knew that she always drank a glass of champagne when we were together in South America, in New York she seemed to want to have two or three glasses with each meal. Since eating out in these restaurants was terribly expensive—and the champagne added to the expense—I decided to try cooking in the apartment on a couple of occasions, but it was clear that Rosario was not at all happy with that arrangement.

The biggest adjustment that I had to make with Rosario was to share the apartment with her. I had lived alone since fleeing Switzerland thirty years previously, except for the time that I lived with Naomi in Beverly Hills. But at Naomi's I was really alone, since my room was in a separate part of her house, and Naomi let me come and go completely on my own. But living in a one-bedroom apartment with someone required considerable flexibility on my part, and I think on Rosario's part as well. I don't know if she had lived with anyone before, but at times I felt that she was not as considerate as she should have been. She totally took over the one bathroom so it became impossible for me to use it except for a shower in the morning. As a result, I had to brush my teeth and shave in the powder room. And I don't think she had any idea as to how to make a bed since, unless I made it, it never got done.

But despite the little irritations that arose from time to time and the adjustments that had to be made in our daily routines, I really think that both Rosario and I were extremely happy throughout the summer. I was absolutely convinced that I loved her and—despite the fact that I was so much older than she—I was totally convinced that she loved me too.

This almost idyllic situation with Rosario continued as August rolled into September when I knew that I would soon have to take another trip to South America. I would have loved to take Rosario with me, but the expense of the trip would be too great—especially since I was paying the rent on the apartment on 72nd Street and had never gotten around to getting rid of my old apartment in

West New York. In addition, since Jim Turner would now be travelling with me, it would have been far too awkward to try to bring Rosario along. When I told her that I would have to take another trip starting around September 10, would be gone for two weeks, and could not take her with me, I was very disappointed that she did not seem at all upset. She explained that it had been too hot all through August so she had stayed in the apartment most of the time, but now that it had cooled off somewhat, she looked forward to starting to explore New York. While somewhat disappointed, I was also relieved at her reaction, and was able to leave on my trip with Turner feeling pretty relaxed.

The two weeks in South America seemed to go very fast—three days in Lima, a week in Sao Paulo, and then three days in Buenos Aires. I found that there were actually some good points to traveling with Turner since he was a very pleasant guy, and I could also have him to write up the call reports for all of the prospects we had called upon, relieving me of that chore. Traveling with Rosario had been more exciting, but it had also been more exhausting. So this trip almost seemed like a short vacation, and I was surprised that Friday seemed to come around as fast as it did and it was time to return home. We flew back to New York on American Airlines, and it was a nonstop flight from Buenos Aires to Kennedy Airport. I could not help telling Jim Turner about my first long flight on Lufthansa when I was at Schleswigbank and how thrilled I had been to fly first class then into Buenos Aires. Now thirty years later, I was leaving Buenos Aires on a Boeing 767 that was a lot bigger and a lot more powerful than the DC-8 had been back in 1965. In a way, I felt sorry for Turner since he did not seem anywhere near as excited by this trip as I had been thirty years previously.

The flight home was right on time, and I had a car service meet Turner and me at Kennedy Airport to take us to our homes. The car dropped me off first, and I went up to the apartment full of anticipation at seeing Rosario again. I had thought of her repeatedly on the trip and kept imagining how she would look when I walked into the apartment again. Even though I was tired from the long trip, I was hoping that we might have sex that very night. So I opened the door and saw her sitting on the couch in the living room. She did not rise as I had expected her to, so I hurried over to her planning to embrace and kiss her, as I always did when I came back to the apartment. But I was stunned as I started to lean down to her, and she said very harshly, "Don't touch me!"

"Rosario, what's the matter?"

"You've been lying to me, you bastard. You've been lying to me."

"What do you mean 'lying'? About what?"

"About everything—every single thing that you ever told me."

I always knew, of course, that there had been a number of things that I had not explained as fully as I might have, but I did not consider most of these things to be outright lies. I had simply let her believe some things that were not entirely true. However, I still could not figure out what she knew now, so I said, "But you haven't told me what it is you're upset about."

"You told me that you were the president of your bank. But that was a lie—you aren't the president, you're just some little vice-president."

"I never told you that I was the president. I think you just assumed that because I was able to spend a lot of the bank's money on you. And because of that crazy chauffeur that we had back in Lima who kept insisting that I was El Presidenté."

"Why didn't you tell me the truth—what you really were?"

"Rosario, what difference does it make what my position at the bank is or was? I think I've shown you that I really love you and have been willing to bring you here to New York and set you up in a nice apartment. I wanted you to live with me here in New York permanently, and I've gotten you out of Lima, which you really wanted. And I thought you and I were getting along just great ever since you got here."

Rosario glowered at me as she said, "You told me that you had this big estate out in New Jersey, and I was going to ask you to take me there when you got back from this trip because I wanted to see it. But I was humiliated when I found out about the place where you claim that estate is."

I realized now that she must have found out something about the whole estate in New Jersey fiction, so I said nothing and waited for her to go on.

"I was shopping two days ago and I went down to Bloomingdale's, like you suggested, instead of going to all those fancy, expensive stores on Madison Avenue. And I had this nice young man waiting on me when I was looking at some gloves. I never had gloves in Lima and knew that I would need some here when the weather got cold. We got to talking and he asked me where I was from. Since he was Hispanic, we talked in Spanish for quite a while. I finally mentioned that I had a friend with a big estate in New Jersey, and the man waiting on me said that he lived in New Jersey and he asked where this estate was. It took me a minute to remember the town where you said you have your estate, so he suggested a couple of towns that I had never heard of. When I remembered, I told him that the name of the town was West New York. He laughed when I said that, and he told me that there were no estates in West New York. It turned out that he lived in West New York himself, and he said that it was primarily a Hispanic community and was very poor. I argued with him and said that my friend lived on Boulevard East overlooking the Hudson River, but he kept laughing, saying that he knew Boulevard East and, while this was the best part of town, there were only some big and fairly old apartment buildings there. I think he took pity on me then when he saw how upset I was becoming, and he said that I must have misunderstood where my friend lived in New Jersey. He said you must have said 'west of New York' and not 'West New York'. I had to agree with him so I could get out of that store before I broke down and cried, but I'm sure he was laughing at me as I left."

She was crying as she finished her explanation, and I thought I should try to comfort her and decided to sit on the couch next to her. As I tried to put my arm over her shoulder, she drew back, saying, "What are you doing? I don't want you to touch me. I thought that you were this great, wealthy man, and I gave up everything in Lima for you, but you're nothing. I gave up Jorge Alvarado for you—I know I could have convinced him to marry me—but I gave him up to come here with you. And now I find that you're absolutely nothing. I thought the money that you were spending down in Lima was your own money. But it wasn't—you don't have anything. And you're not the president of that bank, like I thought you were."

It suddenly crossed my mind that maybe Imad had talked to her while I was away and had told her what my position was at the bank, and I said, "I always told you that I wasn't the president of the bank, but why do you believe that now?"

"After I got back from talking with that man at Bloomingdale's, all I had to do was to call up the bank and ask who the president was. I got a phone number from some operator who spoke Spanish. When I called the bank, they told me that the president was someone I never heard of, so I asked what your job was and the girl I was talking to said she would look it up. I had to spell Wenner for her two or three times because she could not find your name in the bank's phonebook. It took a long time but she finally found your name someplace. Your job must be so unimportant that they don't even list you in their phone book."

Everything that she had been saying since I arrived was pretty irritating, and I finally decided that I had had enough. I looked at her for a minute and said, "Rosario, what you're complaining about now is that you thought I had more money than I do. So it's not that I treated you badly or don't love you or anything really meaningful—it's only that I don't have enough money. That's what's upsetting you. You've been trying to make me believe that you love me, when what you're saying now tells me that you're only after my money. And that's a much worse lie than it was for me to let you believe that I was very rich. Because I did sincerely love you from the minute that I first met you, and you used to tell me how much you loved me. But based on what you've just said to me tonight, you must have been lying when you said that you loved me."

"Love you? How could I love you? You're old. If you were still young and still had a chance to amount to something, maybe I could put up with you. But you're too old and you're not going to amount to anything and you don't have any of the money I thought you had. No, I never loved you, and I don't want to have anything to do with you anymore."

I had been sitting next to her while we argued, but I now got up and stood there for some time looking down at her, knowing that the scales had finally fallen off my eyes. I now realized what I had tried to ignore until tonight—no matter what you tried to call it, she was a woman who made money out of sex. I still didn't want to use the word 'prostitute' but it was becoming almost impossible not to. I could not believe how quickly my feelings for her had changed. Minutes before she had been the most important thing in my life. Now, after what she had just said, I knew that our so-called love affair had been a fake from the very beginning, and that her only concern had been my money—what she thought was my great wealth. As that realization hit me, she not only became unimportant, but I wanted to get her out of my life as quickly as possible.

Continuing to look down at her as I stood over her, I said as coldly as possible, "Rosario, the rent on this apartment is paid through the end of September. It's now the twenty-fourth, so you have six days to get out of here. And I mean you have to get out by the end of this month. And I'm also going to immediately cancel the credit cards that I gave you, so don't try to use them again. However, because I want you to get out of the US as quickly as possible, I'm going to buy an airline ticket for you to go back to Lima—but it's going to be in coach—no more first class for you. I will get a ticket for you to fly on the 30th, and while I can't force you to be on that plane, I strongly advise you to be on it."

She seemed shocked at my decision and said, "You can't do that—you can't give me only six days to leave New York. What if I don't want to go then? What if I can't go then?"

"Frankly, I don't give a fuck at this point what you do. You weren't very smart ending our relationship this way, Miss Martinez, but it was your decision, and after what you've just said, there's nothing I can do about it or even want to do. You're on your own from now on, so *buenos dias*, Rosario."

With that I turned my back on her, picked up the two suitcases that I had carried up to the apartment when I came in, and walked out the door. I went downstairs and got a taxi for the Port Authority Bus Terminal and there transferred to a jitney—one of those cheap little jitneys—for the ride through the Lincoln Tunnel back to West New York and Boulevard East. It was kind of humbling going back there after the glamour of the Upper East Side, but somehow tonight I felt more at home there than I did in Manhattan. Once in my apartment, I phoned both American Express and Citibank to cancel the credit cards that I had given Rosario. While cancelling them, I checked on the balances and found that they were substantial in both cases, so she had done a fair amount of shopping while I was in South America.

When things finally settled down that night and I was able to sit with a scotch on the rocks to consider what had happened, I found that I was not terribly upset. I knew that Imad would say that I had been thinking about Rosario solely with my penis, but now that my sexual illusions had been shattered and I was able to think more clearly, I realized that Rosario was not Ingrid, and she was not even Susan. Both of them were bright, intelligent women with whom I had had things in common at one time. Rosario was great in bed, and I had been captivated by that, but I realized tonight that I was not the type of guy who could build a long-term relationship simply on sex. And her interests beyond sex focused solely on money. So I consoled myself with the thought that the fact that our relationship had broken up as quickly as it had undoubtedly saved me a great deal of money.

What rankled the most, however, was her taunting me by saying that I was "nothing" and was too old to ever amount to anything. She had kept repeating that over and over. With all the women in my life—Ingrid, Susan,

Naomi, Rachel—not one of them had ever said I was 'nothing'. Susan, Naomi and Rachel had all lavished attention and praise on me, at least while our relationship was going on. Susan, of course, had apparently become bitter when I stopped paying attention to her. But I had always considered myself to be special—to be a cut above everyone else and certainly to be smarter than anyone else. And I think I can say that I also knew that I was pretty damn handsome, even if I was now fifty-nine. Being told that I was "nothing" and that I was too old ever to amount to anything was a blow to my ego. I knew it would take me some time before I could forget the things that Rosario had said to me that night.

I called American Airlines in the morning and bought a coach ticket for Rosario back to Lima, asking the airline to call her and give her the details. I then contacted the owner of the apartment and told him that I would only be using it for one more month, since I was required under the terms of our lease to give him thirty days' notice if I decided to leave. I also decided to go to the apartment to be sure that Rosario had not done any damage or taken anything before she left. So I waited until my deadline for her to leave had passed and, after work on Friday, October 1, I walked up Park Avenue to 72nd Street and then over 72nd Street to the apartment. I checked the entire apartment and was pleasantly surprised to find that there was no damage and nothing was missing as far as I could tell. The apartment was a mess, however, and I spent about two hours cleaning things up, particularly in the bathroom and our bedroom.

After finishing the cleaning, I had a drink and phoned out to have dinner delivered, something Rosario and I had never done. I ended up spending the night there and decided in the morning that, since I was paying for it, I might as well spend the entire month of October there. By the end of October, I had become so used to living in this very pleasant apartment in this very nice neighborhood that I decided to give up the apartment in West New York and to execute a one-year lease for the apartment on 72nd Street. It was a lot more expensive than the apartment in West New York, and would put a great deal of pressure on my financial situation. But with Rosario now a thing of the past, all of the expenses that had been associated with her had ended, so I felt I could afford to indulge myself with a better place to live. Ironically I ended up living alone in the apartment that I had originally leased as a love nest for Rosario and me. Surprisingly, I rarely thought of her even though I was living in what had been 'our' apartment. When I did think of her, it was only to be saddened by those last stinging insults that she had hurled at me just before our final parting.

CHAPTER XXXVII

The first day back in the office from the South American trip was terribly busy—catching up on all the work that had accumulated while I was away; meeting with Turner to review all of our calls on the trip; and late in the day, meeting with Ana Maria to tell her about all of the calls that we had made. I have to say that I was a little irritated during the meeting with Ana Maria since Turner made a point of talking Spanish with her, apparently to show her how competent he was to deal with our Spanish-speaking clients. I could speak Spanish myself, of course, and could have joined in their conversation, but I did not want to play the game Turner was playing of trying to impress the boss. Turner also made a big deal out of giving her all of the call reports that he had written, and I realized that it had been a mistake for me to let him write all of them. Aside from that, the meeting went pretty well, and I think that Ana Maria was now fully convinced that her decision to have Turner join me on these trips was the correct one.

That entire week was quite busy and I only had time to speak with Imad briefly when I happened to run into him around the office. So I had not had a chance to explain to him what had transpired with Rosario. I have to confess that I was also trying to avoid telling him about it since I was sure that he would tell me that he had never believed in her in the first place. However, on Thursday I made a point of going by his office—he had a small one like mine—and suggested that we get together on Friday evening.

He looked surprised when I suggested that and said, "Are you being given a night off?"

"I'm afraid I've got every night off now."

"You mean she is no more?"

"She is no more."

Imad shook his head, saying, "Wow! That's big news. You've got to tell me what happened."

I smiled and said, "Well, you're going to have to wait until Friday to find out, and you'll have to buy me at least one drink then in order to get the full story."

When we got together on Friday evening, Imad insisted that we go into the dining room at the Bull and Bear right away, rather than staying at the bar where it would have been too noisy to talk. When we were seated, and after we had ordered, I repeated to him as objectively as I could what had happened with Rosario when I got back from South America. When I finished relating the whole story, I said to him, "And I would guess that you are not at all surprised."

"No, I'm not surprised, Kurt. I think it was pretty inevitable that you would wake up to the situation at some point, and bringing her to New York seemed to me to be a way that would accomplish that. I hope you understand that I think that you're a pretty smart guy, and I always felt that at some point you would figure her out."

"I have to confess that I felt relieved the night it happened when I was able to get back to my little apartment over in West New York. However, this has been such a blow to my ego that after this I'm convinced that I will never have sex again in my whole life. I guess that's the price I have to pay for getting involved with Rosario in the first place."

Imad raised his eyebrows and said, "Yeah, I'm sure that's the case, but I won't start feeling too much sympathy for you just yet."

Nothing much was said as our dinner was served, but as we had our usual after-dinner brandy, Imad said, "I hope you're not mad at me for suggesting that you bring her here."

"No, why should I be mad?"

"Having her here in New York ended the relationship."

"Look, I recognize the fact that I could not have kept up the pretense that I was very rich and had this great estate out in New Jersey. She was going to find out at some point what the truth was, so I think it saved me a lot of money by having her find out as soon as she did."

Imad sat sipping his brandy for a while, and then said, "What I don't understand is why she ended it the way that she did. You said that she had made some pretty outrageous statements."

"Yes, she said that I was old and poor, and would never amount to anything. I guess that she was really disappointed when she found out about me, and she must have had great hopes for becoming a wealthy woman residing here in New York. I'm pretty sure that she was crushed when those hopes were dashed, and I guess that's why she struck out the way that she did. But the more I think about it the more I think that maybe she was right—I am old, if you consider being fifty-nine as old, and I am certainly poor. Whether I will amount to anything in the future is pretty doubtful."

"Kurt, I've told you before that you don't have to be poor. I'm sure that if we put our minds together I know that we can find a way to get a few millions out of the bank, without anyone having any idea what happened."

"Yes, you said that before, and since I've been caught twice trying to do just that, I really don't see how it can be done."

Imad grimaced as he said, "OK pal, you just wait. I'm going to come up with a plan that will be foolproof, and you and I will both walk away as millionaires."

I finished off my brandy, put the glass down on the table and said, "I can hardly wait."

The rest of 1991 passed relatively quietly. I saw Imad regularly for our Friday-night dinners, but I made only one more trip to Latin America in the fall. Turner pretty much arranged the whole thing, and I was happy to let him do it. He was clearly very ambitious but I did not feel that I should be in competition with him. The trip itself was uneventful, and I did not see Rosario when we were in Lima. Several times I looked in at the bar where I had first met her, but she was not there and I did not ask the bartender about her. Since I really did not want to see her and was always afraid of running into her, it was a relief when we left Lima and flew on to Sao Paulo. Turner had arranged all of the meetings for the rest of our trip, and the time that we spent in Sao Paulo and Buenos Aires passed fairly quickly.

Imad took two weeks of vacation and went back to Cairo in mid-December. I don't think he was going there for the Christmas holidays, although I suppose he could be a Copt, but I don't know if they celebrate Christmas at the same time that we do in the West. He and I had never talked about religion, and since I am not a religious person, it was not an important issue for me. However, with his absence, I quickly realized that I would be totally alone through the holidays. There were, of course, a few office parties, but I ended up going home to my apartment on 72nd Street entirely by myself throughout the holiday season. I think there is something about the Christmas/New Year's period that tends to make people sad. All the media focus on the expectation that everyone will be with family or loved ones throughout the holidays, so that if you end up being totally alone, as I did, you feel almost completely abandoned. I thought of going out and trying to meet a woman at one of the hotel bars, but never seemed to have the energy to do it. After losing Rosario during the year and having to face my sixtieth birthday in the forthcoming new year, I was probably more depressed as 1991 ended than I had ever been before.

Imad and I got together on the first Friday in January and we brought each other up to date with what we had been doing. I tried to be as upbeat as possible that night and hoped that I convinced him that this had been a great vacation for me after the trauma of earlier in the year. Whether or not I succeeded, I don't know. It had been almost three weeks since he and I had had dinner together the last time, and as we sat eating our dinner, the thought hit me that I had really come to depend on him. Other than Imad, I had virtually no friends in New York and, at this point in my life, I was not very likely to make any new ones. I had to suppress a smile as it occurred to me that Imad was somewhat akin to Naomi, except that she was always insisting that I do the right things, while he was trying to convince me to do the wrong ones.

As we sat having brandy that night, Imad said, "Well, Kurt, I've got the whole thing worked out. We're going to be millionaires."

"You mean we're going to win the lottery?"

"Very funny. No, I mean that I have a foolproof way of getting at least five, and maybe even ten, million out of the bank, and I'm sure that no one will ever realize that there was a scam practiced on them."

Knowing how unlikely it was that such a plan existed, I said, "OK, tell me about it."

Imad said, "Here we are at the beginning of 1992 and what is the hottest market that everyone wants to invest in? It's China, of course. And what do most investors know about China? Nothing. I'm sure that you have had a number of your clients tell you that they want to buy stock in some Chinese company, haven't you? I sure have. But the bank has nothing to offer them. So my idea is to create a company, maybe in Hong Kong or Singapore, and this will be a company that you and I own, although our ownership will be completely hidden. Using this company as a vehicle, we can offer investors stock or convertible debentures, and we'll be raking in the money."

I tried to go along with his fantasy, and said, "It sounds too good to be true. What exactly is this company supposed to do that will attract all these investors?"

"It's got to be some kind of Chinese technology company—y'know, a company that competes with someone like Shen Wei Computing."

I hated to interrupt him but I had to ask, "What is Shen Wei?"

"It's like the Chinese Intel. All we have to do is to put together an impressive private placement memorandum saying all the exciting things that our company is going to do, and the bank's clients will flock into it. Since it will be a private placement, it will never be quoted anywhere, so no one can check on how the company is doing on a day-to-day basis. We can provide quarterly earnings reports for several years, always saying how great the company's prospects are, until a few years down the road we admit that it's gone bankrupt. But that wasn't our fault; that was management's fault, and management was a bunch of fictitious Chinese. Somewhere along the line, you retire and take your five million back to Switzerland, or wherever, and a year or so later I quit and take my five million back to Egypt. And the only result will be that the bank will have suggested an investment to its clients that did not work out as everyone had hoped. It almost sounds to me as if it's too easy."

"How are you going to put together a private placement memorandum that is impressive enough and credible enough so that we can get approval from the Investment Committee? Because without that approval, we can't offer it to our clients. And if we did that without the Committee's approval, we'd never be able to put in orders to buy any of those securities or, even if we managed that somehow, when the company does go bankrupt the focus would really be directly on us."

"In the first place, have you seen some of the crap that the brokerage firms are putting out about China? Some of their offerings are so amateurish that no one in their right mind would put money into them. So I don't think that it will be at all that hard to put together a really first rate PPM. I'll write the first draft and let you read it, and I'm sure that between the two of us we can produce something 100 percent believable. And with all your broker contacts, you should be able to find one that will act as the sponsor of the deal or the underwriter, or whatever you call it."

I immediately thought of innumerable problems that Imad would have to face—or we would face, if I were to work with him. So I said, "I know I've told you that I had tried to con two different companies that I worked for out of money twice before, and I failed both times. There was always something that I didn't anticipate. You really ought to think twice before you take a step like this."

Imad waited a minute and finally said, "Kurt, I should have told you before that this would not be my first run-in with the law. I used to work at another bank here in New York—Manufacturers Hanover—and I tried to make $250,000 disappear from an account that that bank was about to lose. Since it was a very large account and it was being transferred away from Manny Hanny, I thought that no one would notice a mere $250,000. What I was trying to do, however, was so dumb and my explanations were so amateurish that my little theft was discovered very quickly. As a result of that experience, I do understand how necessary it will be to plan every single detail as meticulously as possible. That's one reason that I hope we can work together on this, because between the two of us we should be able to consider all the angles."

"You mean to tell me that the Second National Bank has hired two people with criminal records and the bank didn't know about either one of us? I understand how I did it, but didn't you have a record?"

"No, Manny Hanny was able to get the money back—all too easily—and, after firing me, they referred the case to the US Attorney's office as an attempted embezzlement. But the DA at the time was too busy going after high-profile people, including a bunch of big-name brokers, so he never did anything. As a result, I was never indicted and don't have any kind of record. I guess you can say that I lucked out."

"Yeah, you did luck out. They weren't as easy with me. But I still think that it's a big step that you're thinking about taking right now."

Imad merely smiled, and finished off the last of his brandy.

Back at the bank the next day, a memo was passed around announcing that Jim Turner had been appointed Director of Marketing for Latin America. There was no question in my mind that I was infinitely better qualified than Turner for that position, and I was convinced that he had been given the job, first, because he was younger, and second, because he had carefully and consistently played up to Ana Maria. I re-read the memo that Ana Maria had written in which she extolled Turner's many virtues—his long experience in international private banking, his years of living in Brazil, his knowledge of the South American culture and, of course, his fluency in both Spanish and Portuguese. Having traveled with him to South America twice, and having seen him interact with clients and prospects, there was no question in my mind that while he was very personal and could be perfectly charming when dealing with clients, he simply did not have sufficient experience in investments to discuss these matters knowledgeably. I had not been looking forward to becoming head of marketing for South America myself—that was certainly not a goal of mine— but it seemed to me that it was a slap in my face that Turner was given that job and Ana Maria did not think that it was even necessary to talk to me about it. I was very involved in Latin American marketing—far more than anyone else in the department—and in my opinion, she should have tried to make sure that I would cooperate with Turner in his new job. My first favorable impression of her was beginning to fade, and I was starting to think that she was not as great a manager as she thought she was.

As I sat re-reading the memo, it brought home to me again what Rosario had said, that I was too poor, too old, and would never amount to anything. Here I was, not yet sixty years of age, being passed over for what was really a very insignificant position. I knew that I should shrug the matter off and not let it bother me, but it did bother me because it seemed to be a confirmation of Rosario's opinion of me. And I had to face the fact that what I was doing now was a real come down from the life I had been living in Los Angeles, and the money I had been making there; and it was even more of a come down from the job I had had at Morris, Brunner. I had been forced to give up the Morris, Brunner job when my little escapade there was discovered, but it had been stupid of me to give up my own company in LA and become a small cog in a big bank like The Second National.

The Turner promotion seemed to crystallize things for me. It reminded me of my run-in with Petersen over my correct decision to buy Aussie dollars for my clients accounts. It made it clear that going forward I would have to put up with Jim Turner, and any other young guy who would come along at the bank and become the hot prospect of the moment, whether he knew anything or not. And it brought home to me that Rosario was really right: I was too old for a place like the Second National Bank and would never amount to anything there. I sat for a long time thinking about all these and came to the conclusion that Imad's idea of another embezzlement suddenly started to look a whole lot better.

I thought about Imad's idea a great deal over the next few days. And I was surprised that I had so few second thoughts about contemplating another embezzlement. When I think back now to that night in the room at the Hotel Lotti in Paris after I had fled Switzerland, it's hard for me to understand today why I had been wrestling with the question of whether or not I had become a criminal. Looking back on it, I don't think that I was a criminal then; Ingrid had encouraged me to take some money that had, in effect, fallen from the sky into our laps. And I don't think that I was a criminal because of what I did at Morris, Brunner. There were a great many circumstances that caused me to do what I did at Morris, Brunner, and none of them were criminal in nature. I was only trying to get even with Sam Brunner for what he had done to me. I have to admit that in both cases, I had crossed the line and resorted to embezzlement, and technically I broke the law. But I really feel that I did what I had to do;

if I have to do it again at the Second National Bank, I felt sure that I would. However, the fact that I was not as excited about the plan this time must have been due to the fact that I still did not really believe in Imad's scenario.

I had pretty well put Imad's draft PPM out of my mind since I was convinced that it would be almost impossible to develop something that would be a believable document; instead, I was more concerned with the formation of a company that would be our vehicle in which to invest some of the clients' money. Where could we form a company where at least the ownership could be kept completely secret? All the off-shore tax havens—the British Virgin Islands, the Channel Islands, the Turks and Caicos—all of them would provide officers and directors for any company that was created in that country. And each of them had secrecy laws that would almost certainly protect Imad and me as owners if we formed a company in one of them. But companies formed in those locations were generally considered to be more than a little questionable, and I knew that we could never get a company that was formed in one of those locations approved by the bank's Investment Committee.

Imad had suggested forming the company in Hong Kong or Singapore since that would add credibility to the company, but neither of those locations would provide the degree of secrecy that we needed. I actually went to the Singapore Consulate in New York and they were very helpful in giving me several booklets that explained the formation of holding companies in Singapore, but it was clear, after reading them, that there was no Swiss-type secrecy there. The Hong Kong Chamber of Commerce also had an office in New York, and they were able to give me enough information to make it clear that Hong Kong was not a good location for what Imad and I wanted.

The following Friday night, Imad and I got together again, and again we ordered the same dinner at the Bull and Bear—beef tenderloin, baked potato, and asparagus. After we had eaten, he laid a copy of his plan on the table. When he saw that I was willing to discuss it, he said, "You seem to be more positive about my plan than you were a week ago. What happened?"

"I've been thinking about it and I guess that what Rosario said convinced me."

"You mean it convinced you that you had no future at the bank."

"Yes, I guess, in a word."

Imad quickly responded, "Look, I want you to work with me on this plan of mine, but I want you to do it because you believe in it—you really should be convinced. But don't do it because of what Rosario said. Do I have to tell you that all that stuff was a bunch of crap? You aren't old—anyone in his fifties or sixties is not old anymore. As you know, life expectancy keeps growing. And you're far from poor. You're making close to a hundred thousand a year. If you would just exert yourself and take a few chances, you'll find that you have a great future. So forget all the stuff from that bitch. Just forget her. And I'm going to put a rule into effect—when you get all this money from our plan, you may not go anywhere near Lima because I don't want you spending one penny on her. OK?"

"You're the boss, Imad." I thought I had said that ironically, but he seemed to take me seriously.

"And don't forget that. Now let's talk about my PPM."

He had given me a draft of the PPM a couple of days earlier, and I said, "Look, before we talk about it, we have to decide if there is someplace that we can form a company and keep our ownership secret. Neither Hong Kong nor Singapore works. Is there some other place that will provide credibility to the offering and still provide the secrecy that we want?"

I don't think that Imad had focused on this problem, so he really had nothing to suggest. We discussed it for a while, but came to no conclusion. Later that evening, we did spend a lot of time going over his PPM, but I kept thinking that there was just something wrong with this whole approach.

The next week I still found it hard to get my mind to focus on the PPM since I kept thinking that we had to have a credible location that would also provide secrecy. We were at our usual dinner table on a Friday night early in May, and Imad was discussing his PPM in great detail. I really was not listening to him, when a thought suddenly struck me and, waving my hands in front of me, I said, "Listen, Imad, we're always stuck on the question of where we can form a company that will provide iron-clad secrecy. We keep insisting that we can't let anyone know that you and I created and own the company that we're putting our clients' money into. But it just occurred to me: what do we care about secrecy? I don't care about it because once I get the money, I'm going off God knows where. And I don't think you care about it—you said that you were going to run off to Cairo with your money, and I guess you can disappear into the Khan el Khalili bazaar. So as long as we are both willing to run off right away—and that would be as soon as the shares of our phony company get purchased—why should we worry about secrecy? We can form a company wherever we want and let everyone find out after the fact who owns the damn thing. Let's make it 100 percent clear who formed the company and took the money and how brilliant we were in getting away with it. We not only get the money, think of all the satisfaction we get from having carried off the whole thing and letting all those idiots that we work for, know that we did it. What do you think of that?"

Imad leaned back in his chair and, shaking his head, said, "Kurt, I've always felt that the only way we could do this is with absolute secrecy. I mean, you've got an interesting idea, but I don't think it's very realistic."

"Imad, this idea just occurred to me, but I'm sure we can do it. I haven't thought through all the details, but I think we would first form the company in some place like Switzerland. Then we'd have to have a pile of the company's stock put into an account with some brokerage firm. I think I know a couple of brokerage firms that we could use. Then when all the bosses are away— Peterson travels all the time, and Engle takes a vacation whenever he can—we enter orders to buy the stock in this company that we created. You enter orders for about $5 million from your clients' accounts and I do the same from mine. It will be a stock that is not approved by the Investment Committee so someone will have to approve the orders when they're entered, or we'll have to make all of them directed orders. Either way, I can always convince the trading desk to put in the orders.

"The really critical things will be to keep anyone from questioning the purchases for several days in order to let those purchases close. As long as we make sure that the broker has the stock in good delivery form, there will be no reason for him not to make delivery and get payment in the usual five business days. We leave instructions with the brokerage firm to have the money transferred right away to Switzerland or some other place, and as soon as the money gets transferred, then you and I take off for wherever the money is going to end up. And by the time Peterson and his whole crew get back to the office and find out that the company is a complete phony, and that you and I created it, we will be sitting on millions of dollars somewhere where we can never be touched."

We sat for a long time as Imad had his eyes closed thinking about my idea, until he finally said, "There are a helluva a lot of things we're going to have to figure out, but I think your idea might just be the way we ought to do this thing. As long as we aren't worried about secrecy, everything ends up being much, much easier."

Once we decided that we did not need secrecy—that we would make it 100 percent clear to everyone that Imad and I had planned and carried out the embezzlement—the whole project took on a completely different dimension. All the problems that we faced as we tried to think through Imad's old plan disappeared. We could form the company wherever it seemed to make sense to do so. Imad and I would be the sole shareholders, officers, and directors, so when anyone checked on the company, they would see that we formed and owned it. And it would no longer be necessary to work up some elaborate and believable private placement memorandum since we were no longer concerned about having to convince the Investment Committee or our clients that this was an attractive company in which to invest. All we had to do under the new scenario was to get some stock certificates printed, arrange to deposit those with a brokerage firm, and give that firm wire transfer instructions for the funds that would be received when the stock was purchased by our accounts. Then all that Imad and I would have to do would be to enter the orders to buy that stock when the time was right—it was almost too simple.

It really did not make much difference anymore what our proposed company—what had we decided to call Company X—was supposed to do. I did not like Imad's idea of having a Chinese company because neither of us knew anything at all about China. We were not going to have to explain the company to anyone, but there might be a couple of questions from the traders or from other investment account managers when we put the orders in, and I wanted to be able to answer those questions as confidently as possible.

Chapter XXXVIII

Before Imad and I were able to get together again to discuss my idea, Ana Maria asked me to come to her office. A very important African client was in London and had been meeting with the International Private Banking office there. He was from Cote d'Ivoire, was extraordinarily wealthy, and spoke only French. Bill Welles, the head of the London office, felt that this client was fairly knowledgeable as to investments since he had been educated at one of the better business schools in Paris. Bill was concerned that none of the investment staff in London spoke French, nor did any of them have in-depth knowledge about currencies, commodities, and other specialized fields in which the client was interested. Ana Maria said that she had considered having someone come to London from our Geneva office since that was the bank's main investment office in Europe. However, she felt that the investment professionals in Geneva were pretty stodgy and would not be able to provide the client the advice that he wanted. It was not so much a question of ability, as the fact that the two top professionals in the Geneva office generally took the traditional Swiss attitude of telling the client what he should do, and they were not at all likely to be responsive to the client's own investment ideas. As a result, she felt that I was the perfect advisor for the client because of my language capabilities, my willingness to work with clients, and my broad investment background with long experience in currencies and the gold and silver markets.

I did not have much choice in the matter and was told that I would have to leave for London the following morning. I was, of course, somewhat flattered by what Ana Maria had to say, although a little upset that I would not be able to pursue the embezzlement plan with Imad. However, I flew off to London the next morning, arriving at Heathrow that evening, so that I was able to be at the bank's International Private Banking office on Curzon Street early the next morning. When I got there, I met Bill Welles for the first time. He immediately said, "This is, of course, an honor for me to meet you since I've heard so much about you. Ana Maria tells me that you're the only one who could possibly handle this client, and that we have no one here in Europe who could possibly do so."

I could tell that he was not terribly happy about my being there since his greeting did not sound at all sincere, so I answered, "I have to say that I wasn't particularly happy at being asked to come here. I was just back from Latin America and was not looking forward to another overseas trip. But Ana Maria is the boss, as you know, so I had no choice but to come. Please tell me something about the client I am to meet."

"Our potential client is the son of the man who must be the wealthiest man in Cote d'Ivoire. The family—meaning the father—apparently made their money in diamonds. Somehow or the other, the father obtained control of the largest diamond mine in the country or, for that matter, in Central Africa. The son, whose name is Ahmadou Kuada, is now in his midtwenties, was educated in France, and, while he does understand English, he much prefers to speak French. I found him to be a rather impressive young man."

We did not have time to talk any longer since Welles's secretary interrupted to say that the client had arrived. After all the introductions were over and we had gotten seated in the conference room, I asked (in French) Mr. Kuada if he and his family had any specific investment objectives that they were interested in achieving. He smiled and said, "As you can imagine, my father would like everything—very good current income with great capital gain possibilities. I'm afraid that he has been spoiled by his success with the diamond company. I assume that Mr. Welles has told you that many years ago, my father bought stock in Diamants Brut, CIE, a company that owned diamond mines, not just in Cote d'Ivoire, but throughout Central Africa. I have to say that diamonds are unique since there is a fairly constant demand for them, and prices have been in an almost uninterrupted uptrend for many, many years. So there has been great income for the family from the different mines, and the value of the shares, which are listed on the Abidjan market has risen continually. You may not realize that there is an Abidjan market, but there is one. It's very small, but the shares in our company trade there quite a bit. As I was saying, the value of the shares has gone up dramatically. All that my father wants is for the bank to achieve something comparable with the money we give the bank to invest." Fortunately, the young man was smiling as he said all this.

I replied, "It would be my fondest wish to repeat the investment success that your family has had with the investment in the diamond mines, but I cannot in all honesty claim that the bank could realize such returns. However, we do think that it is important for you to diversify your holdings so that you are protected against any downturn in the diamond market. I know you think that is impossible, but what if another huge diamond mine were discovered somewhere in the world, such as Siberia, Mongolia, or Alaska? Diamond prices might come down and the value of the shares in the mining company could fall dramatically. So all that I am arguing is that any investments that the bank makes for you not be tied to diamond prices—or to any commodity prices—but rather be primarily in the common stocks of the great companies of Europe and the United States, and particularly the technology companies. I suggest that you gradually put up to 50 percent of your family's money into the common stocks of those companies, since stocks would be the best way to provide growth over time as well as provide a protection against inflation. I really believe that inflation is the greatest problem that you have to guard against in your investment program. Diamonds, of course, have to be considered as another major hedge against inflation, but you already have a substantial investment in that asset class."

Mr. Kuada said, "I'm glad to hear you say that, Mr. Wenner, since I hope that you would agree that diamonds are a truly alluring investment—probably even more alluring than gold—and not just a hedge against inflation. It would seem to me that many people would like to own shares in a diamond mine or in a company like ours that has a number of mines."

It suddenly hit me: he was not just in London to talk about investing all the cash that the family had—he was considering selling some of the stock in the diamond company that they controlled. I immediately said, "I have no doubt that if your family were to decide to sell any of the shares that they own in your company, there would be a very positive reaction from the market. Yes, of course, diamonds are very alluring, as you put it, and I know that the bank's Corporate Underwriting Department would be delighted to discuss with you the details of handling any sale that you and your father might decide upon."

The meeting with the client lasted for several hours that morning. We also discussed currencies at great length and I recommended that he keep a substantial portion of his investible funds in the US dollar, if for no other reason than its security. I tried to convince him that with his family's overall wealth, this was not the time for him to be taking unnecessary risks. But I concluded by again encouraging him to move forward with the possible sale of some of the family's holdings in the diamond company.

Most of the conversation that morning was between the client and myself since the others from IPB did not speak French. Bill Welles hosted a rather elegant lunch in the afternoon. This was a typical English lunch that started off with cocktails at the bar just outside the bank's private dining room before we went in to sit down for lunch. There was sherry with the shrimp appetizer, a white wine with the fish course, and a red wine with the main course—a filet mignon—and then there was port with dessert. I have unbounded admiration for the ability that the English have in being able to consume such a great amount of alcohol and still go back to work in the afternoon. Whether or not they are able to do anything after all that drinking seems to me to be an open question. As we finished lunch, the client expressed great appreciation for the investment recommendations and for the luncheon. He indicated that he wanted to consider everything that I had said, and that he would speak with his father back in Abidjan. Welles also arranged for Mr. Kuada to meet the next day with the bank's Corporate Underwriting Department as to the possible sale of shares in the diamond company. We parted with the understanding that we would all meet again the next day.

I had dinner alone that night, and simply spent some time walking around the West End, since Bill Welles indicated that he had other plans and could not ask me to join him. I really did not mind; London is a great city and it occurred to me as I walked that this might be the perfect place to locate a major part of the plan that Imad and I were hatching. I decided that I should look into the question of forming Company X right here in London. There would be more credibility attached to a UK company than there would be to any company formed in one of the offshore locations. I still did not consider credibility to be terribly important, since according to our plan, there would not be time for anyone to challenge the purchases. But it was always possible that someone might question the orders to purchase stock in Company X at the time that they were entered, and I felt it would be best to form the company in a noncontroversial place. I was also struck by what the client has said about diamonds, and was beginning to think that Company X could very well be involved in diamonds.

The next morning we had another fairly long meeting with the client, and I was pleased that he had accepted most of what I had recommended. Bill Welles invited the client to have lunch with us again, but he declined, claiming a previous engagement. I have to say that I was really quite impressed with Mr. Kuada—not only the fact that his family was so extraordinarily wealthy, but with the knowledge and sophistication of the young man himself.

After the meeting with the client was over, I decided to follow up on my idea of the previous evening of forming Company X in London, so I asked Bill Welles if he could refer me to a solicitor. I explained that my ex-wife might want to send my daughter to school in England, and I needed to understand if any tax laws would apply. Welles referred me to Sir Wilfred Tancred, a solicitor with whom the bank worked from time to time. He had offices in the city, and I asked Bill's secretary to make an appointment for me to meet with Sir Wilfred the following day.

The British legal system has always confused me, since you first talk with a solicitor who tries to understand what your problem is, and he then refers you to a barrister who actually does the work for you. The solicitor always remains the "instructing solicitor" but it seems to me that it is always the barrister who does all the work. Sir Wilfred's office was in the city—that part of London where all the banks and the financial firms are located. And I have to say that he had a most impressive office. It was in a very old building, perhaps four or five stories high, but there was a gleaming brass plate beside the door on the street with only the name Sir Wilfred Tancred etched on it. One walked up a fairly long flight of carpeted stairs into a rather elegantly furnished reception room: it was paneled in dark walnut, had heavy leather chairs next to the fireplace, and very expensive looking oriental rugs on the floor. I only had to wait two or three minutes before being ushered in to meet the great man himself.

The meeting with Sir Wilfred was very pleasant, but I was not at all impressed with him. We got to talking about wines—of which he is quite a connoisseur—and I thought we would never get off the subject. I think he was surprised that I was able to match him in the discussion of vintages and years, and that my opinions showed that I was at least as knowledgeable as he was on the subject. We then spent a great deal of time talking about guns. I had made the mistake of mentioning that I had gone into Purdy's (the famous up-scale London gun shop) and Sir Wilfred wanted to show me that he was an avid gun collector, so he related virtually everything he knew about guns. I had a big gun collection back in the States, and I had planned to visit Purdy's to get an idea of what some of the guns might be worth since I would have to dispose of them before fleeing the United States after the proposed embezzlement. Sir Wilfred seemed to be quite impressed that I had known about Purdy's, even though I had never bought anything there.

We did finally get around to talking about the reason that I had come to see him, and I explained that an investor that I represented wanted to form a company in London that would own stock in the family's business. I explained that the investor intended to sell that stock in the near future and had decided that London would be the best place to accomplish it. Sir Wilfred felt that what my investor wanted to do would be no problem at all, and he immediately indicated that he would refer me to a barrister with whom his firm frequently worked. This was a woman named Julia Larwood who had an office nearby. I left Sir Wilfred's office, giving his secretary my address in New York to which his bill could be sent, knowing full well that the bill would never be paid.

Sir Wilfred's secretary had made an appointment for me with Miss Larwood and I went to see her the next morning. Her office was also in the city, but was nowhere near as plush as Sir Wilfred's. And she herself was surprisingly vulnerable looking. For some reason, a woman barrister in London had conjured an image for me of a rather stern, forbidding-looking woman—rather like Maggie Thatcher—whereas Miss Larwood seemed quite feminine and rather disorganized at the same time. She smoked incessantly, dropping ashes everywhere, and was constantly thumbing through piles of papers on her desk, causing many of them to fall to the floor. It took me some time before I came to realize that she did seem to know UK tax and corporate law quite well. And for the first time since Rosario, I found myself becoming interested in a member of the opposite sex.

I started off by saying, "Miss Larwood, I'm delighted that you were able to see me this morning. Sir Wilfred indicated that you were frequently very busy."

"I've been known to be a little busier than I am right now. Referrals from solicitors have not been exactly dropping from the sky lately."

I was a little taken aback by her candor, but continued, "I assume Sir Wilfred has told you why I wanted to see you."

"Yes, he said that you wanted to form a UK company. Perhaps you could explain to me exactly why you want a UK company."

"The principal for whom I act is a very wealthy individual from Africa who wants to sell a least a portion of the mining company that he controls. He received advice from a lawyer in Abidjan that he forms a company to which he would somehow transfer the ownership of his diamond company, and then to sell shares in that company, while retaining control of the company. My principal felt that the London market would be the most appropriate place for that sale to occur."

Miss Larwood smiled rather primly—if not condescendingly—and said, "But you still haven't told me why you want a UK company, unless, of course, you would really like to pay UK taxes."

"Obviously I don't want to pay UK taxes, or to incur taxes for my principal. Where would you suggest that the company be formed?"

"I have had great success in forming holding companies in the Channel Islands and, more recently, in Andorra. Andorra is up in the mountains between France and Spain and I can tell you that they have the most wonderful wines there. They are able to get them from both sides of the Pyrenees, and I can never decide whether I prefer the French or the Spanish wines, since they are both quite excellent. However, I assume you would not want to form a company in Andorra just because of its wines, although I can assure you that Andorra has all of the tax and administrative advantages of any of the other tax free locations."

I was beginning to wonder about this obsession that solicitors and barristers in London seemed to have with wine, but I decided to say nothing about that matter, and simply explained, "I have advised my principal, Mr. Kuada of Abidjan, Cote d'Ivoire, that it would be necessary to have a UK company for the sale of his shares in the mining company. If we were to use one of the off-shore tax havens . . ."

Miss Larwood interrupted to say, "I always consider them to be off-shore financial centers."

I went on, "If we were to use one of these off-shore places, it might reflect on the credibility of the company itself, so I'm afraid that we do need a UK company."

She exhaled rather melodramatically and said, "Well, if you insist, I can certainly form one for you. But please understand that with a UK company the Inland Revenue Service may very well become interested and, if nothing else, they might audit the company to see if they can collect any taxes. They really haven't discovered Andorra, since they're trying to deal with places like the Channel Islands, Luxembourg, and the British Virgin Islands, and you could sell all the stock you wanted out of an Andorran company without any concern about taxes."

I was becoming a little frustrated with her and said, "I'm afraid that you will have to believe me that my principal has decided upon a UK company, and our potential underwriters at the Second National Bank of New York agree that we should form our holding company here." Obviously, there had been no discussion with the bank underwriters at this point, but I felt that mentioning them would help get her off of the idea of using Andorra.

Miss Larwood now said, "Very well, to summarize what you've been telling me, I understand that Mr. Kuada—that is your client's name, isn't it?—Mr. Kuada wants to sell stock in his diamond mines so he wants to form a company in London. But the London company will not have any assets. I presume that all of the assets are in whatever company Mr. Kuada now owns. Isn't that correct?"

"Yes, of course, but his company was formed in Cote d'Ivoire and Mr. Kuada felt that it would be very difficult to sell stock in a company formed there. So the proposal is to merge the Cote d'Ivoire company with the London company before the offering takes place."

"Well, I really don't know much about the tax laws in what we here in England call the Ivory Coast, but I assume you will want our firm to manage the merger. Did you discuss this with Sir Wilfred?"

"I'm afraid Sir Wilfred was more interested in guns at Purdy's than he was in potential mergers, but, of course, I will recommend that your firms handle the merger."

Miss Larwood seem somewhat mollified by my reply, and again spent a great deal of time rooting through a pile of papers on her desk, finally coming up with the one for which she had apparently been searching. She then looked up and said, "Now, since it will be a UK company, I need to fill out this form, and the first thing that you have to tell me is what the name of the company will be."

Up to that point, I had not even thought about what the name of the company should be, and sat thinking for a couple of minutes. Miss Larwood said, "In Andorra and the other off-shore financial centers they could come up with a name for you, and we could do that here is London also, but I thought since you were so determined on a UK company that you already had a name in mind."

I was somewhat taken aback since I had not been considering a name, and said, "We have been referring to it as Company X in all of our discussions, and my associates and I have not really talked about a name for it."

Miss Larwood said, "I could always form the company with whatever name might be convenient—use what is known as a shelf company—and whenever you decide we could change the name at that time."

I did not want any delays—I wanted to get this plan moving -- and suddenly remembered the name Katanga. This was a province in the Congo that had gotten a great deal of publicity because of some problem they were having down there a couple of years ago. I thought that the name "Katanga" sounded authentically African, so I said, "No, I don't think we should delay. Let's call the company Katanga Minerals."

She responded, "Let's make that Katanga Minerals, Limited. OK?"

When I nodded, she asked, "And who will the officers and directors be?"

I told her that I would be chairman and that Imad would be president, explaining that Mr. El Kasim also worked on Mr. Kuada's behalf. I added that if we needed additional officers or directors, I hoped that either she or Sir Wilfred would be willing to serve, since the Kuada family would like to avoid any possible publicity. She explained that a UK company required four directors and she agreed that Sir Wilfred and she would be willing to serve, but said that there would be an annual charge for those services.

I then asked her what the total charges would be for forming the company, and she mentioned the government fee and also her own hourly fees. Again, I was not particularly concerned about the amount of the fee since I was sure I would be off in Brazil or someplace with all the millions I would be getting out of the bank and the fee would never be paid.

There was a lull in our conversation as she again seemed to be looking for something on her desk, until she said, "And how can I satisfy my KYC requirements?"

All I could say in response was, "Your what?"

"My KYC requirements. I'm sure you understand that I'm required to know all about my client and to know where his or her money is coming from. So the UK government, all the European governments, and the US, you name it, everyone now requires that if you're dealing with international clients, you have to 'know your customer'. They seem to be concerned about money laundering, or something like that."

"Yes, of course, I am certainly aware of that. I'm in the International Private Banking Department of the Second National Bank of New York and we have to deal with KYC all the time."

I waited for her to say something, but I then added, "The IPB office here in London has, of course, done everything that's required to ascertain the veracity of the client on whose behalf I'm working, and the fact that his money has all been earned legitimately. Could I, as an officer of the bank, sign something assuring you that the bank has done everything necessary to satisfy the KYC requirements? I'm sure I could get permission from the bank to sign anything that you were to draw up."

Miss Larwood smiled and said, "Well, that will make it very easy for me. I should have realized that since Mr. Welles had referred you to Sir Wilfred, that you were acting as an officer of the bank. Generally, I hate having to deal with that KYC issue since it means having to ask the client so many personal questions that they don't particularly like to answer. But as long as you can provide me with assurance that the bank has dealt with it, I think that I'm in the clear."

It then occurred to me that I needed to be sure that Imad and I could control the company that we were creating. "Miss Larwood, as I have indicated, that Kuada family owns all the stock that will be merged into the new company, as well as the stock in the company that we are creating, and the proceeds of the sale of the new stock will go to them in the accounts that they have in various off-shore financial centers. But I assume that Mr. El Kasim and I, as officers of the company, will be able to provide instructions not only in connection with the merger, but also to the brokerage firm handling the stock sale and to the various banks, to make the necessary transfers."

"Mr. Wenner, all you have to do is to explain what it is that you want, and I will make sure when drafting the corporate documents that there is no impediment that would prevent you from doing it."

I said, "Well, that's all the questions that I have. Will you be able to get papers drawn up so that I can sign them in the next few days, or would it be better if you sent them to me in New York?"

"When are you returning to New York?"

"I had hoped to leave on Friday—two days from now."

"In that case, I think it will be better if I put everything together and sent it to you in New York. I assume that Mr. El Kasim is with the bank in New York, so you both will have a chance to review everything and then return them to me here so that I can have Sir Wilfred join me in signing everything."

"And there will be no need for Mr. Kuada or his son to sign anything."

"No, their name will not appear on the records of the company."

This seemed to conclude our discussion, and I got up to leave. Before leaving, I asked if it would be at all possible for us to have dinner that evening, an invitation that she declined all too quickly. As I got to the door, she said, "Incidentally, before you leave, please arrange to leave a retainer with my secretary." Apparently I had impressed Sir Wilfred far more than Miss Larwood.

Chapter XXXIX

Back in New York, I immediately told Imad that I had formed a company in London and that it was called Katanga Minerals, Ltd. He really liked the name and the idea that it would be in the diamond business. He quickly suggested that, when the time came, we should tell anyone who asked about the company that I had learned, while in London, that Katanga was to be bought out by DeBeers, the big diamond cartel, and that we expected to make a big profit in a fairly short period of time. This seemed like a good idea to me, and Imad and I spend hours discussing all the details of our plan.

The papers from the barrister in London were received a few days after I returned to New York, and when I sent back the signed copies, I asked Miss Larwood if she could arrange to open checking accounts for the company in both the Channel Islands and in Geneva. I had originally wanted an account in London as well, but Miss Larwood insisted that the money go offshore as quickly as possible. She felt that if the money were transferred directly from the brokerage firm to an offshore account, it was fairly likely that the Internal Revenue would not attempt to impose any taxation. She and I were able to work out all the details of these matters by exchanging a few faxes.

It suddenly struck me that things were moving almost too fast. We now had a company and the next step would be to have stock certificates. But we still needed an arrangement with a brokerage firm, and that was the most important thing that I planned to work on. On Friday night over dinner at the Bull and Bear, I said to Imad, "For the first time, I really think that this is going to happen; we're going to pull it off."

He slowly nodded in agreement, saying, "I think you're right. With the company having been formed, we're moving into the final stages of our plan."

"Getting a brokerage firm to handle the stock is really the only significant part of the plan that is still not settled. And Monday I'm going to start talking with David Green; he's a broker with Forgen and Company, which is a Philadelphia firm that I've been buying a lot of bonds from. And our fearless leader Petersen has specifically approved my trading through that firm. David was just transferred to London to head up a new office there, and he's a very nice guy—not the brightest guy in the world—but one who will do anything to make a buck."

"Have you told that woman lawyer in London how many stock certificates she should have printed, and what denominations they should be?"

"No, I haven't done that yet, since I haven't yet figured out how many certificates we will need in order to settle our trades."

Taking out a ballpoint pen, Imad began doing some calculations on the tablecloth. "Let's see, if we're each going to buy $5 million worth of Katanga Minerals for our lucky accounts, we've got to decide on a price per share. What's your thought?"

I also started doing some computing on the tablecloth. "I think that the price ought to be fairly high and that we buy an even number of shares." I kept trying different combinations, and finally said, "What would you think if we priced the stock at $85 per share and each bought 60,000 shares? That would cost a total of $5,100,000 for the accounts that we use to put into the deal, and that extra $100,00 could come in handy some day for each of us."

Imad laughed and said, "Every little bit helps. And with 60,000 shares, we could each enter orders for 15,000 shares in four different accounts."

"That's really great. We would be entering orders for an even number of shares for each client, so we just have to make sure that we provide the brokerage firm with enough thousand share certificates so the transactions can close without any hitch. And since the investment for each of the eight accounts would be only $1,275,000, I can tell the trading desk that these are speculative investments for eight of our biggest accounts, and that these clients want the bank to take more risk to try to get higher returns."

Imad said, "That's the great thing about the investment business; you can always come up with some phony excuse for anything you want to buy. Incidentally, I would tell that lawyer in London that we want about most of the 120,000 shares to be 1,000 share certificates, and any balance to be 100 shares."

As I thought about it for a few minutes, I said, "Maybe we should not ask that lawyer to have the stock certificates printed. She thinks that our African client is going to merge his company into Katanga, and she's looking for a big legal fee in handling the merger. From her viewpoint, there would be no reason to have stock certificates printed until that merger takes place. So let me see if I can get someone else to print the stock certificates."

I was now becoming tremendously excited by the whole scheme. When I thought back on my previous embezzlement attempts, I could see that what Ingrid got me to do in Zürich had been child's play in comparison to this. And while I had spent a lot of time on the embezzlement in New York, the amounts involved in that case were relatively small and my preparations had been amateurish. I kept telling myself that I had to hold back my enthusiasm now and be sure that I did not make any stupid mistakes again, as I had done in the past.

The next day I called David Green at Forgen's London office. After the usual pleasantries, I said, "David, I'm sure you know how much I've appreciated all the great bond deals that you've given me over the last year or so since I joined the bank. I think the fact that some of my clients were pretty happy with their returns was one of the reasons that I got a good bonus at year-end. So I've got a little deal here that I'd like to refer to you and your company."

Like any broker, David was always anxious to hear about possible new business, and said, "That's very nice of you."

I continued: "The Second National Bank has a very important client from Africa, and the family owns a diamond company called Katanga Minerals. The company has hired the bank because they want to diversify their holdings—all their wealth is connected to diamonds—so we have agreed to buy some of their stock in a number of our most important accounts. This will be a private placement, and I had thought that we could simply exchange stock certificates in one of our conference rooms at our Private Banking office on Curzon Street in London. But you know how banks are—they have lawyers looking at everything you try to do, and they feel that the stock should be traded through a brokerage firm. So I have suggested that the company—Katanga Minerals—open an account at your firm and deposit something like 150,000 shares of stock with your firm. We would then buy those shares—or at least most of them—at $85 per share for our accounts in New York. Do you think you'd be interested in this?"

"Kurt, that sounds very interesting. We would, of course, have to charge a brokerage commission for something like this, maybe $2 per share, but I don't think it should be any problem. I'm sure you will think that $2 per share is a high number, but, as I understand it, this comes close to being a private placement and my company will have to do a lot more work analyzing the thing before we can act as the broker."

I didn't say anything, but his comment reinforced my belief that brokers never think of anything but commissions.

David went on, "And I'm sure you know that we will have to deal with the 'Know Your Customer' rules, but since the family owning the company being sold is a customer of the Second National Bank, you should be able to provide us with all the necessary papers."

"Yes, I'm sure I can. Our solicitor in London is Sir Wilfred Tancred and we also have a barrister, a Miss Julia Larwood, so between the two of them, I know that we can provide you with what you need. Miss Larwood has chambers at 63 New Square in the City and you may wish to send her whatever forms need to be completed for Katanga Minerals to open an account with your firm. And David, I should mention that the bank's client is quite anxious to have this sale occur as quickly as possible."

"I'll plan to contact her first thing in the morning."

This discussion had seemed almost too easy and after it was over I began to think of all the things I would have to do before leaving New York -- a departure that would essentially last forever. Once the embezzlement took place and I had the $5 million, I would be traveling the world for the rest of my life and could only return to New York if I was prepared to risk arrest and imprisonment, and I could not envision ever wanting to do that. I sat at my desk after talking with David Green thinking about places in which I might like to live or at least visit, and they would all have to be places that did not have an extradition treaty with the US. I stayed in this reverie for several days until late in the week when I received a phone call from David Green at my office in the Second National Bank.

"Kurt, this is David. I'm calling you from a pay phone outside the office, so we will have to make this very brief. I've run into a little problem on my end, but I think it can be taken care of. If you have a pen, take down my home phone number and call me at home tonight. And you might want to call from your home phone too. I just want to discuss that wonderful recipe that you told me about the last time that we talked."

This conversation was a total surprise and I was unable to concentrate on anything for the rest of the day, although I had a pretty good idea what he was going to say. I got back to my apartment a little before 6:00 p.m. and immediately called David's home number where it would have been 11:00 p.m. in London. He answered right away and we quickly got down to the main issue. David said, "Kurt, I'm sorry about this, but I did talk with that Larwood woman and she told me that she is just now in the process of forming this Katanga Minerals company. She tells me that there will be nothing in it until it merges with some company down in the Ivory Coast."

I couldn't help saying, "Yes, in the Cote d'Ivoire."

David laughed and said, "You continentals are so sophisticated. But if you are in a hurry to get this sale accomplished, as you indicated that you were the other day, then you might be selling stock in a company with no assets. Isn't that right?"

I had not thought that he would have the brains to figure that out, so I said, "David, how could you possibly think that the bank would put their clients into a worthless stock. No, no, no, of course, a merger will take place at some point in the future and these shares will become very valuable. You have to believe that this is a perfectly legitimate transaction."

"But the shares are not very valuable today."

"David, if you want to be crass, I suppose you could say that, but one always has to have a long-term view in the investment world."

"I agree 100 percent Kurt, and my long-term view is rather personal. And being involved in the sale of a worthless stock can result in certain liabilities, so I really have to understand all the factors that might affect my personal decision."

It was really necessary to have a brokerage firm that would handle this transaction, and I was quite surprised that David had figured out what we were doing as quickly as he had. I had known the moment that he had suggested having this call from home that he would want a part of the deal, and this conversation made his intention very clear. So I said, "David, let's talk again in the next day or two since I have a partner here in New York that I need to discuss this with, but I feel sure that we can come to a very nice agreement that will be a win/win for all of us."

I had dinner the next night with Imad and told him how things had developed with David Green. Imad thought about it for a couple of minutes and then said, "What was that old perfume commercial, something like, 'Promise them anything, but give them Arpege.' We can promise this guy anything, but all he's going to get is the $2 per share brokerage commission. He probably thinks that he can blackmail us somehow after the deal is done, but he doesn't realize that everyone will know that you and I carried out this thing and will have disappeared with the money, so blackmailing is not going to be possible."

"You're right, but remember, all of the sale proceeds go into an account at Forgen and Company in London. What if Green won't let the money be transferred out?"

Imad immediately said, "Yeah, but remember, all the money has to be transferred out of the Forgen account right away. As soon as the bank wakes up and discovers what has happened, they will try to get the brokerage firm to cancel the trade and return the money. Green won't want to lose the commission, so he has to let it go through. In that case, the Katanga Minerals account at Forgen has got to be zeroed out ASAP. And what is Green going to do? Set up an account in his own name and have money transferred to that account? No, he can't do that, so he really has no alternative but to trust us. All the money has to go out of the Forgen account to the Katanga Minerals account in the Channel Islands, and then it will immediately go on to Geneva. We can always promise him that we will put $1 million—or whatever amount you and he agree on—in a safe deposit box for him in Geneva. But, unfortunately, you and I might forget to do that. So like I said, promise him anything but give him Arpege."

I had to lean back and laugh; this was another indication that our decision not to worry about keeping our involvement secret, but to end up being perfectly open about it, was making everything so much easier. I ordered a glass of champagne for each of us and felt more and more confident about our plan, as I toasted Imad: "To our brilliant success!"

Saturday morning I called Green at home. We had a long discussion that started out when Green said, "I think I've got a pretty good idea of what you guys are trying to do."

I said, "And what is that?"

"You're going to buy this worthless stock in some of your accounts at The Second National in New York. But what I haven't figured out is how you think you can get away with it. If it works, each of you guys would stand to make millions."

"Why would you think that we're going to make so much money?"

"Well, I don't know what you plan to sell it for, but all the sale proceeds probably go to you, so it's gotta be several million each."

"Wow, wouldn't that be great, but that's not what's going to happen. I haven't told you the whole story about this deal, so get a piece of paper and a pen because I want you to take down some information.

"First of all, take down the name Ahmadou Kuada. This guy is the son of one of the biggest diamond mine owners in Africa. The family lives in Abidjan in the Ivory Coast. You got that name? OK, when we finish talking, you can go and look the family up in *Who's Who in Africa* and you'll see what they own.

"The next name you should take down is Diamants Brut, CIE, which is the company that the family owns. That name, incidentally, translates into 'rough diamonds'. Now ordinarily you would think that these people are among the wealthiest in the world, and they probably are, but the son has been spending money like water, and the family has had some other problems, so they are in a cash squeeze. That's why they want to sell stock in this holding company. They talk about eventually having Diamants Brut merge into Katanga Minerals, but I don't know when that will happen. However, the shares in Katanga Minerals are supposed to have some kind of option to buy shares in Diamants Brut.

"So the way it will work is that all the sale proceeds received in the Katanga Minerals account will be transferred to an account for that company in the Channel Islands."

I stopped talking for a minute to see what David would say, and after a minute or two, he asked, "And then where does it go?"

"David, all you need to know if anyone asks you after the deal has closed is that you understood that this was a perfectly legitimate transaction on behalf of Katanga Minerals, a company that either had options to buy stock in Diamants Brut or would eventually merge into it. Personally, if the deal falls apart and I'm asked about it, I'm going to claim that I was convinced by that guy Kuada, and that I understood the same thing—that it was a perfectly legitimate transaction. In point of fact, this whole thing was really the son's idea and he will probably end up with most of the money. My partner and I will hopefully get something like 5 percent of the sale proceeds."

"Well, you've got to admit, Kurt, that this looks like a pretty fishy transaction, and there could be a lot of questions about it, but if those names check out and I have a creditable story so I can explain why I handled the transaction, then we've got a deal. The only thing we still have to decide is what I get paid for taking all this risk."

I think I was pretty tough in bargaining with him and after close to an hour of negotiating, we agreed that in addition to the $2 broker commission on 120,000 shares (which he would have to split with his firm), Imad and I would give him another $200,000 in cash so his total take from the deal would be a little over $300,000. I think I convinced him that it was impossible today to say how that extra $200,000 would be paid to him, but promised that I personally would see to it that he got that money. He finally recognized that it was going to be very difficult for him to receive money from us and still preserve the fiction that he knew nothing at all about the embezzlement. Unfortunately for David, he could not speak six languages as I could, which would enable me to run off to any corner of the world that suited me, nor could he flee back to a country like Egypt, where he would be almost certain to disappear. So his attempt to share in the embezzlement proceeds only made it more certain that he would want to cooperate with us, but his chance of getting anything extra was absolutely zero.

Chapter XL

With a UK company having been formed and with an agreement in place with David Green covering the use of Forgen and Company as the brokerage firm in the transaction, the only thing remaining to be done was to get some stock certificates printed in London that would look credible. I checked with the Public Records Office in London and found that there was a company called London Printing Company that indicated in their advertisements that they could produce high quality stock certificates. As a result, I contacted them by phone and reached a Mr. Paul Hastings, explaining to him what we needed. We discussed costs and, as is generally the case with printing, all the costs are associated with the original setup, and a greater or lesser quantity makes little difference in the total price. Mr. Hastings and I quickly came to agreement as to the quality of the paper and the fact that it would be multi-colored printing, and this led to the total cost that would be involved for this order. I asked Mr. Hastings if they would send the bill for the stock certificates to Katanga Mineral's solicitor, Sir Wilfred Tancred, and he saw no problem with that at all. Since quantity made no difference as to cost, and since neither Imad nor I were going to be paying the bill, I told Mr. Hastings to have one thousand certificates printed at 1,000 shares each and an equal number at 100 shares each. All of those shares were to be delivered to Forgen and Company. I felt that having a larger quantity gave more credibility to the order.

As a result of this conversation, the only thing left to decide was the design of the certificates. I wanted London Printing to just go ahead and use one of their regular designs, but Mr. Hastings explained that they had to have written confirmation that the design was approved by the client before they would begin working on the order. After discussing various elements of the design for some time, Mr. Hastings said that he would work up a proposed design and fax a copy to me for my approval. I suggested that he keep in mind the fact that the flag of the Ivory Coast was green, orange and white, and that an eagle was an important symbol in that country. He explained that it would probably take until the next day before he would be able to lay out a proposed design and fax it to me. As a result, I gave him the fax number in the International Private Banking Department, feeling that I would have to watch the fax machine very carefully the next day. I also asked him to call me just before he faxed it, so that I would be sure to get it.

I spent the rest of the day working on some of my accounts until just before 5:00 p.m. when Jim Turner came into my office, which was something that he had rarely done before. He handed me a two-page fax, one page of which was a facsimile of a stock certificate, with the name Katanga Minerals Ltd. in large letters in the very center. Turner said, "Kurt, I just found this on the fax machine—it seems to be for you. What the heck is it?"

I was, of course, stunned to see that it had come just a few hours after Hastings and I had talked, and it was also a real blow since Turner had found it. To gain time, I said, "Let me see it." After a minute, trying to keep my voice calm, I went on, "Oh yeah, this is for that diamond company that that client in London owns. You know, Ana Maria sent me to London to meet with this very wealthy African client, and this guy's family owns a diamond mine—or actually several diamond mines. They want to sell at least part of their company, so the bank is probably going to handle that sale in London. Bill Welles had the client—someone named Ahmadou Kuada—meet with the bank's Corporate Underwriting Department, and they will be the ones handling the sale."

Turner said, "OK, I see. But why are you dealing with the stock certificate?"

"You know how these really wealthy clients can be. I didn't want to have anything to do with the stock sale. We just talked about how to reinvest the sale proceeds. But the son kept saying that he would have to show his father a sample stock certificate, and he said that he would value my opinion on what one should look like. He said that his father always valued the opinion of older people. So I asked this company in London to make one up."

"I assume that could be kind of expensive."

"I suppose it could be, but I didn't even ask what the charge would be just for the design. The real expense would come when the certificates are actually printed. And I got the printing company to agree to send any bill directly to Kuada's London solicitor."

Turner seemed to be satisfied with my explanation, and finally said "OK" and left my office. I was almost trembling after Turner left, and was cursing that idiot in London who sent the fax to me a day earlier than he had indicated he would send it. All I could think was to thank God that the company I formed was based on that meeting with Ahmadou Kuada in London so that I had a credible story to tell Turner. I was so shaken that I did not even look at the design for almost an hour as I tried to calm down from the fright that Turner had given me. When I did look at the design, it seemed unremarkable to me; it was just an eagle soaring in the background, with the company's name in large green letters on a field of white in the foreground, and with an orange border. As far as I was concerned, it looked like a normal stock certificate, and that was all that mattered to me.

This happened on a Thursday so the regular meeting with Imad was the next day. I explained to him what had happened and how furious I was at the guy in London. Imad was not as upset as I was and said, "Look, he was just trying to show you that this was an important order and he could respond real quick. So what did you do with the design that he sent you?"

"When I finally calmed down last night, I studied it and it looked perfectly OK, so I sent a fax back to him approving it on behalf of Katanga Minerals. He indicated when we were talking that they could have the certificates printed within two weeks of getting that approval."

"OK, Kurt, now let's go over everything to be sure that everything is ready so that we can act any time after two weeks, whenever the time looks right. I made up a list of things that we need to have accomplished, and I'd like to go over it with you. First, are we sure that the UK company is formed?"

"Yes, that Larwood woman—our barrister—sent me the formal incorporation papers, or whatever they call them in England."

"And did she set up the accounts in the Channel Islands and in Geneva?"

"All the papers have been signed, but both banks—the one in Guernsey and the one in Geneva—require initial deposits to actually get the accounts open. Larwood didn't think it was necessary to do anything now, but I convinced her that the family would feel better if every possible detail had been taken care of at the earliest possible date."

"So what do we have to do?"

"We have to wire transfer $5,000 to each of those accounts, and I'll take care of that the first thing Monday morning."

"Do you need any money?"

"No, I can handle it. But I'll take it out of your share when the money gets to Geneva."

Imad rather drily responded, "I'm sure you won't forget to do that." He went on, "Now, has the Katanga Minerals account at David Green's firm been opened?"

"Green has sent all the opening account forms to Larwood, and I think she may already have had them signed. Remember, she and that solicitor guy are officers of Katanga Minerals, and they can sign on behalf of the company."

"Kurt, I'd feel better if you had her send you a copy of the agreement."

"She'll probably want to fax it. But don't worry, I'll see to it that no one else gets to see it."

Imad now leaned back and said, "Let's see, we've got a company, we've got an account at Forgen, we're getting accounts in the Channel Islands and Geneva, and the stock certificates are being printed. Now all we've got to do is figure out when Engle and Petersen are going to be away."

I said, "Imad, I've been thinking about the timing issue, and I think the best time for us to enter the orders would be the first thing on a Monday morning. That would mean that we would close five business days later which would be the following Monday, but I could instruct the settlement division to wire transfer the money to Forgen on Friday to make sure that it was there in London for the Monday closing. That way the money would already be gone if either Engle or Petersen came back on that Monday and questioned the trade, and, because of the five-hour time difference, Forgen would already be transferring it to the bank in Guernsey."

"And don't forget, Kurt, you and I would also have flown out over that weekend to Geneva."

"That's right, but since I assume that we intend to fly first class to Geneva, I'm sure that we can get tickets at the last minute. Incidentally, we are going to fly together, or is there any reason for us to fly separately?"

"What the heck, let's fly together. If the money gets transferred next Friday, we can leave from JFK the following day and be in Geneva on Sunday, ready to greet the $10 million on Monday."

We had another drink to toast our forthcoming success and agreed that we should meet again on Tuesday, rather than waiting until next Friday.

Chapter XLI

We were now into the last weeks of August and since many people only took vacations during the summer, the vacation season was drawing to a close. Therefore, I had to find out when Engel and Petersen were planning to be away. I decided that the easiest thing to do would be to simply ask Engel when his vacation was scheduled, saying that I did not want to be away at the same time that he was gone. As an officer of the bank, he was entitled to four weeks of vacation, and I seemed to recall that he had only taken two weeks so far. He responded that he would be away during the last two weeks of September, and told me that he and his wife had tickets for a cruise in the Caribbean. That was reassuring since he would definitely be away during those two weeks. Then I also talked with Petersen's secretary, but found out that Petersen had no travel plans at all for September. Knowing about Petersen's plans was important since it was essential that both of them be away when Imad and I entered the buy orders for Katanga Minerals. If either one of them were there, the trading desk would require their approval before executing the purchase orders of a non-approved stock.

The news about Petersen was somewhat upsetting, but I knew that an opportunity would surely arise in the not too distant future when the orders could be entered, and decided that I had to concentrate on getting everything in order for what I started to call 'D-Day'. The first thing I did was to call our barrister in London, Julia Larwood, to be certain that all of the accounts had been opened. She agreed to send me by FedEx copies of the opening account forms for the account with Forgen and Company and the two checking accounts.

I then wire-transferred the $5,000 to the officer at the Guernsey bank who I understood was handling the Katanga Minerals account and informed him that in the next week or two this account would receive a wire transfer from London of $10,200,000. As soon as that money was received, $10,100,000 was to be wire transferred to the Banque de Genéve, and I gave them the specific wire transfer instructions for the Geneva bank. I felt that giving the impression that $100,000 was to be left there would indicate to the Guernsey bank that

Katanga Minerals would continue to use their account in the future. But I did, of course, have other plans for that $100,000.

Imad and I had decided that the money should quickly be transferred from Guernsey to Geneva since the authorities would immediately find out from Forgen and Company that the money had gone to a bank in Guernsey, but it would probably take several days before they could pierce the bank secrecy laws in Guernsey to find out where it had been sent from there. These extra days would be important to us in getting the funds out of the Geneva bank and to wherever we had decided to hide the money.

I then sent what was really the crucial fax to Banque de Genéve. I said that I had given instructions to wire transfer $5,000 to them that morning. And I told them that in the next few weeks they would be receiving a wire transfer into the Katanga Minerals account of $10,100,000, and that they should immediately wire transfer $5,000,000 to a bank in Cairo. This was an account that Imad had opened and on which he indicated to me that he had full signature authority. I also told them that they should begin accumulating $5,000,000 in gold coins issued by governments anywhere in the world, and said that I would give them further instructions with respect to those coins when I was in Geneva.

When I had finished with all the faxes, wire transfers and the phone call to Ms. Larwood, I sat at my desk feeling quite satisfied with myself to have accomplished so much that morning. The originals of all the faxes were still lying on the top of my desk when a few minutes later Jim Turner came into my office again. Last Thursday was one of the very few times he had ever been in my office, and to come back again so soon seemed to me that it could only be a harbinger of bad news. I tried to move the *Wall Street Journal* from the side of my desk over on top of all the faxes without being too apparent that I was covering something up.

He started off by saying, "Kurt, I wanted you to know that I talked to a friend of mine in the bank's Corporate Underwriting Department in London. He seemed a little upset that I knew about the potential IPO by that diamond company from Africa."

I quickly responded, "I would think he would be. That deal is supposed to be very hush-hush."

"Yeah, that's what he said. He said it was very preliminary and the bank was just putting together a formal proposal to the family in the Ivory Coast for us to handle the deal. But he wanted to know how I had heard about it. So I explained that you had met with the client and were working on the design of the stock certificate."

"I'll bet he didn't like that at all."

"Yeah, at first he seemed a little upset, but he finally agreed that he could understand how the old man who owned the company would want to be involved in some of the details of the deal, and the design of the stock certificate was one of the few things that he would understand. It was such a minor point that my friend was almost happy to let you handle it."

I then said, "Jim, don't tell your friend since they haven't even made the formal proposal to the family yet, but the son told me that they were not talking to anyone else, so the Second National Bank will definitely be selected."

"I'm going to have to tell Ana Maria so that you get some of the credit for this deal."

"I think you ought to really wait until the agreement with the Kuada family is finalized. I'm pretty confident that the son will let me know when that happens, and I'll be sure to let you know."

Turner finally left my office and I could not decide whether it was a good thing or a bad thing that he knew as much as he did about our cover story. As long as he did not find out that the firm Imad and I had created, Katanga Minerals, had nothing at all to do with Diaments Brut, the Kuada family firm, and would never have anything to do with it, I think it was probably a positive that he knew that something was going on concerning a diamond company.

After getting all the accounts set up, there was really nothing more than either Imad or I could do. The two-week wait before the stock certificates were delivered seemed interminable, but I finally got a phone call from David Green letting me know that they had arrived. I made sure that he opened them up to be certain that he could have them put into good delivery form. The opening account form with Forgen and Company had authorized them to put any securities deposited into the Katanga Minerals account into street name, so there was no reason that there should be any delay when it came time to deliver them.

Now all we had to do was to wait to see when both Engle and Petersen would be away at the same time. Engle went on vacation starting on Friday, September 15th, and was planning to be gone until the 30th. Petersen, however, was back at work on Monday, the 18th, as expected, and there seemed little chance that he would be away while Engel was gone. I kept fantasizing about ways that I could get him out of the office, but clearly could not think of anything at all likely to succeed. However, just when I thought that we would have to put 'D-Day' off indefinitely, he did not come into the office on Thursday, the twenty-first. I debated with myself for most of the day whether or not I should ask about his absence, but finally went to his secretary about 4:00 p.m. I made up an excuse for wanting to see him, telling her it was something personal, and she told me that he had unexpectedly been called to London and would be gone all of the following week. This was what we had been waiting for—tomorrow would be 'D-Day.'

Imad and I got together that night in my office, after everyone else had left, and we made up orders for each of us to purchase 15,000 shares of Katanga Minerals in four of our accounts at a price of 85 or better. As we had previously agreed, the orders would be entered in the morning and I would inform our trading desk that they should contact Forgen's trading desk in Philadelphia. Forgen's London office will already have told their Philadelphia office that they had a customer that wanted to sell this stock.

Even after all of our preparations for "D-Day," there still seemed so much that we had to do. With Imad sitting there, I called Swiss Air and got two first-class tickets for the flight to Geneva on Saturday the twenty-fourth, putting the cost on my Visa card—a bill that I knew would never be paid. We then agreed that we should probably start cleaning out our desks, and also get rid of things in our respective apartments. Since we would have to wait a week before leaving the country in order to be sure that the money was transferred prior to our departure, we still had plenty of time to pack. However, I'm sure that both of us were struck by the enormity of what we were doing, and I know that this thought gave me both a real thrill as well as a sense of panic.

The next morning at about 10:30 a.m., I dropped off my four orders at the trading desk, and said to the head trader, Chuck Lindsay, "Incidentally, that stock that we're buying is kind of like a private placement and the only firm that makes a market in it is Forgen and Company."

Chuck looked at the orders and shook his head: "This stock isn't in our approved list, we can't buy it. And I thought that we were only authorized to buy bonds from Forgen, not stocks."

"This is a very special situation, Chuck, and both Imad and I are buying it for some of our accounts. You know some of the big accounts want us to take more risk to get higher returns, so we're buying a little over $1 million of this stock in several of our accounts. And Forgen happens to be handling this deal and brought it to our attention, so we have to trade through them."

The trader continued to argue, "But either Engel or Petersen would have to approve this."

"Yeah, of course, and usually they would. But Petersen was supposed to be here and he just got called out of town yesterday and won't be back for a week. You can call his secretary, and she'll tell you that this trip was unexpected. And we had agreed with the seller over in London to buy this stock today, or else he plans to sell to someone else."

Chuck continued to look at the orders and I was beginning to become afraid that he might refuse to enter them. However, after a couple of minutes, he looked at me and slowly said, "So you're going to take full responsibility for this?"

"Of course."

"OK, you're the boss, but give me a memo telling me that I should execute these orders."

I promised to do that, and within a half hour, Chuck had talked with the Forgen trading desk in Philadelphia and eight accounts at the Second National Bank of New York had each bought 15,000 shares of Katanga Minerals at $85 per share, or $1,275,00 per account, and at a total cost of $10,200,000. We had also agreed that the brokerage commission of $2 per share would be paid by our accounts so the net sale proceeds going to London would not be reduced.

The next week seemed interminable, just waiting for time to pass until the money could be transferred on Friday. On Tuesday, I was surprised when Jim

Turner came by my office again and asked to see the stock certificate. I said, "What do you want to see that for?"

"I'm just curious. I really would like to be over in the Corporate Underwriting Department, doing this kind of private placement deal. I think that would be more challenging than being in private banking."

I handed him the mock-up of the stock certificate and we kept talking for a little while, when all of a sudden Chuck Lindsay came to the door of my office. He saw that Turner was there and I was sure that he saw Turner holding the Katanga Minerals stock certificate. For a minute I was horrified as to what Lindsay might say and reveal that the trading desk had just bought stock in that company on my direction. However, all Lindsay said was, "Oh, pardon me, I'll come back."

As soon as Turner left and I had calmed down somewhat, I went to the trading desk and asked Chuck what he had wanted. He said, "Well, I was waiting for that memo you were going to give me. But I have to tell you, I felt a lot better seeing Turner holding what looked like a stock certificate in that Katanga company. If he knows about our buying that stock, I guess it's gotta be OK that we put in those orders."

"Chuck, I hope to God that you don't think that Imad and I would be doing something illegal."

"No, of course, not. But you have to admit that it was a pretty unusual transaction."

I was tremendously relieved as I walked away from the trading desk.

Things stayed quiet for another day or so, and time seemed to pass incredibly slowly until Thursday afternoon. I then received a phone call from Petersen's secretary telling me that Petersen would be in the office the next day, and since I had indicated a few days ago that I had wanted to see him, she wanted to set up an appointment for me. She suggested that we could do it at 11 am or 3 pm, and I chose the appointment at 3. I don't think I slept all that night since I was so afraid that Petersen would question the Katanga Minerals purchase and hold up the transfer of the $10,200,000, and Friday was the last day that the money transfer could be stopped. I knew that I would have to think up some story that would keep him from questioning that transaction.

I don't think I was able to do anything on Friday morning except work on the story that I was going to tell Petersen, and then rehearse it and try to anticipate any questions that he might have. The time for our meeting finally came, and I went into his office and sat down. He was working on a paper, making me wait for several minutes before he finally said, "I've got a couple of things I wanted to talk to you about. But first of all, my secretary tells me that last week you had asked for an appointment to see me. What was that about?"

"Since Dick Engel is away, I thought I should mention this to you. It turns out that I have prostate cancer, and I have to go into the hospital on Sunday for an operation on Monday. They don't think that it's life threatening, but I will have to be away for two or three weeks. This just came up late last week, and I assume that someone will have to be designated to cover my accounts while I'm gone. And the doctor tells me that after the operation I will still have to have radiation treatments, and I think that those will last for six weeks."

I could see that playing for sympathy was working, and Petersen immediately said, "Kurt, I'm very sorry to hear that. It seems to be such a common thing to happen these days to men in their sixties and seventies."

"The doctors seem fairly optimistic since it's been caught rather early, so I'm trying to be just as optimistic myself about the whole thing."

"What hospital are you going into?"

"Lenox Hill."

"Yes, of course. Well, if there is anything we can do for you, just let my secretary know. And I will talk to Engel next week about who should cover your accounts. I would guess that Turner should be able to do that."

After a pause of almost a minute or two, I finally said, "Was there something else you wanted to talk to me about?"

"Yes, those purchases of Katanga Minerals. As you may know, my secretary reviews all the purchases each day—a report comes to me from the trading desk—and part of her job is to review all transactions for unusual items. She had these eight items circled when I got back this morning. You know that you are not supposed to buy a stock that is not on our approved list. I hope that this wasn't another case where you were giving your own investment advice to our clients."

"No, I was not doing this on my own. As you may know, Ana Maria had me go to London to meet a wealthy African investor, and in talking with him I found that his family wants to sell some of the stock in their diamond mine. The son tells me that DeBeers is going to buy them out eventually, apparently at a big profit. But the family wanted to establish a market first, so we were given the opportunity to buy some of their stock for our accounts. Turner and I have talked about it at great length and Imad bought some for his accounts. We've done a complete analysis to make sure that the price that we're paying is supportable."

"OK, if Ana Maria and Turner know about it, there must be a good reason that this was done. But when you get out of the hospital, we have to talk about this a lot more, since I really do not like this kind of transaction. As I told you before, we have to have rules and we have to follow them. You and Turner and Imad do not constitute the Investment Committee."

"I agree, Mr. Petersen, and I think when you hear the whole story you will understand why that stock was purchased."

"I hope so."

As I was about to leave his office, I turned around to face him, and I could not resist saying, "Just let me tell you this: we're gonna make a helluva lotta money on that stock."

Petersen looked very dubious about the whole thing as I walked out, but I could tell that he was not going to do anything to try to stop the wire transfer of the money to London. I could not resist laughing as I walked back to my office for the last time.

Chapter XLII

Saturday afternoon, Imad and I sat in the first class cabin on the Swiss Air Boeing 747 as it roared down the runway of JFK airport and slowly lifted off. We had done it; the $10,200,000 was in London now, but on Monday practically all of that money would end up in Geneva and Cairo. It seemed to both Imad and me that this was an absolutely stupendous achievement, and we had several glasses of champagne to celebrate. As we were eating dinner, I said, "Imad, I never really thought that we would get this far. It seemed too fantastic—I just did not think that it could be done."

"Kurt, if it had not been for your idea to give up that whole idea of keeping our involvement secret, I don't think we could have worked everything out."

"The money is going to be waiting for us—or at least for me—when we get to Geneva. Your share should be in Cairo by then, but we can check on that on Monday. I haven't quite figured out how I'm going to put my share away so it can never be found, but do you mind telling me what you plan to do with yours?"

"There's no secret, since my $5 million is just going to disappear as soon as it gets down there to Egypt."

"But how? I don't know much about Egyptian banking, but won't the authorities be able to trace the money?"

"Look, Kurt, maybe you should move your share to Egypt too. Money laundering is the name of the game in Egypt. That $5 million in the bank in Cairo is going to be transferred out of Egypt right away and it will then come back to banks all over the country. And it will appear as if it is being used for a lot of different things. But 90 percent or so will end up in accounts that I control one way or another. The other 10 percent will have been used to grease a few wheels. And there will be no record that anyone can trace."

"Why haven't I ever heard of this before?"

"Well, Egypt is an important friend of the United States, and they want their banking system to look as if it is just as legitimate as the US system. But, you know, Saudi Arabia is right next door and all those little countries in the Gulf seem to be loaded with sheiks and emirs and princes that have all this money that they don't know what to do with, and they look to the Egyptian banks to take care of things for them. And very frequently that means hiding some of it. Egypt is just trying to be a good neighbor."

"I can only hope that the Swiss banks can be as accommodating." I decided to say nothing to him about the gold coins that I had ordered the Swiss bank to accumulate, since he might not agree with what I was planning to do, and I really felt that I needed to keep the whole matter to myself, at least for now.

We had another glass of champagne as we finished dinner, and I turned to Imad and said, "I think it's been great working with you on this project, and I have to thank you for the basic idea that we pull off a deal like this, and to keep me motivated despite all my initial doubts. It would not have happened without your constant encouragement."

"Kurt, I have to tell you that I had had a vague idea of doing something like this almost from the first day that I came to work at the bank. I realized when I met you that you were a pretty smart guy, and when I found out at that cocktail party that you had some kind of background that was not 100 percent kosher, I decided that we had to find a way to work together."

"Well, you were right, so thanks again for the inspiration."

After a minute or two, Imad said, "You know, Kurt, one of the things I have never understood is how the bank ever hired you considering the fact that you had a conviction and were banned from the securities industry, at least that's what that guy at the cocktail party said."

I had to laugh as I thought back to that day when I had my fingerprints taken in the bank's Human Resources Department. "I guess I never told you how I had to raid the bank's personnel office to take back, so to speak, my fingerprint records and to delete my name from the list that was going to the FBI. If the information on me had gone to the FBI, I would never have been hired."

"You're kidding. How did you do it?"

"I just waited until a very nice young woman who was responsible for the whole process left for the night, and then managed to get into her office and you might say that I cleaned up the files. She had already given me a bank ID card, sot it was easy to get in. It was kind of a desperate act at the time, but what else could I do? I needed the job."

"And you always look so distinguished and so honest that no one would ever suspect you of anything, whereas everyone thinks that a dark, swarthy guy like me has just got to be a crook."

We both laughed and sat sipping our champagne, until Imad said, "So, Kurt, how do you plan to spend all that money?"

"You know, I haven't really thought about it all that much. It will certainly let me lead a pretty nice life—traveling, staying in all the best hotels, maybe having a house in the south of France—things like that. Do you have any plans for yours?"

"I've been thinking of buying one of the banks in Egypt. There's so much opportunity there and the local banks are not really aggressive enough, and not just in lending, but in helping the wealthy people in Egypt and the Gulf get their money into one of those off-shore tax havens, like that tax lawyer in London was talking about."

"But you can't use your own name, can you?"

"The name 'Imad El Kasim' will totally disappear once I leave Rome. My entry into Egypt will be with a different name and a different passport."

I had to agree with him that that was a smart move; I only wish that I had done the same thing when I was in Los Angeles. Although if I had changed my name, Imad may not have discovered my record at Morris, Brunner, and he probably would not have encouraged me to get involved in this embezzlement. If it hadn't been for him, I would almost certainly still be working at the Second National Bank of New York. And I couldn't help thinking—going back to the beginning of my problems—that if it hadn't been for Ingrid I would probably still be working at Schleswigbank in Zürich and might even be heading it up now.

The more we talked, the more apparent it became that we had different ideas as to what we would each plan to do going forward, and we finally touched our champagne glasses in one last toast to each other. I felt truly sad to think that this long relationship with Imad, as well as our challenging embezzlement project, would now be coming to an end. He and I had worked together extremely well and I had come to look upon him as my best friend, and in reality my only friend. It was hard for me to think that this relationship was now to all intents and purposes over.

Our dinner on the plane was really the last time we had any kind of meaningful discussion. I had taken a suite at the Richemond and, since the flight arrived in Geneva early Sunday morning, I had reserved the suite for the night before our arrival to make sure it was available as soon as we got there. It was seven in the morning when we checked in, and we immediately went to our respective bedrooms in the suite to rest for a few hours. There was nothing that we could do on Sunday and since it was a gray, rainy day we spent most of the day just sitting around, making small talk, looking at TV, and simply trying to kill time. We had dinner in the dining room of the Richemond on Sunday night, but we did not exchange confidences as we had done on the plane the night before. In fact, our conversation that night, for probably the first time since our original meeting, seemed rather stilted. We both decided to go to bed fairly early in anticipation of what would occur over the next couple of days.

As we went to our bedrooms, I'm sure that both Imad and I were focused on what was about to happen, since Imad would leave early Monday morning for a flight to Rome, and a connecting flight to Cairo, and by Tuesday, if all my plans worked out, I would have what I had fantasized about almost from the start of this entire project—the $5,000,000 in gold coins. I knew that it would be difficult to get to sleep that night since all the details of the plan kept swirling in my head. Therefore, rather than lie in bed trying to sleep, I stayed up and decided to concentrate on those details, not only from my perspective but from the bank's perspective as well.

As I sat in a chair in the bedroom thinking about it, the current situation seemed so comparable to what the situation with Ingrid had been after Elsa Wilhelm had unveiled the Schleswigbank embezzlement. I remember having to tell Ingrid in great detail what was likely to occur after I had fled Zürich. Now, as I thought about what was likely to happen back in New York the next day, the situation seemed very similar. I was sure that on Monday morning someone at the Second National Bank would start looking into Katanga Minerals. It probably would be Dick Engle, if he were back from vacation, but it was almost impossible for the bank to find out until Tuesday at the earliest that Imad and I were the ones who had formed that company. They would probably ask the bank's counsel in London to find out about the company, and this would take a day or two for London counsel to get the required information from the Public Records Office or wherever such information was kept. In point of fact, considering the time difference between New York and London, it would probably be Wednesday or Thursday before the bank realized that this was a fraudulent company that Imad and I had formed.

Their next step would be to demand that Forgen and Company return the sale proceeds, but, of course, Forgen would have to tell them that the money had been transferred to Guernsey. Then it would probably take two or three days for the authorities to pierce the client secrecy laws in Guernsey before they would learn that the money had been transferred again, this time to Geneva. And by the time the bank traced the embezzled money to the Banque de Genéve, it would be much too late, since my $5,000,000 would already be outside the banking system, and could no longer be found, while Imad's money would have been transferred to Cairo, and then on to who-knows-where.

I had to smile to myself as I considered the fact that they would also almost certainly check with Lenox Hill Hospital, probably to send me flowers or a sympathy card, only to find out that I was not there and had never been there. They would then rush up to my apartment on 72nd Street and find that all my personal effects had been removed, and the only thing that was left there was my gun collection, since I had not been able to come to an agreement with Purdy's or anyone else as to its sale. They would also be checking on Imad, who had told the bank that he was taking a few days of vacation, and when they found that he had disappeared too, and when they finally discovered that we had brazenly used our own names in forming Katanga Minerals, they would finally have to face the fact that we had pulled off one of the most amazing embezzlements of all time.

From my viewpoint, everything had gone according to plan up until now, but some critical points lay just ahead. As I continued to sit in the chair in my bedroom, I tried to enumerate all the things I still had to do. First of all, the Banque de Genéve had insisted that I bring at least two people with me who could identify me, before they would turn over any of the gold coins to me.

They explained that since they had never met me, they had to be sure that I was, in fact, Kurt Wenner, an authorized signer on the Katanga Minerals account, before they could turn over all that gold. I had several discussions with Henri Larcier, a vice-president of the bank, as to who might be acceptable, and we finally agreed on Ingrid, since she was a Swiss citizen and she and I were still married, and on Julia Larwood, the company's barrister from London. In addition, David Green had indicated pretty strongly that he wanted to be there, and I had no choice but to agree. I explained to M. Larcier who Green was and he seemed pleased that an additional seemingly reputable person would be there. Ingrid was due to arrive in Geneva on Monday afternoon, and Miss Larwood and David Green on Tuesday morning.

The other problem concerned how to physically handle the $5,000,000 in gold coins. Many years ago the volume and weight of that amount of gold coins would have been too enormous for me to try to deal with. But with gold having soared to about $400 per ounce from $32 when President Nixon took the US off the gold standard in 1973, and with a significant premium now attached to gold coins issued in many cases by governments that no longer existed, the price of the coins had risen dramatically and, as a result, the physical volume of the coins had become manageable.

When Monday morning finally came, a continental breakfast was served in our suite for Imad and me and, as soon as the banks were open, I checked with M. Larcier at Banque de Genéve to make sure that my $5,000,000 was there and that the gold coins had been obtained. I also asked if Imad's $5,000,000 had been transferred on to Cairo. I was assured by M. Larcier that all of my instructions had been carried out. After I told Imad that the bank had confirmed his wire transfer, Imad placed a call to Cairo and spoke in Arabic to someone there. When he finished that call, he was beaming as he turned to me and said that the money had arrived and was already being dealt with as he had planned.

Since Imad's plane left at noon, he had to leave for the airport as soon as these phone calls were over. He then quickly came over to me and we briefly embraced and shook hands, seemingly reluctant to finally part. We talked about meeting in Cairo in the next few months, but I somehow sensed that this was a more permanent parting. I had felt terrible when Naomi died, and I now had almost the same feeling as Imad walked out of that room. The thought kept recurring to me that an important part of my life was just ending.

As soon as Imad was gone, the first thing that I had to do was to visit the Rolls Royce dealer in town. We had been talking by telephone for several weeks, and I pretended to be a Brazilian multi-millionaire, using a Brazilian passport that I had obtained in Sao Paulo on one of my frequent trips there while I was so infatuated with Rosario. I had ordered a black Phantom Rolls Royce sedan, and agreed that I would pay cash for the car upon delivery. The car, with all the extras, came to over $200,000 and I had been told the exact amount the previous week. The dealer and I had agreed that I should bring a cashier's check, which assured the dealer that the check was good, and avoided my having to use the name 'Kurt Wenner' to sign a check on the Katanga Minerals account since I was buying this car in the name on my Brazilian passport. It was very easy for me to buy such a check in the morning at the Banque de Genéve, and as a result I was able to complete the purchase very quickly. So within a very short time, I drove out of the dealer's showroom with what has to be the absolute ultimate automobile. The only problem with the Rolls was that it was a very highly visible car, and I knew that I would have to get rid of it fairly quickly or risk being discovered. On that Monday morning, I had not yet decided how I would be able to do that.

The next thing I had to do was to open two safe deposit boxes at local banks. I could not use the Banque de Genéve since I again wanted to use my Brazilian pseudonym and the Banque de Genéve knew me as Kurt Wenner. The Swiss banks that I called on were wonderfully accommodating and within a very short time I had two large safe deposit boxes rented in my Brazilian pseudonym. I put both of them on one-year leases, with payment in advance, and gave both banks an address in Sao Paulo to which they could send their annual fee invoices. The address was for a post office box that I had rented in the central post office, again on one of the marketing trips to Brazil for the Second National Bank. After the safe deposit boxes were rented, I drove the Rolls back to the Richemond and told the doorman that I would not need it until the following afternoon.

I rested for the remainder of the afternoon until a little after six when the front desk called to say that Mrs. Wenner was in the lobby. I responded that she should wait and I would be right down. It took me a few minutes to get fully dressed again and, after I had finished, I took a deep breath and headed out of my room to face Ingrid, after not having seen her since that meeting in Zürich over fifteen years previously. There had been that long period after the Morris, Brunner embezzlement attempt came crashing down when I did not have enough money to send to her and Petra, but I had tried to make that up after Good Win Investments had been fairly successful.

When I got to the lobby I saw Ingrid sitting off to one side, and was surprised to see that she had brought Paulo with her, or a young man whom I assumed to be Paulo. However, I decided that all I could do was to try to ignore the situation and be as pleasant as possible. Having dinner with your wife and her young lover was not exactly the easiest thing to have to deal with, but at this point I was only thinking about getting control of those gold coins. I needed Ingrid for the meeting at the bank the next day, and was determined not to argue or fight with her on that Monday evening.

I went up to her and kissed her cheek, and she and I exchanged the usual pleasantries. After she introduced me to Paulo, I then led the way into the dining room. Once at the table, I ordered a bottle of wine, but Paulo asked to have a whiskey and soda. After we had ordered, Ingrid rather brusquely said,

"So you want me to go to the bank tomorrow as your loving wife and assure them that you really are Kurt Wenner?"

"That's the idea, yes."

"Don't you think it's rather risky for you to admit your identity to a bank here in Switzerland?"

"It is risky, of course, but I have to assume that that old problem with Schleswigbank has been forgotten a long time ago. How long has it been now—over twenty-five years?"

"And why do you need me to identify you now? Is this another one of your—what do you say in English—one of your scams?"

"Ingrid, there has never been a scam. You know what happened in Zürich, and essentially the same thing happened in New York—the money just fell into my lap and I picked it up, just like we did in Zürich. One of Morris Brunner's richest clients moved his account offshore but forgot that there was about $300,000 cash in the account. I waited for months and months, and it became clear that he had forgotten about it. So I transferred it to my own account, but some accountant discovered it, and I was sunk. And for all those years in Los Angeles—what was it thirteen years?—there was never a single problem. This is something quite different."

Ingrid waited a minute after I had finished, and then said, "All right, then please tell me what this 'something' is."

"Well, as you know, I have invested in the stock market for as long as I can remember—going all the way back to Zürich. And in recent years I have made quite a bit of money and incurred some fairly large US capital gains taxes. I decided that it would be ridiculous for me to pay those taxes, so I have liquidated my entire portfolio and am moving the money out of the US. The money is now at the Banque de Genéve and they will require identification before they let me take any of it out. It's really quite simple."

At this point, Ingrid turned to Paulo and said, "Does anything he just said make any sense to you?"

Paulo smiled and said, "No one likes to pay taxes. I can understand that."

I was beginning to be glad that Ingrid had brought him along, until he continued, "But as to how he got the money in the first place, I have no idea about that."

Nothing was said for quite a while after Paulo's last comment, as we all started eating our dinner. Ingrid ate very little, and soon put her knife and fork across her plate indicating that she had finished eating. She now looked directly at me and said, "I brought Paulo along since I want him to hear you say that I am not going to get in any trouble by vouching for your identity tomorrow at the bank, and that this entire transaction is perfectly legal."

I waited a few seconds, and then said, "Ingrid, there is absolutely no reason why you should get into any trouble simply by identifying me at the bank tomorrow afternoon."

"But you haven't said that the entire transaction is perfectly legal."

"Ingrid, I've already told you that the transaction is not perfectly legal, since it is a crime to avoid paying US capital gains taxes, whether you're a US citizen or not. If you incur gains in the US, you owe US capital gains taxes."

"Then what do I say if the authorities ever were to ask me to tell them what I knew about this whole matter?"

"Well, in the first place, I don't think anyone is ever going to ask you anything at all about what will happen at the bank. There is no reason for the Swiss authorities to look at the transaction, and I can't imagine why the US authorities should. But if anyone should inquire, I think you have to tell them exactly what I've told you—that as a Swiss citizen, which I am, I did not want to pay US capital gains taxes and so I was moving money out of the US. You personally do not know anything about US tax laws, but you are aware that a great many people move their money to Switzerland to avoid taxes in their home countries, so you did not think that this was anything unusual. And as to my conviction over twenty-five years ago, I had convinced you that there was a statute of limitations so that conviction was no longer a problem. You can say that since the bank was willing to work with me, they obviously did not think it was a problem, so you did not think it was a problem either."

She looked at Paulo again, and he smiled at her and simply shrugged his shoulders. I could tell that she was debating with herself, until she finally said, "Kurt, if you're lying to me, I hope you end up rotting in hell. But I'll do what you ask and just hope to God that I don't get in trouble for doing so. Now you did promise me something for doing this for you, didn't you?"

"I was hoping that you had forgotten, but, yes, I have a check here" and I then took an envelope out of my coat pocket and handed it to her. It was a check for $100,000 drawn on the Guernsey bank—the $100,000 that had been left there after all the rest of the money was transferred to Geneva.

Ingrid looked at the check, and said, "Katanga Minerals, what is that all about?"

"Oh, that's the name of a holding company that I created, and a name that I just pulled out of the air on the spur of the moment. In fact, the lawyer from London who created the company will be at the meeting tomorrow, and you can ask her, because she was asking me for a name when I thought it up."

We sat for a while longer having coffee and finishing up the wine, until it was clear to all three of us that it was time to go. As we walked out of the dining room, I wanted to tell her not to bring Paulo to the meeting the next day, but decided that saying that might irritate her, so all I could do was to trust to her judgment. When I got back to the suite, I took a Courvoisier out of the mini-bar and collapsed in a chair. I sat sipping the cognac while reviewing everything that I had accomplished that day, and was extremely satisfied the way things had gone. I actually fell asleep in the chair and awoke about two in the morning and staggered off to bed.

CHAPTER XLIII

I was really surprised that I slept so well that night, apparently because I was exhausted from everything that I had had to do the previous day. This day, however, Tuesday, September 27, was the day that I had been awaiting for several months since Imad and I had first conceived our plan. After waking up at about 8:00 a.m. and lying in bed until 9:00 a.m., and after a leisurely shower and breakfast, I called M. Larcier at the bank to make sure that everything was ready for the meeting that afternoon. I felt that I remained remarkably calm as I looked forward to the luncheon meeting with Julia Larwood, who was flying over that morning from London. I called the airport to see if flights were arriving on time, and found that everything was perfectly normal. I assumed that David Green was on the same flight as she was, but I did not have time to see him before the meeting at the bank.

At about 11:45 a.m., I received a call from the front desk telling me that Miss Larwood was waiting for me in the lobby. Again, I had to finish dressing before I could descend to the lobby, so it was almost noon when I was able to greet Miss Larwood. We quickly went into the dining room and ordered; all that I felt able to eat was a cup of soup and a salad and Miss Larwood had something similar. The real point of this lunch was to be sure that Miss Larwood was satisfied that I had the authority to carry out the action that I had planned, and would tell that to the bank. She would also, of course, be required to tell the bank that I was, in fact, Kurt Wenner. I felt unsure how I should proceed to explain to her what was likely to occur that afternoon.

I was spared that problem, however, since my guest took the initiative and very quickly asked what exactly she would be required to do at the bank meeting. I told her that she needed to confirm that I was the Kurt Wenner who had been referred to her by Sir Wilfred Tancred, her instructing solicitor, that I had directed her to open the account here at Banque de Genéve for Katanga Minerals, and that I was an authorized signer on the Katanga Minerals account. I said to her, "You may find the transaction this afternoon to be somewhat unusual, but I'm sure you understand that Mr. Kuada Sr. is rather old-fashioned and prefers real assets, such as gold, to bank accounts and things like that. I am merely carrying out his instructions."

She replied, "You seem to be implying that some funds are going to be taken out of the Katanga Minerals account in gold. How can that be? We are in no position to be selling stock at this time. It will be several months until the merger is completed before stock sales can occur. I don't understand how there can be any assets to disburse."

"I understand, of course, that that is the way things would appear from your viewpoint, but I probably should have told you previously that the family has had a significant stock portfolio at an account in the Channel Islands. Some stocks were recently sold there, with the sale proceeds being transferred to the Banque de Genéve. That's the money that will be taken out this afternoon. I was making use of the Katanga Minerals account that you had opened here in Geneva, since the money had to be transferred to Switzerland, which was the most convenient place to convert it into gold, and that is what Mr. Kuada wants. The money that is involved today came from the family's stock trading account in Guernsey, and I had not anticipated that I would need you to be present here in Geneva to vouch for me. If I had known what the Banque de Genéve would require, I would have tried to use some other account or some other bank. However, I assume that I would have faced similar requirements from any other bank, since gold coins cannot be traced once they leave the bank and therefore banks like to be sure that they know the person who is taking them out."

Miss Larwood closed her eyes and seemed to be thinking for a few minutes. At last, she said, "You retained Sir Wilfred and me to open several accounts on behalf of the Kuada family for Katanga Minerals, one of which is here in Geneva. You tell me that there was a trading account in Guernsey for the Kuada family. You also say that the proceeds of stock sales in that account have been transferred to the Katanga Minerals account here in Geneva, which is owned by the Kuada family. You must have had some type of authority over the Guernsey account in order to have the stock sale proceeds transferred to the account here in Geneva, and you are an officer of Katanga Minerals, with signature authority on the Geneva account. Isn't that right?"

I merely nodded.

She continued, "Well, then I cannot see any problem. You come highly recommended and I doubt if Sir Wilfred would have referred you to me unless he was assured of your credibility. I have to assume that the Second National Bank knows what you are doing, but I have to ask: why isn't this transaction taking place at that bank?"

"The Second National does not deal in gold or gold coins, at least not to any meaningful extent. Their branch here in Geneva does have a small retail operation for people who collect gold coins from time to time. But the amount of gold that is involved in this transaction is far beyond the normal trading capabilities of the Second National Bank. And I should mention that I had requested the head of their Geneva Private Banking Office to attend this afternoon's meeting, but he is traveling in the Middle East and was not able to be here."

Miss Larwood merely nodded at my last explanation, and we sat there for a few minutes while I kept hoping that she would not ask to call the Second National's Private Banking Office to see if its leader really was in the Middle East. I finally broke the silence by saying, "If you have any other questions, please ask them now before we go to the bank."

She said nothing, but looked very pensive as the waiter came to ask about dessert and coffee. I suggested to her that we have a glass of champagne instead and while she seemed surprised at my suggestion, she readily accepted. We drank the champagne in relative silence, with neither of us saying anything of significance. As we left the restaurant, I explained to her where the Banque de Genéve was and said that I would meet her there. Since the bank was within walking distance and it was a beautiful fall day, she said that she would be only too happy to walk.

After she left, I went back to my suite and stood at the window looking down at Lac Léman and thought about the meeting that was about to take place. There would be three people there ostensibly vouching for me, and each of them would have a different understanding as to why I was taking all this money out of the bank. I had told Ingrid that it was to avoid US capital gains taxes; I had told Miss Larwood that it represented the proceeds of stock sales and that my principal, Mr. Kuada, wanted to have those proceeds removed from the bank in gold; and I had told David Green that Mr. Kuada's son had thought up this fraudulent stock sale as a way to alleviate his cash flow problems. Had I been at all religious, I would have gotten down on my knees and prayed that these three people would not start explaining to the Banque de Genéve the three very different assumptions underlying their presence at the meeting that afternoon.

I decided that I had to go forward and could not let doubts stop me now, so I went to the phone next to the bed and called the front desk. I explained that I was suddenly called away and had to check out immediately. I asked to have someone come up to my room to get my bags and also asked to have my car brought around. Within minutes someone was in my room taking my luggage—four heavy suitcases containing everything that I had brought from New York. I went down to the lobby, stopping at the front desk to go through the formalities of paying my bill, and shortly thereafter, I was seated in the Rolls Royce driving to the Banque de Genéve.

The Banque de Genéve had a doorman at their front entrance who would take the car of their wealthy clients (if the client did not have a chauffeur) and park it behind the bank. So I left the car with the doorman and walked into the bank, where M. Larcier and several of his associates from the bank were waiting for me. After introducing me to his associates, he showed me into a conference room where Ingrid, David Green, and Miss Larwood were gathered. I was glad to see that Ingrid had not brought Paulo to the meeting. Since I had not seen David Green in Geneva before this, I spent several minutes exchanging the usual pleasantries with him.

Once everyone was seated, M. Larcier began by saying, "I would like to explain why we are having this meeting, but I have to be very circumspect as to what I tell you so that I don't run afoul of Swiss bank secrecy laws. We will be discussing an account on which Mr. Wenner has signature authority—an account that was opened by his counsel in London. He and his barrister, Miss Larwood, sent me an authorization from London that allows me to discuss a few of the details concerning that account with you this afternoon. Now, do any of you have any questions before I go on?

"If not, I think you may all be aware that Mr. Wenner is an officer of a company called Katanga Minerals. He has indicated to us that the principal for whom he works has directed Mr. Wenner to withdraw a fairly sizeable sum from that account. Normally, Mr. Wenner could write a check, since he has signature authority on this account, and checks would leave a clear trail as to where the money had gone. In this case, however, since Mr. Wenner has been instructed to remove the funds using a precious metal that could not be traced, the Banque de Genéve must be certain that this gentleman here is, in fact, Mr. Wenner. I am very reassured that Mrs. Wenner has come here from Zürich to help confirm Mr. Wenner's identity, and that Mr. Green, who will be handling the sale of some stock for Mr. Wenner's principal, has come from London for the same purpose. I am particularly pleased that Miss Larwood is here, since she has been involved in establishing the accounts in question.

"Again, if you have any questions, please let me know. If not, I have prepared a simple form for each of you to sign merely attesting to the fact that you recognize this gentleman seated here at the table as being Kurt Wenner."

Ingrid looked quite puzzled when she heard these references to my principal and that I had been instructed to remove funds using a precious metal, but she merely frowned and did not say anything. I began to think that perhaps I should have told her a story similar to what I had told Larwood and Green. M. Larcier then passed out a form that asked each of my witnesses to affirm that the person who had identified himself to the Banque de Genéve as Kurt Wenner was known to each of them as being a person of that name. It was very simple, and each of the three quickly signed the form.

Miss Larwood really frightened me as she decided to ask a question: "M. Larcier, it is my understanding that the funds being disbursed today were received in the Katanga Minerals account from an account in Guernsey in the Channel Islands. Is that correct?"

He answered, "Oh, yes, the funds came from Guernsey. Do you have any other questions?"

She merely shook her head, and I tried to restrain myself from showing too much relief.

M. Larcier then said, "Well, Mr. Wenner, I think that with that having been settled, you and I and my associates from the bank should proceed to the vaults."

I replied, "If you have no objection, M. Larcier, I would like to have my friends here join us in the vaults, at least for a few minutes, since I think it will be educational for them." I really wanted to impress them by showing them the tremendous amount of gold that I expected would be waiting for us in the vaults.

Since he had no objection, the entire group left the conference room and proceeded down a broad, sweeping staircase to the vault area of the bank. M. Larcier then led us to another smaller conference room within the vault itself. The room was too small to allow everyone to get in, but it was possible to look in from the doorway and see that a great number of very secure-looking bags were piled up, not just on the table but on the floor as well. I had been hoping that all the gold coins would be visible, since I think everyone would have been stunned at seeing between $4 and $5 million dollars of gold lying before them, and I was rather disappointed that all they were able to see were these bags. I said, "Even though you can't see the gold itself, I'm sure you can appreciate that what you are looking at represents a pretty impressive amount of money. I know that my principal will be delighted when I deliver these bags to him."

With that Ingrid, David Green, and Miss Larwood left and went back upstairs. I told them to wait until I had checked everything out and then went into the small conference room with M. Larcier and his associates from the bank. One of those associates handed me a list, documenting what was in each of the bags. The list described the coin in great detail, indicated how many were in each bag and provided a value for every coin and for the contents of the bag. M. Larcier said that it would obviously take several hours, if not well into the night, if I were to try to count the contents of each bag. He suggested, therefore, that I select five or six bags at random and check those, trusting that the Banque de Genéve had accurately counted the coins in all fifty of the bags. This seemed like a good suggestion to me, particularly since I was in a hurry to drop off some of the bags at the other banks in which I had rented safe deposit boxes, and I wanted to get on the road and get out of Switzerland as soon as possible. I had also studied the value of the coins in great detail and had memorized their value so it was easy for me to quickly check the bank's list to be sure that the coins had been valued properly.

It did not take me long to check five of the bags, trying to look at a different type of coin with each bag that I checked. When I finished, I reminded M. Larcier that I had also asked to receive 500,000 in Swiss francs, since I knew that I would need cash before I had any chance of selling any of the coins. This, of course, reduced the value of the coins that I was removing from the bank by that amount. The value was also reduced by the $200,000 I had used to purchase the Rolls Royce, since I had taken that amount of cash out of the Katanga Minerals account to buy the cashier's check for the Rolls Royce purchase. One of his assistants quickly handed me an envelope that contained the 500,000 Swiss francs. With the cash in hand, and having checked the gold, I was satisfied that everything was satisfactory and that I was prepared to sign a receipt. Another of his assistants produced a receipt, and when this had been signed, all of the bags were loaded onto a dolly to transport them up to the street.

I accompanied the dolly into the elevator and out to the area behind the bank where my Rolls Royce was parked. It took some time for the bank employees to load all the bags into the car, and I was thankful that I had bought a Rolls Royce with its extremely large boot, as the English would say. Even so, it was necessary to move my luggage out of the boot and place it on the front seat next to me and on the floor, so that some bags containing the coins could be placed on the back seat and on the floor adjacent to the back seat.

At long last the packing was done, and I shook hands with M. Larcier and several of his associates. I thanked him and suggested that he ask Ingrid, David Green and Miss Larwood to step outside in front of the bank. I waited several minutes to give him time to deliver my message and, judging that the time was right, I slowly drove around to the front of the bank and pulled up where my friends were waiting. I got out of the car and went over to them saying, "I really can't thank all of you enough for being here today. Working everything out has taken a great deal of effort on my part, but it probably could not have been done if you had not been willing to vouch for me today."

I went over to Ingrid who was now standing with Paulo, and I kissed her on both cheeks. However, she seemed very stern and unresponsive, saying, "What that man from the bank said when we were in that meeting just did not make any sense based on what you had told me at lunch yesterday. And I cannot believe that you're about to drive away with all that gold in your car, and you still maintain that this is a perfectly legitimate transaction. I know you too well to believe that, Kurt."

"Ingrid, I can't tell you what to believe. All I know is that this is something that I will always be proud to have done; it's a quite stupendous accomplishment." After a short pause, I said, "Oh, and incidentally, be sure you cash that check right away."

She responded, "You can be sure of that; you can't imagine for one second that I would trust you on a check. I was at the bank the minute it opened this morning."

All I could say in response was, "Don't spend that money foolishly, Ingrid."

I then shook hands with Paulo, wishing him good luck since I could not think of anything else to say to him. I then turned to David Green and we both smiled at each other as we shook hands, but neither of us said anything. I finally turned to Miss Larwood and said, "As soon as I deliver everything to Mr. Kuada, I will let you know, and we can proceed to work on the merger."

She very forcefully said, "I had no idea that you were planning to load all that gold into your car and drive away with it. I think that that is a totally imprudent think to do; it's really quite mad. The risk you are running is absolutely enormous. There must be another and more secure way to deliver those coins to Mr. Kuada."

"Yes, there may be, but this is the course of action that was decided upon and it is what I have to do now."

She insisted, "I really think that what you ought to do is to have the Banque de Genéve deliver all those coins to the Second National Bank's office here in Geneva which is just down the street. I am totally appalled at the thought of what might happen with all that gold in your car. As your counsel, I must insist on giving you this advice."

I said, "Miss Larwood, I appreciate your opinion very much, but at this point there is nothing else that I can do."

With that I turned and waved to the group, which also included M. Larcier and all of his associates and got back into the Rolls. As I started the car again, I blew a kiss to Ingrid and I again waved to everyone else, and then drove slowly away with almost $5,000,000 in coins and cash loaded into that car. I don't believe that I ever felt such a great sense of self-satisfaction and accomplishment as I did at that moment. Driving away in a Rolls Royce with all that gold in the car seemed to me to be like a dramatic scene out of a James Bond movie. This was the culmination of everything that Imad and I had been planning for at least a year, but it was far more than that. It was the crowning accomplishment of my life after all the failures with the previous petty embezzlement attempts. I wanted to yell with joy, I felt so triumphant. I can't remember ever having felt as ecstatic before.

Within days, everyone would know that I had just pulled off one of the greatest embezzlements of all time. I was so elated that I thought of driving around in front of the bank again, blowing the horn the whole time, to celebrate what I considered to be my victory. The only reason I did not do so was because I wanted get to the two banks in Geneva where I had rented safe deposit boxes so I could put some of the gold coins in each, and I also wanted to get out of Switzerland as quickly as possible. But it still took great self-control on my part not to drive around once more to flaunt the gold-laden car.

CHAPTER XLIV

$\mathbf{M}$y immediate destination in leaving Geneva was to get to Luxembourg, which was about 250 miles almost straight north through France. I had checked the map well in advance and had plotted out a route to Luxembourg by going up through Dijon, Nancy, and Metz. The route was mainly on secondary roads that were fairly hilly, but I stayed to the west of the Jura Mountains so it was not a very difficult drive. I arrived in Luxembourg the next day, after spending a night at a small hotel that I discovered along the way. I immediately drove directly to the airport, since this was part of my plan to get rid of the Rolls Royce, a too easily identifiable car. I parked the Rolls at the airport in one of the most remote corners of the long-term parking lot—with the gold still packed inside. I had determined in advance that I would have to leave the car and the gold at the airport overnight, so that I would not be associated with the Rolls at the hotel where I would be staying. After parking the car, I went over to the terminal and got a luggage cart, went back to the Rolls and took out all my personal luggage, and then went and got a taxi to take me to Hotel Belair Bourscheid. This hotel was more of a resort hotel, outside of the main part of the city of Luxembourg, but I felt that it would be a good place to use as my headquarters while there.

I finally got settled in my suite and, as I sat sipping my gin and tonic, I think I felt more self-satisfaction and a greater sense of personal accomplishment than I had ever felt in my entire life. Here I was at almost sixty years of age, and for the first time in my life, I felt that I had really done something of which I could be proud and which would cause other people to be amazed at what I had done. My first thought, of course, was of Eric Petersen, who had irritated me so badly when he tried to tell me what I should do about currency investments. The irritation with Petersen had grown over the months as I thought about that confrontation where I had been forced to swallow my pride and agree to take orders from that young idiot. And I had also been irritated with Ana Maria for choosing that young guy Turner to head up Latin American marketing. I didn't particularly want that job, but having her choose someone else without even talking to me about it rankled. So I could sit back now and think about how chagrined each of them must be by what I had accomplished since I had reported to both of them and both would be held responsible for my achievement.

In thinking back, I also had to admit that there had been a certain feeling of accomplishment after I had succeeded in taking the 250,000 Swiss francs from Schleswigbank. But then I had had to flee Switzerland only several months after that embezzlement, and I could remember sitting in the Hotel Lotti in Paris morosely trying to convince myself that I was not a crook and that I had done nothing illegal. There was some small sense of victory at that time since that money was still there in Kusnacht, but that sense was more than mitigated by the necessity of fleeing my home, my wife, and my country to avoid a certain prison term.

Today, by contrast, I left Switzerland in a Rolls Royce carrying the equivalent of $5 million dollars with me, knowing that there would be astonishment and grudging admiration for all that I had done.

And as I sat thinking about my past, my thoughts fell upon my first experience in New York and my time at Morris, Brunner. I really could not recall that I had ever felt that there had been anything glorious or heroic about the embezzlement from that firm. While that whole escapade was going on, I think I always knew that I was not going to get away with it. Looking back on it, I think that that furtive bus ride to Florida really represented my poor, failed embezzlement attempt at that time, and I can only compare that terrible bus ride down to Florida with the Rolls Royce drive to get to Luxembourg. The comparison between the two rides represented for me just how much more impressive this embezzlement was as compared to all my previous attempts.

I even thought of Los Angeles for a minute but never had a great sense of accomplishment there. I had a certain pride in having built a successful business when Good Win Investments became profitable, but there was nothing like the tremendous overwhelming sense of accomplishment and victory that I felt as I sat in that suite in Luxembourg. The thought that I could ever be caught for what I had just done, or that there could be another prison sentence, were things that I could not even conceive of as I sat there.

I stayed at the Hotel Belair Bourscheid for three days, since I really felt that I needed to relax and unwind after the drama of the embezzlement. Those three days also gave me a chance to buy a new Mercedes Benz (in cash, of course) that enabled me to transfer all the gold out of the Rolls and into the new car. I even managed to steal some license plates in the airport parking lot, while transferring the gold coins from one car to the other, and put them on the Mercedes. And I also rented two more safe deposit boxes in Luxembourg, so I could leave some of the gold coins there. By the time I left Luxembourg, I could not have felt more pleased with what I had accomplished and how well things continued to go.

I had planned a long trip from Luxembourg, going to as many of the European tax havens as I could—places where I could open safe deposit boxes in which to leave more of the gold coins with very few questions being asked as to who I was or anything else. The trip initially took me straight south through France to Andorra, a tax haven that Miss Larwood had so strongly recommended. Andorra is up in the mountains between France and Spain, and after spending a few days there, I then went back east through France to Monaco. Both of these places have great tax and confidentiality laws that are designed to attract wealthy people from around the world to entrust some of their wealth to those countries.

Then I had a rather leisurely trip going across northern Italy, finally getting to Venice. I was ultimately heading for Vienna and then Liechtenstein, both of which have very favorable tax and confidentiality laws, but Venice would be a good stopping point on the trip. It was interesting that throughout my entire journey I kept reading, either in the Herald Tribune out of Paris or in the local newspapers, about the incredible embezzlement that had occurred in Geneva. When reading these stories in restaurants or outdoor cafés, I wanted to get up and tell people at adjoining tables that those stories were about me. I was the one who had done this incredible thing.

It was mid-November when I finally got to Venice and I found a little apartment in a building not far from Piazza San Marco and started to settle in for a fairly long stay. I was, of course, tired from the long drive from Luxembourg, and while I had not driven terribly far in any one day, I was happy to think that I could stay here in Venice for a considerable period of time without any pressure for me to move on. Most of the time I would go to one of the many restaurants adjoining Piazza San Marco, but twice during my first week in Venice, I went to the dining room at the Danielli for absolutely wonderful meals.

I soon realized that one of the things I had to face up to was that I had embarked on a rather lonely existence. Not being able to talk with anyone about the newspaper articles concerning the embezzlement was one thing; but it began to bother me that there was absolutely no one with whom I could carry on any kind of conversation. The dinners at the Danielli should have been very enjoyable, but I have never really liked dining alone. And I kept wondering if there was another guest in the dining room who might be from Switzerland and who might recognize me. Having to maintain a low profile while I had the equivalent of $5 million available to me whenever I wanted it was, if not depressing, at least disconcerting and something that I had not anticipated.

If only Imad had been with me I don't think I would have felt as I did, and the feeling of loneliness was unsettling. I had no one to talk to—no one with whom I could share what I considered to be this tremendous accomplishment of embezzling $10 million out of the Second National Bank of New York. (While $5 million was now with Imad, I felt that I should have primary credit for the entire embezzlement.) I thought of running to Cairo and trying to find Imad again. I thought for a second that if Naomi had still been living, I would have wanted to fly to Los Angeles to see her, until I remembered how much she would have disapproved of what I had just done. So I reminded myself that I had made the adjustment to living alone when I fled Switzerland and began living in New York many, many years ago, and I was sure that I could do it again.

Venice is a lovely city when the weather is good and one is able to walk along the canals and contemplate all the charming buildings and other vistas, but after I had been there several weeks and, as days passed one after another, I realized that the fall had slipped away and we were now in the second part of November. The weather became very unfriendly; raw, rainy days were frequent, and the chill invaded my little apartment. When I first arrived in Venice, I had made arrangements with my landlady to have her bring me coffee and a roll every morning, so that going out for a light lunch and for dinner were two of the principal events of my day. But now, with the cold, bleak weather, venturing out became a real inconvenience, and so I felt I had no choice but to simply rush to a nearby restaurant for my meals, which were no longer the most enjoyable parts of my day. And I soon noticed, if I did venture into the Piazza, that Christmas decorations were appearing on many of the stores and on the Piazza itself, and that had a disquieting effect on me.

I have to confess that the mood of elation and accomplishment that I had felt when I drove away from the Banque de Genéve had now given way to a feeling of, if not depression, at least one of unease or dissatisfaction with my present situation. Not knowing quite what to do or where to go, I spent time thinking about going just about everywhere, including Cairo, Rio, and Hong Kong. I finally decided on the spur of the moment one day to call Ingrid, since she would at least be someone who would understand what had happened, and I would be able to talk with her about everything. There was a phone in my apartment so I had no trouble placing a call to her, and she answered very quickly.

"Ingrid, this is Kurt."

"Kurt, I am surprised. I don't think that you should be calling me."

"Well, I'm not in Switzerland, so I'm not worried. But I called to ask how you are."

She seemed to laugh a little, and said, "Oh, I don't think I can say."

"Is everything all right?"

There was a long pause, and she said, "Well, not exactly."

"What's wrong? You don't sound very good. In fact, you sound rather depressed. Are you ill?"

"Physically I'm all right, but you'll probably find out at some point, so I may as well tell you that Paulo has left me."

"I'm sorry, Ingrid. I'm sure that's a terrible disappointment for you. I hope he didn't take any more money from you."

"I think he felt that with all the publicity surrounding the event in Geneva, it would be more prudent for him not to be associated with me anymore. I'm probably not telling you exactly the way he put it when he left, but he clearly felt that he wanted to get away."

"Have the police been harassing you?"

"You know how persistent the Swiss police can be. Since I was in Geneva at the time of the embezzlement, they try to claim that I was somehow involved in the whole thing."

"But I told you what to tell them. Hasn't that deflected them?"

"I think so. I think so. I don't hear from them all that much anymore."

"Ingrid, I'm in Italy now, and I think that you should join me here. It's not very pleasant where I am, but we could go to Sicily—some place like Taormina in Sicily and just relax in the sun. With Christmas coming up, that might be a nice place to spend the holidays."

"Oh, Kurt, I'd love to, but I couldn't bring Petra with me, and I absolutely have to spend Christmas with her. I wish there were some way you could come to Zürich, but that, of course, is impossible."

"What if you both came to Lugano? I would think that you and Petra could get away from Zürich for a few days, and it would only take a day to drive to Lugano. It wouldn't be prudent for me to stay at the Splendide or in Switzerland itself, but I could stay across the border in Italy and I'm sure we could find ways to get together."

There was another long pause in our conversation, until Ingrid finally said, "Let me talk to Petra about that. Getting together in Lugano might be possible—it just might be possible."

Our conversation ended and I was very glad that I had called her. I began to think that maybe, after all these years, we would be able to get together again. I waited about two weeks until early December and then called her again. After the usual preliminaries, I asked her if she had thought any more about our getting together at Lugano.

"Kurt, I've talked to Petra and she likes the idea. You know that she's a young woman now – actually in her 30's – and she really seems interested in getting to know her father."

"Does she know—let's call it—my history?"

"Yes, she does. I'm not very happy to tell you this, but you know how these young people can be. She seems to find it very exciting that she has a father who is a successful and rather notorious embezzler, and she's dying to meet you."

"Well, that's something for me to look forward to. But you agree that we can get together in Lugano?"

"Yes, I think so. I thought that Petra and I would come to Lugano around the twentieth of December and we'll stay at the Villa Principe Leopoldo Hotel. I think you probably know it. It's a little outside of town, but I understand that it's very nice, and I've made reservations there for Petra and me; I've taken two rooms. You may prefer to stay on the Italian side of the border, but we should be able to get together without too much difficulty."

I was more than a little surprised that she had moved ahead so promptly, deciding upon specific dates, and making reservations, but I hoped that she was as anxious as I was for us to get together again. And I recognized the implications of the fact that she had reserved two rooms. So I said, "That sounds great. I will really look forward to seeing you again, and I hope that I can get to know Petra somewhat better. I will try to convince her that I am not just an embezzler but have been a pretty successful businessman."

We ended the conversation, and I began to count the days—about two and a half weeks—until we would meet at Lugano.

CHAPTER XLV

I left Venice a few days after my conversation with Ingrid and drove back southwest through Florence to Sienna. The weather was much better in Sienna than it had been in Venice, and Sienna is also a very charming town. My spirits improved significantly in Sienna and the next two weeks passed rather quickly. The time finally came when I could travel up toward Lugano for the long-awaited reunion with Ingrid and Petra. I drove up to Como, Italy, which is just on the Italian side of the border from Lugano, and booked into the Hotel Villa Flori, right on the shore of Lake Como. Since this was a very nice hotel, and the location was beautiful, it occurred to me that Ingrid and Petra should come here, rather than for me to risk going into Switzerland.

On December 20, I called Ingrid at her hotel in Lugano and, while I would have liked to get together that evening, she suggested that we wait until tomorrow since she was tired after traveling from Zürich. Although I tried hard to convince her to come to Como, she insisted that I come to her hotel the next day, and I agreed to go there for lunch. And so the next day, I left Como in my Mercedes, which still had bags of gold coins in the boot, and drove up to the border crossing. I was using my Brazilian passport that day, and stopped for just a second at the Italian crossing point, merely waving that passport at the guard, and then driving on. At the Swiss entry point, the guard came up to the car and asked to see my passport, as they always do. I handed it to him, and he asked me to wait just a minute.

The wait lasted more than just a minute and I was becoming impatient when the guard returned and said, "I'm afraid I'm going to have to ask you to step out of the car."

My heart skipped a beat and I asked, "Is something wrong?"

The guard replied, "Please, sir, if you will just step outside for a moment."

I immediately noticed that two other guards had come up to the car, one standing directly in front of it, and I realized that I had no choice, but would have to go into the small border crossing building. I still had confidence that I would be able to convince these guards that I was, in fact, the Brazilian whose name was on that passport.

The guard led me inside and as I entered the room he said, "This is Chief Inspector Giovanni Cecchi of the Canton of Ticino police force."

My heart almost stopped beating as he said that, since it was clear that for a Chief Inspector to be waiting at the border crossing, they had to be aware of who I was and they had to be aware that I would be entering Switzerland that day.

The Chief Inspector made that very clear when he said, "Mr. Wenner, how nice to meet you, at long last."

It took me a full minute before I could say anything, but I was finally able to say, "I gather that this was not an accidental meeting. You must have been expecting me."

"Yes, Mrs. Wenner has been so helpful in keeping us apprised of your movements recently."

"Mrs. Wenner has done this?"

"Yes, in a way I suppose you can say that she has done this. She's here in Lugano and she has said that she would like to talk with you after you and I take care of some preliminary matters."

I rather grimly responded, "I don't think I care to see Mrs. Wenner now."

The Chief Inspector smiled all too broadly, in my opinion, and said, "I would hate to have you think too badly about her cooperation with us. She was, of course, very upset when the check that you gave her bounced."

I interrupted to say, "You mean the check on the account in the Channel Islands? That check should not have bounced."

"I think you forgot to take into consideration the wire transfer fees when all that money was transferred from London to the Channel Islands and then to Geneva. As a result, there was only $99,950 in that account and the $100,000 check to Mrs. Wenner had to be returned, causing her to be most upset. Then I'm afraid that the Zürich police added to her unease by putting some pressure on her since she had, after all, played a role in the embezzlement in Geneva. And they had begun to think that she had also played an important role in that long ago embezzlement from Schleswigbank. So they were able to convince her to cooperate with them."

"But why do they think that she was involved in the Schleswigbank matter?"

"Well, she had apparently given this young truck driver with whom she was living quite a bit of money to buy his truck, at least according to him, and she could not explain—to the police's full satisfaction—where that money had come from."

"And may I assume that the truck driver has fled the scene?"

"Why would you think that? No, from what I hear from my colleagues in Zürich, Paulo, or whatever his name is, has been very supportive of Mrs. Wenner throughout all of her meetings with the authorities."

So the full truth of the situation suddenly became clear—the whole Ingrid/Petra reconciliation thing was a come-on—a lie. That bitch Ingrid, instead of telling me about the problem with the check, had vindictively decided to turn me in to the Swiss authorities. The knowledge of this fact was a staggering blow. There was only one other thing that I wanted to know, so I asked, "And do you know what has become of Mr. El Kasim?"

"It's very odd. From what I'm told by Zürich, Mr. El Kasim left Rome on an EgyptAir flight to Cairo, but never seems to have arrived in Cairo. He has apparently disappeared."

Yes, I thought, he's disappeared into the Khan al Khalili bazaar as he said would. That Imad was going to get away with the whole thing probably bothered me more than anything else—that and the fact that I've been caught. But Imad would never have done what Ingrid did, so I could never be mad at him.

There was a chair in front of the desk at which the Chief Inspector was sitting, and I collapsed into it, putting my head down and I buried my face into my hands. All I could think was that those two wire transfer fees—a total of $50—had caused Ingrid to turn me in. It was hard to accept how drastically this had not only changed my entire life but also destroyed any hopes that I might have had for the future. After a few minutes, I looked up at the Chief Inspector and started to laugh. I decided that I must be the most unsuccessful and incompetent embezzler of all time, and there was nothing left to do but to laugh. All the embezzlements were over. I had failed again, and I would never have another chance.

Note: I have written these Reminiscences in the Regensdorf Prison in the Canton of Zurich, Switzerland, where I will be spending the remainder of my life. Kurt Wenner